Send Me

Send Me

Patrick Ryan

THE DIAL PRESS

Published by The Dial Press
A Division of Random House, Inc.
New York, New York

Portions of this book appeared in somewhat different form in the
following publications: "Getting Heavy with Fate" in *The Yale
Review,* "Ground Control" in *The Iowa Review,* "So Much for
Artemis" in *One Story,* "Welcome to Utica" in *Cairn,*
"That Daring Young Man" in *Bloom.*

Book design by Virginia Norey

ISBN-10: 0-385-33874-0
ISBN-13: 978-0-385-33874-5

Printed in the United States of America

To Fred Blair

Send Me

Send Me

Somewhere between Rome and Dixie, he fell asleep behind the wheel. This had happened to his father once, long before Frankie was born: he'd drifted off just outside Grand Rapids, Michigan, and when he'd opened his eyes, his car was somersaulting out of a ditch and across a field, the view through the broken windshield a rapid slide show of sky, grass, sky, grass, sky, grass. One of the doors came off. The backseat was torn loose and expelled. The bumpers, the hubcaps, the headlight rings, the trunk lid, and the jack shot out like shrapnel from a grenade. When the car finally came to rest on its wheels over fifty yards from the highway, it was so mangled that the state trooper who arrived on the scene was unable to make a visual identification of the vehicle's year, make, or model. These details were learned from the young man sitting behind the wheel, dazed and disoriented, but with nothing more than a bruised elbow and a superficial cut on his forehead. "It's a miracle of God," the trooper had said, but Frankie's mother, deserted by two husbands by the time she told him the story, had footnoted the remark: "More like dumb luck."

Frankie's luck—dumb or otherwise—held him steady as he dozed. When his head snapped upright and his mind pulled out of what had seemed like a long stretch of darkness, he found an early afternoon intensely radiant with greens and blues. He was on a road in the Conecuh National Forest of Alabama, both hands on the wheel, and he was centered perfectly in his lane.

The road turned into a bridge, and the Volkswagen skimmed a level path across the river, like a hovercraft. Then the bridge turned back into a road. The trees began to thin out. He saw a sign for Damascus, then another, smaller sign made of two flat wooden triangles nailed to a post. The triangles were painted white and bore words so small that Frankie had to come to a full stop and lean into the windshield to read them.

Turn
Here for
The Gallery of
The Eleventh Coming

said the top one, and beneath it:

Rev.
Damien Lee
Wheeler (Every-
Thing Seen Is for Sale.)

Just in front of the sign stood a mailbox with a number that matched the one on Frankie's Rolodex card. He steered the Volkswagen along the dirt road that led into the marsh.

He'd sketched a road just like this recently. Smears of brown pastel rose on one side of it, snakes of blue pencil reaching across a green plain on the other. But in the sketch there'd been a church as large as an airplane hangar, made entirely of polished steel, and all he saw when he rounded the bend in the dirt road was a small, salmon-colored shack of a house.

It sat on cinder blocks in the middle of a clearing of damp grass. The clearing was fronted by a thick wire strung waist high between a series of fence posts and hung with wooden placards that nearly reached the ground: calendars, he noticed as he pulled up alongside them, each one heavily illustrated. When he shut off the engine, a kinetic silence rose from the ground and hummed against his ears, hindered only by the sound of a cicada, and then shattered completely by the shriek of a screen door.

At the top of three bowed steps, a man stood in an open red bathrobe, a V-neck undershirt, dark slacks, and a pair of hunting boots. His fingertips beneath the cuffs of the robe, his exposed wedge of chest, his neck and face—all were a deep, rich brown. His bald scalp reflected the sun as if his skull were a light source. He was staring at Frankie behind the wheel of the Volkswagen.

He looked livid.

Frankie got out of the car. He stood holding his keys with both hands, dodging the angry gaze by studying the calendars strung along the wire.

"Have you been sent?" the Reverend asked in a voice so low that he seemed to be speaking through a cardboard tube.

"Yes," Frankie said. A gallery owner in Jacksonville had introduced him to the Reverend's work, showing him several original pieces, and slides of a dozen more. But then he added "No," because the owner had refused to give him the Reverend's address, and when she'd left the room, he'd swiped it from her Rolodex.

"You're not sure which one?"

Frankie shrugged. "Maybe both."

"I understand." The Reverend descended the steps carefully and crossed the lawn. "More and more citizens arrive all the time. Three last month alone. Some folks are sent by art dealers too sneaky to do their own buying; some just show up, no idea on Earth why they're here." When he reached the other side of the wire, he made a flourish with his hand to indicate the row of calendars. "Everything seen is for sale. Of course, I'd be a liar if I said the sent ones weren't preferred. No wisdom for fools; I know what butters bread. Which is why all of my prices are not negotiable but *reasonable*. And that's generous, because this is not a reasonable world. You look like someone who knows that."

Frankie had stepped back from the wire at the Reverend's approach. He glanced at the hunting boots, the sides of which were coated with mud. When he looked up, he saw the Reverend studying him. The man's head was a sieve of perspiration. Where his eyes—bulbous, thyroidal—should have been white, they were yellow clouded with pink: spheres of amniotic fluid that had allowed his pupils to evolve into the receptors that now scanned rapidly over every part of Frankie's body, collecting information. Frankie felt as if he were being x-rayed. Then the Reverend dipped a hand into a pocket in his terry cloth robe and brought a folded handkerchief to his face. He passed it over his eyes. "I'm the Reverend."

"Frankie Kerrigan," Frankie said. "Where's your church?"

The hand that held the handkerchief lifted above his head, and with a long finger he drew a horizontal circle in the air, seeming to indicate the entire sky. "The sent ones come from Atlanta, mostly. Some come from Savannah, or Charlotte. Never west, always east. I got a letter some time back, an art dealer up in New York City wanted a price list. At least *she* was honest enough to say what she was. I used her paper and sent her back a vision—with the list. I called it 'Twenty Johns and a Whore Are Not Selected.'"

"I saw your work in a gallery in Jacksonville," Frankie offered. He bent his legs against the ache in his knees.

"So you *were* sent."

"Not really. I just saw your work and ... decided to come."

The Reverend dragged the handkerchief across the dome of his head. "You might start at the beginning," he suggested, nodding toward the far end of the row of calendars.

Frankie walked down one side of the wire; the Reverend walked down the other. The first placard, Frankie now noticed, wasn't a calendar but a painting of an open white hand against a grid, with orange flames on the tips of each finger. On the palm was a dollar sign. Above it, in green, were the words "Five Dollars Payable for Viewing." He glanced up and saw one of the Reverend's hands extended toward him, palm up.

"Thank you," the Reverend said, once Frankie had dug the bill out of his wallet. "I'll let you be for a while." He stuffed the money into a pocket as he turned away, and walked back toward the house.

Each calendar was laid out traditionally, with the illustration above and the grid for the month below. But the first month was called *Normalary,* and the days, unnumbered, were peppered with notes: "Been good to dear Lila," "Been a good man," "Still good," "Love my dear Lila." Frankie had seen a similar calendar in Jacksonville. It had been called *Lovepril,* and had been filled with acknowledgments of having been a good husband. The illustration had depicted, in a pointillist, comic-book style that adhered to no rules of proportion or perspective, a man in a blue baseball cap and a woman in a pink dress holding hands and walking in a field of spiraling colors. In *Normalary,* the same two people were sitting down to a picnic at the foot of a spectral mountain. A tiny spacecraft hovered in the distance in both paintings, a few minuscule daubs of gray paint that might have looked like a bird to someone unfamiliar with the Reverend's work. The next month on the fence, *Betremeber,* showed a row-boat on a river of colors, and in it, a bearded man holding his fists in the air while the woman in pink sank her face into his lap. In the distance the spacecraft loomed, somewhat larger now, its underside circled with blue dots. One of the notes on the un-numbered grid read "Blue Light Special!" and on the next day, "L-I-L-A: Lecherous Insipid Lies Accumulate," alongside "They knew before I did." This was followed by a month called *Whorefest,* and it took Frankie a moment to realize he was look-ing at a close-up of a vagina, surrounded by a dozen thumb-sized replicas of the bearded man's face. Several placards down was a month called *You-Lie,* wherein the spacecraft—larger and shaped like a Bundt cake pan with tentacles—hovered over a house much like the salmon-colored shack and emitted a beam of blue light that fanned out to the ends of the clearing. In *Law-gust,* the man in the blue cap was suspended in midair while the spacecraft above him projected into the swirling night sky what appeared to be a film of the oral sex in the rowboat. *Dismember* was an entire landscape consumed by primary-color flames. Fi-nally, there was a month called *Winter,* subtitled "All Liars and Whores of Babel Are Left Behind / Good People Are Driven." The illustration showed a fleet of tentacled Bundt cake pans as-cending over a charred and smoking crater. In the crater's cen-ter was a small mountain of skulls.

Frankie stepped away and counted the months. There were seventeen. He looked toward the house and saw the Reverend walking out of it, down the steps, backward. It occurred to him that he might have fallen asleep again, might have lain down on the grass next to the fence and slipped into a dream. In trying to confirm this, as he sometimes did while actually dreaming, he squinted and then forced his eyes open wide. The Reverend walked backward all the way across the yard, then turned around at the last post to face Frankie.

"What you see is just a representation."

"Oh, I—I understand that," Frankie said, glancing down at the mountain of skulls.

"I'm saying, there's more in the house." He started across the lawn—walking forward this time—and without looking back, he motioned with a finger over his shoulder for Frankie to follow.

It was a normal house inside, save for the fact that nearly every surface was illustrated. The ceiling was a map of some alternative outer space crowded with planets, many of them triangular or square. The walls were laden with paragraphs of handwritten text framed inside a network of snakes. The coffee table was a mural of an earthquake. The armchair was rendered on fire with red and orange paint that flaked off and collected around it like dandruff, and the floor itself was painted to resemble a flood, scattered with men, women, horses, and dogs, all in the process of drowning. "You might care for this." The Reverend tapped one of his boots against a stool covered with eyes.

"Thank you," Frankie said, eager to sit down.

"I mean, it's for sale," the Reverend clarified. "Everything seen is for sale. Everything unseen is either already gone, or I won't sell it. See this?" He took from one of his pockets what looked to be a perfectly round orb of naked wood no bigger than a tennis ball. "Giotto di Bondone was the only person that ever lived who could draw a perfect circle without even trying. I made this from a branch that fell on my house last summer. I made it with a kitchen knife. It's perfect, and it's for sale."

Beneath the front window, a small plastic tape deck sat on the floor, unplugged. A hammer had been smashed into the top of it, the handle jutting out like that of a hatchet sunk into a tree stump. The Reverend noticed Frankie looking at it and said, "That's a sculpture. It broke, so I turned it into a prophecy. All our machines will fail us."

A small metal fan oscillated on top of a television in the corner, stirring the warm air. Frankie's skin began to itch. He
rubbed his fingertips through his hair and looked around for
something to sit on that wasn't merchandise. "Why were you
walking backward outside?"

"Excuse me?"

"Why were you—can I sit down somewhere?"

"Careful, now. Christmas!" the Reverend said. Frankie felt
a warm hand around his upper arm. He'd nearly toppled,
and was dangling now over a torrid sea. A cow was swimming
for its life beneath him, trying to get a hoof onto the roof of a
half-submerged barn. "Careful," the Reverend said again.
"Right over here." He guided Frankie to the flaming armchair.
It crackled beneath him. "Just sit. I'm going to get you a glass
of water."

Frankie closed his eyes. He felt the breath of the fan across
his face, heard a faucet running in the next room.

"Drink that," the Reverend said.

He opened his eyes and took the glass. The Reverend sat
down on one end of the coffee table, facing him, and leaned forward to rest his elbows on his knees. His red bathrobe dipped
into the floodwater around his boots.

"Tell you what I don't see—not that it matters to me one way
or the other. I don't see somebody who came here to buy something."

Frankie had nearly reached the bottom of the glass. He
looked over the rim at the Reverend as he drank.

"Let me ask you something, son. How old are you?"

"Twenty-nine."

"That's a hard twenty-nine. You eat anything today?"

"Breakfast," Frankie said. And then, remembering, "Lunch
too."

"Where are you from, again?"

"Jacksonville. But I grew up lower down the coast, on Merritt Island. Where NASA is."

The Reverend glanced at the ceiling. "*Those* whores of Babel." With a thumb and forefinger, he wiped the sweat from his eyes. "The heat does catch up. It makes you slow, is how it does it. Really, now. Tell me what you're doing here."

"What's the Eleventh Coming?"

Frankie saw the dark skin tighten over the man's forehead. "Don't toy with me. You weren't sent, so why do you want to know?"

"I saw it on your sign, out by the road. It's not about God. It's about them, isn't it? On the calendars."

The Reverend's lips moved thoughtfully against each other. "Depends on who you consult."

"I'm ... consulting ... you."

"Mm-hmm. There's a fee for that. Same as before."

Frankie dug into his wallet again and counted out five one-dollar bills.

The Reverend took them with his free hand and tucked them away. He leaned back and seemed once again to x-ray Frankie with his stare. Finally, he said, "The Eleventh Coming is the eleventh time they come. They've been eight times, which I know only because they told me. The tenth time, they take final inventory."

Frankie looked down into his empty glass. "Inventory of what? Of ... souls?"

"Of who they're taking with them," the Reverend said. "They see what's going on from a distance. Hiroshima. Nuclear waste. Radioactive glow around certain government buildings. The entire state of California shaking like Jell-O, about to slide into the sea. People talk about half the film being already gone, eaten up because it had acid in it, and, oh my god, save the film! Save the movies! They're nothing but movies of us being stupid. What about save the *frogs*? Used to be a million frogs out in that forest, making a sound so loud, it would keep a man up at night if he wasn't used to it. Well, what I'm not used to is the frogs being *dead,* and wondering what killed them all. Frogs are the next unicorns, and unicorns maybe used to be men, and maybe we got a second chance, and we've *ruined* it, plain and bold, we have *ruined* it."

Frankie had no idea what the man was talking about. "They're going to take people with them?"

"Focus, son!" the Reverend snapped. "You're lucky to be hearing this once. They're going to take some people with them, yes. *That* is the Eleventh Coming. And they're going to turn off the lights on their way out—finish the job this century started. It's going to be the hurricane-flood-earthquake-*and*-fire next time. They'll do it with our own weather, polish the whole planet smooth, and when the smoke clears…" He'd been rubbing his hands over the wooden ball, and he held it up now between them and focused his gaze on it proudly. "Beauty. And not a living soul left on Earth to see it." The ball sat balanced on his fingertips for a long time; then it disappeared back into his robe.

"The eleventh time," Frankie said.

"The eleventh. Which may be next year or ten years from now; I'm still working it out. Understand, since approximately 1865 they've come here eight times to take note of the particulars, and they've done a hundred and eleven good deeds each time they've come. There will be nine hundred and ninety-nine good deeds before they're finished. And then that's it. You get me?"

Frankie nodded.

The Reverend seemed unconvinced. *"They know what we're like,"* he said, leaning forward again. "They witness it. Do something wrong to another human being, they witness it. Do something destructive, they witness it. We destroy each other"—he drew a line back and forth between them with his index finger—"it's what we do best. And *some of us* they don't want destroyed. Like me. Because the Reverend Damien Lee Wheeler's going to be around for the Eleventh Coming, and he's going with them, for sure. That is why they showed me my lying whore of a wife cleaving to another man. They knew it would destroy me if it didn't stop."

Lila. Frankie nearly uttered the name, but caught it before it left his mouth. He said, "And the tenth time, they're coming to take inventory."

"Believe it," the Reverend said.

"What about the ninth time?"

"That is the last official help visit. After that, they're making their list, checking it twice, going to torch who's naughty and take who's nice."

"The reason I ask..." Frankie leaned forward, inching closer to the Reverend's damp face. He'd never said it aloud before. He'd kept silent about it the way he did with any potentially good but uncertain thing: because he didn't want to jinx it. But the Reverend seemed beyond jinxing things. "I've met them."

"You met who?"

"Them. Ten years ago. I was at school, in Tallahassee, on this stretch of grass." He cleared his throat. "It's called Landis Green, and people sit all over it during the day like it's a beach. But I was there at night by myself, right in the middle of it, lying on my back on the ground. And it just came... floating over my head. I mean, it was up there—it was pretty high, but it was right over me. It was dark, and round, but with these little points of light all over it, no bigger than the stars. I think it was supposed to look like a constellation."

The muscles of the Reverend's face had gone slack while Frankie was speaking. Slowly, like ingredients floating in a thick sauce over flame, they began to shift, simmering into the look of anger Frankie had seen when he'd first arrived. Then the eyes squinted shut and the mouth winced and the entire head seesawed right and left violently. Frankie drew back.

"What do you think you're doing?" the man snapped.

"Just telling you—"

"I mean, what are you up to? Do you paint?" he demanded.

"No. I—I draw, sometimes. With pastels and markers."

"Christmas, you've got balls! Coming into my home to tap my head!"

"It's not that," Frankie said. "I don't . . . I'm not an artist. I don't sell my stuff or even show it to anybody. I just mean . . . I've met them."

"Met them."

"Yes."

"And they talked to you?"

"Yes."

"And you don't sell?"

"No. I swear."

"Why didn't you tell me about this when you first got here?"

"I don't know." Frankie felt his dizziness return. "I've never told anyone before. It just happened that one time."

"And they actually talked to you," the Reverend said. "That's a . . . rare . . . thing." He isolated these last words as if his doubt was spacing them apart. "What did they sound like?"

"Like . . . regular people, I guess."

"Maybe they sounded like you."

Frankie shrugged.

"They do that. There's some that speak Spanish, too. They know every language we've got, except maybe German."

"They didn't say a whole lot. They just made a prediction, and a kind of . . . promise."

"End of the world?"

"No," Frankie said, "not exactly."

"The list?"

"No. It was something else."

The Reverend's tongue appeared and pressed against his upper lip. He nodded a slow, abbreviated *yes,* which seemed to indicate that the cross-examination was over. "Well, be careful, son," he said, leaning back. "You may not want to see what they have to show you."

"It was just that one time," Frankie said again.

"And you're sure you don't sell?"

"Positive."

"If I only had your hair," the Reverend said, dragging a hand over his scalp. "Hair holds sweat like a sponge, you know? You never think about it till you go bald, and then it's just a free-for-all. Gives my eyebrows too much to do. Did they take you on their ship?"

"No. They just talked to me."

"Then let me show you something that's not for sale."

Frankie followed him through the kitchen and out the back door. Behind the house, across several feet of muddy grass, sat a rusted aluminum shed with a peaked roof. They walked out to it with the ground sucking at their shoes. The Reverend dug into one robe pocket, then another, and produced a single key. With his elbows tucked into his body he turned completely around on his boot heels, then turned around again in the reverse direction. He passed the key from his right hand to his left, and back to his right. Then he unfastened the padlock and slid open the door. The key vanished into his robe and his hand passed over the wall just inside the shed, illuminating a single lightbulb mounted over the door.

"If it wasn't about the end," he said, stepping up onto the

plywood floor of the shed, "and it wasn't about the list, what was it they talked to you about?"

The shed reeked of paint. Along the back wall, several planks had been laid across a pair of sawhorses, and on them sat a bottle of Old Crow, a large coffee can stuffed with brushes, and at least a dozen quarts of paint clustered together and stacked on top of one another, their colors striped and smeared across their sides. Frankie felt tired again, and slightly dizzy from the fumes. He wanted to find out whatever he could, finish this conversation, and get back on the road, maybe pull over somewhere and sleep. He felt warmer than he thought he should; his fever had returned. "They told me that everything I'm ever going to do is already written down," he said. Stacks of painted boards stood a foot deep against the walls on either side of him—all calendars, from what he could tell.

The Reverend walked over to the makeshift table and opened the Old Crow. He swigged from it, watching Frankie.

"They didn't say too much."

"Heh," the Reverend said—to the whiskey. He set the bottle down. "Look up here."

He pointed to the shed's peaked ceiling. Frankie looked up. Suspended over their heads was a round, three-dimensional object with a hole cut out of its bottom. It was painted silver (rough brushstrokes were visible in the dim light), was at least as wide as the makeshift table, and was sprouting tentacles. The Reverend unwound a nylon cord from an anchor on the back wall. "The hull I made from specifications they gave me—scaled down, of course. The inside is all my own." He gathered the cord in his hand and then carefully started to let it out. The object jostled back and forth, and descended. Frankie stepped out of its way. "It won't fall," the Reverend said. "It goes to right . . . there." He kept his eyes on the spacecraft as it turned gently, hanging now just above their heads. His hand found the bottle again. He drank from it. "Look like what they showed you?"

"Sort of," Frankie said. "It was dark."

The outside of the model, he saw now, was covered not in brushstrokes but in words that had been etched into the paint before it had dried, possibly with a toothpick. The effect was a paisley-like relief that hurt Frankie's eyes when he tried to read it. He caught only the words *cast* and *eventual*.

"Slide that box over here."

He looked down and saw a wooden crate next to the door. He pushed it toward the center of the shed with his foot.

"So what did they tell you?"

"This is good," Frankie said of the ship, beginning to move around it. "They told me I was going to get sick." He heard the slosh of liquid as the whiskey bottle was tipped up again.

"Go on."

"They told me I might die."

"Christmas."

"And I understand. I mean, I see it. I know it's been happening. Everywhere. It's just that some of it isn't really like being sick. It's strange, more than anything else."

"'Strange is this vision into the future of our future,'" the Reverend said, quoting something Frankie didn't recognize.

"But they said they were coming back. And when Ms. Kotula—the gallery owner—told me about you, I thought maybe you'd know something about when they were coming."

"I can't tell you the exact date of the end of the Earth." The Reverend sighed. It sounded like an admission, not a self-imposed rule.

"It wasn't that. I wanted to know about the...the *Ninth* Coming, I guess it would be. The last time they come to help people. They told me they were going to come back after I got sick, and that when they did, they would know how to help. Not just me. Everyone who's sick. From anything."

"Tall order," the Reverend said.

"I'm curious, more than anything else. About what's going to happen. If there are going to be antidotes. I mean, whether or not I'm still here, I want to know. And if it *is* going to be a time when I'm still…around, that would be great too. It would just help, knowing."

"I don't know anything about the Ninth," the Reverend said. "Everything up to and including the Tenth? They don't let out that information. They don't want us to know."

"I don't draw the way I used to," Frankie said, focusing on the spacecraft. "My hand movement, I mean. Even my signature doesn't look like it did a year ago."

"Flip that crate over."

He reached down and turned the crate so that its bottom was facing up. The Reverend extended one of his long legs, and with his muddy boot he centered the crate under the spacecraft. He nodded to Frankie.

"Go on. Stick your head inside. Mind you, it's not for touching; it's for looking."

"What is it?"

"I call it 'The Diorama of My True Abduction.'"

Frankie hesitated. The Reverend glared at him over the bottle. Rubbing his palms against his hips, Frankie moved forward, bent down, and stepped onto the crate. Slowly, he stood upright. His head ascended into the dark bowels of the spacecraft.

He heard a scratching sound, and sensed the craft moving around him. Then the inside of it lit up gradually as if controlled by a dimmer switch.

"I can't tell you the date of the Eleventh Coming," the Reverend said, his deep voice sounding radioed in, "because I don't know it yet. But it's wrapped up in a package they placed in my brain, and they put it there on purpose. I didn't pick them, *they* picked *me*. Just like they picked you. They came and showed me the deception and whoredom going on in my life so I could get pure enough to be on the list."

Inches from Frankie's nose was a struggle, or rather, a single moment of a struggle: frozen in time, miniaturized, rendered in intricate detail. Seven blue-bodied aliens handmade out of clay, with black almond-shaped eyes, held tight to the twisting figure of a man wearing a blue baseball cap. They surrounded him, holding on to his feet, his arms, the back of his head. The man's face was a tortured grimace rendered with what must have been a single bristle torn from a brush. The scene was enclosed on either side by silver walls, each cut with a portal-like doorway. Frankie shifted his gaze—and his body—to the right, where in a second room the aliens held the man in a kind of dentist's chair. He seemed to be sleeping. In the next room, each of the aliens stood around him, holding instruments.

"They didn't cut me," the Reverend said. "What nobody understands is that these beings don't have anything to learn from us. What's to be learned from a species of whores and thieves who'd just as soon destroy each other and their own planet as scratch their noses? They come here to *teach*. They come here to *save* us. Some of us. They take your own situation and they use it to show you what you need to know. They illuminated my life, and in that same moment, they gave me a vision of the end of this world. I've just got to get the right information so I can do the math and find out *when*."

"What math?" Frankie asked. His voice bounced back at him from the inner walls of the craft.

"Haven't you been listening? The math gives you the *when*, son. Everything that's going to happen, that's ever happened before, only matters if we know *when*. I need to figure out the exact date of her first betrayal. I've got everything else: our birthdays, old phone numbers, Social Security numbers, anniversary, number of years we were together, number of months, number of days. If I get the *exact date* of her first betrayal, I'll be ready to put numbers on all these calendars, and *then* I'll be able to tell you the date of the Eleventh Coming."

"You can't ask her?" Frankie chanced.

"She's not talking to me anymore," the Reverend said in a tone that was both frustrated and disappointed.

Frankie shifted again.

"I've got one calendar I'm writing in a book, from the last page backward. It's a record in reverse of our lives together. I'll figure it out on that one soon enough."

In the next room of the spacecraft, the man in the blue cap was still unconscious and was suspended, by no visible means, from the ceiling, while the aliens stood beneath him with miniature clipboards and pencils. "So you don't have any idea about the Ninth?"

"There's something I need to do," the Reverend said, his words overlapping Frankie's question. "What's that?"

"The Ninth—"

"I'm not withholding information, son. That would be my understandable *right,* but I'm not. I'm telling you what I know. Some of us are the real thing, and some of us ruined what was handed to us. I mean, some of us are among the most special and patient citizens that ever walked this Earth, and that's who's going to be delivered from it. It's all about what you do with what they show you. I paint because I know I should. If you draw—and I mean really draw, from your head and not your heart—it's because you know you should draw. Forget about the Ninth. Just be patient, in the meantime, about this . . . help they promised. The fact is, it comes with a price that's probably not going to be negotiable."

There was writing on the miniature clipboards. Frankie strained to read it, but it was too small. "Okay," he said.

"Where are you headed when you leave here? Not to Prophet Mulvaney's place, I hope."

"Who?"

"That fool up near River Falls building the Apocalypse Boat."

"No," Frankie said. "I'm—I'm going home."

"Jacksonville?"

"Merritt Island."

"You got family?"

He had two brothers and one sister, but they weren't there anymore. Sometimes it felt like they'd been carried away in separate ships, to separate planets. But there *was* someone waiting for him at home. He said, "My mom's there."

"She know what shape you're in?"

He shook his head no.

"Is she expecting you?"

"Yes," he said. "Not me . . . like this, but I called and told her I was coming."

"Home." The Reverend pronounced the word like a new sound he was testing out. He coughed suddenly. He coughed again, and then, from what Frankie could tell by the noises that entered from the bottom of the diorama, he spit. "What we do on this planet, we won't do on the next. You realize that, don't you?"

"I'm not sure."

"That's what it *is*. That's what it *has* to be. Otherwise, there's no point." The Reverend spat again. Then, sounding both sad and irritated, he asked, "You got a tape deck in your car?"

Frankie hesitated inside the spacecraft. He bent his legs and pulled his head out, and he had to turn around to face the Reverend again. "Yes."

"Can I use it?"

He glanced around the inside of the shed. "What for?"

"What do you *think*, son? For a minute, that's what for. I just got to hear something."

"Okay." He dug his keys from his pocket and stepped down off the crate.

"No, no, you stay here," the Reverend ordered. He took the keys. "I know how to work it. Just let me use it for a minute. Keep looking in there; you might learn a little." He indicated the spacecraft with his jaw, and then walked straight out of the shed with Frankie's keys in one hand and the bottle of Old Crow in the other, his red bathrobe flowing behind him like a cape.

Frankie watched the Reverend climb the back steps and disappear into the house. He stood for a moment on the plywood floor, surrounded by the unnumbered calendars. Then he stepped up onto the crate and eased his head back into the diorama.

His strength—what was left of it, for the day—was waning. He felt it, sometimes, trying to find a way out, slipping through his veins, pushing at the ends of his fingers or traveling with gravity down his legs and collecting in his feet. Going home now made sense. Going home might even be what they wanted him to do, what they had already decided would happen. Could they steer the future? Not just predict it, but guide it down a particular path? He would ask the Reverend about that when he got back.

Then it occurred to him that the Reverend might be stealing his car.

From outside the spaceship, he heard the loud, repeated banging of a piano chord. Then an explosion of violins. He pulled his head out and stepped down off the crate.

Someone—an anguished-sounding man—began to sing: *I saw the light on the night that I passed by her window.*

Frankie crossed the yard and entered the house through the back door. In the living room, he saw the tape deck still had a hammer sticking out of it, but its front panel was open, the chamber empty.

The song was getting louder. The singer's voice seared the air like a bolt of heat lightning. Frankie pushed through the screen door and was descending the front steps when the chorus started, carried on a wave of mariachi horns.

Why, why, why, Delilah?

The Volkswagen was parked where he'd left it. The driver's door was open and the Reverend was sitting behind the wheel. Between Frankie and the car, the row of calendars hung with their backs to him, unpainted, rippled by humidity, blanched by the sun, like an unfinished fence that had never been properly primed.

He eased toward the car. The Reverend's head was hanging down. His robe was open, the bottle was in his lap, and his face was in his hands. His entire body began to shudder.

So before they come to break down the door, the singer bemoaned, *forgive me, Delilah, I just couldn't take anymore.*

Frankie would wait until the song was over, wait until the Reverend had stopped crying. But he was more tired than patient, and time was running out. They were coming. And whether it was going to be beautiful or tragic, tomorrow or ten years from now, home was where he wanted to be when they arrived.

Getting Heavy with Fate

1965

You don't know who I am, Teresa writes. We've never met. That was Dermot's doing.

The candle on the plate next to her hand is a votive, caving in on itself like a little melting Colosseum of wax. The walls of the room—a room that triples as living room and dining room and bedroom—are an ashy avocado, more gray in this light than green. I don't hate him, she writes. She scratches through the sentence, tears off the page, and starts again: You don't know who I am. We've never met.

She wants to be direct. She wants to sound—to be—*smart,* to fill the page with evidence that she is a smart young woman, a scholar, that there is nothing irresponsible or gold-digging about her. *I've just completed a course in art appreciation. Dear Mr. and Mrs. Ragazzino, you don't know who I am. We've never met. But I'm your daughter-in-law, Dermot's wife, and I've just completed a course in art appreciation. I'm taking another course in American poetry now, and have received an A on my first test. Enclosed are pictures of your grandchildren, Matthew, 5, and Mary-Katherine, 2. For a likeness of me, please see Watteau's* Ceres.

It's important to be clear about it all. Articulate. Factual.

Matt and Katherine share the bedroom opposite the little

kitchen. Between Matt's single bed and Katherine's crib is a path so narrow, Teresa brushes both sides when she turns around between them. Sometimes, coming into their room late at night to check on them, she finds Matt's smooth white arm stretched out in sleep, his little fist closed around one of Katherine's crib posts like a tether. They feel too warm at night. The apartment is on the top floor of the building; inches above their ceiling is a long rectangle of black tar that soaks up the heat during the day and drips it down into the apartment after dark.

She can't think of how to word any of this without sounding ridiculous (and what if they don't believe her?). She wants them to know the facts. The pictures are factual; there's no arguing with them. Matt's is a kindergarten photo, and he looks undeniably like Dermot: blond-haired and broad-faced. Katherine's is a portrait made at a professional studio and paid for by Uncle Phil. In it, she's a happy, round-headed, universal baby, though in reality Katherine is capable of expressions weighted with annoyance and cynicism. Some nights, when Teresa comes home from work and extends her arms toward her daughter, Katherine pulls away, looks insulted, hugs her ballerina doll as if Teresa means to steal it, and gives her a scowl that seems to say, *Why are you bothering me?* Teresa writes their names and respective ages on the backs of the photos and stacks them next to the envelope she's already addressed.

You don't know who I am, she writes. We've never met. But I'm your daughter-in-law, Teresa Malloy Ragazzino, and I'm trying to reach my husband.

✳

There's a war starting up, but it feels very far away. Nearly everything outside of her day-to-day life has become remote. She's paid almost no attention to the holidays this year, completely skipped Easter, forgotten her own birthday and has barely managed to celebrate the children's. July 4th slipped her mind entirely, and when the fireworks blasted over the Capitol she thought, just for a moment, that they were under Russian or even Chinese attack. Because Uncle Phil has gotten her a subscription to the *Washington Post* she reads the headlines while she makes breakfast each morning. Winston Churchill dead. T. S. Eliot dead. Stan Laurel dead. Lyndon Johnson looking edgy as he's sworn in again and Robert Kennedy still looking sad, but excited too, wading through a field of outstretched hands. "You're keeping up with this, right?" Uncle Phil asked her one evening. He sat at the aluminum table that took up part of the living room, touching one of his thick fingers to a headline.

3,000 Marines to Da Nang to Fight Vietcong

"I looked at it." Teresa was making a sandwich for Matt to take to school the next day.

"I believe I may be the only bona fide veteran of a world war who's against this nonsense." Uncle Phil is her father's younger brother. He and her father—the Malloy boys, they once called themselves—went to their local college together, enlisted in the Navy together, and moved in tandem across the lily pads of aircraft carriers and destroyers and destroyer tenders off the coast of Japan. Her father, having ascended to the rank of captain, died in combat—an event Uncle Phil witnessed and refuses to talk about beyond saying there was a storm, and they were transporting Sean from one ship to another with a pulley system and a swinging metal chair. The storm was bad and there was an accident—no fault of the Navy's. You were somebody important if they put you in that chair. Ten years later, when her mother died from TB, Teresa would have been without any family at all if it hadn't been for Uncle Phil. He's fifty-five and has never married. He lives in Alexandria and does something for the Pentagon, which he won't discuss. He drinks. He'd been glad when Teresa had married a man with a solid job (Dermot worked as a desk clerk at the Westmeyer Hotel), but as soon as Dermot took off, Uncle Phil said he'd never trusted him and had expected as much. Because of the drinking—a chronic hint of gin lingers on his breath, and on his neck like cologne— Uncle Phil looks more Irish than he did ten years ago. His nose is a knobby map of river lines. His face looks like a partially deflated punching bag framed by a thin white beard. But he comes by the apartment weekly and makes regular offers of money. "We're doing okay," Teresa told him recently, and he frowned at her doubtfully, glanced around the room—its undecorated walls, her folded sheets and pillow stacked alongside the couch where she slept—and then dropped his gaze to the newspaper.

"You ask most people on the street, they couldn't even tell you what Communism is, but they'll tell you we've got to fight it, *wherever*. We'll be fighting it in space soon, I guess, because they've got that commie-naut up there right now turning somersaults. This whole Harry Truman containment idea is just foolishness. And I say that as a man who spent six months throwing shells at Okinawa—which I'd do again tomorrow, God knows, if they needed me to. But this whole Vietnam thing is getting out of hand. This whole Communism thing. It isn't even about Communism anymore, it's about money. We have to have Japan, so we have to have Southeast Asia. So what are we doing? Sending air-loads of boys to a jungle halfway around the world to get shot to pieces. Half of *them* probably couldn't tell you what Communism is."

"What is it?" Teresa asked, dropping Matt's wrapped sandwich into a paper bag.

"What is it?" Uncle Phil took his finger off the newspaper and cleared his throat. "It's the red without the white and the blue. It's you standing in a breadline, instead of making a sandwich in your own kitchen. Are you sure you couldn't use a few bucks, just till payday?"

Watteau was French, she imagines writing. *His first name was Jean-Antoine, and he lived in the seventeenth and eighteenth centuries. He painted religious pictures and military scenes and elaborately costumed women enjoying the outdoors. I was one of his models. I know that sounds strange, but the likeness is undeniable. He put a sickle in my hand, draped a sheet over my body—*

Matt, a phantom in underpants and T-shirt, is standing in the doorway to the bedroom, watching her stare at the blank page.

"What's wrong? Do you feel sick?"

He shakes his head no. His blond hair is standing up in wild corkscrews around his scalp. He walks over to the television and turns the knob, staring at her.

"No television," she says.

"It doesn't work."

"You should be in bed."

"Nothing works," he says. "All the lightbulbs broke."

"You don't need them when you're asleep. Can't you sleep?"

"Is Uncle Phil mad at you?"

"No. We just had a discussion, that's all."

He turns the television knob on and off, watching her. "Are you writing Dad?"

"No."

"Let's call him." He crosses the room to where the telephone sits on a brass-legged table that came with the apartment. He has the receiver in his hand and is suddenly wide-awake, obstinate, his head tilted back and his eyes gazing at the phone, one little finger hovering over the dial.

"Matthew," she says, "put the phone down."

He waits another moment, then drops the receiver back into its cradle. "It works," he says.

"You're going to wake your sister. Do you want to sleep here on the couch awhile?"

He hesitates, shrugs. "Not especially." A grown-up expression, and one he hasn't learned from her. Maybe from Becky, the girl who lives in the twin building opposite theirs and who, as the babysitter, spends more waking hours with Teresa's children than Teresa herself does. Becky took them to see *Mary Poppins,* and Teresa was the one who then had to snap at Matt when he tried to mount the railing of the cement staircase outside the apartment.

I'm not the villain. She wants to say this to her son and write it in the letter to the Ragazzinos, but she can't, and it makes no difference to Matt; he's already wandering back toward the bedroom, his white shirt fading into the dark outside the candle's perimeter.

This may sound strange to you, but I remember the feeling of his calloused fingers closing mine around the handle of a sickle. He set a woven loop of straw on my head and draped a sheet over my torso. He told me there were going to be children in the painting, that they would be at my feet, adoring me.

✳

She's part of a typing pool for an auto insurance company. She doesn't make much, but for a while after he took off, Dermot was mailing her cash—sixty, sometimes eighty dollars a month—without a note, wrapped in butcher paper, as if he'd taken a job somewhere cutting meat, though she's certain he's gone back to his parents and is probably selling cars in the family business. The first envelope he sent had their return address in Utica, New York.

She knows the Ragazzinos own a car dealership and a few other businesses in Utica. By Dermot's own description, his stepfather and uncles are a tough Italian family, a *business* family. Dermot is blond and has no Italian blood at all; he's the product of his mother's first marriage, to an Irish electrician. But he acts Italian when he's angry. "Trust me," he told Teresa when they made plans to elope. "You don't want to meet my family."

Dermot, in fact, had first made his way down from New York to Washington, D.C., on family business: he'd been delivering a new deep-blue Cadillac to a buyer in the capital, and whatever was supposed to have happened on that errand (he'd once told her the buyer hadn't shown up; another time he'd said the buyer had changed his mind when he saw the cream-colored interior), Dermot remained in Washington, kept the car, and got the job at the Westmeyer Hotel. He met Teresa not long after, in the diner that sat between the hotel and the insurance company where she worked. He courted her in that Cadillac. He allowed her to place a Virgin Mary on the dashboard, though he'd stopped going to church years before, and after they married he moved her into the suite the hotel had given him to live in. He had no communication with his family whatsoever—at least none that Teresa was aware of. Then one day, somewhere in between the births of Matt and Katherine, the Cadillac vanished from its parking spot in front of the hotel. "We should call the police," Teresa said, and Dermot said no, they should definitely *not* call the police. "What about your family?"

"What about them?" he shot back. "You think they don't know where that car is? You think they don't know where *I* am?"

And so no one was called, and the car was never mentioned again.

The rooms they lived in at the Westmeyer Hotel were nice—not honeymoon-suite nice, or Teresa's idea of what that would be, but the walls were white and clean and the furniture matched, and even though they were rooms relegated to employees and their families, there was housekeeping and discount room-service meals, and during the time they lived there Teresa's life came close to how she imagined rich people lived; now she thinks it was simply that she hadn't felt poor. She suspects that the note Dermot wrote her when he left was not as elaborate or as elegant as the one he wrote for the hotel management. (Unlike her, they seemed to have understood completely why their evening desk clerk was suddenly gone, understood why it would take her two weeks—till the end of the month, they emphasized—to find a new place to live.) His note for her, written on Westmeyer stationery, sealed in a Westmeyer envelope, and left under a reading lamp on one of the nightstands, read simply: *T, please don't take this personally. I'm just not cut out for it.* That, and a postscript: *I'll call you.* He never called her at the hotel, nor has he called the new number, listed in the D.C. phonebook under her married name. At first, she came home each day from the job she'd managed to get back (after quitting it to be a wife and a mother) and asked Becky if there'd been any calls. The girl always seemed to say "nope" a little too quickly and unsympathetically, seemed to know that Teresa was asking about the absent Mr. Ragazzino, and Teresa caught herself wondering whether Dermot had left her for another woman, and wondering if that other woman might be Becky. The lunacy of this thought made her afraid she was going crazy, so she stopped asking.

＊

Mr. Hardy, who was a manager in the claims department at the auto insurance company where she worked, told her one day that she was doing a fine job. "Honestly," he said, "if it were up to me, you'd get a big fat raise."

"Thank you, Mr. Hardy."

"Call me David?" That he put this as a question went far

with Teresa. It was a kind of invitation. He was a thin man, a little younger than she was, maybe twenty-five, with Hershey-bar
hair that he parted on the side and combed back over the top of
his squared-off head, though a few wayward sprigs always
hung over his brow. He never passed through the large room
where Teresa worked among seventeen other women without
making eye contact with her and mouthing hello. The day he
asked her to call him David, he'd stopped on the other side of
her Underwood and rested one hand on the machine's gray
body; his other hand held a doodle-covered manila folder. "You
do a bang-up job," he said. The woman to the left of Teresa
sniffed, or snorted, her fingers pecking at evergreen keys.

"I'm serious," Mr. Hardy said. "Some of the girls here use
correction fluid like spackle, but you don't." He bent forward
so that his head was alongside hers and said straight over her
shoulder, "I've asked Mr. Rand if we could get you moved over
to Claims so you could be my secretary. He told me fat chance."

Teresa, dressed in a plain white blouse and an olive skirt, was
wishing she'd worn something prettier that day. She was wishing she owned nicer clothes. "The pool's the pool," she said.

"That's what he said. 'The pool's the pool, it serves the whole
company.'" David Hardy straightened back up. "He knows a
good thing when he sees it."

He smiled at her. Then he was gone, long-striding the path
between the desks and cutting a comic, military turn at the wall
beneath the large round clock.

"Missy," the woman to her left said without looking at her.
"Send me a postcard."

Teresa hadn't been flirted with since she'd met Dermot in
the diner. She looked down at the memo wrapped around the
platen, and sent her fingers flying.

The break room was smoky and filled with black formica-
topped tables and yellow plastic chairs, and for a while she took

her lunch there, bringing her schoolbooks with her and reading chapters for class while she ate. There was a soda machine, a coffee urn, and a large round wall clock identical to the one in the room where she worked. The other women from the typing pool pushed the tables together in groups of two or three and talked incessantly, and none of them ever acknowledged Teresa other than the occasional nod when she first came in, though they sometimes looked her way and lowered their voices. They were better dressed than she was: they had outfits—skirts that matched jackets, shoes that matched purses. They talked about her, and it was flattering at first because she imagined they were calling her "brainy" or "bookish." Then she heard one of them say "Mr. Hardy" before the voice dropped to a whisper.

She started taking her lunch outside. There were pebbled concrete benches on the strip of grass between the building and the parking lot, and she chose one and ate her sandwich with her art history book open across her lap. When a shadow fell over the page one afternoon, she knew before looking up that it was David Hardy, that he'd noticed she was no longer eating in the break room and that he'd come looking for her. He was holding his manila folder out for her to see. "What do you think?" One of his doodles was circled and indicated by a large arrow. It was a cartoon version of her, on the bench, holding her book and biting into her sandwich.

"You made me a mouse," she observed.

"That I did. Round ears, black nose. And this is your tail coming out behind the bench. I'm always drawing mice."

"You've been watching me eat?"

"I drew this as I was walking up the sidewalk. I do it fast, like the pros."

She dropped her eyes from his face to the drawing again. Her mousy backside looked a little large.

"Disney, Warner Bros.," he said, as if she'd asked which pros. "The big boys. I was going to be an animator before I discovered the true joys of the auto insurance business. Mind if I sit down?"

She scooted over and he sat. Immediately he slouched his back and dropped his hands into his lap, his long legs stretched out in front of him and his feet resting on the heels of his brown shoes. He was staring hard across the parking lot and he narrowed his eyes, letting her study his profile; then he reached into his suit coat for his cigarettes. She caught the scent of butane from his lighter. "I hope I'm not bothering you," he said.

"You're not. I'm just eating."

"And reading." He tilted his head toward the book. "What is that?"

"It's for a course I'm taking in art appreciation. I want to—"

"Better yourself," he interrupted. "That's a good thing, nothing wrong with that." He seemed nervous. He was staring at the parking lot again, smoking.

"I want to be a schoolteacher," she said. "An English teacher, really, but you have to take a lot of different courses."

"That's one thing I never wanted to be: a teacher. I wanted to do a lot, when I was younger—a lot of stuff I never ended up doing. Like be president of the United States. And be an animator for Walt Disney. I even wanted to be a soldier, but I've got a gimp foot."

She wasn't sure what the proper response was to the admission of a deformity. "Something you were . . . born with?"

David Hardy laughed. "Nah." He leaned back on the bench, lifted his leg, and planted a shoe between them. "It happened in college. I lost a battle with a farmer named Boone. Who, it turned out, was in cahoots with a Daniels named Jack."

She was confused, and then startled when he hiked up his

left pant leg and pulled down his sock. Suddenly she was staring at his bare ankle and shin.

"That line, right there," he said, pointing to a satiny, lipstick-red trail as wide as a pencil that climbed out of his shoe and curled at the end.

"Oh," Teresa said, wincing. "Ouch."

He shrugged. "Doesn't hurt anymore." He uncapped his pen and drew a pair of mouse ears and a little black nose on one end of the scar. "See, this other part becomes the tail. I don't even have to draw it." He wiggled his bare ankle, flexed the scar, and said in a pinched voice out the side of his mouth, "Hi, Mrs. Ragazzino."

She gave him the same smile she gave Matt when he was trying to tell a funny story. "So you got into a fight?"

"Only with a reservoir wall," he said, shucking the pant leg down. "Which was in cahoots with a broken pop bottle. I got it cut up *and* broken, two for the price of one. Anyway, they told me I shouldn't play tennis anymore—not that I was any Rod Laver—but I can't really run, either, and it's kept me from being shipped out."

"Well, that's a good thing, then."

"I guess it is. I wouldn't mind, you know, defending my country."

"Against Communism?"

"You betcha."

He was staring out over the parking lot again and she felt she'd steered them into a different conversation. She felt responsible for saying the right thing next. "My super's brother was killed in . . . Chu Lai? He stepped on a land mine. I saw a letter from a priest over there, and another one sent by a colonel."

"War is hell," David Hardy said around his cigarette.

"You've got kids, right? I'm sorry, that was nosy. It's just what I've heard around the coffee urn."

"I have two children," she said.

"Two kids. Wow. You're a young mom."

"I'm twenty-seven."

"That's young. I'm twenty-five myself, but I feel"—he shrugged, grinned—"twenty-seven. It's admirable work you do."

"Thank you again."

"No, I don't mean just here. I mean working here and raising two kids on your own. There ought to be a medal for that."

She hadn't told him she was on her own. He'd heard that around the coffee urn too. As she took the last bite of her sandwich, he stood up, and she exhaled around the bite. Enough for one day, she thought. It was exhausting, trying to feel worthy of all this attention.

Then he turned around and asked if she would go out to dinner with him that Friday, and she said yes.

✳

It becomes little more than wordplay, after a certain hour. *I've been proposed to* sounds less decisive than *I'm considering a proposal of marriage. A certain man I work with* sounds more mysterious yet somehow less promiscuous than *a gentleman I know.* She won't actually mention the Watteau. She knows she would sound crazy if she did. But declaring herself the reincarnation of an eighteenth-century model does lend a sense of importance to who she is, and she really has come to believe that it might be true. Maybe she just stared at the textbook reproduction of the painting for so long one night during her first pregnancy that she dreamed herself into it, and in the morning that dream felt like a memory that had always been there. But maybe not. *He preferred the morning light* sounds more impressive than *He painted mostly in the mornings.*

There is a thread of movement in the corner of her eye, and it's so late and the apartment is so silent that it startles her. She jerks in the chair, her leg knocking against the aluminum leg of the table. By the light of the candle burning in the kitchen she sees a cockroach skirting the puddle of water in front of the refrigerator and crossing the floor. *Dear Mr. and Mrs. Ragazzino, I intend to remarry.*

I intend to accept the proposal of a certain man I work with.

Your son needs to know that I am seeking a divorce.

Your son needs to come home.

※

She got tipsy on her date with David Hardy. David Hardy got drunk. She chose to meet him at a steakhouse near Dupont Circle, though he'd offered to pick her up at her apartment. When she arrived at the restaurant, he was waiting for her in a red leather booth, looking almost exactly as he did at work—clean-shaven, wearing a dark-blue suit, his hair combed but falling over his forehead. His eyes were banded in dark, end-of-the-day circles. He moved as if to kiss her cheek but didn't. He pumped her hand nervously and said, "You look great."

"Thank you."

"How about a drink?"

There were two water glasses on the table. "Maybe some wine?" she said. She'd had wine with Dermot on their first date, a glass or two of red wine she hadn't liked but had drunk anyway, and it had made her less nervous. She'd grown talkative, chatting about Khrushchev's wanting his own electric toaster, playing *Ben-Hur* with the salt and pepper shakers. She'd felt amusing. She sat across from David Hardy with her hands in her lap, her purse next to her in the booth, and he tilted his head back as he gazed at the wine list, called the waiter *my good man,* and ordered a bottle of burgundy. He did most of the talking, skillfully asking her something about herself, listening to her answer, then directing the conversation toward his own experiences: the various jobs he'd held in Washington and, before that, in Baltimore; the town where he'd grown up in central Virginia; his three semesters at U.Va.—"I was more interested in the Everly Brothers than in my classes." What did she think of Simon and Garfunkel, he wanted to know, and then told her what he thought: "Good music, but they're so *serious,* like someone ran over their dog. They could take a lesson from the Beatles, you know? 'In restless dreams I walked alone,' fine, but 'I wanna hold your hand' too. 'Mi-chelle, ma belle.'" He opened his hand, palm up, on the table between them, and she thought for a moment he wanted her to hold it; then the steaks arrived.

"You know, I really admire you," he said halfway through the meal.

She was on her second glass of wine. It was necessary that he admire her, she wanted him to admire her, but she said, "There's no reason to."

"Sure there is. You've got a lot on your plate. And I don't know who this husband was, but he's a fool for not being here, right now, instead of me. I'm sorry, I've got no business saying that, but I've said it. There it is."

"Well—"

"You know, I was engaged once. I was all set to tie the knot. But it didn't work out."

What was the right response? Some statement, maybe, about how things happen for the best—but would she sound lonely, saying that? Would it underscore the fact that it was he, David Hardy, sitting across from her now, instead of Dermot? She opened her mouth.

"Fate," he said, sitting back. "I don't question it. I accept it with open arms." His steak was finished, reduced to a twist of gristle. Where his baked potato had been, there was an empty husk of foil. The lower half of his shirtfront, she noticed, was pushing out against his tie; he was like a puppy that balloons around its middle after it eats.

"Was she your high school sweetheart?"

"God, no. Those two were old maids before they reached fifteen. Sarah I met at U.Va., and she was *the one,* I thought, but there were problems. She didn't want to have kids—can you imagine that? A woman who doesn't want kids?"

She could imagine such a woman, but she would never admit it. She wanted only to say whatever would be right and true to his mind, even while part of her felt appalled by the deceitfulness of wanting such a thing.

He asked her if she was Catholic.

"I am," she said. Her steak was half-eaten. She'd barely touched her potato.

He smacked his hand against the table. "I knew it. Why are you Catholic?"

"*Why?* What do you mean?"

"I mean, do you really believe it? The whole three-days-in-the-cave, roll-back-the-boulder business? Purgatory-as-heaven's-waiting-room?"

She believed it all. True, she'd slipped some. She'd forgotten how to say a rosary. But she wanted to learn again, wanted to be a good Catholic and wanted her children to grow up belonging to the church. It was the only religion she'd ever known. Believing in its rewards all these years—since childhood—felt like an investment she would be a fool to pull out of now. It felt wrong to even think about not believing in the sacraments, in the teachings of Christ, as out of practice as she was. "I do," she said.

David Hardy dug a St. Christopher medallion from beneath his shirt collar and wagged it at her. "Where do you go?"

"Well, I haven't really gone since...I became single. You know how the church is."

"About divorce? Just show up. Tell them your husband's a Methodist. What are they going to do—come to your house?"

That she'd gotten a divorce was apparently part of the coffee urn gossip. She didn't correct him. "The church is pretty strict. I do miss it, though."

"So just fib. Go to church if you want." He smacked the table again. "We should go together sometime. I've been remiss myself lately." He looked down at the plates, then brought a hand up and tucked his St. Christopher medallion back under his collar. "Patron saint of travelers," he said, patting the knot of his tie. "Hey—do you want to take a drive?"

Something caught up with him, once they were sitting in his Mustang. He slumped behind the wheel for several moments, then bolted forward. "Whoa," he said, rattling his head a little. "Okay."

He turned the ignition.

They drove down Connecticut Avenue, then turned west on Constitution, following the edge of the Mall and the Reflecting Pool, and made a complete circle around the Lincoln Memorial. Then they headed back east, past the Washington Monument, and north. She watched the White House glide by the left side of the car. Somewhere beyond McPherson Square he cut a sharp corner and jumped the curb, grazing a mailbox. The side mirror on her door snapped away clean. "Oh!" Teresa said, and closed a hand over her mouth for a moment. "I think you just lost your mirror."

"Did I?" He stopped the car. She waited, exhilarated and worried at the same time, while he got out and went back for it. When he returned, he held the mirror up for her to see, as if it were some oddity he'd found, and tossed it onto the backseat. "I guess we can live without it," he said, climbing back behind the wheel.

They parked on a residential street, and she knew they were in the vicinity of his apartment. He kept a hand on the key in the ignition after the engine was off and seemed absorbed in studying the odometer. She said, "I told the sitter I'd be back by midnight."

His two-room apartment was filled with clutter: newspapers and ripped-opened mail and clothes dropped randomly about the furniture and floor. A coffee mug bearing the name of the company that employed them anchored a T-shirt to one end of the coffee table. In the bedroom there was no closet, just a rod suspended from the ceiling with wires, and hanging from it, next to a raincoat, were three other suits she recognized from work. He stood next to the bed, tapping his foot and bobbing his head slightly, as if he were hearing music. When she reached up and tried to loosen his tie, he stiffened, then dug his own fingers into the knot, pulled it off and flung it over a chair. She undressed herself.

"Okay," he said when they were on his bed, his voice that of a man starting a serious project. He centered his body over hers, resting his weight on his elbows and looking at the wall just beyond her head. "Okay." In the faint light from the street lamp outside the window she saw his jaw edge forward. He was rigid from head to toe. She put her hands on his lower back. "Okay." With what seemed to her to be as little movement as possible, he pushed forward, then began to rock his entire planked body back and forth, saying "okay" every few thrusts, the St. Christopher medallion winking between them. He finished almost immediately—"O-*kay*"—and then froze, suspended, his eyes still fixed on the wall.

As he rolled to the side, he exhaled and folded his arms across his stomach.

That was it for him, she thought. She hadn't been with anyone since Dermot, had barely had the chance to be in bed with
David Hardy before he was done, and now, in all likelihood, he
was done with her entirely.

But in the car on the way back to her apartment, he said,
"Marry me."

Her throat closed up. She swallowed and said, "We hardly
know each other," which sounded awful, given what they'd just
done.

"I'm serious. I love kids. I want to be a father and a husband,
it's what I was meant to be, and you can't argue with fate, can
you? I mean, who are we to start getting all heavy with fate?"

⁂

There is only so much she can be expected to do. Only so
much—and she's doing it, isn't she? Watteau expected her to sit
entirely still on a table, her leg folded against a chair, her hand
clutching the sickle that would, in the final product, be curled
under the chin of a child hovering in the background—and she
imagines she did just that. Uncle Phil expected her to tell him
when she needed money, and she did that too, now and then, because there was nothing coming in from Dermot anymore and
her paycheck was usually spent before she saw it; but asking felt
awful to her, made her feel as if she were always exhausted for
nothing, as if her efforts at keeping herself and Matt and
Katherine fed and cared for were feeble and would never be
enough. So she'd let that one bill slip, and then let it slip again
because they didn't seem to have cared, had sent no warning
notice. And then one night, halfway through *The Big Valley*,
the picture shrank to a pinpoint on the television screen and the
apartment went dark and the fans slowed down to nothing. The
silence was so sudden it seemed loud. The children were already
asleep, thankfully. Teresa saw light coming from the apartment

building beyond the living room windows and knew immediately what had happened. Thinking—trying only to think—that tomorrow she would buy candles, she reached over in the dark for her pillow and sheets, and stretched out flat against the couch.

Uncle Phil came by the next afternoon, a Saturday, with a bag of groceries resting on one arm. Matt ran up to him and hugged his leg and said, "Nothing works."

"Nothing works? Well, I brought the works, right here. Vanilla ice cream and peanuts. If you have some ginger ale, we'll make Boston coolers."

He was already at the refrigerator before Teresa could stop him. He opened the door and stood in front of its darkened, warm interior, its carton of ruined milk, its dripping freezer compartment. She saw the back of his neck turn red above the black collar of his sport shirt. He turned around and his sagging face sagged a little more as he spotted the candles she'd set out on plates, not lighted yet but ready for sundown. He looked at her.

"Don't," she said softly, touching a finger to her lips.

"Don't what? You didn't pay the light bill?"

"There's a problem with the electric company," she said, glancing at Matt, and at Katherine, who was drawing jagged red lines across the pages of a coloring book. "We were just talking about it, weren't we, Matt?"

"Teresa," Uncle Phil said. He seemed baffled, irritated. "Teresa, what have you let happen here?"

"We were just talking about it," she said more firmly. "It's a problem with the electric company. They're fixing it."

"And how are they going to fix it if you don't tell me about it? My God, it can't be that much money."

"We're doing fine," she said. It was all she could think to say.

"You're not doing fine. You've got no power! You have to *tell* me when you need these things. I'm right here, I want to help!

I mean, what kind of mother... You've got, you're paying money for those classes, and for that babysitter when you want to step out, but you let them cut your power? What kind of mother—"

He didn't finish the sentence. She'd stood up from the couch and was walking toward him, a ship steering into a storm. There were tears in her eyes—of anger or desperation, she wasn't sure which—and she blinked slowly and took the bag of groceries from his arms, setting it on the counter. "Ice cream," she said loudly, reaching into the bag. She looked past Uncle Phil at the wall behind him, then leaned sideways until the children came into view. "Who wants ice cream?"

※

Dear Mr. and Mrs. Ragazzino, she wants to write, *I'm not what I expected to be.* In truth she hadn't expected much. It's just that what her life has become, what *she's* become, is so much less than what even she thought she would be. There is some basic formula she isn't privy to, a force that works like a mixer, swirling all the ingredients into a smooth, digestible stock. This shouldn't be so hard, after all. Uncle Phil will take care of the emergencies. Sometime Monday, he'll get the power turned back on. He'll make some excuse—as he shuffles through the newspaper, head bent down—about his mind being somewhere else, on his job, maybe, when he said what he had about her mothering skills. David Hardy, who hasn't smiled or said hello once since she declined his proposal the day after their date, will most likely come around and apologize for being so standoffish. Just as the men who threw her and her children out of the Westmeyer Hotel apologized on that last day, saying that the decision wasn't theirs but the owners'. All men, she imagines, perpetually get themselves into situations that call for apologies, and eventually apologize—except for Dermot.

Please, his note had said, *don't take this personally.* But there was no apology in what he'd written, or for what he hadn't done since.

※

After Uncle Phil had consumed his share of ice cream and left, she called Becky and asked if she could come over for an hour or so, and when Becky knocked on the door, Teresa opened it and said, "The power's out," before the girl could make the observation herself. Teresa already had her purse in her hands. "Be good," she said to the children. She walked along the concrete balcony to the steps, followed them down to the street, and walked to the corner. There were three people waiting for a bus: two men seated on the bench and a woman wearing an aqua-blue dress, with a matching pillbox hat, standing next to the sign. The woman was sweating, smoking a cigarette, and waving her free hand like a large feather in front of her throat. Teresa stood next to her. She commented on the heat, and the woman smiled. Then Teresa asked her if she might have an extra cigarette. The woman's eyes ran the entire length of Teresa's body, as if she suspected Teresa was not a real smoker. But she reached into her purse and gave her one, then produced a flame from the corner of her cigarette case. "Thank you," Teresa said. She closed off her throat and pushed the smoke out of her mouth. "That's lovely." The woman gave her a strange, almost worried look, then turned and resumed watching for the bus. *I'm just not cut out for it,* Dermot had written. How long would Becky wait for her to return before panicking? How long before Becky found Uncle Phil's number stuck to the refrigerator and called him, and how long before he, assessing the situation in his blunt and practical way, called the police? The thought was like a train speeding through Teresa's mind, and she caught herself smiling as the ash of the neglected cigarette dropped onto the sidewalk. Changes in sound, changes in light, a whole new cast of characters. "Is this you?" the woman in the aqua-blue dress asked, for the bus had arrived, was standing in front of them, and Teresa hadn't even noticed.

❊

It's August. Sunday evening. She's in her apartment, her children are asleep, she has written by candlelight the date, the city. *Dear Mr. and Mrs. Ragazzino, You don't know who I am. We've never met. But I'm your daughter-in-law, Teresa Ragazzino, and your son, Dermot, walked out on me.* "Honey," the woman asked, "is this you?"

It is and is not. It's for another Teresa, perhaps, one who might board and be carried someplace else, to live out a different life and become—who knows?—the model for someone's painting, or the title of someone's song, or just a person remembered for having vanished. "Is-this-your-bus?" the woman asked, articulating her words as if Teresa were a foreigner. "I don't know," Teresa said, taking in the length of the bus, its massive, openmouthed tires, its dark interior. "Well, you ought to find out," the woman said, placing one aqua shoe on the first step. "Otherwise, you'll be standing here all day."

Dear Mr. and Mrs. Ragazzino, she writes. You don't know who I am. We've never met, but I'm your daughter-in-law. Dermot is with you, I believe, or at least you know where he is. Please tell him I've been proposed to by someone, and have declined the offer. Should your son wish to contact me, my number is listed. But there's no immediate need.

She signs the note with her initial, T., folds it and slips it into the envelope without the pictures of the children. Better, she thinks, to let them guess a little. Better to keep her options open.

So Much for Artemis

At the beginning of the summer Jennifer hypnotized him with her MedicAlert bracelet. "You are in my power," she said. "You will do exactly as I say." She told him to bark like a dog, and he barked. She told him he was a car, and, sitting across from her on her bed with his eyes closed, he honked and lurched forward, screeched and reared back. "Now you're a beggar," she said. "Go ask my mother for a dollar."

Frankie got up and walked out of her room and down the hall, fluttering his eyelids, his arms raised in front of him like a zombie. Jennifer's mother was in the aboveground pool in the backyard, floating in a donut-shaped raft that had a holder for her iced tea tumbler. Her hair was piled onto her head with bobby pins, and she was reading a book through a pair of large round sunglasses. At the top of the metal steps, his arms still raised, Frankie said, "Mrs. Woodrow, I need a dollar, for I am a beggar."

"You certainly are," Mrs. Woodrow said.

Standing next to Frankie on the deck, Jennifer told her mother she'd hypnotized him.

"Well, I don't go swimming with my purse," Mrs. Woodrow said.

"You can promise," Jennifer said. "You can give it to us later."

Mrs. Woodrow promised and asked them to please go do something else.

Back in the bedroom, Frankie sat cross-legged on the floor and said, "Half that dollar's mine, right?"

"You will have no memory of this," Jennifer said, and snapped her fingers.

*

He was never, ever, to push her, hit her, or throw things at her. He didn't want to do any of that, but his mother had told him not to anyway, saying it was Mrs. Woodrow's rule for any child she babysat. "And don't ever ask Jennifer if she's sick," his mother had told him. "Mrs. Woodrow said other children have asked that, and it isn't nice. Jennifer's not sick. She's just— fragile." Frankie was seven and small for his age, but Jennifer was eight, and smaller. Her nose came to a sharp tip and her jaw was almost not there at all, as if it had been pushed into her neck. Her skin was wrinkled and dry-looking, like a thin layer of papier-mâché. She always wore some kind of hat, indoors or out—a cowboy hat, a plastic fireman's helmet, or, most often, a soft white Gilligan cap with the NASA logo and an elastic strap that hung loosely in front of her throat. That afternoon, when Frankie asked if they could take turns hypnotizing each other, she led him into the bathroom and took off the cap, showing him her bare head for the first time. She was almost entirely bald. Her scalp was dimpled with pink and gray spots and had just a few strands of white hair. "You have to be very smart to hypnotize a person," she said, looking at herself in the mirror. "My brain is so big, there's hardly room for hair roots." Frankie stared at her too, and then the two of them looked at Frankie's head, which was covered in dark, wavy hair. "The less hair you have," Jennifer said, "the more brains. It's just a fact of nature."

During dinner at home that evening, Frankie, the youngest, looked at the five other heads around the table, each one covered with hair, and said, "Do you think we'd be a smarter family if we were bald?"

Matt and Joe burst out laughing, and Katherine bucked forward and pinched her nose. "God!" she said. "I almost snorted milk!"

Frankie's mother had more hair than any of them; it was straight and the color of palm bark. She frowned while they were laughing, and her mouth started moving soundlessly, as if she didn't know what she wanted to say. Finally she snapped, "All right, that's enough now. Your father's had a *very* rough day."

At the other end of the table, Frankie's father kept his head down and his hands close to his plate, sliding his knife through his Salisbury steak. When he put a piece in his mouth, his jaw moved like a machine with a worn-down battery. He glanced at Frankie's mother, and between bites he said, "Why don't you tell them?"

She swallowed and pressed her napkin against her lips. "Roy, let's just have a nice dinner."

"They're going to find out anyway," his father said.

Matt, who was fourteen and the eldest, said, "You don't have to tell me. I already know."

"Oh, Matt, be quiet," his mother said. "You *don't* know."

"Yes I do," Matt insisted. "Paul Krieger's father is in the same boat. He told Paul, and Paul told me."

"Why does Matt get to know and I don't?" Katherine asked.

"There's nothing to know," Frankie's mother said, glaring at Matt. "Everything is fine." She glared at Katherine and at Joe, too, and finally at Frankie, whose mouth was full of food. "Just eat," she said.

The next morning she got dressed and left for work without taking Frankie to Mrs. Woodrow's house. His father was at the table for breakfast, as usual, but he didn't go anywhere afterward. He stayed in his robe and pajamas, reading the newspaper.

An hour later, Frankie was sitting on the couch and Matt and Joe were on the living room floor, watching *Ultraman*. Frankie's father was still at the table. Katherine stood between the two rooms, holding a glass of milk, staring at him. "Aren't you going to work?" she asked.

"No." He lit a cigarette and turned a page of the newspaper.

Matt looked at Katherine and Joe. "Told you."

"I'm supposed to go to Mrs. Woodrow's house," Frankie said.

"You don't have to go today," his father said without looking up. "I'm going to be here."

"Are you sick?" Katherine asked.

"No, I'm not sick. I'm just going to be here."

Frankie heard Katherine groan softly as she walked toward the back of the house. When their television show ended, both his brothers followed.

By lunchtime, the three of them were gone. Matt and Joe had ridden their bicycles to the mall, and Katherine had walked to the end of the street to play foursquare with her friends. Frankie's father made him a baloney sandwich and Frankie sat on the couch eating it and watching *The Andy Griffith Show*. His father ate his own sandwich standing up. He stared out the window at the front lawn for a while. Then he turned around. "Do they usually do that? Just leave like that?"

"Who?"

"Matt and Joe. Katherine."

"I don't know," Frankie said. "I'm supposed to go to Mrs. Woodrow's."

His father looked at him. He turned back to the window. "God, that grass looks pale."

"I'm supposed to be playing with Jennifer."

"It looks *awful*," his father said. "Probably the soil. Who's Jennifer?"

"*Jen*nifer," Frankie said.

"Oh, that little girl who—that's Mrs. Woodrow's daughter?" Frankie nodded.

"Well, you're not going over there today, I told you that. Wouldn't you rather be here with me for a change? Have some fun?"

The walls on either side of the front window were lined with pictures from his father's job. He worked with cameras at the Space Center, and after each big launch he was given photographs, framed in thin black metal, that hung like award certificates all over the living room: trios of smiling, orange-suited astronauts; the enormous building where they constructed the rockets; silver capsules drifting down over the ocean, beneath orange-and-white-striped parachutes. Above the television was a large picture of Neil Armstrong standing on the surface of the moon, saluting a stiff American flag. His father ate dinner most nights with his NASA badge still dangling from his shirt pocket. He liked reading the paper and working on the lawn, and his favorite television show was the news, which seemed, lately, to be on all the time and had turned into nothing but men sitting around in suits, talking to one another. Frankie couldn't picture what kind of fun the two of them might have.

"So," his father said, turning away from the window. "What do you want to do?"

They looked at each other. His father raised his eyebrows and held them that way for a moment. Then he let them drop and walked over to the television. *Andy Griffith* was over, and he turned the dial to the men in suits. Lowering himself into the armchair next to the couch, he said, "You let me know when you think of something."

✳

The next morning, Frankie begged his mother to take him to Mrs. Woodrow's. She was standing in the kitchen, about to leave for work, and she looked toward Frankie's father at the dining room table. His father turned his eyes down to the newspaper and lifted one hand with the fingers spread wide, which somehow conveyed that it was fine with him.

They played Mousetrap. They played Battleship and Don't Break the Ice! They played Lava, a game Jennifer had invented, which involved stepping cautiously around her room with their arms raised while she determined which pieces of furniture and which squares of her checkered carpet would incinerate them. Mr. Woodrow came home in the middle of the day and ate lunch with them, his yellow realtor's blazer hanging over the back of his chair, and when he was gone, Mrs. Woodrow set up her card table next to the television and worked on her decoupage. Jennifer and Frankie watched *The Big Blue Marble* and sang along with its spooky theme song. "That song says the planet's turning slowly, but it's really spinning at a million miles per hour," Jennifer told Frankie. "If it stopped, we'd all fly off into space."

"That's not true," Frankie said.

"It is true. Isn't it true, Mom?"

Mrs. Woodrow was leaning over a plaque of wood, spreading shellac onto a picture of a pelican she'd cut from a magazine. "It's true," she confirmed.

"Let's play Science," Jennifer said. "You can be my assistant."

In the kitchen, they mixed baking soda with mustard and red food coloring, and spooned the result into a glass filled with pickle juice. "It might be poisonous," Jennifer said. "But it might be a cure for the most deadly disease in the world. Test it." She pushed the glass toward him.

"You test it," he said, nudging it back toward her.

"If it's poison, I'm the only one who can make the antidote. It has to be you."

Frankie took the smallest sip he could from the glass. It tasted awful, and he swallowed it with his head shuddering.

"Your vital signs are good," Jennifer said, resting her tiny, shriveled fingers on his wrist. "Let's play *Wild Kingdom*."

Their neighborhood sat alongside a patch of swamp, and armadillos and possums sometimes crept out of it and waddled down the sidewalk. Glass snakes and black snakes wound across the road and curled up against doorsteps. There were palmetto bugs, slugs, roly-polies, and dragonflies. A turtle as big as a suitcase lived in a cavern beneath the house at the end of Jennifer's street. But when they played *Wild Kingdom,* it was about the lizards, which were everywhere. Jennifer had developed a tracking system for the ones they caught in her backyard. They would name them, tag them by tying bits of colored string to their legs, and use index cards to keep track of the information: *Zeus, five inches long, lime green, white belly, found near back fence next to magnolia bush. Red string on right foreleg.* They had never caught the same lizard twice, but if it ever happened, they were prepared to record its new location and note any changes in its appearance.

"Herman," Frankie said, holding up a lizard he'd caught on the warm metal side of the swimming pool. Its stomach felt spongy between his fingers.

Jennifer peered at it and shook her head. "Artemis," she said, and wrote the name down on an index card. She pulled a couple of inches of blue thread from the spool her mother had given her, and bit it off. Frankie cupped his hands around Artemis and felt the lizard charging against his palms, ricocheting back and forth like a miniature Superball. Lizards were so fast, they sometimes seemed to vanish before his eyes: one moment they'd be clinging to the side of the house, or to the edge of the patio, or to a slat in the fence—and the next moment, they'd be gone. "We should do a magic show," he said. "We could be a husband-and-wife magic team, and we could have the Amazing Vanishing Lizard, and put Artemis in a box, and when we opened the box, he'd run away so fast, it would look like he disappeared."

"Red ants," Jennifer said.

"What would they do?"

"You're standing in red ants," she explained, pointing down.

He bent over and saw at least a dozen of them crawling over his sneakers and around the folds in his socks, heading for his bare calves. By the time he got done jumping and smacking at his legs, the lizard was gone.

"So much for Artemis," Jennifer said, still holding the piece of string.

"Sorry."

She shrugged. "I don't like magic, anyway. It's silly. If we're husband and wife, we're an explorer team doing a study on Bigfoot."

"Okay," Frankie said.

"One's been spotted right over there"—she pointed to a corner of the yard where a thatch of bamboo stood higher than the fence behind it—"and we have to go investigate the sighting."

Frankie nodded. They started across the grass.

"The husband's always rescuing the wife from quicksand," Jennifer said.

"Okay."

"And she's his assistant."

He nodded.

As they neared the bamboo, Jennifer put one of her bird-claw hands against Frankie's chest and stepped ahead of him. She said, "You be the wife."

✳

For the next couple of weeks, Frankie continued to go to Mrs. Woodrow's during the day. In the mornings his father would be at the dining room table, reading the paper. In the afternoons, when Frankie and his mother walked through the front door, he would be on the couch in front of the television. He stayed in his pajamas some days, and if he had a cowlick at breakfast, it would still be poking up at dinner.

One afternoon Frankie and his mother came home and the living room looked bigger. It took Frankie a moment to realize that all of the NASA pictures had been taken down from the walls. The nails were gone and the holes had been filled with white putty.

Frankie's mother stood next to him holding her purse and looking at the walls. Then she walked out of the room. His father was standing at the sliding glass door in the dining room, staring out at the backyard. He was turning a book of matches in his hand.

"Where'd all the pictures go?" Frankie asked.

"Away," his father told him.

"Where?"

"Just away." He looked over his shoulder at Frankie. His chin was turning dark with stubble. "What do you say we go to the library tomorrow?"

"I'm supposed to go to Mrs. Woodrow's house."

"I know. But let's go to the library. I have to look up some information. We have a project to do, you and me."

"What kind of project?"

"The lawn," his father said.

The next day they drove to the library, a squat one-story building made of brick and large, flat rectangles of concrete. His father opened a drawer in the card catalog and Frankie headed for the children's section, but he never made it past the curved, carpeted wall that held tanks of gerbils and garden snakes and a frowning, putty-colored iguana hugging a plastic branch. Before long his father was tapping his shoulder. He didn't have any books, but he was tucking a folded piece of paper into his pocket and there was a ballpoint pen behind his ear. "You ready?"

They drove from the library to Mr. Krieger's house, in the neighborhood next to theirs, and parked in his driveway. Frankie waited in the car while his father knocked on the front door. Mr. Krieger stepped outside wearing a dress shirt and a bathing suit. He was growing a beard. Frankie's father did most of the talking, motioning toward Mr. Krieger's pickup truck. Mr. Krieger shrugged, said something, and disappeared into the house. Frankie's father came back to the car. "That's all set, then," he said, getting behind the wheel. He glanced at Frankie. "Isn't this fun?"

At dinner that night, someone had a Gas Attack. It was either Matt or Joe, and they both clutched their throats and leaned sideways while Katherine pretended to throw up and Frankie pressed his hands against his face.

"Can we please?" Frankie's mother said.

"Please what?" Katherine asked.

"Have a quiet meal, young lady."

"Why? Did Dad have another rough day watching TV?"

"That'll do."

Matt said, "Dad watches more TV than we do."

"That's *enough*."

Frankie's father cleared his throat. "I don't know how you'd know that, since you're never home during the day."

"I'm just saying," Matt said. "It was on when I left and it was on when I got home."

Frankie's mother put her fork down. "You'll clean up that sass mouth, Mr. Man, or you'll spend the rest of the summer in your room, with no television at all."

Matt was silent for a moment. Then he said, "Fine with me." He reached out to the Parmesan cheese shaker and picked at its green foil wrapper with his fingernail. "Maybe I'll just hitch-hike up to Utica and spend the summer with my real dad."

Matt and Katherine had a second father who lived up north. Frankie didn't understand it, and he'd been told by his mother that he didn't need to.

"Hitchhike?" his mother asked Matt.

"Yeah." Matt stared at the cheese shaker. "Up to Utica."

She looked down and turned her spaghetti with a fork. "As if he'd want to see you."

Frankie's father leaned over his plate. "It just so happens that *fake* Dad, here, has been busy. I've been working with Frankie on a little home improvement project."

Joe looked at Frankie and crossed his eyes.

"Can kids get married?" Frankie asked.

His mother set her fork down and touched her temple. "What are you talking about?"

"Me and Jennifer. We want to get married and be an ex-plorer team that investigates Bigfoots."

Katherine and Joe broke into laughter. "Good one!" Katherine said, and Joe held up an imaginary scorecard. "Ten points!" Katherine leaned into Frankie. "I mean, *look* at her! That would be like marrying your *grandmother.*"

"Enough!" Frankie's mother nearly shouted. "Enough, enough, enough!"

The next day his father watched the news all morning and through lunch. When he and Frankie had finished their sandwiches, he changed out of his pajamas into shorts and a white T-shirt, walked out to the storeroom at the end of the car- port, and came back into the living room with a shovel. "Time to get to work," he said.

They walked to the end of their block and down the next street, where a little concrete bridge crossed a ditch into the next neighborhood. His father smoked along the way, occasion- ally tapping the blade of the shovel against the sidewalk. At Mr. Krieger's house, he let Frankie hold the shovel while he knocked on the door. This time Mr. Krieger came out wearing only his bathing suit. His chest was broad and pale and covered with gray hairs, and he had a popsicle in his hand. "AC died," he told Frankie's father. "How's that for timing?"

"Real bad," Frankie's father said.

Mr. Krieger looked down at Frankie. "You must be who is it. Joseph."

"I'm Frankie," Frankie said.

Mr. Krieger said, "I don't know, Roy. It's not looking good out there. The whole Apollo program's been dying a slow death for a while now, and the big boys are finally starting to get scared. I thought they'd take a few of us back, maybe pawn us off on Quality Control. But it's a contract situation. Techni- color's shaking in its boots."

Frankie's father nodded. "I thought we'd borrow that truck now, if it's all right."

Mr. Krieger sucked his teeth. He took the keys from a hook inside the door and handed them over. "Take your time with it. I'm not going anywhere."

The truck was old and noisy and dirty. Its grille was speck- led with smashed lovebugs. Frankie's half of the wide front seat was swollen and bounced him up and down in front of the glove compartment. They took the road that ran behind the two neighborhoods and alongside a patch of swamp, then followed the edge of the swamp to where a Publix supermarket sat at the corner of the mall parking lot. Behind the Publix was a small, sandy jut of land that stuck out like an elbow into New-found Harbor and was dotted with palmetto bushes. Frankie's father slowed the truck down and turned off the pavement into the sand. He rolled forward a little ways, looking out both sides of the cab, humming to himself. Then he shut off the engine. "Let's steal some beach," he said, opening his door.

It wasn't a beach; the sand dropped almost immediately into the brown-green water of the inlet, and there was no place where Frankie would have wanted to put a blanket. He stood at the back of the truck and watched his father open the tailgate and then stab the shovel into the ground and toss a blade's worth of sand into the bed, where it scattered across the ribbed metal. "You watch the road for cops," he directed, winking at Frankie. "What we're doing is technically illegal. There's nothing wrong with it, we're just relocating a little bit of land, but the cops wouldn't see it that way."

He scooped and tossed, slowly covering the bottom of the truck bed.

After a while, he said, "There's a man I know up at the Space Center, his name is Mr. Swilly, and he used to work at the Chamber of Commerce. He's seen pictures of Merritt Island when it was nothing but swamp. Then people came along and did just what we're doing. They relocated soil—brought it over from Cocoa and spread it around so they could build houses and roads." He looked at Frankie. "Mr. Swilly told me something else, too. You know what this whole island used to be covered with?"

Frankie glanced toward the road. He shook his head.

"Take a guess," his father said.

"Cops."

"Nope." His father kept shoveling. "You're just one letter

off, though. *Cows.* It was cattle country. There were ranchers who used to let their cows just wander through the swamp. You know that big concrete bridge we take to get into Cocoa? It used to be just a little wooden bridge. When it came time to take the cows away, they'd round them up and herd them across that bridge. A cattle drive right across the Indian River. Can you imagine that?" He was starting to breathe heavily. His arms and neck were shiny with sweat. "We went from land cowboys to space cowboys, all on the same island," he said. His T-shirt had turned flesh-colored. "What kind of cowboys do you think will come next?"

Frankie looked at the truck bed. It wasn't even half-filled. He said, "Sea cowboys."

His father snapped his head to get the sweat off his face. "We already have those. They're called sailors."

"Sky cowboys?"

"We have them, too—airline pilots," he said. "There may not be any cowboys left."

It took a long time to fill the truck bed. Frankie sat down on the ground and was drawing Bigfoot prints in the sand with his finger when his father announced that they were finished and motioned him back into the cab. On the way home they stopped at the Minute Mart and got Freezies. Frankie's father pinched his cup between his legs so that he could steer the truck and shift gears at the same time. Glancing at Frankie across the wide, bulging front seat, he said, "I don't know about you, but I'm having fun."

At home, he unloaded the sand at the side of the carport. Then they went back for another load. They kept Mr. Krieger's truck overnight, and the following day they did it all over again, twice, only this time when they got home he drove the truck right up onto the lawn at the opposite end of the house and shoveled both loads of sand over the fence into the backyard. The mound reached halfway to Katherine's bedroom window.

All his father would tell any of them, when they asked about the sand, was that it was part of the project he and Frankie were working on. They were a team, he said, and it was a secret.

"So," Katherine said to Frankie that night while he was brushing his teeth, "talk."

"Huh?" Frankie said through a mouthful of toothpaste.

She took hold of the skin over his Adam's apple and twisted it. "What's with all the sand, dingus?"

"I don't know!" He leaned into her hand and dipped his head, dripping toothpaste down his chin.

Matt walked into the bathroom and reached around the two of them for his hairbrush.

"He won't talk," Katherine said.

"Let him go. Talk about what?"

She let go of Frankie's throat and wiped a drop of toothpaste from her arm onto his shirt. "The sand."

"I don't know anything!" Frankie said.

"Who cares about the sand?" Matt looked at himself in the mirror. He drew the hairbrush across each side of his head, reestablishing his part. "I'm just glad he's not my real dad. No job. No friends. *And* he voted for Nixon."

Frankie asked his father the next day if he could *please* go to Mrs. Woodrow's house to play with Jennifer. His father looked irritated. "We're a team. You're not going to quit on me now, are you?" He got Frankie a can of Pix soda, handed him an entire bag of potato chips, and told him to sit on the front porch and keep an eye out for squad cars. Frankie sat in the middle of the porch and ate the potato chips while his father distributed the first two piles of sand across the lawn one shovelful at a time.

"So," Frankie's mother said when they were all at the table

that night, her eyes tired-looking and her mouth bent into a smile. "I thought it might be nice if your father told us about what's happening with the yard." She shrugged as if it didn't matter one way or the other.

"We're replenishing the soil," he said. He glanced around the table as if he was waiting for an argument, or a burst of laughter. "This island's technically three feet below sea level. I don't know if you knew that. There's a lot of dampness in the ground, and then we get all that rain on top of it. Over time, the soil gets washed away and the roots get exposed, so the soil needs to be replenished. I've researched this."

"Don't the Petersons have the same soil we do?" Matt asked.

"Yes."

"Their grass looks great. It's like a golf course."

"That's because the Petersons have WonderLawn come out and hose their yard down with expensive chemicals. And their grass is St. Augustine. Ours is Bahia. It's thinner."

"And," Frankie's mother said, shrugging again, "how long will the sand be there?"

"Until it sinks into the ground. It's for the *soil*. It'll sink in on its own, and the grass will look a thousand times better." He reached for a slice of bread. "Two weeks, tops."

The next day was devoted to distributing the two remaining piles of sand over the backyard. Frankie knew by now that it was no use asking if he could go anywhere. His father told him after breakfast that it was another project day for the two of them, and that it was Frankie's job to sit on the back patio and keep an eye out for police helicopters while he worked. Frankie didn't see any helicopters, or police of any kind, though later that afternoon several neighbors slowed their cars down while passing the house and stared at the sand-covered lawn as if they were witnessing an accident. One of the cars belonged to Mrs. Woodrow. She came to a stop next to the sidewalk and rolled down the passenger window. "Hello, Frankie," she said. "We're just on our way home from the doctor's. It was check-up day. What on earth's happened to your yard?"

"We're fixing the soil," Frankie said. He looked at Jennifer in the backseat and waved. She waved back, then scooted over to the open window and leaned out, peering at the lawn from under the bill of her cap. She said, "There's *sand* all over the grass."

"I know," Frankie said. "My dad says it's good for it."

"That's stupid. Grass needs sunlight. Anyone knows that."

"Frankie," Mrs. Woodrow said, "we miss having you around. Come back and see us."

"I'll try," Frankie said.

The window went up and the car began to roll. Frankie waved as they rounded the corner.

✳

The sand remained right where it was. The sky was clear and the air stayed hot, day after day, until what little grass there was, poking above the surface, began to curl and turn brown. Frankie's father added a soap opera to his afternoons, and several times a day he got up and stood at the front window, or at the sliding glass doors that opened onto the backyard, smoking as he gazed outside. They were sitting on the couch when they heard a rumble in the distance that grew until it nearly blocked out the sound of the TV. The door knocker rattled like a tele-graph knob. Frankie looked toward the front window, then at his father. His father's eyes didn't leave the screen, but his nose twitched and his nostrils flared and, as if he'd identified the rocket by smell alone, he said, "Weather satellite."

One morning, after Matt, Joe, and Katherine had cleared out of the house, he stood in the kitchen talking to Frankie's mother, who was calling from work, and Frankie heard him say that he'd figured out the lawn problem, and that he and Frankie were going to get to work on it that day. "We just haven't had enough rain, that's all. If this were last summer, with all the rain we had, everything would be fine. But we're going to take care of it—give it a little jump start. We're working out a whole sprinkler system." He paused, listening. He began tapping a finger against the kitchen counter. "Teresa, I go through that paper every day," he said. "But the fact is, there's nothing out there.... Yes, I do.... Yes, I have, but it's not going to happen overnight. That's a lot of people they let go, and there are only so many jobs in one county. I mean, I'm looking at a whole career change. Do you really want to get into this now? Here, talk to Frankie." He waved Frankie over to the phone.

"Hi," Frankie said into the receiver.

"Hi, honey," his mother said. "Are you having fun?"

"I guess," Frankie said.

"Can I talk to your father?"

Frankie held up the phone.

They drove to the hardware store and bought a sprinkler that sat on a spike and spit water and shook its head *no* continuously.

The sand turned to mud, dried out, and turned to mud again; but it didn't go anywhere.

His father still made him sandwiches for lunch but stopped making them for himself, grazing instead on whatever snack foods he found in the cabinets. Some nights he didn't eat dinner with the rest of the family, claiming he wasn't hungry, and there were mornings when Frankie came out into the living room and found him asleep on the couch.

One evening, just after they'd finished a meal without him, Frankie's mother was doing the dishes and his father walked into the kitchen and started eating a piece of baloney. A fight broke out. They yelled, and then whispered, and then yelled for a long time. Katherine and Matt closed themselves up in their bedrooms and turned on their record players, and Joe dropped down onto his bed to read a comic book, but Frankie stood and listened in the doorway of the room they shared. He heard his mother shouting about how embarrassed she was, how tired she was, how frightened, and his father shouting about which boat he was in, what didn't fly with him, what was driving him up a tree. Frankie waited to hear the word *sand,* but he never did.

✳

His father yanked at the garden hose and stretched it across the yard until the sweep of the sprinkler was just short of the fence. Then he dodged the water, making footprints in the sand. A neighbor came out of the house behind them and walked slowly over to the chain-link fence that ran between the two yards. He was old. His head hovered in front of his body. He pointed at the sand and started talking to Frankie's father, who straightened up, dried his hands on his pants, and folded his arms, listening.

Frankie was stretched out flat on the patio. He closed his eyes for a while and looked at the sun through his lids; then he rolled onto his side and turned a Superball in front of his face and sang *The Big Blue Marble* song. Finally, he got up and walked to the side of the house, where the gate stood open and a thin band of living grass ran between the fence posts. Lifting his arms out in front of him, his fingertips stretched toward the street, he stepped over the grass and, as if hypnotized, walked across the sandy front yard until he'd reached the sidewalk.

Two streets later he was at Jennifer's house. He rang the bell, and she answered the door wearing a plastic Viking helmet. "Who brought you?" she asked, looking past him down the driveway.

"Nobody."

"Oh. I'm Poseidon, ruler of Atlantis. Do you want to be the citizens?"

Atlantis was at the bottom of the tub in her bathroom. She'd filled the tub with water and submerged several overturned cereal bowls and coffee cups, along with the upright plastic cover for the tissue box, and grouped them together to make a city. Lined up along the edge of the tub were the citizens: wavy-armed rubber finger puppets from the dime machines at the grocery store, plastic monster figurines she'd gotten out of cereal boxes, a Pez dispenser with a clown head. Frankie knelt down on the floor next to the tub and Jennifer sat on the lid of the toilet. "Poseidon's problem is that the citizens are being unruly," she said. "They're refusing to stay underwater." She reached over and flicked one of the monsters into the tub. It sank an inch or so, but then rose to the surface. Frankie poked at it with his finger.

"See?" Jennifer said. "That behavior is unacceptable. There's a curfew, and everyone is supposed to be indoors, asleep."

Frankie put on one of the finger puppets and jiggled it up and down, making its rubber arms flap. In a high, squeaky voice, he said, "We can't help it!"

"Yes you can," Jennifer said. "You're being unruly, and you're all going to be punished."

"Have mercy!" Frankie said, jiggling the puppet. "Give us one more chance!"

"Poseidon is not a patient god," Jennifer replied.

Frankie looked at the submerged city, and at the row of citizens. He reached into the water, covered the opening in the tissue box, and tilted it back. With his other hand he took the citizens one by one and made them jump into the water and swim under the bottom edge of the box. When they were all inside, he replaced his hand with one of the overturned coffee cups, so that the cup became a domed roof. He sat back then, his hands dripping, and smiled proudly.

"Poseidon is not pleased," Jennifer said.

"Why?"

"Because you've changed the whole kingdom around without permission."

"Just one building."

"It's a serious offense," she decreed. "I'm afraid everyone will have to be banished to the Outer Sea."

"Where's that?"

"Gather your people," she said, "and follow me."

Frankie pretended to weep as he removed the cup and the citizens rose to the surface. He collected them in one of the cereal bowls and followed Jennifer out to the backyard.

Mrs. Woodrow had just gotten out of the pool when they climbed the metal steps. Her book and her iced tea tumbler were on the deck next to the ladder, and the donut-shaped raft was drifting away from the side. She took her towel from the white metal railing and wrapped it around her body just below her arms. "Hello, Frankie," she said, pushing her sunglasses up on the bridge of her nose. "I didn't know you were here."

"He's leading the citizens of Atlantis to the shores of the Outer Sea, by order of Poseidon," Jennifer said. "They're all being banished."

"All right, then," Mrs. Woodrow said. "Would you kids like something to eat?"

Frankie nodded.

"I'll make PBJs." She carried her book and her tumbler down the steps and disappeared into the house.

"Phineas R. Wigglethorp," Jennifer proclaimed.

"Who's that?" Frankie asked.

"The first citizen to be banished. We're doing it one by one."

Frankie looked into the bowl. He took one of the finger puppets and tossed it into the middle of the pool.

"William B. Kootchapapa," Jennifer said.

They kept on until the bowl was empty. Then, because Jennifer deemed that punishment not severe enough, they took turns holding the citizens down against the bottom with the pool net. Mrs. Woodrow reappeared, still wrapped in her towel and carrying a tray that held two sandwiches, two glasses of Kool-Aid, and a bowl of potato chips. She set the tray on the picnic table next to the patio, called them over, and went back into the house.

They were eating when Frankie's father came into the backyard through the side gate. He was walking slowly, holding a cigarette down next to his hip, with his head cocked as if he were listening for a particular sound. When he spotted Frankie, he frowned openmouthed.

"What are you doing?" he asked.

Frankie felt his stomach tighten up. He swallowed and said, "Eating."

"You just walked over here, without saying anything?"

"You were talking to that old man."

"So you just *left*? You don't do that! What were you thinking? How was I supposed to know where you were?"

"He's eating his lunch," Jennifer said. She was still wearing the Viking helmet. The horns teetered as she gazed up at him.

"No he's not. He's done."

Frankie pushed the last bite of sandwich into his mouth.

"He hasn't finished his potato chips," Jennifer said. She reached into the bowl and took a small handful of chips and dropped them onto Frankie's plate.

"Stop that," his father said.

"You're not the boss of me," she said. "How come you're killing your lawn?"

Frabkie glanced up nervously. His father's jaw was clenched.

The Viking helmet tipped forward, and Jennifer reached up to lift it away from her eyes. "You *are* killing it, you know. Grass needs sunlight. And air."

"You don't know what you're talking about."

"No plant can live buried under a bunch of sand." She dropped another handful of chips onto Frankie's plate.

"*Stop* that," his father said. "Frankie, I'm not going to tell you again—"

Just then the back door opened and Mrs. Woodrow stepped out, holding the chlorine tester in one hand.

"Who are you?"

"I'm Frankie's father."

"Oh! You're Mr. Kerrigan," she said. "I'm Jill Woodrow. It's nice to finally meet you." She stepped across the patio, extending her free hand.

"Let's go," Frankie's father said to him. "I don't know what you were thinking, coming over here, but you're in big trouble."

Mrs. Woodrow lowered her hand. "He's been perfectly well behaved."

"Excuse me, but—I'm talking to my son. And no, he hasn't been well behaved, because he left the house without permission, and I didn't know where he was."

"He isn't through *eating,*" Jennifer told her mother. "Does he have to go with this lawn killer?"

"*Frankie,*" his father said. He put the cigarette in a corner of his mouth and set his hand on Frankie's shoulder.

Frankie felt his eyes going damp. "I'm not finished yet."

"Well, then, I'm going to stand here until you decide just how much trouble you want to be in."

"I'm sorry," Mrs. Woodrow said, approaching the other end of the picnic table, "but I don't allow smoking around my daughter."

Frankie's father frowned, causing the cigarette to droop. Around it he said, "We're outside."

"She doesn't have a normal resistance to pollution, and I don't allow smoking anywhere in my house, or on my property. It's a rule."

"A rule," his father said. He inhaled through the cigarette, then blew smoke around his words. "You know, if you're so concerned about kids, you might think to call us when our son just shows up by himself, without an adult."

"I think," Mrs. Woodrow said, "that I do a *very* good job of babysitting your son, and that it's your responsibility to make sure he stays in your home when you're there. Now, would you *please* put out that cigarette?"

His father sucked hard, and then in one swift motion plucked the cigarette from his teeth as if it had roots, threw it down onto the grass, and stepped on it.

Jennifer put a single chip onto Frankie's plate.

"That's it," his father said. "Come on."

Frankie ate the chip.

She dug into the bowl again, and brought another chip across the table. His father was reaching down to haul him up by the arm, but he closed his hand over Jennifer's arm instead, and hissed, *"Stop it."*

"Hey!" Mrs. Woodrow snapped.

He let go.

Jennifer looked startled, but she wasn't hurt. She pulled her hand back and looked at Frankie and stuck the chip into her mouth.

"You don't touch my daughter!"

"I didn't hurt her," Frankie's father said.

"Who do you think you are? No one roughhouses my daughter! Do you realize how frail she is?" Mrs. Woodrow stepped forward, waving the chlorine tester in front of her. "Get off my property!"

"Jesus," his father said. And then, more loudly, "That's what I'm trying to do."

"Then go! I'm sorry, Frankie, I know this is awkward, but your father really does need to leave now, and I think you should go with him."

Frankie looked across the table at Jennifer. "Bye," he said.

"Bye," Jennifer said.

His father turned to leave, and Frankie got up from the picnic table.

*

They didn't talk during the short ride home. In their driveway his father turned off the engine, but instead of getting out, he just sat there, one hand resting on top of the steering wheel, his gaze fixed on something beyond Frankie's side window.

Frankie said, "Sorry."

"You know," his father said, "I'm just trying to do my job here."

Frankie nodded.

"You're the one who's supposed to stick around. You're the one I can depend on. Your brothers and your sister, every day they're off somewhere—"

"They're allowed," Frankie said.

"Yes. *They're* allowed. But you're not, because you're not old enough. And you know that. I thought we had a project going on here. I thought we were a team."

"Is Mrs. Woodrow still my babysitter?"

His father slid his palm back and forth across the top of the steering wheel. He tilted his head to one side and rifled air through his nose. "I don't think so, Frankie. That woman...if her daughter—what's her name? Jennifer?—if she's so sick, then maybe it's not such a good idea for you to be playing with her."

"She's not sick," Frankie said. "Mom said she wasn't sick."

His father blinked and looked at him, one brow hitched up. "She *is* sick. You should know that, Frankie. She has an illness. It makes her very old, even though she's just a little girl."

"Will she get better?"

"I don't think so," his father said, frowning. "Plus, you saw what just happened. People like that, if you hurt them—even by accident—they'll sue you. You know what that means? They'll take you to court. The cops will come, and they'll take you to court and *make* you give people like that a whole lot of money. And if you don't have a whole lot of money, then what do you do?"

Frankie didn't know the answer to the question. His father was looking past him again, out the passenger side of the car, at the sand-covered lawn and the row of houses beyond it.

"I don't want to be on your team," Frankie said.

His father pulled his focus in and looked at him as if he'd uttered a swear word. "Get in the house. We'll talk about this later."

Frankie stayed where he was.

"Go on," his father said. "Get in the house." Frankie didn't move. His father reached down and unbuckled his seat belt for him. Then he stretched over, unlatched the passenger door, and shoved it open.

Frankie didn't want to stay in the car; he didn't want to go inside, either. He didn't feel like doing anything his father told him to do.

Finally, growling under his breath, his father opened his own door and got out of the car.

But instead of going into the house, he walked into the

middle of the yard and stood with his back to Frankie and the driveway. Surrounded by sand, he looked like a man standing on a beach.

A breeze moved through the open windows of the car. Frankie smelled salt in the air. He imagined he heard the sound of the ocean carried on the breeze. The citizens of Atlantis had been sad as they'd stood on the shore and heard their names called out, one by one, but his father didn't look sad. He looked angry and impatient. He had his hands on his hips and was tapping a foot against the sand, as if ready to march into the waters of the Outer Sea the next time someone said his name.

Ground Control

1981

I was morphing into something I didn't want to be. My nose was growing bulbous, my neck was elongating, my hands were thickening into fleshy paddles that batted against door frames and knocked over drinking glasses. When I looked in the mirror, every part of me was out of proportion to whatever it was attached to. I would wake up in the middle of the night freezing beneath the unremitting current of the central air unit—humping the mattress, desperate for contact, like the last animal of its species.

Frankie was two years younger than me and infinitely better-looking. Because he slept with his door open, I could listen to his breathing—hear the back of his tongue clicking against the roof of his mouth each time he inhaled, a sound he'd been making in his sleep since he was a baby. My sister, Karen, kept her door shut. Clawing out of another warm, slick dream, I stepped into the refrigerated hall and stood between their two rooms and Matt's old room—now mine—an erection lifting the front of my pajamas and the blood pounding in my ears. I wanted something I believed was not of this world. Beyond that, I wanted to be someone else, getting it.

My father left during the summer of the bicentennial, when I was eleven. His name was Roy and he was Frankie's father too, but not Karen's or Matt's, and he had moved out so abruptly that he hadn't even taken most of his things. He was married to another woman now, less than fifteen miles away, at the north end of Merritt Island near the Space Center, and within a year we understood not only that he wasn't coming back but that he wasn't very interested in knowing us anymore. Trace evidence of his existence had remained in our house for a while after he'd left—including not only the smell of his cigarettes but the Pall Malls themselves, along with his lighter, an arrangement my mother preserved on the lower level of the end table next to the couch. She'd told us he would be back by that first Thanksgiving, and by that first Christmas, and by Easter, and then by the time Matt, who was the oldest, graduated from high school. Finally I came home one day to find my father's picture extracted from the faces on the dining room wall. His coffee mug was missing from the cup tree in the kitchen, and his cigarettes and lighter—along with the ashtray my mother had dusted for a full year—were gone, in their place a candy dish and a copy of the *Florida Catholic*.

Roy was the second man to move out on my mother. The first man was named Dermot, and I knew very little about him other than that he lived in Utica, New York, and that he was Matt's and Karen's father. Matt, as soon as he'd graduated from Merritt Island High School, left home and took a bus up to Utica, and not long after that, Dermot started calling our house to complain about him. I answered the phone one morning before school and heard a clotted voice say, "Teresa?"

I started laughing. "I'm not Teresa," I said. "I'm a boy."

"Just put your goddamn mother on the phone."

I got my mother, then lingered close enough to listen to her end of the conversation. She said "All right, Dermot" several times, and "All *right,*" and then, "If you don't want him getting into trouble, maybe you should think about what sort of example you're setting." Dermot's voice, coming through the receiver she held away from her ear, sounded like a tiny car engine trying to turn over. "No," she said. "Matt's an adult. He's eighteen and he can do what he wants. Besides, it's my understanding that when he called you, you told him moving up there was a good idea.... Well, you ought to know by now, Dermot, that you shouldn't tell your child something you don't want his mother to hear. If it doesn't come out in confidence, it'll come out in an argument.... Maybe something like *'If she's that crazy, then you should get away from her.'* Sound familiar? ... Oh, don't feed me that bullshit!" She slammed the receiver down hard enough to make the ringer chime. Then she closed her eyes, let go of the phone, and crossed herself: Father, Son, Holy Ghost.

She wasn't so tough with us. That is, she gave orders—told us to come to the table, straighten our rooms, get ready for church—and she yelled if we didn't follow through, but she didn't really seem to care anymore. Karen, who, at seventeen, reigned supreme now that Matt was gone, did nothing she was told and had turned mouthy. "So?" had become her favorite refrain. "It's almost time for mass," my mother would say, to which Karen, legs splayed open on the couch in front of the television, would respond, "So?"

"So, I'd like you to get up, get dressed, and come with us."

"So?"

My mother would work her mouth around a string of unsaid words, then finally spit out, "Fine. Stupid me for suggesting it."

She wasn't a wife anymore; she'd been fired from that

position—twice—and motherhood was the work she'd been stuck with.

At least, that was how my sister put it. In our backyard at night, in her uniform of short shorts and tank top and bare feet, her shoulder blades spiked against the cinder block wall of the house and a cigarette wedged between two stiff fingers that hovered in front of her chin, Karen glared at the chain-link fence that separated our backyard from the next and said, "You can hear it in the woman's voice. She's still got the volume, but she's phoning it in."

"Maybe she's tired," I said.

"Maybe she's dead. As in *Night of the Living*. She keeps the house freezing, like a morgue, you know? She's like a zombie, but instead of eating you, she just nags you to death."

Karen was sailing toward the end of high school and she'd lost her pudginess and grown sleek and dangerous during the past year. She'd chopped her hair off at the neckline (just as our mother was growing hers long), she'd gone skeletally limp, and she'd perfected a look of absolute hatred that she wore now along with her makeup.

"If you were smart, you'd do whatever you wanted," she told me. "Mom's not going to care."

"I do what I want. I'm taking two electives."

A little bubble of adult laughter and smoke burst at the back of her throat. She stared at the fence and shook her head wearily. "I'm not talking about your little *Romper Room* poetry classes. I'm talking about having some fun. You're so afraid of getting into trouble, it's pathetic. You don't even ask if you can hang out with your friends. *I* don't ask anymore—I tell her what I'm going to do or I just do it. You have friends, right?"

I tried to mimic her laugh. "Yeah."

Her head tipped sideways as if her neck were broken. "I mean, not just the people you sit next to in class. You have *real* friends?"

"Screw you," I said. *"Yes."*

"And I'm sure you can't get a date to save your life—not till your face clears up, anyway—but if you could, you would, right?"

"Screw you twice."

"Just asking," she said. "Just trying to get an idea of where the family registers on the freak-o-meter."

"What about you? I don't see you dating anybody."

"Because I've already done the whole dating scene. I get straight to the good stuff now."

"What does that mean?"

"Two words," she said to her cigarette. "Seth Colby."

She was a senior. I was a sophomore. Seth Colby was a short, drum-playing junior who had shaggy blond hair and who'd been kicked out of band for having a joint behind his ear during a pep rally. He glowed with the fame of that scandal, and there were plenty of kids who longed to be part of his inner circle.

"Good stuff," I said, trying to sound indifferent, even bored. "I suppose you're just dying to tell me all about it."

"What I'm dying to tell you is that Mom doesn't give a shit what you do, so you ought to start doing what you want. This goody-two-shoes thing is embarrassing, if you want the truth. I don't bring my friends over anymore because they'd just see this whacked-out ghost-lady, this sixteen-year-old dork, and this little *Star Wars* freak who's, you know, kind of old to still be playing with dolls, and they look at me and say, literally, where's the two-headed chicken?"

This was mean, but not entirely off the mark.

Try having a friend at school ask where your father was, and explaining that you *thought* he lived on north Tropical Trail but that you weren't positive because you'd only seen his house once, from the backseat of a moving station wagon, and your mother had ignored the question *Is that where Dad lives now?*

Or try explaining why your mother had been pulled out of the Communion line during mass more than a few times and escorted to the back of the church by whichever off-duty priest had been assigned to keep an eye on her.

Or why your little brother, who was fourteen, taped aluminum foil over his bedroom windows (which faced the street) and spoke sometimes in a language of his own invention called Sub-Middle-Earth Glocken.

And just try explaining to anyone—your friends, your mother, your fire-breathing sister—what exactly it was that was happening to *you*.

✣

I tried practical reasoning. A fat person who wants to lose weight shouldn't bake desserts for a living. A kleptomaniac shouldn't get a job in a jewelry store. An alcoholic shouldn't work at the drive-through beer barn, and an ax murderer shouldn't become the tool guy at Babcock's Hardware. I didn't want to be gay, and when I masturbated, I was incapable of thinking about anything but boys. Therefore, I resolved never, ever to masturbate again. Two days later I chose a different strategy: proactive normalization. Alone in the house, I rooted through Matt's belongings for anything even vaguely pornographic. Like my father, Matt had left a lot of stuff behind. Guitars and amplifiers and wah-wah pedals. A metal Nabisco snack rack he'd pulled from a dumpster and filled with handgrips and nunchucks and empty shotgun shells. From under the bed I dug out surfer magazines, scuba diving magazines, stacks of *Rolling Stone,* but not a single copy of *Playboy* or *Penthouse*. Finally, I resorted to Farrah Fawcett-Majors. She was still hanging on the wall between a poster of Jimi Hendrix and a cross fashioned out of crumbling palm fronds. She flashed a set of teeth as perfect as shuttle tiles, her face floated in a storm

of blond hair, and her nipples punched at the backside of a
bathing suit the color of a circus peanut. *Come here, darling,* I
thought as I took the poster down from the wall. Utilizing a
pair of scissors, I acted with all tenderness and good intention,
tried to become hypnotized with the visual of it, and succeeded
only in giving myself paper cuts in the last place you would ever
want them.

※

Frankie was on the floor surrounded by action figures, multicolored dice, and sheets of hexagonal graph paper. He was
drawing what looked like a rainbow that had been run through
a blender.

"Did you take my new colored pencil set?"

"I did," he said without looking up, "but only for purposes of
intergalactic peace."

"Frankie." I reached down and took hold of the ear I saw
sticking out of his wavy black hair.

He moved his head sideways with the tug. "Gravitational
pulls! Misunderstood trajectories! There's no interspecies language for this; the only way to keep track of them is to assign
each one a different color!"

I let go and he jerked away from me, rocking the four-inch
Luke Skywalker doll that hung from a shoelace around his
neck. A week ago, when we were all fanned out across one side
of the living room, eating dinner on TV trays, my mother had
asked him out of the blue why he was wearing that doll. Without looking away from the television, Frankie had answered
her in Glocken.

My mother cleared her throat. "Translation, please."

"It's not a doll," Frankie said. "It's an action figure."

"Well, you don't wear it to school, do you? I'm just afraid the
other kids will . . . that the other kids might . . ."

"Beat him up?" I offered.

Through a mouthful of spaghetti Karen said, "If he ν
that to my school, *I'd* beat him up."

But Frankie was unfazed by whatever we had to say abou
him. He would be fifteen and starting high school next August.
In one corner of his room, he'd hung a model of the *Millennium
Falcon* and suspended on fishing line around it a little cluster of
foam rubber asteroids. On the back of a sheet of butcher paper
taped to the inside of the aluminum foil that covered his bedroom windows, he'd drawn with an El Marko a picture of
Yoda, the *Close Encounters* alien, dwarfs, wizards, the cookie-
tin-shaped robot Dr. Theopolis from *Buck Rogers in the 25ᵗʰ
Century,* Starbuck, and Apollo, all gathered around a long con-
ference table with Luke Skywalker at the center, his hands outstretched like a clean-shaven Christ. There was a drawing
taped to the closet door of the first space shuttle, the *Enterprise,*
clinging like a pilot fish to the back of a 747, piloted by a tiny
figure who looked a lot like Frankie. He had yet to throw out
the light saber he'd made from a gift wrap tube when he was
ten. He walked around in Matt's old karate vest and called the
backyard Tatooine. There was less than a two-year difference
between me and Frankie, and while Karen made me feel like a
child, around my little brother I became an abusive adult.

"Give me the pencils," I said with as much venom as I could
put into my voice.

He said, " 'What has roots as nobody sees, is taller than trees,
up, up it goes, and yet never grows?' "

I kicked the side of his leg.

"Ow! All right!" He made a few clicks and whirs out of the
side of his mouth and moved his arm like a robot's, his fingers
clawing at the colored pencils. He gathered them back into
their clear plastic sleeve and held them up to me.

I took them. "What are you drawing?"

nebula. But I really needed the pencils for
dy I'm presenting in front of the council."

is smooth, narrow face up toward me. There
of cuteness, sarcasm, or lunacy in his voice; he could
easily have been talking about his homework.

Well, I have to fill in a chromosome chart for biology. You
can use them after that." I started out of the room.

"Roger," he said. "Would that be alien, or pure human?"

"What?"

"Some of us are one or the other, some of us are a mix," he
said, blending the nebula with his finger. "The mixed ones have
the most complicated chromosomal structure."

*

Our mother's somewhat pronounced cheekbones had grafted
themselves onto the four of us. Beyond that, we took after our
fathers. Matt and Karen were of Dermot stock; I'd seen the
snapshot Matt used to carry around in his wallet, and there was
the blond hair, the slightly flattened bridge of the nose, the full
lips that distinguished my two older siblings. On Matt these
features looked masculine; on Karen, somehow, feminine. As
for Frankie and me, we were children of Roy: faces narrow,
noses sharp. Our hair was wavy and nearly black, and our ears
were smallish and round, like side mirrors on a toy motorcycle.
That's how I'd been up to the age of twelve, anyway, and I kept
waiting for Frankie to start mutating as I had, to start growing
ahead of himself in some misshapen way, or at least to start getting acne. We were of the same blood; it only seemed fair that
we should suffer the same disfigurements. But it wasn't happening, which only made me feel like more of an aberration.

At school, Karen had begun making a project out of denying
I was her brother. This was done in the style of a grand joke, a
running gag that no one in her clique ever got tired of hearing.

I stepped out of English class one day to go to the bathroom, and when I entered the commons area of C wing, there was Karen stretched out in one of the benched recesses along the wall with Seth Colby across her lap. Another girl sat on the floor in front of them. And leaning against the wall was one of Colby's followers, a guitar-playing pothead named Wes Markham.

They were all focused on Colby. He was folded into the recess, his sneakers against one side and his shaggy head against the other, his blue-jeaned butt cradled in the valley between Karen's thighs. As I approached them, Colby finished whatever he was saying and the rest of them finished laughing at it, and the commons fell silent. One of my shoes screeched on the terrazzo floor.

"Not my brother," Karen said, "these are people. People, this is not my brother."

The girl sitting on the floor bent her head backward to look at me upside down. Colby peered at me with one eye squinted shut. He said, "Nice hall pass."

"Oh—yeah, really." I hefted the piece of plywood that was larger than a dinner plate and strung with a rope handle. "Mr. Watley's been going crazy in shop. I've got Mrs. McInerney, and he calls her 'Mac,' so he made her this hamburger-shaped thing, like a Big Mac, that everybody's supposed to carry around. It's total bullshit," I added, in an effort to sound like someone they'd want to listen to—but Colby had already turned away and was looking up at Karen, who rolled her eyes.

"As you can see, there's no family resemblance whatsoever," she said.

The girl on the floor stretched her legs out in front of her, kicked off a sandal, and worked her toes over one of Wes Markham's white-socked ankles.

I knew Wes Markham because he was in two of my classes. He was long and lanky and had thick red hair that rose up from his forehead like the bristles of a push broom. He walked like the Pink Panther, with a spring in his knees and a swing to his hands—the hands that were now buried in the pockets of his corduroys. His elbows were locked, lifting his shoulders so that the hem of his T-shirt rode high and revealed a quarter-moon of bare stomach. When I looked up, he was staring at me, his mouth crimped into a slightly lopsided grin as if he were piecing together a punch line.

"You'd better get going," Karen said. "McInerney times you when you've got the hamburger."

"Right." She was making that up, I thought, but I wasn't positive, so I walked with my best what-do-I-care shuffle to the other side of the commons, the plywood disk bouncing off my thigh and then banging loudly against the door as I entered the boys' bathroom. Before the door closed behind me, I heard them break into a laugh.

"Am I the ugliest person in the family?" I asked my mother the following Saturday. We were in the station wagon on our way to Divine Mercy for confession. We'd left Karen at home because she'd told us she wasn't handing her sins over to anyone, and we'd left Frankie because he'd started confessing things that weren't real—hoarding spice mélange on the planet Arrakis, or breaking flight patterns on Y-wing patrol missions—which had finally prompted Father Gillespie to pull my mother aside (in the same manner he used when she tried to crash the Communion line) and ask if this wasn't some sort of code for larger and more relevant sins.

She took her eyes off the road and stared at my face for a moment—maybe to see how much it had changed since the last time she'd looked at it. "No," she said leadenly, turning forward. "None of my children are ugly. None of them look like me, and none of them are ugly."

Because she wasn't allowed to take Communion, she refused

to go to confession herself. I knelt in the booth and mumbled generic offenses into the screen. The priest, sounding bored, asked if I had anything more (meaning, I thought, anything *good*) to confess; I said no, and we wrapped things up. When I emerged, my mother was sitting alone in the middle of the church, staring toward the altar as if waiting for a movie to start. I walked down the aisle and was standing beside her before she realized I was there and made a small, startled noise. "Joseph. Jesus, you nearly gave me a heart attack. Did you say your penance?" I nodded yes, marking the first sin on what was supposed to be my clean slate. In truth, I hadn't bothered saying penance because I hadn't confessed any of the actual offenses I'd committed. They were unutterable, and they were dwarfed by all the things I still wanted to do.

The next week, Karen and Seth Colby were caught cutting class and making out with lit cigarettes in their hands two days in a row, and they were suspended for the next three—a punishment they celebrated by riding around the island in Colby's Firebird listening to homemade tapes of his band. Their first day back in school, Colby made his lunch entrance by delivering a karate kick to the cafeteria door—slamming it into the head of Mr. Salkind, the history teacher. Mr. Salkind took two stitches, Colby was immediately suspended again, and Karen skipped school in solidarity.

I was moving with the herd of students between fourth and fifth periods when I felt a sharp pain on the back of my neck. Wes Markham was walking close on my heels. He had "thumped" me—cocked his middle finger beneath the inside of his thumb and then snapped it against my neck—and he was sneering with his hand poised, ready to do it again. Our schedules overlapped for two hours a day; he slept through political science several desks away from me, then followed the same path through the halls to the chorus room. Like Colby,

Markham was a "problem case" who had no actual interests and was constantly getting kicked out of one elective class after another, shuffling from art to the newspaper staff and, most recently, to chorus. He had no enthusiasm for singing and couldn't carry a tune, but Mr. Tepper seemed satisfied with just letting him sit high up at the back of the room with his unplugged electric guitar on his lap, quietly picking out riffs.

We worked on "Brian's Song," "Both Sides Now," and a 1960s medley that began with "Blowin' in the Wind" and ended ten minutes later with "The Age of Aquarius." Between songs I heard the distant, tinny plucking of Markham's guitar. I glanced back at him only once during class and he was staring right at me, his feet propped up and his pick hand fumbling inside the pocket of his Ron Jon's T-shirt. When class ended I looked again, and his chair was empty.

I gathered up my books and was walking past the row of darkened practice rooms when a hand reached out of one of them and grabbed my forearm. In the next moment I was dragged inside, the door was shut, and a voice said out of the darkness, "Kerrigan."

"What?"

"Keeerrrrriiigan."

"I know who it is," I said. "Open the door."

The fluorescent light tube flickered against the low ceiling, flooding the tiny room with light. Markham was standing in front of the door. "You want to suck my what?"

"Let me out."

"Not so fast." He towered over me by half a foot. One of his hands reached out and pushed my breastbone so that I fell backward onto the piano bench. Then he dragged a folding chair between me and the door, sat down on it and stretched his legs out, planting a shoe on either side of the bench. "You've seen the junk," he said.

"I've seen the what?"

"Junk," he said. "Sucking dick must be making you deaf. You've seen the *junk.*"

"I don't know what you're talking about."

"Your sister really isn't your sister, is she? She's, what, a cousin or something?"

"She's my sister."

"Your last name's Kerrigan. Hers is Ragazzino. And she's right—you don't look anything like her."

"We have different fathers."

"Yeah, and both of them split, right? What's wrong with your old lady? I mean, your old man lives, what, fifty feet away? Karen said you never see him. That's got to be fucking weird."

I stared at him, my face burning.

He folded his arms over his chest and mortared the heels of his sneakers into the green carpet. "Thing is, if you were really Karen's brother, I wouldn't worry about it. It would be cool because there'd be that blood tie."

"We have the same mother," I said. "There *is* a blood tie," though I didn't know what he was getting at.

He dug his fingers into the pocket of his T-shirt. "Then I can half trust you. At best. Because I know you saw *that.*" His hand snapped, and on the bench next to me landed a small plastic bag of white powder.

I felt my stomach implode. "I didn't see that. I don't even know what it is."

"You saw me moving it from my notebook to my shirt pocket. You looked right at me while I was doing it."

"That wasn't why I looked."

"Then why'd you look? 'Cause you want to chew on my bone?"

"I just looked over," I said.

"If you were Karen's brother, I wouldn't care. But you're some kind of half-breed. I don't know *what* you'd do with information like this." He was staring at me, his eyes heavy-lidded. Then he reached a hand up and pulled a joint—à la Seth Colby—from his forest of stiff red hair. He was already palming a book of matches.

Each practice room had a square foot of glass set into its door. Mr. Tepper had a rule that these little windows were to stay unblocked, but students were constantly taping sheets of paper over them. The window just beyond Markham's head was covered with black construction paper. One corner of the paper had been torn away, revealing an eyelet large enough for someone to peer through, but it was the beginning of lunch hour and the chorus room was empty.

Markham lit the joint and his entire face came to life, lifting into a comedy mask and then puckering as if the pot were a lemon. He made a whoopee cushion noise at the back of his throat. "Primo," he said, exhaling. "But, now, you probably shouldn't have seen *this,* either. Unless you want some."

I'd never had and didn't want any pot. I did and didn't want to leave the practice room. I shook my head no.

"See, this problem's only getting worse." Markham took another hit. He licked his thumb and forefinger, pinched the joint out, and put it inside his sock. Then he reached over and brushed the outside of my leg with his hand as he retrieved the bag of white powder. "I'm going to have to get something on you."

"What do you mean?"

"The only way I'll know for sure you're not going to go nark is if I've got something on you. It keeps us honest."

"What's there to get on me?" My hands, I realized, were shaking. I closed them over the edge of the piano bench.

"Think about it," Markham said. "You tell anybody about me, you're going down for what you did. You tell your sister what you did, you're going down *plus* some."

He stood up from the folding chair. I started from the piano bench but he put a hand on my shoulder and kept me down. "I don't get it," I said. "What did I do?"

He reached behind him and turned out the light. "Plenty."

We were in the middle of *Hart to Hart*—all four of us—when my mother turned to Karen and said, "I'd like it if you'd at least tell me about the major events going on in your life." They were sitting at opposite ends of the couch. I was in the recliner on Karen's side and Frankie was on the floor in front of the coffee table, wrapped head to toe in a bedsheet with only his face showing.

Karen looked across the couch and said, "*Hart to Hart*. It's a major event in my life."

"I don't appreciate sarcasm," my mother said.

"So?"

"If you've been suspended, I'd like to learn it from you, not from some school secretary."

Karen made a halfhearted attempt at swallowing a laugh. "They *just* called you about that?"

"This is why you've been sleeping late," my mother said. "This is why you haven't had any homework, why you've been staying out till two A.M.—"

"*Mother,*" Karen said, shaking her head, "that suspension is over. That was last week. This week I'm not going because Seth got suspended again and I'm his girlfriend."

Frankie began to rock back and forth: a metronome wrapped in swaddling clothes.

"I don't even know who Seth is," my mother said. "You

could meet me halfway, you know, just give me the highlights. Is that too much to ask?"

"Seth *Colby,*" Karen snapped, as if the name should have impressed my mother. "You want the highlights? I hate school, I love Seth, he's screwing me, and it's great. How's that?"

I had the recliner's footrest up and felt as if I were floating—not free of all this, but a part of it, drifting alongside the rest of them, like a bona fide member of the ragtag fleet of spaceships following the battlestar *Galactica* in the mural taped to Frankie's ceiling. I felt a pain when I swallowed: the spot Wes Markham had battered as he held on to my head, his hands stretching from my jaw hinge to the top of my spine. There was an ache in my jaw and a sour fold in my stomach. My mother's daunted face was just one more item adrift. "I don't want to hear that," she said. "I don't want to hear that at all."

"Well, then, you shouldn't have asked."

"I *have* to ask," my mother shot back, raising her voice. "I'm your parent. I'm the one who's *here.*"

"Bok, bok, bok, *braaack!*" Karen darted her head forward and flapped her elbows like a chicken.

I thought about television. There was that character on *Dynasty,* and another one on *Soap.* There were those two men on *Barney Miller* who wore scarves and blousy shirts and swished around the police station with their hands dangling from their wrists. That was four characters out of what, a million? And as for actual people, the only one I'd ever known whom I even suspected of being gay was a boy named Jeremy in my American Lit class who wore eye shadow to school one day (and had it washed off for him in a toilet that afternoon) and who had since moved to Vermont. The odds of Wes Markham and me being at the same point on the map, at the same moment in time, seemed beyond remote and infinitely lucky.

Karen had stopped clucking and both she and my mother

had turned back toward the program. Frankie was swaying between me and the television screen.

I said, "Hey, Twiki, you make a better door than a window."

"Don't be a fool," Frankie said. "This is my transparency wrap."

❋

I heard his guitar plucking but didn't look at him at all during chorus the next day. He didn't call my name from the practice room after class. But when I stepped into it, he was there. He was sitting back on the same folding chair, with his legs spread apart and a cigarette pinched sideways above his upper lip like a mustache. A hard-on pushed against the front of his jeans. I said, "I wasn't sure if, you know—"

The cigarette dropped into one of his wide palms. "Shut the fuck up and close the door."

I did what he said. He palmed the light switch without getting up, the room went completely dark, and I got down on my knees. On the previous day, he hadn't touched any part of me other than my head, but this time he dropped one of his hands and closed it over my crotch. I was soft. He squeezed a couple of times as if trying to identify what he was touching, then grunted and took hold of my head again. Seconds after he came, he stood abruptly and left the practice room without another word passing between us.

❋

"My children are all named after saints," my mother said. She was talking to Frankie and me as if we weren't her children but were two strangers having breakfast at her table. I was eating toast. Frankie was doodling behind a fortress of two cereal boxes. My mother hadn't looked up and it occurred to me she might actually be talking to the *Florida Catholic* opened in front of her. "Matthew. Mary-Katherine. Joseph. Francis of Assisi. What could be more Catholic than that? Not good enough for the wafer club, though." She sipped her coffee and turned a leaf of the newspaper. "I should have named one of my children Jesus. There's a Mexican woman at work who's divorced and has a son named Jesus. She even says 'Jesus' when you sneeze. I'll bet they let *her* take Communion."

Karen was leaning against the kitchen counter eating an Oreo. She said, "Who's Mary-Katherine?"

Mary-Katherine was Karen. She'd refused to be confirmed when she was twelve and had chosen, instead, her own unofficial, "unconfirmation" name: Karen Carpenter Ragazzino. My mother said, "Someone I used to know. I take it, since you're up and dressed, that you're going to school today?"

"Yeah," Karen said to her Oreo, "I thought I'd go. Seth's back today, and anyway, I have to clean out my locker."

"Why?"

"I just told you why. Seth's back."

"Why do you have to clean out your locker?"

"Oh. Because I'm quitting."

My mother looked up from the paper, then looked back down and began to fold it. "I don't want to hear whatever it is you're trying to hurt me with right now."

"I'm not trying to hurt you, Mother. I'm dropping out of school. But I'm not *trying* to hurt anyone."

"I don't want to hear it," my mother said. She kept folding the newspaper until it was the size of a biscuit, then, squeezing it tightly, she looked at Karen and said, "What do you think is going to happen to you if you don't get an education? What do you plan on doing?"

"Well, I don't plan on shooting any rock stars or presidents, if that's what you're worried about."

"That's not even funny."

"Maybe I'll head up to Utica," Karen said.

"Maybe you should! If I'm doing that bad of a job, maybe you should all just run to your fathers! That will solve everything! It's clearly worked out just peachy for Matt!"

Matt, we all knew, had called from Utica the previous week asking my mother for money, which she'd mailed to him only after adamantly refusing to do so.

Karen was walking forward, poking another Oreo into her mouth. My mother was folding and unfolding her arms, shifting around in her chair as if deciding whether or not to storm out of the room. The top of Frankie's wavy head of hair rocked over the cereal boxes. There was room for all of this in our family, I thought; there was even room for me: one of everything in a ragtag fleet drifting through space. Then Karen stepped up behind Frankie, looked down at his drawing, and said, "You ought to fix her hair, twerp. That looks like two guys."

"It *is* two guys," Frankie said, without looking up. "It's me and Luke Skywalker."

"You and Luke Skywalker? So that makes you, what, Princess Leia?"

"I'm *me,*" Frankie said. "We're *rescuing* each other."

"Great," Karen snorted. "Gay astronaut lovers."

"*Yes,*" Frankie said, as if bored with such petty inquiries.

My mother reached out and took away one of the cereal boxes. "What is that? What are you drawing?"

With his felt-tipped pen still moving, his head bent down in concentration, Frankie said, "Me. Luke. The chasm."

She pulled the other box away, and all four of us stared down at the drawing of a chasm shrinking in one-point perspective into the center of the page, and in the foreground, holding on to some sort of cable-shooting pistol, Luke Skywalker was in mid-swing, his other arm wrapped around a young man with dark, curly hair who looked an awful lot like Frankie. Frankie's arms were wrapped around Skywalker's torso. His eyes were gazing into Skywalker's, and his lips appeared to be touching the blond man's cheek.

"Queers in space!" Karen said gleefully.

"*Yes,*" Frankie said. He reached for the cereal boxes. "May I have my shields back?"

"Karen, stop it," my mother said. "That's not what he means."

"It *is* what I mean," Frankie said.

"No, it's *not.* You don't mean that the two of you—in that picture—are . . . that way."

"In the picture, *yes,* I mean that exactly. It's a *fantasy,* Mom."

Karen snorted again and said, "Fag Wars!"

"Karen, shut up!" my mother said.

Frankie glanced at the two of them calmly. "She doesn't bug me, Mom. None of you do."

I had never given a thought to actually telling them I might be gay. Suddenly, I saw that it was possible, and that I wanted to—and at the same moment, I realized I never could. In his calm, innocent way, Frankie had seized that moon in the galaxy of crazy and had raised his flag.

Karen was laughing around a cookie. My mother was staring aghast at her youngest son, who had returned to his drawing and was shading in his own curly hair. I wanted to shrink to a pinpoint and vanish from the room.

❊

Wes Markham and I were never alone again. I didn't want it that way; in fact, after Frankie's announcement, I conjured up a very Frankie-esque fantasy about me and Markham in the new-fangled space shuttle, using it to zip from moon to planet to asteroid, never having to confront another member of our own species except for each other—and with each other we would be entirely happy. Two days after our second encounter in the practice room, I was walking along the outside of the school, heading for driver's ed, when Markham leaped from between two portable buildings with his arm out like a lance. His fist, bony and solid, drove straight into my upper arm hard enough to fold one of my legs and knock me down onto the sidewalk. My forehead burned against the cement. I heard clapping and a small eruption of laughter. "Shit, Markham," Seth Colby said, "you're crazy." Colby and Markham were with someone else, a boy with long hair who looked just as shocked and amused as Colby and who grinned down at me and blew me a kiss. Then the long-haired boy and Colby were gone. Markham was retreating, too, his hand still drawn into a fist and his eyes conveying a message that would have been crystal clear from a thousand light-years away.

I could raise my left arm—but slowly, painfully, and not without its trembling in its socket. I didn't go to driver's ed, but walked instead to the boys room off the main commons, where I sat in a stall and cried, angry at myself for not getting hard, that last time (though I realized now it was only because he'd terrified me); for being so pathetic; for having such a stupid family; for crying. When I left the bathroom, I headed straight for the bike racks at the front of the school, unlocked my bicycle using only one hand, and pedaled off with my left arm hanging loose at my side. I didn't want to go home, so I rode north for a while, then west, toward Tropical Trail. I told myself I didn't know where I was going, though I did; I just wasn't sure if I could find it.

Tropical Trail was winding and narrow. The palm scrub grew out over the road in spots, and the inlets to neighborhoods buried among the palms and citrus trees came out of nowhere, marked only by little sections of wrought iron gate or cinder block entrance walls. My father's house wasn't sunk back into a neighborhood but sat right off the trail by itself, surrounded by its own low concrete wall painted light blue and cut through with starbursts. It was only from my memory of this wall that I recognized the house. There was a white plastic box for the *Today* newspaper at the end of the driveway, and a black mailbox bearing no name at all, as if he'd done his best to sink himself into a little compound of anonymity. My mother had told me he was selling real estate now and was doing well for himself. Behind the wall, the house, like nearly every building in town, was one story, but given what I knew of Merritt Island, it looked like the home of a rich person. The lawn had a built-in sprinkler system. There were two Buicks in the driveway. I stopped my bike just across his property line.

A woman was carrying groceries in from one of the cars. She was small and had permed hair and her name, if I remembered it right from listening to the arguments just before my father left, was Leona. The trunk to the Buick nearest me was open and she had a bag in each arm. She spotted me as she was rounding the car. I stood perfectly still over my bike at the foot of the driveway. She looked toward the trunk, where another couple of bags sat, and then at me again, as if worried I was going to steal her groceries or maybe wanting me to help carry them. I didn't move. She walked up the drive, through the garage, and into the house.

Cars whisked by on the road behind me. A dragonfly, like a miniature Huey chopper, zigzagged across the lawn and hovered in front of my face for a moment, then darted away. The door inside the garage opened again, and my father walked out with one hand holding a cigarette. He was smiling slightly. He emerged into the sunlight and, with his head tilted forward, walked between the Buicks to the foot of the driveway.

"Joe," he said. His dark hair was combed back and straighter than I remembered.

"Hi."

"Your head is bleeding."

I touched my forehead with my right hand and felt the sticky beginnings of a scab. "I ran into a branch," I said.

"You want a Band-Aid?"

"It's okay."

"You want to come inside? Wash it off?"

"No, thanks."

His smile leveled out. He drew on his cigarette and looked at my face, then glanced up the trail and exhaled. "You, um . . . we haven't talked in a while. How's school?"

"Fine," I said.

"You're still doing well in those art classes?"

"That's Frankie," I said. "I'm the one who's doing well in English."

"That's right. That's great. And what about Frankie? He's doing okay?"

"Yeah," I said, but I wanted to say, *Frankie's gay.* I wanted to say it so badly. *Frankie's gay, and Karen's dropping out of school, and Mom's getting into trouble at church, and I've been blowing a pothead in the music room but I'm never going to have sex with anyone, ever again.*

"Karen?" he said. "And Matt?" He looked tired already, running through this short list of names.

"Matt's in Utica."

"Right," he said. "I know." Then he glanced up and down the trail again as if disappointed anyone could ever leave such a setting and said, "I guess he likes it up there."

I looked at the house behind him. "Do you have a pool?"

"No," he said, as if he'd expected this question, "not me. Boy, if I did, I'd have you kids over to swim in it. That would be fun, huh?"

I nodded.

"Listen, Joe. What brings you around today?"

I thought about what I might tell him. I shrugged. "Nothing."

"So everything's all right? The house— Is it...cool enough?"

"It's freezing."

"Ha, ha. That's good. I bought that central air unit, you know. Right after I...When your mother and I...The old air conditioner broke. You all would have baked alive, but I had a new one put in. I wanted to contribute, you know, and I told your mother I'd pay the electric. The bill comes straight here every month. You all don't even see it."

"She keeps it pretty cold," I said.

"Ha, ha. Well, that's her right. Good for her."

"I have to go," I said.

"Do you?" He drew on the cigarette, burned down now almost to the filter. "Well, don't be a stranger, all right?" Then, without warning, his hand came up and patted my left arm. Pain shot into my chest and I felt tears come to my eyes. My entire body flinched and drew away from him, and when I looked up at his face I saw that his own eyes had gone damp. The hand he'd touched me with was lowered and turned palm up, as if to show me he wasn't armed.

I said, "Okay," making little more than a whisper of sound, and I nodded yes, then turned the handlebar with my right hand, rolling away from him.

He was saying something about putting in a swimming pool as I began to pedal.

※

For the next couple of hours I rode around the island, down back roads with narrow shoulders, alongside ditches and swampy lots marked for development. I rode back and forth across a darkened square of repaired parking lot next to the First National Bank, where the previous summer a water main had broken and washed away the underlying dirt and a man's car had fallen through the asphalt crust, nose-diving halfway into a soupy muck of earth. By the time I got back to our house, it was after five and my mother was home from work. I pushed my bike into the backyard and came in through the sliding glass door off the dining room, and it was obvious there was a major fight in the works. Karen was sitting forward on the recliner and her face was red from crying. My mother was at the dining room table, her own face buried in the boxed well of her arms. A suitcase was standing by the front door.

For an instant I thought I understood. They'd been fighting about Karen's quitting school, and Karen had blown her top and threatened to run away again. But they looked so flipped out that I started wondering if the suitcase belonged to someone else. My mother might have packed it. Or even Frankie—though he was leaning against the wall where the living room funneled into the hallway, observing the two of them like a scientist taking mental notes.

"I think my arm is broken," I announced.

Karen cut her eyes toward me. Slowly, my mother lifted her head from the table. She said, "What?"

"My arm." I wasn't holding it. I was just standing there feeling it throb and wanting to be acknowledged, though I didn't want to tell them anything about what had actually happened.

"What's that on your head?" my mother asked.

"I cut it."

She looked straight up at the ceiling. She stared at a particular spot in the plaster as if the word of God were written there. Dropping her eyes again, she said, "I don't believe this."

"My arm—"

"Your arm looks fine! I don't want to hear that it's broken, all right? There's entirely too much going on right now!"

I glanced over at Karen, who made the slightest squinting gesture with her already pinched, damp eyes, declaring herself the winner of the moment. Then I walked through the living room, past Frankie, and down the short hall to my bedroom, where I closed the door behind me.

※

When I didn't come out for dinner later that evening, it wasn't because I was vying for attention (I'd given up on that as quickly as I'd tried for it) but because I felt nauseous—just enough to keep me prostrate and miserable. The house was nearly silent; there was only the soft timpani roll of the air conditioner. Eventually I heard the clinking of silverware, and then a flow of unruffled conversation that could only have been coming from the television.

He tapped on my door sometime after that. I didn't answer. The doorknob was locked but was made with a small hole in the middle so that a nail could be pushed into it in case of an emergency, and a few minutes later I heard the sliding and poking of the nail, then the click of the lock giving way. I was lying on the bed, on my side, with my back to the door. Suddenly, I was afraid of him: he was so calm and smart and direct; how could he *not* have realized what was going on with me? I felt as if he were a magician, and that he was about to guess all the cards I was holding. But he didn't speak. The mattress dipped behind me as he settled his slight weight onto it. His hand reached around and in the hollow of my stomach he dropped one of those odd little cigar-shaped snacks he'd collected over the years: a waxy, vaguely chocolate rod called a Space Food Stick.

My arm, it turned out, was indeed broken. My mother drove

me to the hospital on the mainland the next afternoon as the space shuttle *Columbia* climbed into the sky behind us on its maiden voyage, sounding out a rumble we could hear through the closed car windows and carving an arc of gray smoke into the sky over the island. She brought her hand to her mouth as the doctor showed her the faintest indication of a fracture in my humerus, so insignificant that he wouldn't put a cast on it but would merely give me a sling to wear for a week—yet significant enough to make her suffer horrible guilt for not having believed me. Before Wes Markham had a chance to see me in my sling, he was suspended for selling a bag of crushed aspirin to a fellow student in his P.E. class. Karen, who turned out to be the one who had packed the suitcase that had sat by the door that night, would unpack it and pack it again several more times over the coming year, but would prove herself not in much of a hurry to go anywhere. Frankie would hold fast to his desire to be Luke Skywalker's intergalactic true love, until *Star Wars* met New Wave and Skywalker eventually yielded to Simon Le Bon. And I wouldn't hold fast to any of my desires, or to any truth about myself, for a long, long time.

But as for that night, as for that moment in my room, I felt temporarily less than miserable. I felt, even, okay. For Frankie, who could say anything regardless of the sense it made, who could speak his own invented language at will, said nothing at all. He bent over and, so gently that I almost didn't feel it, kissed my upper arm the way our mother used to when we'd hurt ourselves. Then he lay down behind me, eased his body against mine, and rested his hand against the side of my neck, and for an eternity, for an hour, we drifted just like that—immobile and weightless.

The Last Time I Knew You

1984

Karen positioned herself in the neutral zone of asphalt between the bowling alley and the religious bookstore, and leaned against the driver's door of the Datsun. She was watching the neon cartoon of the Shore Lanes Bowling sign, on which a man in profile bent down and sent a ball blinking toward a set of pins, exploding them outward and prompting S-H-O-R-E L-A-N-E-S to flash in bright pink sequential letters, over and over again.

If they ever arrived, they would see her just like this: illuminated by a pole lamp, posed with one foot crossed over the other and a cigarette in her hand. She'd changed clothes in the car after work and was wearing a pair of black low-heeled boots, cutoff shorts, a *Quadrophenia* T-shirt, and a black leather jacket with metal studs across the shoulders. It was November, the day after Thanksgiving, and the jacket was making her sweat. Though the air was stagnant, she bent her head and cupped her hands around the match to light the cigarette, then rose out of this posture as if the smoke were pulling her upright. Cars moved up and down Courtenay Parkway. The lights in the drugstore across from the theater went out a third at a time, and a moment later the drugstore sign went dark.

Ten o'clock, they'd said, and it was thirty minutes past that now: a half hour spent standing in a parking lot, her eyes trained on every car that turned in at the bowling alley. Holding the cigarette over the roof of the Datsun, she stuck her head and one arm through the open window and turned the ignition key halfway, then switched on the radio. Her fingers rolled a Winn-Dixie commercial into Phil Collins into Billy Idol, and she turned up the song. She'd give them five more minutes.

Finally, a pair of headlights veered off the road and made a beeline across the parking lot, aiming right for her. She heard the gurgle of the muffler, the ratchety knock of the motor, and then the radio coming through the Chrysler's open windows: *Pa-na-ma-ah-ah-ah-ah-ah!* She tilted her head back and blew smoke and pretended not to see them until the Chrysler lurched to a stop alongside the Datsun.

Ronnie Talbot raced the engine before turning off the car.

"You're late," Karen told him.

"And for that I humbly apologize," Talbot said. "Lam had to bow out at the last minute because his mother's a little pickled. But we have a special guest with us tonight. My cousin Jason, direct from Boca Raton."

Karen dropped her cigarette and set a boot heel down on top of it. "I'm thrilled." She dipped her head down and peered at the figure in the passenger's seat. He was dressed in khakis and a light blue oxford, the sleeves buttoned around his wrists. He sat with his wide shoulders slumped against the seat, appearing at the same time both muscular and soft-boned. His hair was parted at the side and just covered the tops of his ears. He eyed Karen through a pair of large silver-framed eyeglasses. She said, "Happy Day After Dead Turkey Day."

Talbot nodded toward the bookstore behind her. "You could have found Jesus while you were waiting."

"Uh-huh. We're going somewhere," she said, "right?"

He nodded.

She locked up her Datsun, then opened the back door of the Chrysler—a dented yellow Newport that Talbot had dubbed the Forehead during their senior year because of its long, wide hood—and climbed inside.

"This is J. Jason Winkle," Talbot said in his game-show-host voice. "I'm calling him Lefty because I can't say 'Winkle' without cracking up. We're cousins by some marriage twice divorced or once annulled or something. His family just moved up from Boca, and he's transferred to our very own Merritt Island High. Lefty, meet Karen."

Winkle smiled and said, "Hey."

"He's still in high school?" Karen asked. He had the look of a seminary student, a young Baptist who planned to go out into the world and improve it.

"That he is," Talbot said. "A senior facing the abyss. I thought we'd show him the ropes." He tapped Winkle on the side of the head and wagged his thumb toward the backseat. "Karen, here, is one of the island's most lovely creatures."

"Right," Karen said. "That's me."

One of the young man's hands extended over the seat as if to shake Karen's, but she didn't take it. "So you graduated?" he asked her.

She looked at Talbot again. "Um, beer?"

"It's right there between our good friend Lefty's feet." Talbot started the engine. "Lefty, imbibe the lady."

Winkle bent forward, dug a beer out of the box, and passed it to Karen.

They drove a half-circle around the Datsun, then rolled across the bookstore parking lot and back onto Courtenay Parkway. "Ol' Lefty here is interested in becoming one of the Midnight Ramblers," Talbot said, adjusting the rearview mirror so that he could see Karen. "Lam's against it, but I'm working on him. I've explained that it takes great amounts of public humiliation to become a Rambler, but Lefty still wants to do it. Don't you, Lefty?"

"Yeah." Winkle grinned and glanced back at her. "I guess."

"There's no 'I guess' about it. There is being a Rambler, and there is not being a Rambler. Ask Karen."

Karen had her beer can against her lips. She finished her swig and grimaced. "Don't ask me. I don't know what happens in your stupid little club, and I can't believe you haven't dropped it by now."

Talbot clucked his tongue. "Well, when *is* a good time to stop being a Rambler? No one's quite figured that out yet."

"I've always been a little out of the loop," Karen said. "I *assume* it's about penis size—like a club for little dicks." She glanced at Winkle. "You may want to think twice about joining."

Winkle looked down at his lap.

"Don't mind Karen. She's just jealous because of our men-only policy. But it's not a matter of *joining;* you have to be approved for membership."

"And Lam had to do what, exactly, to get approved?" Karen asked him. "Walk through the mall in his underwear and a fright wig, if I remember right."

"Let's change the subject," Talbot said. "Where are we going? I was thinking about Mather's Bridge."

Karen groaned.

"Kelly Park?"

"We could," she said, trying to sound indifferent. "Or we could just go to the airport."

"The airport it is."

They crossed 520 and drove south, past clusters of darkened neighborhoods, the yellow glow of the Shell station, the Minute Mart, and the elementary school, to a dark, narrow road that peeled off the parkway and led to the Merritt Island Airport. The wind sock over the little terminal hung limp against its pole. The terminal was dark, save for a single light burning in the tower. The runway, which extended out between the airport's two black-mouthed hangars and ended abruptly in the distance, looked like an enormous spike laid down over the marsh. Talbot backed the car into a spot opposite the terminal and turned off the engine. "How are we set for beer?"

"We've got some," Winkle said.

" 'How are we set' means 'how many do we have left?' "

"Oh." Winkle leaned forward and stirred his hand through the box. "Nine."

"We have a beer problem," Talbot declared.

Winkle looked at Karen, who was drawing a circle in the air with the bottom of her can. "That's not enough?" he asked.

"No," Talbot said. "Tonight will not be brought to you by the number nine. You're a drinking man, right?"

"S-Sure," Winkle stammered. "I mean, I'll have a few."

"Well, there you go: that's only three more apiece."

Karen took her cigarettes from the inside pocket of her jacket, opened the box, and shook one out an inch. She tapped Winkle's shoulder. He flinched. "You're Baptist, right?"

He nodded.

"I thought so. Want one?"

He glanced at the pack. "No, thanks," he said.

"Your funeral."

He grinned and cracked open a beer for himself, then clamped his lips on it to catch the fizz.

Out of the darkness beyond the far end of the terminal, a pair of headlights low to the ground flashed on and off.

"Holy shit. Is that who I think it is?" Talbot asked.

"I wouldn't know," Karen said, though of course she did.

She'd marked the time on her calendar and knew this was the week of Colby's return to the island. She knew he'd be out on the prowl the first chance he got, and that the airport was a likely spot to find him.

The headlights flashed again. "It *is* him. What did he end up with?"

"Six months," Karen said. "One of those baby prisons."

"Half a year. That seems harsh for a little hemp."

"Intention to sell. Plus, he was drunk and had his dad's pistol in the glove compartment."

"Ah, yes," Talbot said, nodding. "Lam told me he did community service for the last part of it. Delivered meals to old people."

Karen blew smoke out the half-open window and tapped her ash against the edge of the glass. "I wouldn't know," she said again.

Talbot started the car. A moment later they were rolling, the tires crackling over the gravel as they crept along the front of the terminal toward a Firebird, its red-orange grille watching them like an angry face. Talbot inched the Newport forward until the two bumpers touched.

"Hey!" a voice called from the other car. The driver's door opened and Seth Colby emerged, his pale T-shirt glowing in the lamplight. He stepped around the door, pushed a hand through the blond wings of his hair, and fixed his eyes on the meeting point of the two cars. "Get your shit off my shit."

Talbot backed the Newport up a foot. He turned the engine off, got out of the car, and hopped up onto its expansive hood.

Colby took a stance and pulled a flask of something from his back pocket. When he drank from it, his shoulders twitched.

"Welcome back to the land of the living dead. Give us a swig."

"Chew me," Colby said. "There's beer, though—we picked up a case. Who're you with?"

"Who're *you* with?"

"Couple of bastards."

Colby snapped his fingers toward the Firebird and Talbot followed his lead, knocking his fist against the Newport's hood. "Send in the clowns."

Doors opened on both cars, and two young men spilled out of the Firebird. Karen recognized them as the identical twins with Boston accents who transferred to her high school during her junior year. Stoners, she remembered, double trouble, though as far as she knew, they'd graduated. They swaggered up to either side of Colby and stared down at the bumper of the Firebird. The one hugging a case of beer against his chest said, "He banged up ya cah."

"Gentlemen," Talbot announced, taking a slight bow and doing a double flourish with his middle fingers, "this is Cousin Lefty, just in from Boca. And ..." He let his voice trail off.

Karen remained in the backseat of the Newport. She watched Colby, who had opened a hunting knife and was already launching into a story, moving around the gravel like an overly wound toy.

"So I just told him, 'Shitwad, one more crack about my height and I'll put you in a box, even if it means going right back to the place I just got out of.' I told him it was Raiford. He didn't know any better."

"What did he do?" one of the twins asked.

"He made another crack. So I lunged for him, and he ran like a son of a bitch. I never saw anyone leave a bar so fast. Then they kicked *me* out of the place for pulling a knife, but I didn't care because at that point it was about, you know, *honor*." He glanced at the twins, and at Talbot, and finally settled his gaze on Winkle. "I looked for him when I got outside. Tool must have hopped a bus or something. Otherwise, I would have finished him."

No doubt, Karen thought. Colby had long ago nicknamed himself "El Destructo," and together, the two of them had destroyed all the plans for their respective futures made by parents and guidance counselors—even the ones they'd made themselves. At the height of their rebellion, the vice principal had caught them having sex in one of the portable buildings, and on the following Saturday night, Karen served as lookout while Colby set the portable on fire. He was lead guitarist for his band Jake and was going to hitchhike with the other members to Athens, Georgia; Karen was going to go with them and be their manager. But last summer, the bassist somehow got himself accepted to one of the state schools, the singer became a Jesus freak, and the drummer coaxed his Mustang past ninety at the south end of Courtenay Parkway and rolled the car into the swamp, landing upside down in the water with a broken neck.

Karen assured Colby he was good enough to be a solo act, since he'd written all the songs himself, and told him she still wanted to go to Athens and be his manager. Colby, in response, smashed his Gibson against the side of a dumpster. A week later, he proposed. She accepted, and told her mother the news, which started a fight culminating in Karen's threatening to move out and never be heard from again. But it didn't matter. Within days she caught Colby lip-locked with a girl from Cocoa Beach, and shortly thereafter he was arrested, sentenced, and sent away.

Watching them gathered now in the gray-blue light of the pole lamp, she realized her late entrance would be seen as a strategy, and that it was doomed because it was going to make her look nervous. But she wasn't nervous—not very. She'd planned on running into Colby. She'd dressed for it. She'd insulated herself with Talbot and, instead of Lam, this dingus of a bonus prize, Winkle. Seth was Colby-the-ex-con now, but he was also Colby-her-cheating ex-fiancé, and that, if anything, ought to give her grounds for striking a pose. She took a deep breath and dug a cigarette out of her jacket pocket.

Colby tried to close his hunting knife and dropped it. He danced a sandaled foot out of its path.

"Did you get any tattoos in the Big House?" This came from Winkle, standing perfectly straight, one hand in his pocket and the other around his beer. He had a stupefied, delighted expression on his face.

"Big House?" Colby asked, staring at him. "Yeah, I got a W tattooed on each ass cheek. When I bend over, it says 'WOW.' You want to see?"

The twins guffawed simultaneously.

Karen opened her door.

The sarcastic sneer on Colby's face melted away as she rounded the front of the Newport, leaned back on the grille, and closed her lips around her cigarette.

His mouth moved without sound for a moment. Then he said, "Hey, woman."

"Capone."

"What are you doing here?"

She raised both hands toward her shoulders and opened them outward.

"You're hanging out with this guy now?" He looked at Talbot. "You didn't tell me she was in the car."

"I didn't know she still was."

Colby looked at her and asked again, "What are you doing here?"

"I've been doing whatever—and whoever—I feel like for a while now," Karen said.

"Yeah?" He took the flask from his pocket again. "Give me a list."

"Mr. Colby's been broadening our lives with tales of the world at large," Talbot said, a little louder than necessary. "I'm afraid we don't have much to report from the island. Wait—I stand corrected. There was that plane."

"What plane?" Colby asked.

"One of those old ones that look like an Airstream trailer. No communication with the tower—it just appeared, and landed. A couple of guys jumped out and ran into the swamp. So the airport crew called the cops, and when the cops stuck their heads in the plane, it was *packed* full of the magic weed."

"Come on."

"I speak the truth. Packed full of it, baled up and ready to go, and it all went to the Brevard County blues."

"And they bust *me*," Colby snorted, shaking his head. "So why'd the two assholes land in the first place?"

"They were running out of gas," Talbot said. He turned and tossed his empty can into the brush. Winkle did the same. When he reached for another one, Talbot edged the box away with his foot. "What's the first rule of being a Rambler?"

Colby burst into a laugh. "The first *what*? Don't tell me you still have your little horseshit gang going. I mean, grow fucking up."

"I tried to tell Lefty it's a club for little dicks," Karen said. She indicated Winkle with her chin, then looked directly at Colby and said, "He's got no business being in a club like that."

"And you'd know?" Colby asked.

Karen shrugged.

"We need to talk," Colby said.

"We're talking. Isn't this talking?"

Colby wagged a thumb toward the Firebird. "My office."

Karen rolled her eyes, but pushed away from the Newport.

Sitting on the red bucket seat, the interior smelling of cigarettes and the console between them a mosaic of cracked vinyl,
she felt like nothing had changed at all. She stared forward,
watching one of the twins light a joint. Colby switched on the
radio and immediately switched it off. He said, "Boy."

"Boy," Karen said.

"This is a hell of a reception."

"If you were expecting some kind of parade, I'm sorry. They
don't give parades for two-timing assholes."

He tapped his fists against the steering wheel. "I get the feeling there's something you want to say to me."

"You called this meeting," she said, then turned and found
his face just inches from hers.

She pushed her tongue into his mouth. He tasted like
whiskey.

When they broke apart, she said, "You can go to hell, by the
way."

"Jesus, you're one crazy girl. You know that? You're a certi-
fied lunatic."

She glared at him. "Who *was* that blond slut?"

"Blond slut . . . you mean, back before I got busted?"

"I mean the one I caught you with. The one you had your secret rendezvous with on the beach."

"You were following me."

"Of course I was following you—because I knew you were
screwing around."

"She was a friend of Darryl's. And for the record, you didn't
catch us doing all that much."

"It was enough."

"Remember your little trick with my license plate?"

"How many times have you been laid since then?"

"Since then? Jesus, Karen, I've been in *prison*. It's not the best
place to pick up girls."

"That doesn't mean you weren't getting laid," she said with a smirk.

"You're a riot. I was half the time in that hellhole, and half the time doing community bullshit. And since I've been out, well, that's my business. You're the one who broke up with me, remember?"

She wiped her mouth and refolded her arms, staring forward again. After a minute she said, "So what now?"

"How should I know? Day by day, baby. I'm not going to be pushed around anymore, I'm sure of that much."

"Nobody ever pushed you around."

"*Plenty of people* pushed me around!" he all but yelled. "And I'm telling you, I'm done with it. I'm different." He jutted his head forward to kiss her again, but she pulled back.

"Different how?"

Instead of answering her, he started the car and put it into drive, rolling forward without turning on the headlights. They barely cleared the passenger side of Talbot's Newport. The group standing alongside the terminal stepped back against the wall and watched as the Firebird passed close by them like an errant parade float. Colby steered around the side of the building.

"What are you doing?" Karen asked.

"What I feel like doing. Get it?"

There was a tall metal fence at the back of the terminal. The gate was standing open, a broken padlock hanging from its latch. They rolled through it and onto the tarmac. A porch light glowed from a trailer near a row of palm trees, and a bulb burned in each of the two side-flanking hangars. Other than that, the only light came from the half-moon over the Banana River. Colby steered the Firebird around a forklift and a stack of wooden pallets. He maneuvered close to a trio of Sandpipers, their propellered noses pointing toward the treetops and their tails moored to the ground. "I think that story about the pot plane is bullshit," he said as they coasted out into the middle of the tarmac. "Who'd let all that go to the cops? I'd rather crash."

"I guess that's the difference between you and other people," Karen said, trying to sound bored, though she was consumed with what he had in mind, driving them around this off-limits area. It soon became at least partially obvious. He was aimed for the perimeter, where a black stem of tarmac led to the runway. "You're not going out there," she told him.

"Baby, you still don't get it. I'm done being told. I'm the action and the *re*action. I'm the subject and the predicament."

"Predicate."

He performed a rough mouthing of the word *predicate* with his tongue hanging over his lower teeth. "I don't care. You've got the book smarts; we figured that one out a long time ago. But look at me, free as a bird, and you all holy with your piss-ass job at the Sizzler—"

"I work at Provost now."

He steered the car in a half circle and eased them to a stop. "Remember that James Bond movie with the sharks?"

"I want to go back."

"He had that car he drove right off the end of a pier, and it turned into a submarine." The runway stretched out before them, extending onto a man-made jut of land surrounded on either side, and beyond its tip, by the darkness of the river. "Want to play James Bond?" he asked.

"You're such a child."

"Or we could play *Grease*. You liked *Grease*. That part at the end where they flew that faggot convertible into the wild blue yonder."

"What if we play adults?" Karen said. "You're twenty-one years old, Colby. You think you can play adult for five minutes of your life?"

His upper lip curled. It was the same twisted smile he'd

given her after stepping away from the burning portable, the gas can still dangling from his hand. Being blown to smithereens with him would have been perfect, that day: the ideal comment on their misunderstood lives. Now she only felt roped into another one of his meaningless stunts, and terrified.

He winked at her as he took his foot off the brake and gently pressed it down on the gas pedal. "Pick a game." He was facing forward now, lifting his butt off the seat to dig a hand into the back pocket of his jeans. The hunting knife reappeared, folded inside its wooden case. "You can hook your seat belt, if you want. If you pick James Bond over *Grease,* I won't let you drown. I'll cut you out, when the time comes."

"You're not funny, Colby."

He sang: " 'Nobody does it better ...' "

"I mean it," she said, trying to suppress the tremor in her voice. "You always take everything too far. You got busted for having a gun, and now you're fooling around with a knife—"

"Let's talk about *why* I got busted," he said, dropping the folded knife into his lap so that he could steer with both hands. "You took my license plate, that night at the beach. Don't tell me you didn't."

"So? What's your point?"

"My point is, I was a little high, and I had some weed on me, and I had my old man's clip-loader in the glove box. And I would have gotten home just fine if I'd had a goddamn *license plate* on my car. *That's* why they pulled me over. Believe you me, Ragazzino, I ended up 'playing adult' for that one."

"I want to go back," she said, raising her voice.

"No can do."

"I mean it. I want to go back to Talbot and Lefty." They were picking up speed now. The grass and trees fell away from either side and the river loomed ahead. She felt her body draw back against the vinyl seat.

"You should have thought of that before."

"Fuck you!" she yelled. "You fucking asshole! Take me back to Talbot, *now*!"

He slammed his foot down on the brake pedal. The tires locked but the car kept moving, rubber shrieking against cement, sliding sideways until her body lifted from the seat and her elbow slammed against the door. They stopped.

"Why?" Colby asked, still gripping the steering wheel and staring at her. "You screwing Talbot? Is that why you're out with him?"

The pain in her elbow throbbed with the thumping of her heart.

"Big-dick Lefty must get jealous," he said. "Or do him and Talbot share you?"

"I'm not—" She winced, and tried to level her expression while deciding on the best response. There were maybe six feet of runway between her side of the car and the river. After a moment she said, "I'm not seeing Talbot."

"No?"

"Just Lefty."

His face drew in as if he'd been hit with a bad smell. *"Lefty?"*

She reached into her jacket for a cigarette. Her hand was trembling. "We've been out a couple of times."

He looked incredulous, but she was achieving the desired effect: he was just surprised enough to be disarmed, and just angry enough to want to get away from her. "You're turning into a cradle-robber in your old age. I mean, what's he, fifteen?"

She glanced again at the speckled surface of the river.

"You fucking him?"

"Not yet." She didn't want to make him too mad. "I just want to go back."

"I'll bet you do."

"Now," she said.

Her hand was clutching the door handle, and he looked over and saw it, then glanced up at her face with a foreign expression that approximated sadness.

A moment later he was steering the car back up the runway. She hadn't realized how shallow her breathing had become until she felt her lungs expand as they reached the strip of asphalt that connected to the tarmac. When they were almost to the gate, the door of the trailer opened. A man in pajamas stepped onto the landing and hollered at them that he was calling the police.

Colby slowed down. He opened the knife and extended one of his skinny arms out the driver's window, pointing the blade at the center of the man's chest. "Do it, you old bastard, and you'll wake up tomorrow with your heart cut out."

The man took a step back into the trailer and watched them drive through the open gate.

When they rounded the corner of the terminal, Winkle and the twins were standing around the Newport. Talbot was stretched out on the hood holding a beer can against his belt buckle, staring at the night sky.

Colby parked the Firebird alongside them. He turned to Karen, his face suddenly dull with disinterest. "You getting out, then?"

She opened the passenger door and stepped out of the car.

"How was the airfield?" Talbot asked, but Colby ignored him and looked at Winkle.

"Lefty."

Winkle straightened up.

"She's all yours."

"She's—?"

"All yours," Colby told him. "You can have her."

"Someone's torn a chapter from this potboiler," Talbot said, glancing from Colby to Winkle to Karen.

Fuming, Karen lifted her purse strap onto her shoulder and walked around the Firebird. She crossed in front of Winkle and puckered her lips at him. Then she opened the back passenger's door on the driver's side of the Newport and got in.

It was warm and stifling in the car. Her face continued to burn, but as she sat waiting for Talbot to get the hint that she wanted to leave, she began to shiver inside her leather jacket. How could she have been so stupid as to think anything good could come of meeting up with Colby again? He was the same now as he'd been when they were sixteen. He'd be the same forty years from now, only gray-haired.

One of the twins started telling them about the nine-foot alligator he'd run over with their uncle's Riviera, but apparently he'd already told the story at some point, because the other twin said it had been their father's station wagon the last time around, and added, "That gatah's getting longah since it died."

"Can we go?" Karen called out the window.

"We can," Talbot said, bending his head backward to look at her upside down through the windshield. "Should we?"

She glared at him until he pulled himself upright, climbed off the hood, and said, "Ladies, it's been a pleasure."

The twins were sharing a roach. One of them passed it to Colby, still inside the Firebird.

Behind the wheel of the Newport, Talbot looked at Karen in the rearview mirror. "So, did he do the flying-car routine?"

"I hate him," Karen said. "He's nothing but a trouble-maker."

"You sound like your mom."

The idea stung; she forced a small laugh and told him to get bent. But he was right. And with a twinge of anger, she acknowledged to herself that her mother had been right: Colby was bad news, a punk who refused to grow up.

"What was all that about my cousin?" Talbot asked. "Did you tell Colby you liked him?"

"Maybe."

"Do you?"

"Sure." She picked up the warm beer she'd left on the seat next to her. "Why not?"

"Well, because he's a dweeb. You don't have to go with Lefty just because Colby—"

"I said, *why not,*" Karen snapped. She didn't want to talk anymore.

"Yeah, okay," Talbot said, "why not." The game-show host was suddenly gone from his voice; he sounded almost sullen. "Fresh blood, I guess." He stuck his head out the window. "We're out of here."

Colby started his engine. The twins climbed into the Firebird, and Winkle folded his stocky, schoolboy frame back into the passenger's seat of the Newport. They left first, and were following the narrow access road back to Courtenay when Talbot said, "So I hear we've got a pair of lovebirds in the car."

Winkle looked at Karen. She gave him her best sarcastic smile.

When they got back onto Courtenay, the Firebird pulled out from behind them and sped past. The twins shrieked out the open windows and Colby's arm reached into the night sky with his middle finger raised.

Karen muttered, "There goes nothing."

Talbot grunted. He suggested they stop by the drive-in.

"Can we not and say we did?" Karen asked. "I've had my fill of car antics for one night."

"Always thinking of yourself," Talbot said. He turned onto

520. When they reached the drive-in, he killed the lights. The theater had been closed for nearly five years and the speaker poles had all been removed, but the gray tattered screen still stood facing the wavy acre of asphalt. Talbot floored it, and Karen saw Winkle tense up in his seat. The car felt like a ship crashing into a series of wakes: up one rise and slamming down after it, up the next and slamming down, over and over, until something metal left the back end of the car and Talbot finally slowed down.

"Was that the muffler?" he asked, glancing at his side mirror.

Neither Karen nor Winkle answered him. They drove back to the parkway without speaking. The Newport rattled across the empty parking lot of the bowling alley to the spot where the Datsun was parked next to the bookstore.

Talbot said, "I guess this is where I drop you two off."

"What do you mean?" Karen asked.

"I'm heading north. Lefty's parents just bought a house in Merritt Ridge, and you live in Bel Air. It only makes sense."

She reached inside her jacket for a cigarette. Tapping the filter against her thumbnail, she asked, "You want a ride?"

"Sure," Winkle said.

The two of them climbed out of the car. Talbot, she expected, would deliver some closing game-show remark, to which she would respond with something gruff and slightly racy. But he said only "Later" and put the Newport into drive.

Karen lit the cigarette and stared at the Datsun. She was the cocky one, out of all her friends. She was the one with the acid tongue, always ready to put *whoever* in his place. But she felt incapable of doing that, suddenly. What could she possibly say to Winkle that would put him in his place? What *was* his place? She didn't even know hers anymore. Finally, to break what would have otherwise been an eternal silence, she said, "That's people for you. You'll find out, in a few years: some people don't ever change; they just get stuck in the asshole stage. Freud wrote about it, the asshole stage, people who'll never be anything more than—"

He was standing less than a foot away from her, leaning forward. His fingers tapped at the sides of his khakis.

"Assholes." She stepped back and felt the warm metal of the Datsun beneath the hem of her shorts. He had a timid, almost doubtful smile set in his lips, as if he were hearing a piece of good news he wasn't sure he could trust. She saw one oxford-sleeved arm lift, and felt the door opening beside her legs. He pushed the bucket seat forward and pressed his other arm against the side of her jacket. She heard herself say "Um" as he guided her into the back. She landed half on, half off the seat, and slid deeper into the car to make room for him. It was comical, this compression of matter and space; there was barely room for the two of them to move. She felt his glasses graze her jaw and his mouth on her throat. His hands were enormous, closing around her ribs. She had no idea where the cigarette had gone. She let one of her arms drift down over his shoulders. "I hear you," she said, because he'd grunted something against her neck. "You're a quick study. But listen—"

One of his hands left her side and closed over her mouth. His weight was pouring, molten, through his hips, and she tried to bring a knee against his crotch, but she could neither feel nor move either one of her legs. He worked his shoulders against hers and wedged the hand that wasn't on her mouth between their bodies to claw at their clothing. She screamed something foul that was absorbed by the flesh of his fingers.

Talbot would be furious when he found out. Colby might still care enough, in the coming days, to put his knife to use. If only it was five minutes ago. The hand that wasn't on her mouth was touching both of them now between their legs, figuring things out. Her right arm was pinned against the seat, and her left hand beat uselessly against his back. He was almost inside her. Everything was about to get much worse. But really, how many minutes could it last? *I could be out of here already,* she thought. *Five minutes, tops.* Her eyes ran across the ratty lining of the ceiling to the back window and the sky hanging low and dark on the other side. *I'm nearly gone.*

Welcome to Utica

My father has taken over the dining room. He's taken over the kitchen. He's turned the den into his personal archive and still his stuff is spilling into the living room. He's got three pairs of broken reading glasses on the phone table, recipe cards on the floor, Elmore Leonard and Dick Francis novels stacked on top of the television and stuck between the posts on the stairs. When I sit on the couch, my leg tips an ashtray into the cushions.

"Dad," I say, "can we clean some of this stuff up? You've got crap everywhere."

"It's my house," he says.

I'm the one who remembers to leave the faucets dripping so the pipes won't freeze. I'm the one who heard wood-borers eating away the inside of the support beams in the basement. And the one who gave a damn, who realized there could be serious damage, when a water stain suddenly appeared on the upstairs ceiling. But it's his house.

I've been awake for ten minutes. He's been awake for hours, most likely. It's 9:30 in the morning. He's in the dining room, in his pajamas and robe, sitting at the table in front of a spill of papers and frowning through his reading glasses at a recipe book.

He has a cigarette going and a cup of coffee in his hand. Without looking up, he says, "Yo," drawing the sound out. "Homeboy. How come you're awake before noon?"

He does two things that really get to me. He does a lot of things, but two of them are when he exaggerates, and when he talks to me like I'm a teenager. I don't think I've slept till noon once the entire time I've lived in his house, and I've been living here almost nonstop since I was eighteen. I'm not a "homeboy" or a "bro" or—when he reaches way back—a "cat." I'm thirty-seven years old. I'm finding gray hair on my chest.

"I don't have to work today," I tell him.

"No? What's Manny, going light on you?"

"Yeah, Dad, Manny's going light on me. He's paying me for doing nothing." This isn't far from the truth.

"Manny," he says, and breathes out through his nose. Then he sucks in air through his mouth so quickly, it's like exhaling was a bad idea, and this is loud too. I can hear every breath. I can practically hear his lungs, that plastic-shopping-bag sound, and I don't want to picture what they look like. "You've seriously got the day off?" he asks, sounding irritated.

"Seriously," I tell him.

He says, "A Thursday," and breathes heavily. He's holding a few recipe cards like a poker hand. "Thursdays I work, you know. Thursday is a business day for me. Have we got any raisins?"

"Yes."

"I think we're out of them," he says.

But I'm the one who does the shopping, which has only become more of a chore ever since an episode of *Emeril Live* inspired him to start baking last year, so I say, "We've got a fucking jumbo bag of raisins in the pantry."

"All right, all right. I'm thinking of making this raisin wheat loaf. *Maybe*. But Thursday's a business day for me, you know.

I've got an appointment this afternoon. Here." The pinky knuckle of the hand holding the cards taps the table. "I've got someone coming by."

"I won't get in your way." I've found the remote and I turn on the TV and click over to the news.

"Hey," he says, "how'd you hear from—" Mid-sentence he breaks up, his lungs heaving, one cough climbing over the next, clawing up his throat for nearly a full minute. On the TV, the local top-dog anchorlady is chuckling at the weatherman, who's chuckling back.

Finished coughing, my father says "Jesus" in general complaint, then calls out to me, "How'd you hear from Manny? I thought you said he never comes by the storage place."

"He doesn't."

"Well, he didn't call here. Did he? I didn't talk to him. I can't remember the last time I talked to Manny. He's all lofty now."

"He didn't call, Dad. He sent me an e-mail. He's got his brother-in-law working there today."

"Oh." He clears his throat. He pushes his chair back but doesn't get up. "That's like a fax in your computer?"

"That's it. That's what it is." We're three years away from the twenty-first century and my father doesn't know what e-mail is. He won't touch the cordless phone I bought, says he can't hear right on it, and he keeps the clunky yellow ground-wired one next to him on the dining room table and gets his feet tangled up in the cord.

He's looking at me now over the tops of his reading glasses. "Does your mother use that e-mail?"

"How would I know that, Dad?"

"I don't know. Maybe you write her that way."

"I don't. And she doesn't write me."

"Well, then, you ought to call her. See how she's doing."

"You were talking about Manny," I remind him.

He lowers his eyes to the table and gives a little shrug. "Manny used to be a good kid."

I get up from the couch and carry my empty soda can to the front window. The snow from last week is packed into a hard, dirty crust along the curb and there's a fresh layer, thin as gauze, over his Cadillac and my Celica. It's March and the house across the street is still decorated for Christmas.

"He's a little full of himself now, though. You know what I'm saying?"

I don't respond to this. I'm thinking about Las Vegas—all the time, lately. I've never been there. But any movie or TV show I've ever seen about Las Vegas, I haven't been able to take my eyes off the place.

My father coughs. "I mean, why does Manny never come around here? He's too busy to be a human being? He's too important, with his little storage facility?"

An icy draft leaks in around the window frame. I feel the cold on my throat.

Then he coughs again and says, "I used to have time for everybody, no matter who—and that was with *half this town* in my pocket," and I know what kind of day I'm in for.

※

He wouldn't let me drive him to the doctor's, the first time he went. He drove himself, then called me six hours later from the hospital. They'd wanted to run some more tests and had moved him over there in an ambulance—"just to jack up the fucking price." When I asked him what kind of tests, he said, "The regular kind." He told me to take a cab to the doctor's office and bring home his Cadillac.

Two days later a male nurse knocked on our door with a plastic briefcase and a canister of oxygen. My father didn't look surprised, and I knew then that he'd decided he wasn't going to tell me whatever the tests had revealed. Not that it was any great mystery. He'd been smoking two packs of Winstons a day since he was sixteen. Over the years, he'd been a big fan of beer and red wine and bourbon, progressively. At fifty, he'd replaced all that with coffee, and he averaged five, six pots a day. He liked eggs, he liked steak, he liked pasta, and he liked iceberg lettuce; nearly everything else he eyed with suspicion, except for snack foods and what he baked himself. As a result, by the time he reached his fifty-seventh birthday, he had an enormous, almost perfect semicircle of a stomach attached to his small frame, and a pair of lungs that could barely move it around. His neck looked inflated and his head had gone the way of Sinatra's, as if the original skull had been replaced with a larger model. The caffeine infusions, combined with his constant need for a nicotine fix, wrecked his sleep pattern, and he'd taken to napping in shifts, three or four hours at a time, so that he was usually just waking up or about to go to bed. The walk from the front door to the end of the driveway and back to get the newspaper—a distance of some fifty feet, round-trip—left him not only winded but exhausted. After the oxygen tank was set up next to the couch in the den, where he'd taken to sleeping because the stairs were too much for him, I went to see Dr. Cox, the one who'd sent him to the hospital, and I asked her what, specifically, was going on with my father.

"It's somewhat complicated," she said. "There are many factors affecting different systems and organs, and the interplay among them contributes to the damage to his body as a whole."

I asked her if she could put that in English.

"The man's a train wreck," she said.

It was how I imagined raising a kid would be. You look at them one day and they're different—different shape, different voice, a whole different feel about them, and somehow all that change has happened right under your nose.

When I'd showed up at his door nearly twenty years ago, he was a solid tank of a man. His arms and chest had been thickened by regular use of a punching bag that hung on the back porch. His hair was still blond, and his jaw was like a cement cradle for his smile. I knew my mother hated him. I knew he'd taken off when I was five and my sister was two, and that he sent us each a hundred-dollar bill every Christmas, which my mother promptly put in the bank, and that he called now and then, and either he fought with her or she fought with him over things that had happened a long time ago.

I'd talked about running away to Utica since I was ten years old, but that's all it was—talk. The idea of actually doing it had been his. I was less than a year out of high school and itching to leave Florida. When I shouted at my mother one afternoon that I was heading for Mexico, she called my father right in front of me and told him this, then handed me the phone and crossed her arms. He was just a voice to me. There was that hundred-dollar bill, but I never got to spend it, and I'd only see him when he was on his way to Miami Beach for vacation once every couple of years and stopped off at Merritt Island to take me and my sister to the Piccadilly. "Let me tell you about Mexico," he said into the phone. "It's a shit hole. You want to get your throat cut while you're wiping your ass with a newspaper?" He asked me this twice, he really wanted an answer, and when I told him no, he said, "I'll send you a bus ticket. You can come up here."

I didn't take him up on it, at first. But then I had another fight with my mother, and I called him and asked him for the ticket. "Done," my father said. And then he started talking like someone in a movie. Like Burgess Meredith in *Rocky*. He told me I could be someone, in Utica. He told me he could help me. I was a Ragazzino, and the name Ragazzino meant something in Utica. If I listened to him, if I stuck with him, I could make something out of myself that people would respect.

I started a new life at eighteen. I got a brand-new family—of one—to replace my sister and two half brothers and ex-stepfather, who by that time had also flown the coop. And to replace my mother. She told me in a phone call a few months later that I'd abandoned her. After all she'd done for me, she said, I'd turned around and swapped her for my father, turned her into the one I never saw and hardly spoke to. She was crying and I started crying too. But I was angry about that last fight, so I told her she was right, and hung up.

And there I was, in Utica. Eighteen years old, then nineteen, then twenty, waiting for the day I would make something of myself. For two years I was engaged to a girl whose name is no longer important, and for six months I was married to her—the only stretch of time since leaving Florida that I didn't live with my father. When that ended, I moved back into his house. Whole years can go by where nothing at all seems to change. But things change. My father turned into a different person, physically. And I don't know what I am, other than the bearer of a locally infamous last name.

❈

"Lucky Ragazzino," he says, bending forward in front of the combination TV/VCR on the cart in the dining room, one hand pressed down on the flanneled knee sticking out of his bathrobe. "Lucky Ragazzino always said it was his idea, that storage facility. Till his dying day he said it, probably his last words on his deathbed. But I'll let you in on a little family secret, my friend. It was my idea. You know what Lucky's real name was, don't you?"

"Luciano," I say.

"Luciano. That's right. He was named after that pansy opera singer."

Lucky Ragazzino's birth predated Pavarotti's, but I've told my father this before and it doesn't go over well. I'm staring at *The New Price Is Right* with the sound off on the living room set. I'm thinking about taking a shower and getting out of the house.

"He'd go ballistic if you reminded him of *that* little fact," my father says. "But Lucky was never big on the truth. We were in your uncle Vincent's Oldsmobile, doing what, I shouldn't exactly say. It was a . . . request. We were on the clock—let's put it that way." He falls silent for a moment and I glance over at him. He's still hunched forward, squinting at the buttons on the TV. His mouth is open and his lips are peeled back, exposing his teeth, and with the hand that isn't supporting his weight he reaches forward and pokes a finger into the tray of the VCR. "Goddamn it," he says. "Didn't I put a tape in here?"

"You asked me to buy more tapes. You said the ones you had were full."

"Oh." He looks over at me. His hair looks like he's been rubbing his head with a balloon. "Well, did you buy any?"

"Not yet."

"I thought I taped the State of the Union. Goddamn it, you didn't buy any tapes at all?"

"I'll get some this afternoon."

"That bastard," he says. "You know what the people of Arkansas said when he got elected? They said, 'Wait and see.' That's all they said. 'Wait and see.' Why didn't you buy any goddamn tapes?"

"I'll get them this afternoon."

"Please do." He straightens up slowly. "Anyway, we were in your uncle's Oldsmobile, and we stopped at a red light right next to what's-his-name, you know, that guy with the knuckle

ears whose sister went crazy after that fake kidnapping." He
stares at me until I give a little shrug. "The guy who drove that
old Chevy pickup," he says, "the one whose ears looked like
knuckles. Anyway, we pull up next to him at this stoplight and
he's got the back of that truck loaded with crap. I mean, there's
a dresser in there, there's an armchair, there's crap till Tuesday.
So Lucky rolls down the window and asks the guy if he's skipping town. 'Not me,' the guy says. 'My mother died.' Turns out
his mother died. She'd lived in a nursing home, and you know
what they're like: those people stick a goddamn room-for-rent
sign in your chest while you're still lying there on the floor. So
this guy had to get all his mother's crap out of there, and he had
no idea where he was taking it. I mean, he *knew* where it was
going—right to his own fucking house, because he didn't know
what else to do with it. And I said to Lucky, 'You know what
you do? You buy an old motel—and I know what I'm talking
about because I used to run one—you buy an old motel, and
you don't worry about linens or room service or any of that. You
just charge people to store their crap. This guy was paying his
mother's rent. If she dies and he doesn't want to give up her
crap, he'll pay to stash it somewhere because it's going to be
cheaper than whatever he was shelling out for the nursing
home. For him, it's a bargain.'"

And so my father becomes the inventor of the storage facility.
On other days, he's invented the leaf blower or the hot-air pop-
corn popper. I lay my head back on the couch cushion and rest
my feet on the coffee table, on top of one of his books of word-
search puzzles and the dog-eared jacket of a Tony Bennett
album. He walks back to his chair at the dining room table and
sits down, out of breath from having examined the VCR.

"Lucky took that one and ran with it," he says. "And I let
him. I mean, what else . . . did he have going on? I had more to
do than I could . . . keep up with. I had half this town." He

coughs—not the out-of-control cough but the deliberate cough, like he's shoving out of the way whatever's lodged in his throat. "Where the hell is Wilson?"

"Wilson," I say, scratching my forehead. I really need to get out of the house.

"My appointment," he says. "He's coming here. He's making a payment today."

I shrug.

"You're not working, huh?"

"I won't get in your way, Dad. I've got stuff to do."

"It's just delicate. Guys like Wilson—" He drops his eyes to the table, to the mess of newspapers, magazines, and sweepstakes forms, as if information about Wilson is buried in there somewhere. "I should just retire," he says, and then the other kind of cough takes over.

※

He's not entirely wrong—not about everything. The name Ragazzino *is* well-known in Utica, particularly among certain people. The family goes back locally three, maybe four generations, and has owned a number of businesses both on and off the books. Car dealerships, soft-drink distributorships, sports bars. A catering company that seems to flourish without ever actually catering anything, and a trucking company that ships something somewhere, I've never been clear on the specifics. Since my arrival here in 1978, three Ragazzinos have been shot (never fatally), at least four have done time in prison for white-collar crimes, and one of them—Benicio Antonio Ragazzino, a.k.a. Uncle Benny—vanished from the area and, as far as we know, from the face of the earth. There's a whole section of one living room wall devoted to family photographs. There's a grade-school photo of my sister, one of me, and the rest are all locals, Ragazzinos, portraits in black and white, in pastel tint, and in full-blown color. Most of them I couldn't name if my life depended on it.

Listen to my father and you'll think we're right in there with the rest of them. The truth is we're marginal, at best. My grandmother, who I never knew, was a Czech woman who married an Irish electrician named McGuire. He died of bone cancer when my father was still a boy, and a few years later she got another husband, Mario Ragazzino, who adopted my father and gave him the last name. When it came time to incorporate this ash-blond kid named Dermot into the decidedly Italian family business, his adopted father hooked him up with one of the Ragazzino car dealerships and made him a drive-away—a guy who delivers cars to out-of-state buyers. Maybe he was unhappy in Utica. Maybe he was just destined to be a fuckup. Whatever the reason, they handed him the keys to a brand-new Cadillac to deliver to a man in Washington, D.C., and my father, at the age of twenty-two, drove that Cadillac down to Washington and got it into his head to keep it. I imagine that in Ragazzino business lore, it's referred to as the time that adopted mick stole the car and vanished for five years. In the history of my own existence, it was the time when my father went on the lam and seeded a family. He met a girl in D.C. (my mother), got married, and had two kids (me and my sister). Then he vanished again—this time from us—tucking his tail between his legs and slouching back to Utica to beg forgiveness.

They forgave him. At least, they didn't disown him. From attending the few Ragazzino family weddings and funerals we've been invited to over the years, and from listening to information gargled up by drunken uncles I barely know, I've gathered that from that point on they gave my father nothing but crap jobs—answering phones for nonexistent companies, overseeing football party cleanups at the sports bars, and delivering not Cadillacs but fruit baskets to business associates.

He lived on what he earned—they handed him at least that much—and he bought the house we live in, far away from the more affluent part of town where all the other Ragazzinos live. And I'm even further removed from the family than he is. I'm the son of a Ragazzino-by-adoption, and the job they've given me, which no one in his right mind would complain about, is to sit in a booth at the entrance to a storage facility three or four days a week and let people in and out. It doesn't have one of those automatic coded security systems. It has a gate, a chain thicker than my arm, and a padlock with a key that looks like part of a spaceship. I let people in, and relock the gate. I let people out, and relock the gate. And the only people who come in and out, a couple of times a day at most, are Ragazzinos. I don't ask questions.

It's a job that pays me well enough—an envelope is dropped off every few weeks with a grand in cash—and I don't really do anything with the money. I buy gas. I buy food. We eat a lot of takeout, which I pay for, and I buy the groceries because my father doesn't charge me rent. I would pay for maintenance on the house, too, but whenever something needs to be done, my father says he'll make a call, and then someone shows up and does the work for free. This work is often sloppy. The men who do it are begrudgingly returning favors—to other Ragazzinos, not to us. But when I point this out to my father, he gets mad. We had the original windows on the house up until last year, when I suggested that we have them all replaced. "I'll make a call," my father said. The next day a couple of frightened-looking Asians came out and took measurements. A month later they showed up again, and crack, slap, dab, we had new windows. But they're crappy. They're single pane, and the cold air just passes right over the sill. If I mention this, my father argues, "There's nothing wrong with those windows. Be a man," and that particular comment always mystifies me, since I don't think either one of us has ever been particularly preoccupied with what that means beyond the equipment we were born with.

"You want New York to be Florida," he's fond of telling me. "You want oranges and girls in bikinis. Well, welcome to Utica."

Vegas, I think. I say the name silently, suck on it like a piece of candy. It's freezing in the living room, which can't be good for him, but I don't want to get into it this morning, so I tell him again I'm going to get cleaned up and head out. I tell him I'm going to return his videos, and I ask if he needs anything from the store besides blank tapes.

"You know what I need?" he says. "Gluten. I want to bake this raisin wheat loaf, and I need some gluten if I'm going to do it right. You think you can find me some gluten?"

I don't even know what gluten is, but I tell him sure, I'll find it.

"I've got to get ready for Wilson," he says, pushing a hand through his papers.

❋

His Cadillac never moves from the driveway. It's a '96 Seville Luxury Sedan, less than a year old, and it was a gift from the Ragazzinos-at-large. That it wasn't given to him on his birthday or anywhere near Christmas made the car a kind of lifetime achievement award in my father's eyes. It did, at least, seem to imply ultimate forgiveness for his fuckup back in 1959. But Utica's not a big place, and my father's doctor was recommended by one of his uncles, so chances are that word spread about the shape he was in and the Ragazzinos felt sorry for him. *Sorry* in the Ragazzino family has the same result as *congratulations.* There's a lot of gift-giving. Envelopes of money, for instance, get handed over in funeral homes just like they do at wedding receptions. The news from Dr. Cox wasn't good, so the Ragazzinos gave my father a Cadillac he was happy to accept, though he's been in no real shape to drive himself anywhere for the past six months. The Seville is metallic gray, and it's a fine machine. Bone leather interior, alloy wheels, North-Star system, and a V-8 engine with 275 horsepower. Not that I've had much use for a car in the past two decades other than local travel, but my Celica's an '84. It's the color of orange chalk, except for one panel on the driver's side, which is more of a root beer shade. The muffler's dangling from a coat hanger and the odometer rolled over to zero a thousand miles ago.

When I pull the Celica away from the curb, the tires slip on a sheet of ice hidden beneath the snow. The back end of the car jerks sideways, like it's been slapped, and then I'm sliding down the street as much as driving on it. I like the feeling. I'm the only car on the road, and just before the stop sign I hit the brakes a little harder than necessary, and I end up in the middle of two lanes with the front end aimed toward a mailbox. From this position, I start a kind of zigzag, back and forth across the centerline, drawing a gray snake in the snow in the rearview mirror.

He hates things like this, my father. He hates senseless, irreverent behavior. His blood boils reading the local crime-watch section in the paper, and he can't even look at *Cops* on TV. "Nobody in this country knows how to *behave* anymore," he's fond of saying. "Most of these punks, they're getting arrested—why? Because they're on the take? No. Because they're acting like assholes in public." It's one of his refrains, and an easy one, since he's too worn-out to get into trouble anymore. Ten years ago, the last time he flew down to Florida for vacation, he got drunk on his layover at JFK and raised a ruckus on the plane while they were waiting to take off. He demanded a bourbon and called the steward a fruitcake. He lit a cigarette. They threw him off, and he had to wait in the airport bar another four hours for the next available flight.

He told me that story himself. Another time, he told me about getting banned for life from a deli for throwing a "light" pound of roast beef at a meat cutter. But when he gave up drinking, he stopped telling the unflattering stories. Now he talks like some retired don who's banked enough respect over the years to be living off the interest.

The parking lots downtown are salted and soppy. I return his videos—*Harper* and *The Drowning Pool*—and buy blank tapes and bulk paper towels at the Big Bear. I walk through the aisles in the grocery store for a while, then ask the woman in the checkout line if they have any gluten. She looks at me like I'm just learning the language and says, "You mean glue?"

"Gluten," I say. "You bake with it."

She tells me there's a specialty store in the mall that has all the unheard-of stuff. But I'm not feeling quite that ambitious.

The roads turn icy again, closer to home. When I stop at red lights, I slide a little. When I go forward on the green, the tires spin and make a sound like a dog yelping. I'm doing this, liking it, slowing way down before a yellow light so I can do it again, when a town cruiser pulls up behind me and gets on the God horn. "Take it to the curb," the voice says, so loud that even through the closed windows it sounds like the speaker's right against my ear.

I pull over. I have not, I should say, been pulled over by the police in I don't remember how long. This cop is tall. He's all legs in the side mirror, walking toward me. I roll down my window and he leans over, his head closed up in a dark blue hat with earflaps. He asks for my license and registration and I hand them over.

"Looked like you were having a little trouble controlling your vehicle," he says. He's peering into the backseat.

"No, sir," I say, trying to sound nothing but pleasant. "I was just—enjoying the slide, so to speak. I thought it was okay, since no one else was around."

"Sir, that is exactly how accidents happen," he says. "Which is why it's never 'okay' to disregard traffic laws."

"I guess you're right about that."

"It's not a matter of opinion," he says.

He straightens up and studies my license, and I'm trying to think of what to say next. I'm wondering exactly how much reckless driving costs, and what it does to your record.

"Matthew Ragazzino," the cop reads off my license. And then he doesn't move or say anything for a few seconds. He's standing there looking at my license, then looking at my Celica, as if he's confused about something. "Mr. Ragazzino," he says, "I'm sorry to bother you. I was just concerned about your safety."

"Oh," I say. His gloved hand is holding the license and the registration card near the open window. I take them. "Well, thanks."

"You have a good day, Mr. Ragazzino."

"You too," I say.

And that's it. He walks back to his cruiser, and seconds later he pulls around me, gives a little wave, and heads off down the street.

*

There's no other car in front of our house to indicate someone else is there. My father's appointment should be over with by now anyway. I carry the shopping bag up the driveway, but when I round the front of the Seville I see a bicycle lying on its side in the snow next to the steps. I walk quietly through the front door and hear my father's voice say, "This is a little light."

Past the wall of the foyer I see him leaning forward in his

chair at the head of the dining room table. He's holding an en-velope. At the other end of the table, standing with his hands fidgeting in his back pockets, is a boy who can't be more than fifteen. I recognize him as the kid who shovels our driveway.

"I can get the rest of it next week," the kid says.

My father breathes loudly through his nose. He looks into the envelope. "How many customers have I gotten you? How many people on this block, and on that new cul-de-sac?"

"Eleven," the kid says softly.

"How many?"

"Eleven. Well, twelve, including you."

"That's right, twelve including me. And those people would have nothing to do with you if I hadn't made some calls. You and I have a very simple arrangement. Ten percent per job with a ten-dollar minimum. Do the math, kid."

"I can get it to you. I'll get it to you next week."

My father catches sight of me standing in the foyer. He ticks his eyes back to the boy, then to me, then to the boy. He breathes through his nose again, a series of three slow, constrained breaths. Then his hand opens and the envelope lands flat against the table. "This time," he says.

"Thanks, Mr. Ragazzino."

"Don't thank me. Just make it right."

The kid is already stepping backward out of the dining room. He turns around and his frightened face looks up at me like I'm the heavy.

"Matthew," my father says, sounding irritated, "this is Wilson. Wilson, Matthew."

The kid tries to smile. He pulls a hand from his back pocket and holds it out for me to shake. I shake it. It's cold as ice.

I've seen similar transactions going down. Last summer my father hired a kid from the next neighborhood over to mow our lawn. Then he called a few neighbors, bargained the kid's price down a little, and brought them into the kid's customer loop. He charged the kid not only a finder's fee of five dollars per customer but a recurring fee each time the kid mowed their lawns. These kids go along with it because it sounds like a fair enough deal at first. By the time they get tired of the arrangement, my father's become an angry, half-crazy, potentially dangerous old-man-with-connections right before their eyes. It's a sad picture. My father's stories about having once had half the town in his pocket are fiction, but I think he actually believes them. He's been telling them for so long now that they've petrified into something that feels real.

※

Wilson is gone. He pedaled away from our house as fast as his skinny legs would carry him. I set the videotapes on the dining room table and carry the paper towels into the kitchen.

"Did you get the gluten?" my father calls through the doorway.

"There's no gluten in this whole town," I say. "Not even in that specialty store in the mall."

"Those bastards," he says. "Would it kill them to put a little gluten on the shelf?"

At some point during the afternoon, I see, he's pulled out all his cooking supplies from the cabinets—his pans and bowls and his flour and sugar, the little sleeves of yeast and the jumbo bag of raisins. But he won't do anything with them now except make the point that he *can't* do anything with them because I didn't buy the gluten, so now the kitchen's cluttered and waiting for me to clean it. I leave everything right where it is, and it's still there in the early evening when I drop some pasta into a pot on the stove.

We eat on trays in front of the TV in the living room. We

watch *Antiques Roadshow*. After only a few bites he sits back from his tray, breathing heavily, and says, "I might just go to bed."

"You want your oxygen?"

"Did that sound like 'I want my oxygen'? I'm tired. Hand me that." He's motioning toward the ashtray on the coffee table in front of our trays. I lean over and get it for him, and he sets it on the cushion between us and digs his cigarettes out of a pocket in his robe. He's got a Winston lit before he notices I'm watching him. "I'm still under half a pack a day, if that's what you're wondering."

"I didn't say a word."

"You don't have to. I'm waiting for them to pass a law that says a man can't smoke in his own living room. That day will come, believe me. Kids will be carrying dope to school in their lunch boxes, and cigarettes will be a federal crime. I'm Nostradamus when it comes to that one."

He stares at me, pulls on the cigarette, and exhales a storm of smoke.

"Your mother—the big anti-smoking radical?" he says, which I take to mean only that my mother doesn't smoke. "I'll let you in on a little family secret. When we were first married and living in the hotel, while she was pregnant with you? She was known to 'court the evil weed' herself." He's nodding his head like we've been arguing about my mother's virtue. "Late at night, when she couldn't sleep, she would sneak cigarettes. I caught her."

I don't know what he's eaten today, and I know he's supposed to eat lots of little meals to even out his blood-sugar level, even though he's overweight, so I say, "You don't like the spaghetti?"

"It's okay," he says.

"You want some bread? There's that loaf of Italian you baked, in there."

"You should call her," he says.

"Call who?"

"Your mother."

"I call her. Now and then."

"You should call her more often." He sniffs and erupts into a fit of coughing that sounds violent and takes half a minute to pass.

"You sound like you're getting a cold," I say. "Maybe we should get out of here, take you someplace warm for a couple of weeks."

"Like where?"

"I don't know. Florida," I say, because it's the only warm place I can picture him going to.

And then he gets this sad look on his face—all the lines conspire to make it happen—and for all I know he *is* sad. He's sick, Dr. Cox has told him more than she's told me, and maybe he knows something more specific that's worth a genuine, heavy sadness. But what he says next surprises me. "I know you'd like it if your mother and I got back together."

I've got spaghetti on my fork. My mouth is open. All I can manage is *"What?"*

"It's natural," he says. "You want your mother and father to be together. Anybody would."

"Dad, I'm thirty-seven. I don't even—I don't *care* about that anymore. I don't know if I *ever* cared about it."

"You did," he says. "Boy, you really did. And you still do."

"Dad." I put the fork back down on the plate. "You don't know what you're talking about."

"You need to listen to me," he says.

"Mom's fucked-up. You know that, right?"

"Don't talk about your mother that way."

"I'm sorry, but she's nuts. She has a way of not seeming like it, but she's really got some problems."

"You only get two parents in this world, Matthew. You're born, and you've got two people who love you from that very moment, who *have* to love you. Just two."

"Well, one of them's a basket case who isn't so happy about being a mother."

"That's not because of me!" he says, his neck and face turning red. I watch him smash a half-smoked cigarette into the ashtray, this man who usually smokes them down to the filter. He's pulling another one out of the pack before he speaks again. "If she feels that way—and she shouldn't—it was because of all that other crap. Roy, your stepfather, he cut out on her with no warning—"

"Like you did." I hear myself saying this. It's strange territory. I've never discussed my stepfather with him. I've rarely discussed *him,* Dermot Ragazzino, leaving his wife and two kids to return to Utica, to start his life over again without us. He's got this look on his face as if out of the blue I've landed a fist in his gut; he looks hurt and mad and confused at the same time.

"That's not fair," he says, his voice weakening a little. "Your stepfather, Roy, he left your mother for another woman. I didn't do that. I left for different reasons. I was scared, I admit that to anyone. Bring in the jury. I was twenty-five, what did I know?" He lights the cigarette and runs his eyes over the junk spread out on the coffee table. "Jesus, you have a kid, and then everything you've ever done gets thrown back in your face one day. I'll tell you this much. Your mother may have got stuck with a bum rap, but if I *knew* ... I mean, if I had it all to do over again, I wouldn't do it like I did."

"Meaning what?"

He breathes through the cigarette. He isn't looking at me

anymore. "I don't know. I just know it would be different. Listen, Matthew, I'm trying to tell you, I'm trying to say, I haven't been much of a father. I know that." He sounds annoyed by having to point out the obvious. "It's not like there's a rule book for every moment of your life. I mean, you just do it, and you hope you haven't fucked everything up in the process. You're not a fuckup, I'm not saying that—and I take partial credit for it too. But what I mean is, God help you if I was your only parent. You ought to just *call* the woman now and then. It wouldn't kill you."

"I don't have anything to say to her."

"You will." He scratches the top of his scalp with the hand holding the cigarette. The smoke makes a spiral in the air over his head and ashes sprinkle into his hair. He looks at me. "How did we get on all this shit, anyway?"

"You brought it up."

He exhales a lungful of Winston. "You're right," he says. "I did. Now can I please just be left alone? Can I sleep?"

"Sure," I tell him, but for a while he nods his head, just barely, as if he has a lot more to say. Then he starts to get up and I stand too, and pull the TV tray out of his path. He looks at *Antiques Roadshow* on his way out of the room. A woman is holding a lamp with a gilded base and a landscape painted across the shade. "They got taken on that one," he says, "it's a piece of crap," and walks down the hall.

※

He must have gotten up, as he usually did, sometime during the night. I find him in the dining room the next morning, on his side, on the floor next to his chair. His legs are bent and his robe is open around him. His right arm is stretched out straight and under the elbow a small puddle of blood has thickened up like a wax seal. "Dad," I say as I step around him and see his purple face against the gold shag carpet, his eyes shut and his mouth scrunched up as if he's just heard a piece of infuriating news. I pull his chair out of the way. I drop down to one knee and say "Dad" again and touch the terry cloth robe over his shoulder. He won't let go of this pissed-off face. A line of congealed blood stands between his nose and the carpet. I want him to wake up, to cut this shit out. And then, because he looks so horrible, and because I'm about to touch his skin, I realize nothing would frighten me more than if he opened his eyes. I'm still saying the word *Dad* and I know I should feel for a pulse in his neck, but I can't make my fingers push into that mass, so I reach down to his wrist and say *Dad* again and touch it. The wrist is hard and cold. The underside is dark purple.

"My father's dead," I tell the operator at 911.

She's astoundingly calm. She tells me to check to see if he's breathing.

I give her my address.

"Sir," she says, "you should feel for a pulse and check to see if your father is breathing."

And this is why I'm a terrible human being: the operator is saying this to me, and I'm thinking about all those envelopes of Ragazzino cash that will be handed to me at the funeral parlor. I'm thinking about what I could do with that money in Vegas.

"He's dead," I tell her. I say the address again into the yellow receiver, and hang up the phone. My bare feet, when I look down, are tangled up in the cord. I'm not skipping out on this. I'm going to take care of it. I'm going to do all the things the son of Dermot Ragazzino should do. But as much as I know this, I know that as soon as I can get away with it, I'm leaving Utica, heading south and due west. And I'm sure as hell not doing it in that Celica.

Woman in a Fan Chair

1975

I

They could only afford one motel room. Roy made that perfectly clear as they climbed the concrete arch of the Hubert Humphrey Bridge, the wind tugging at the station wagon and rain batting the windshield. "I want it understood right now," he said, "because I don't want a big production when we get there about how we have to have two rooms."

The edict was preventive maintenance on Roy's part; no one had mentioned the room. The children were squeezed into the backseat: Joe and Frankie in the middle, Matt and Karen on either end. Frankie was clutching a fishbowl, its top covered with perforated tinfoil. Karen hugged a large purple purse and was slumped against the door with a transistor radio pressed to her ear.

"*There's* one," Teresa said, turning around and squinting back at Merritt Island over the tops of the children's heads. An ice chest filled with perishables sat on the front seat between them, and each time she moved, the chest squeaked against its lid. "Tell me you don't see that."

Roy could barely see the bridge. "I'm driving, Teresa."

"It's a funnel cloud," she declared for the third time since they'd left the house, and for the third time all three boys writhed in their seats and peered through the back window at the ashen sky. Joe said he was pretty sure this one was coming down over the Catholic church, but Matt said it was the high school that was about to get it, and Frankie, nearly panting with excitement, all but shouted that the twister was aimed right for their house.

Roy felt the muscles in his jaw tighten. He gripped the steering wheel as if it were the collar of a man he was getting ready to punch. "I think we all just need to calm down. The wind isn't even that strong."

"This wind is terrible," Teresa said.

"I'll bet it's sixty miles an hour, tops."

"Ninety-four," Karen said from the backseat. Her voice was calm, weighted with disinterest. In the rectangle of the rear-view mirror, she caught Roy's gaze and hinged the radio away from her ear. "The guy just said."

"Okay, ninety-four. That's still low-end for a hurricane."

Teresa gripped the armrest of the passenger door. "We are going to be blown right off this bridge."

Despite this prediction, they rolled onto the mainland and into the town of Cocoa. The first intersection they came to was buried under a lagoon that swallowed the station wagon's bumper and dragged against its chassis. Roy plowed forward, hearing Teresa say his name: a single syllable she managed to bend in half with a nervous wrenching of her throat.

Evacuation of the island and the cape had been recommended by the governor, but it wasn't mandatory, and for a while Roy had convinced Teresa they would be fine riding out the storm at home. They'd spent the morning gathering flashlights and extra batteries and candles, tacking up a blanket over the sliding glass door in the dining room, and making Xs across the windows with masking tape. In the middle of all this, it wasn't Teresa but Karen who had leaned against the doorway in the laundry room and challenged Roy, asking him point-blank why he didn't want to evacuate.

"What do you mean, *why?*"

"Why means why," the girl had said. The extra roll of tape he'd been looking for was dangling from her wrist like a bracelet. "Why stay in the middle of a hurricane?"

She'd caught him off-guard. Knowing, even as the words left his mouth, that he wouldn't be forgiven for the corniness of his response, he'd said, "Ever heard of protecting the home front?"

One of Karen's cheeks had popped up as if snagged by a fish-hook. "Yeah, right."

"I've got this house *and* the store to worry about," he'd added.

"But it's not like you're Shazam. What are you going to do, hold the walls up if they start to fall? Besides, you can't be in three places at once."

"Two places. Here, and the store."

She'd clucked her tongue and handed over the tape.

Then, just as they'd been finishing the preparations, Teresa had gotten on the phone with a couple of neighbors, Mrs. Gardner and Mrs. Taylor, one of whom told her that the storm was ripping roofs off houses along Cape Canaveral and both of whom were gathering their families and heading for the mainland. After hanging up, Teresa found Roy in their bathroom, filling the tub with reserve water, and told him to forget it: they weren't stay-ing. He wanted to argue with her, put his foot down, but she had a wide-eyed, rabbity look and she was holding her rosary, and experience told him there would be no winning.

※

The bickering became explosive soon after they got a room at the Ponce de Leon Motor Lodge off U.S. 1. The children's usual volley of insults and complaints felt like bees thumping against his forehead, and then out of the blue Teresa snapped, pulled Karen into the bathroom, and shut the door.

Following that, the only sound was the television: the closest they ever got to silence. The two older boys were watching some awful program that crossed *Gomer Pyle* with *Lost in Space.* They were stretched out, one on each bed, hands behind their heads and elbows anchoring both sets of pillows, legs spread wide so that their sneakers nearly reached the corners. Frankie had pulled a chair over to the dresser to sit next to his fish and was studying them. There was a boing! and a doink! from the TV set, and Roy heard the low hiss of his wife's voice from behind the closed bathroom door, though he couldn't make out a word.

Some of the bickering had been about who would sleep where, and after watching Matt and Joe do their bed-hogging routine, Roy accepted the fact that they were actually here, and that they were going to need roll-aways. Two of them. Which meant talking to the knothead at the front desk again. He stepped between the beds, picked up the phone, and dialed. He counted eight rings before hanging up, then dialed again and let it ring eight more times. The boys were ignoring him. The sky beyond the rain-spattered window was turning from dark gray to black, and the wind was picking up. It looked to him as if the front window was starting to waffle. He hung up, crossed the room, and tugged on the nylon string, drawing the curtain over the glass. Then he switched on the floor lamp next to the door.

The room seemed to close in around the lamplight. He pictured the two roll-aways eating up floor space, and felt the walls inching forward.

Of course, they could have gotten a second room; the motel was cheap and nearly empty. But Roy had very much wanted to stay on the island and he'd lost that fight, so he wasn't going to budge on this one. They would all just have to suffer one another's company, and he would have to suffer right along with them.

The bathroom door opened abruptly. Teresa's voice shot forth like air from a pump rifle: *"No!"* The door closed again.

Matt and Joe exchanged glances across the beds. Frankie leaned in until his nose was against the fishbowl and whispered something to the fish.

An air conditioner wheezed beneath the hem of the curtain. There was an odor: a vague animal smell of rot, and Roy realized as he crossed the room again that it was the softening ground beef in the ice chest. Around that, the room itself smelled like an empty frying pan someone had forgotten to take off the burner.

He dropped into an orange corduroy chair and stared at the television. Jim Nabors, dressed in a silver jumpsuit, was leaning sideways as if his shoes were nailed to the floor. Ruth Buzzi was attempting to push him upright, producing a squeak overlaid with canned laughter. The lights flickered and the set swallowed the picture and spit it back out again a moment later, as if the program had gone down the wrong pipe.

Maybe what was happening in the bathroom was a female thing. Maybe Karen was having her first period, and it wasn't just her regular difficult behavior Teresa was dealing with but a whole new rigmarole. Roy wasn't sure at what age it first happened to most girls. Thirteen? Eleven? That book *Carrie* was about a girl who hit puberty, went insane, and started lobbing things around the room with her mind. Where, he thought, was the handbook for *that*? Teresa had devoted a shoe box at the bottom of their closet to paperbacks she didn't want sitting out, and right alongside *The Erotic Man* and *The Erotic Woman* was *Understanding Children* and *Dr. Spock on Parenting*. Roy had never been able to get through either one of the parenting manuals; what he really wanted was a book called *Your Stepdaughter: What Does She Know, When Does She Know It?*

"This room stinks," Frankie said, pulling his nose away from the fishbowl.

If it had been anyone else besides Frankie, Roy would have suspected mouthiness. He said, "You're talking about the smell?"

"Well, there are all kinds of ways to stink," Matt said from one of the beds.

"Stow it," Roy told him. He looked at Frankie. "What do you smell? The food in the ice chest?"

"It's like that taste you get when you chew on tinfoil," the boy said.

Roy had never chewed foil, but the idea of an electrical fire passed through his mind. With this storm, there could have been a surge or a spark; flames might be chewing their way through the walls toward room 28 right now. It irked him to be having one of Teresa's worrisome thoughts, but there it was, as if she were telegraphing it his way from the bathroom.

The program inched along.

Two roll-aways.

Possible electrical fire.

"Stay here," he told them, getting up from the chair.

It was raining sideways as he moved along the cement walk. The motel was one story and shaped like a boomerang, and he found his way to its apex and made an unintentionally dramatic entrance into the lobby: tourist pamphlets scattered from a metal rack like roused birds. As they drifted to the floor, the desk clerk appeared in the doorway of a back room, the light from a television blinking on the paneled walls behind him. "The answer to your first question," he said, stepping up behind the front desk, "is yes: we've got rooms."

"We already have a room." Roy said. "I was trying to call you."

"Ah. Well, the phones have been in and out."

"I'm wondering if there's a fire in the motel somewhere."

The man was younger than Roy, puffy around his chin and midriff and even his wrists, in a way that suggested a medical condition. For an instant his face looked distraught; then it leveled itself professionally, and he smoothed a palm across the thin band of hair that rode the top of his head like a bucket handle. Adjusting his horn-rimmed glasses, he said, "Not to my knowledge."

Roy felt rainwater dripping from his nose. "There's a smell in our room," he said. "Like something's burning. Like something metal is on fire."

"Oh, that." The buckethead smiled proudly. "Let me put your mind at ease." He leaned forward and settled his elbows on the counter, folding his hands. "I'm the owner."

"And?"

"I know the smells. I could tell you the smell of the old lady from Dothan who was here a year ago, just from what she left on the towels." His laughter snagged at the back of his throat, and he coughed his way through it. "Seriously," he said, "I know what you're talking about: that chemical smell? It's coming from the carpet—a brand-new pattern called Spellbound, which is actually becoming very popular with some of the finer motels. But it takes a while for the odor of the poly-seal to work its way out. Trust me, that poly-seal's a good thing. Come back a year from now, the carpet will be stain-free and you'll be glad for it."

"We're going to need roll-away beds," Roy said.

The man cleared his throat. "Can do."

"Two of them."

"It's happening as we speak." The man was writing something on a notepad next to the telephone. "Anything else?"

"Not as long as there isn't a fire."

"No fire," the man said, "of that much I'm sure." His smile looked almost willfully grotesque. The fat hand holding the pen skated in the air over the paper, as if ready to take down Roy's every wish.

"Then that's it. Just the roll-aways."

"Two beds," the buckethead repeated, nodding. He dropped the pen and picked up the phone receiver. Without dialing, he said into it, "Me? It's me calling. Two beds to room . . . twenty-eight, is it? . . . and make it snappy, or tell me I'm fired." He hung up, laughed again, and said, "Small business," but Roy was already turning toward the door.

✳

There was a cigarette machine next to the tourist pamphlets; his gaze was drawn toward it like a compass needle to north. As he was leaving the lobby, he seriously considered buying a pack and lighting up for the first time since quitting almost a year ago. Hadn't he earned at least that? To stand under the overhang in front of this dump of a motel and smoke half a Pall Mall? Not so grand a request to make of the universe, really. But it would mean having to ask the buckethead for change and, worse, stepping back into that little hotbed of a motel room smelling of smoke. Teresa and the children would pick up on it immediately, and even if, by some miracle, none of them said anything, he would see that look of disappointment on Teresa's face. He marched into the wind and rain, and by the time he got back to the door of room 28, he was soaked to the skin.

The door was locked. He banged on it.

Frankie's voice came through the painted plywood. "Who is it?"

"Me."

"What's the password?"

The password is open the goddamn door. "It's *Dad,*" he said, framing his lips around the designation.

His molars were grinding together when he heard the bolt turn. Frankie opened the door wide and stood next to it with his narrow arm extended, saying, "All rise."

No one moved. Teresa and Karen had come out of the bathroom and were sitting as far apart as they could, given the space: Teresa was in the corduroy chair near the door and Karen was sitting cross-legged on the Spellbound carpet beyond the far bed. Roy stepped into the room. With the exception of Frankie, they were all watching the television. Some ambitious local reporter was standing in front of Canaveral Pier as the sleeves of his raincoat rippled around his arms. "...absolutely horrible," he was yelling into his microphone. "We've seen palm trees falling onto houses, downed power lines, and one local policeman just told me they're hoping *everyone* has evacuated by now because the roads aren't safe for travel. This is a real class-A storm...."

"We're getting roll-aways," Roy said. He shut the door behind him and felt water running down the backs of his knees, inside his trousers. "Two of them."

"Oh my god," Teresa said, taking her eyes off the screen to look at him, "you're drenched."

"The desk clerk is going to bring them."

"You're just asking to catch pneumonia," she said. She got up, walked to the bathroom, and came back with a thin white towel.

"There'll be room for everyone to sleep," Roy continued.

"Do you want to die?" She handed him the towel. "Get out of those wet clothes."

"I didn't bring anything else to put on. We're only staying for the night." He scratched the towel over his scalp.

"I'm starving," Matt interrupted from the far bed. "Can't we go somewhere and eat?"

Teresa glanced at the boy, then pointed toward the television. "Do you have eyes? It's *deadly* out there. We're staying right here until this passes over." She looked back at Roy. "You've got to get out of those clothes."

"I don't have any other clothes to put on," he snapped, crossing the room. "Should I walk around naked?"

"Not really," Matt said.

"Sure," Joe said from the opposite bed. "Let's streak."

Frankie had resumed his post next to the fishbowl. He glanced around the room as if he'd missed some instruction and wanted to keep up. "Are we taking our clothes off?"

Something was missing from this volley of bees, and Roy realized it was Karen. She was sitting with her back against the wall, watching him. There was no evidence in her face of having been yelled at for the past half hour; it was as if whatever had gone on in the bathroom had had nothing to do with her. She was reading his thoughts, he imagined. She was about to send a lamp through the air and crash it into his skull with her newfound pubescent telekinesis. He had crossed the room only for the sake of moving, too irritated to stand in one place, but there was nothing to cross the room *to;* there was nowhere to sit, no other spot to occupy except for the toilet. He looked at his reflection in the mirror over the sink and dragged a hand across his eyes, his nose, his mouth, running a desperate diagnostic of the instruments set into the melting control panel that used to be his face.

Teresa had been digging through a grocery bag next to her

purse, and when she straightened up, she had a pair of his pants, a shirt, and underwear neatly folded and stacked in her hands. "I packed a change of clothes for everyone."

He looked at her, feeling both impressed and irritated. "Thanks." To the rest of them, he said, "There's food in the ice chest."

"Not *real* food," Joe said.

"Eat it." He accepted the clothes from Teresa's hands, and, like a rat in a pipe, took the next and only turn there was to take: into the bathroom. "Just stay away from the ground beef," he said, and shut the door.

He sat on the toilet lid and stirred the skin over his forehead with his fingertips. Teresa was right, a chill was setting in, and after turning the doorknob lock, he stripped down and got into the shower and stood under its warm spray. He put on the dry clothes she'd packed. He was pressing another towel against his face when the door opened and Frankie stuck his head in.

"How did you unlock that door?"

"I didn't," the boy said. "It just opened."

"Well, you're supposed to knock when someone's in the bathroom."

Frankie tapped his knuckles lightly on the door. "I have to pee, and Mom says dinner's ready."

Roy surrendered the bathroom to the boy, and when he emerged, the atmosphere had changed. Deliberate steps had been taken to calm things down. Teresa had had the foresight to bring paper plates and plastic forks and spoons, and there were six place settings spread out across the two beds. On the nightstand was a selection of what they'd salvaged from the refrigerator. Teresa was standing next to the food. The rest of them were sitting on the floor around the perimeter of the two beds, in front of their paper plates.

"What's this?" Roy asked, trying to sound light and jovial.

"We're survivors," Teresa said, unfolding a paper napkin. "We're riding out the storm, and we're going to have a proper dinner." There was a slight, artificial-looking smile crimped into her mouth. The television was turned off and in place of its noise was a kind of leveling static. There they all were (including Frankie, who had just slipped past him and taken his spot alongside the bed), gathered around food, waiting for Roy so they could start a meal, like regular people. Roy appreciated—and felt guilty about—her efforts.

"Well, then, let's eat," he said, walking over to the chair they'd pulled up in front of his plate.

They passed around a loaf of Wonder bread, a package of baloney, a jar of mayonnaise, a jar of pickles, a Tupperware container of leftover spaghetti, and a container of orange Jell-O Teresa had made the previous day. Roy picked up his plastic fork.

"I think we should say grace," Teresa said. "I think that would be nice."

"I'll say it," Matt offered, and then cleared his throat and said the word *grace*.

"A *real* grace," Teresa said. She looked at Roy. "Would you do it?"

He'd become an atheist in his late teens. Then, when he was twenty, he'd barrel-rolled his car into a field and by all rights should have died in the crash, and because he hadn't, he'd started believing in God again. But at some point over the past year—after he got laid off from NASA and spent a month lumbering aimlessly around the house, fantasizing about waking up dead and wondering what was beyond death—he'd come to the conclusion that people were no more special than blades of grass: they either got rained on or withered up in a drought. There was no set path, no great design. It was all chance, and God was just an invention that people were convinced they needed, like digital watches or steering-wheel wraps. But he couldn't admit his atheism to Teresa, who dragged them all to mass each Sunday and saved the missalettes as if they were concert programs.

O random collision of molecules, thank you for not letting us be born with physical deformities; thank you for not turning us into Richard Specks and Charles Mansons; thank you for televised golf, and prime rib, and . . . good teeth.

"Well," he began, bringing his free hand up against the hand that held the plastic fork, "we're, uh, we're glad that we're here, safe. That we're . . . not out in the storm." There was more. There had to be. He knew prayers; the entire Apostles' Creed fell from his mouth by rote every Sunday, but that was like standing in a choir and lip-synching the words. "We're thankful for this food, and for shelter," he heard himself say. "That's it. Amen."

"Amen," Frankie said, and delivered a forkful of Jell-O into his mouth.

Teresa sighed and lifted her sandwich. "Frankie, that's for dessert."

"You know what?" Joe said around a pickle he was mouthing like a cigar. "We're like the Swiss Family Robinson."

"Yeah," Karen said, "except we aren't marooned, or Swiss."

"Close enough," Roy countered. "We're survivors—of this storm, anyway." He shouldn't have said *anyway*. "We did the right thing in coming here," he added quickly, knowing Teresa wanted to hear this, and when he glanced at her, she smiled a genuine smile, and he smiled back, and winked. Then he shifted his glance to Karen and saw her rolling her eyes. She knew he was looking at her; she wanted him to see this reaction. Worse, she didn't make eye contact with him afterward but looked down at her plate and began pushing dents into her sandwich with her finger. Did she hate him? Resent him on a hunch? He twisted his fork through his cold spaghetti.

They finished off everything save for the packet of ground beef, which they joked about having brought in the first place. How had they thought they were going to cook it in a motel room? Stomachs full and an aggregate tiredness settling over the six of them, they fought very little about what to watch on television, settling on *The Six Million Dollar Man*. They made it right up to the ending, when Steve Austin demonstrated to his doctor why his hand needed adjustment by breaking a table in half with his pinky. Then lightning flashed, thunder cracked overhead, and the power went out.

It was an utter, ink-black darkness. Someone moved and bumped into something, and Roy got up from his chair with an impulse to somehow right the situation, and nearly lost his balance against the side of the bed. "Nobody move," he heard Teresa say. "Roy..." But she didn't follow this up with any instruction, and there was a long pause during which he felt that their lives had suddenly been switched off. Then he heard a fumbling sound and the hiss of a match, and a yellow glow flared up on the other side of the room.

"Any of the Robinsons got a candle?" Karen asked, her face animated by the wavering flame in front of her.

Teresa leaned forward, squinting. "What are you doing with matches?"

There was a knock on the door.

The match went out, and Karen lit another, and by its light Roy made his way to the door and opened it. The glare of a flashlight hit him in the face.

"Whoa," said the buckethead from behind the flashlight. "How's that for timing? I feel like the Red Cross."

He was dressed in a yellow hooded rain-slicker and was standing between a pair of damp roll-aways. With his free hand, he dug inside the slicker and produced two votive candles. "Been carrying these around all afternoon, just in case.

Looks like you could use them." He handed them to Roy, who asked for Karen's matches and then lit the candles, and helped roll the beds into the room. Standing just inside the door, the buckethead moved the beam of his flashlight around the room and made some comment about hoping none of them was nude.

"Thanks," Roy said, stepping toward him, nodding his jaw in an effort to wave him out of the room. "We appreciate it."

The man stepped backward, his flashlight beam still moving. "Hope I didn't interrupt anything."

"Thanks again," Roy said.

"If you need more candles—"

"We're fine." Roy wide-stepped so that the man was forced back out onto the sidewalk, and shut the door. He turned around, and there they all were, his family, in the flickering light of the two votive candles like an old sepia portrait come to life. "Nobody talks to that man," he said. "Nobody goes to the front desk, or has anything to do with him."

As if he hadn't just spoken—much less made a declaration—Teresa took Karen's purple purse from her and began rifling through it. "Young lady, I would like to know what you're doing with matches."

"Mom," Karen said. "Please."

"Teresa," Roy said, suddenly tired and desperate to narrow the focus, "let's just set up the beds and call it a day, okay?"

"Have you been smoking?"

He thought for a second this question was meant for him. But Karen said, "Have I been smoking what?"

"Smoking *what*?" Teresa shot back.

"What's on second," Joe said. "Who's on first."

Roy pocketed the matches and tapped the back of the boy's head. "Help me out, here. You too, Matt."

"Nature calls," Matt said. He took the paper plate that held one of the votives into the bathroom and closed the door.

The room darkened by half.

Karen reached out and snatched her purse out of her mother's hand. "That's personal property."

"I try with you," Teresa said. "I try, and I talk to you, and I try some more. But Jesus help me when it comes to your mouth."

Karen let her mouth hang open.

"Joe," Roy said. "Frankie. I want you to move both those chairs and that lamp out of the way. We need to make room for these beds."

Frankie started meandering around in the flickering light, hunched forward, making chimp sounds. In the space he and his brother eventually created, Roy unclasped the beds and, with their hinges screeching, opened them like two enormous hunting traps, folded linens and little pillows tucked in the middle of each mattress like bait. He inched them as far away from each other, and from the nearest bed, as he could, then stood back while Teresa made them up.

"These beds are wet at both ends," she said.

"They're fine."

"Oh my god!" This came from Karen, who had forgotten Matt was in the bathroom or had known full well that he was; either way, she'd opened the door and was stepping back from it now, her hands thrust open at her sides. The door slammed shut.

"What is it?" Teresa asked, stepping toward her.

"*Oh* my god." Karen sounded mortified and delighted at the same time. She pistoned her feet and slapped her hands against her thighs. Her voice broke into a singsong laughter. "Oh my god, oh my god, oh my god."

"Hey," Roy said, "can you keep it down, please?"

"What is it?" Teresa asked again.

Karen continued to sing.

"Matt?" Teresa knocked rapidly on the door. "Matt, are you all right?"

"Teresa, just leave him alone," Roy said.

"I want to find out if he's okay." She was turning the knob and pushing against the door, which was giving only an inch or so and was being shoved from the other side.

Joe and Frankie, their voices nearly overlapping, asked what was happening.

"Oh-my-god," Karen sang, dancing in place, adapting the tune to "Over There." "Oh-my-god, oh-my-god, oh-my-god."

"Just leave him alone," Roy said.

"Matthew, open this door right now."

"What is it, Dad?"

"What's going on?"

Suddenly, there was power. The lights sprang on, intensely bright, and the television flashed to life and blared at an insane volume. Karen, still singing, looked as if she were jumping rope.

"That's it!" Roy shouted. *"Every one of you—SHUT UP!"*

They all froze, watching him. He was standing next to the television. He raised a hand and, as if smashing an insect, brought it down against the control panel, turning the set off. "Just," he said. "Shut. Up."

For a moment, no one moved. Then Karen, who'd been poised on her toes, slowly lowered her body until her feet were flat on the carpet. She opened her mouth to speak.

"I'm telling you," Roy said. His hand left the set and hovered in front of him, closing into a fist. He knew he should release it. It wasn't a gesture he'd ever made in front of any of them before, not out of anger, not like this. It was an awful moment, but a moment part of him clearly wanted to take place. "I don't want to hear another word spoken in this room tonight," he heard himself say. "Not a single goddamned word from any of you."

Teresa's eyes had grown large. She still had a hand on the bathroom doorknob and was looking at him intently, waiting, he thought, for some indication that she was exempt from this crazy dictum. He wouldn't give it to her; she wasn't exempt. He didn't want to hear from her, didn't want to hear from himself. He wanted only to be somewhere else, and though that somewhere else was not, by any means, either one of the two double beds in front of him, he chose one and stretched out, only then releasing his fist to fold his hands over his chest, his eyes already closed, all sensation transferred, suddenly, to the heat of embarrassment and shame he felt behind his face. He listened to their breathing, and to their efforts at communicating with one another in sighs and low grunts of complaint and the occasional, anonymous whimper.

※

He woke up early the next morning. With careful, quiet movements, he washed his face, brushed his teeth, and pulled on his shoes. He found a pen in Teresa's purse, and on the back of the brown paper lunch sack in which she'd packed their toiletries, he scribbled a note saying that he'd gone to the island to check on the house and the store. "Back soon," he wrote, and signed it with an R.

The perimeter of the vinyl curtain was glowing. When he opened the door, the room was flooded with sunlight. He put on his sunglasses, stepped outside, and eased the door shut behind him.

The asphalt was covered in a damp carpet of palmetto

fronds and pine needles that slid beneath his shoes. The station wagon had leaves stuck to its roof and sides, and a branch as big as Roy's arm lay across the long, navy-blue hood. He lifted the branch and threw it aside, wincing at the dent it had made in the dorsal ridge running down the center. With the wipers smearing pine needles across the windshield, he backed out of the parking space, wound his way around the motel, and accelerated onto the highway.

There had been and were always going to be worse things. Someone had died, maybe, in this hurricane, and it lifted his spirits to realize that he earnestly wished no one had. There may have been lootings, burglary, rape; anything was possible because there were always people willing to take advantage of catastrophes. He imagined a lead story in the *Today* paper about some local shop owner besieged by such villains, and feeling his own disgust at reading such a headline, he felt better about himself. There were some sick people in the world. Men with everyday faces, capable of unimaginable crimes. Child molestation. Cannibalism. Human torture. He veered into the left lane, the right blocked, suddenly, by a mangled roadside marquee, its frame twisted, its red arrow snubbed against the pavement. The car clopped over the train tracks and he drove through the scattered trash of downtown Cocoa, back to the bridge, where, at its summit midway across the river, he saw the island before him, green and silent and abandoned: a floating sliver of calm.

He was the last man standing. He was the Omega Man: torn by circumstance from what he cared about most, piloting his craft through this ruined landscape, resolved and fearless and anxious in the same mile. The electricity was still out here. The neon signs for the Tiki Lounge and the Ping Pong Motel were reduced to dull gray script. The unlit façade of the First National Bank looked tomblike. He turned north onto Courtenay and wove around traffic that was light but moving at an annoyingly slow pace, until at last he reached the parking lot of Driftwood Terrace. Several terracotta roof shingles had been blown off and lay shattered on the asphalt. He drove over this detritus to the end of the row and parked in front of the door to apartment 6.

He used his key. The chain stopped him.

"It's me," he called out.

A padding of footsteps over carpet, and then the door eased shut, the chain rattled, and she let him in.

"You didn't tape your windows."

"I taped the back ones," Leona said. "These face west."

"They could have blown in anyway."

"They didn't." She kissed his cheek. "You're all right?"

"I've been better, but yes, I'm fine." He put his arm around her waist and shifted the two of them so that they faced each other. He kissed her on the mouth, then kissed her again. "You were the one who had to ride this out alone."

"It wasn't bad. I never even lost power."

"No tornadoes?"

Her arms lay across his shoulders and she smiled at him and shook her head no.

"None at all?"

"Well, I wasn't staring out the window the whole time, but I don't think so. Did you see any?"

"A couple of them, in the distance, when we were leaving the island. That's why I was so worried about you. You've got batteries in that radio, right?"

"Yeah. That would have been a real lifesaver," she said. He'd given it to her the previous week. It sat on the coffee table now, turned off, its antenna collapsed. "Do you want coffee?"

"Desperately."

Leona walked into the kitchen, and from the pass-through in the living room wall he watched her take a pair of mugs down from the cabinet and pour from the coffeepot. She had another new hairstyle, one that left her thick, auburn hair cut short and curled outward, revealing her shoulders and most of her neck. He sat down at one end of the beige sectional she'd bought from a neighbor who had moved out—part of her mismatched troupe of furniture. "I'm going to check on my folks," he said. "Do you mind?"

"I'll be quiet as a mouse."

He took the phone off the end table and dialed his parents in Satellite Beach. "It's Roy."

"I told you this storm was nothing," his father replied.

"You all are okay?"

"Of course we're okay. They've got the police going up and down the street with a bullhorn, asking the same question. You'd think it was the end of the world."

"It was pretty rough, Dad. They said on the news it was a 'class A' storm."

"They play these things up because they don't have anything else to talk about. One branch off the weeping willow, that's our damage."

"Well, I just wanted to check on you."

"How's the island?"

"It's okay. I mean, I guess it's okay. We relocated to a motel in Cocoa, just to be safe."

"You did *what*?"

Roy closed his eyes. "We thought it would be better to play it safe."

"So you bought into the whole thing," his father said—not so much a question as an observation.

"Yeah," Roy said. "The whole kit and caboodle. Listen, I should go. I just wanted to check on you."

"Your mother wants to talk to Teresa."

"She stepped out. Listen, I've got to go. Tell Mom we'll call later on, all right?"

His father asked how much they'd paid for the motel room.

Roy forced a laugh that fell dead flat, said again he had to go, and hung up.

"How is everyone?" Leona asked with her back to him.

"The old man's cranky as ever."

"I meant everyone else."

"Oh. Do we have to talk about them?"

"I'm asking. I want to know."

"They're fine. We set up shop in the Ponce de Leon, and at last report no one had been murdered."

"That's not funny," she said, rounding the wall with the coffee mugs. She handed him one and sat down next to him, facing him, folding one of her legs over his. "You know I don't like those kind of jokes."

"I know."

"Where do they think you are?"

"Right now? If they're even awake, they think I'm checking on the house and the store, which I am, eventually."

"And they're okay with that?"

"You say it like they're some sort of committee. They're *asleep*. And I didn't just take off; I left them a note. Besides, after last night, I doubt they're in any rush to see me."

Leona sipped, watching him. After a moment she tilted her head forward slightly and hitched her brow. She was twenty-nine years old, six years younger than Roy. She was in nursing school, had on her dining room table a fortress of medical textbooks, the contents of which sailed over Roy's head. Some of their illustrations sickened him. When she gave him this expression, he felt as if he were being scrutinized by a precocious teenager who fancied herself a psychologist—but with her, he didn't mind. She was waiting for him to elaborate. Finally, she asked, "What happened?"

"Oh, I blew my top. But, Jesus, they had it coming. They can act like a bunch of lunatics when they're locked up together. I'm telling you, the noise alone is enough to drive you out of your skull." She held the look. "What?" he protested. "It is."

"What *happened*?"

"Karen... The thing is, Karen's acting like— Well, never mind that, but Matt is obviously..."

"Tell me."

"It's Teresa, really. She's like gasoline on this flame you just want to... put *out*. She antagonizes them, and me. She doesn't mean to, she's just always so wound up." He felt wound up himself; he was leaning against her leg, holding the mug by its handle and tapping his other hand over its mouth as if he were trying to send smoke signals. "There's something about it," he said, and then shook his head and sat back, and continued to shake his head, craving the attention she was paying him and at the same time wanting to drop the subject.

"Don't do anything crazy," she said.

"Crazy what? I'm there, aren't I?"

"I mean impulsive."

"I'm there, and I'm here. I'm trying. I just... Can we talk about something else? Please?"

"Sure." She lifted a hand and stroked the back of his neck. "You want some breakfast?"

"Matt's masturbating," he blurted out. He was immediately glad he'd said it. There was an arrested look on her face, which smoothed out into its own kind of gladness easily enough, because he never would be able to talk about this with Teresa, and Leona knew it. He could live the next ten years with Teresa, and the two of them would never speak of their oldest son having been caught, by his sister, playing with himself in the bathroom of the motel during the hurricane of '75. That conversation, benign as it might be, would never take place, and this one already was, and the realization held Roy and Leona together like a pair of handcuffed prisoners in a moment that felt, above all things, sexual.

"He made an announcement?"

"No. But he's doing it. I mean, he's fifteen, it makes sense. He's probably been doing it for years. Only, last night he was doing it in the bathroom of the motel and—stupid him, what was he thinking? We're like sardines in there, and the bathroom lock is broken, but *he* doesn't know that, and of course it's Karen who walks in on him, and then Teresa starts to panic for no reason. I just blew up. They get like that, and maybe it's normal behavior, I don't know anymore, but I turn into this . . . *father*."

"I'm sure you're not as bad as you think."

"I am. But the thing is, I don't know how else to do it. And now I guess I'm supposed to talk to him about it. And what am I supposed to say? He doesn't need my approval. He doesn't even want it."

"Maybe you could give him some pointers."

She was grinning at him, and he popped his hand lightly against her leg. "I'm serious. I know myself. I'm not any good at this."

"You just need more confidence."

"That's what I'm talking about."

"You're a smart man, Roy. You'll find a way to talk to Matt. And I'm sure you've already thought of this, but you've got Joe coming up right behind him, and Frankie after that, so you might find yourself in this spot again."

"What I'm trying to tell you is that I don't feel like I can do it."

"You're just tired right now."

"It's not that. You don't know what it's like—the whole thing."

"But you don't have to talk to him about it today. You can wait."

"I don't mean this one situation. I mean *the whole thing*," he said. He'd leapt on her sentence; their voices had overlapped. He ground his teeth and turned toward the front window.

She set her mug down and kneaded the back of his neck, then got up and moved to the fan chair on the opposite side of the coffee table. It was a solid wooden chair meant for a patio, painted sherbet green with red piping. She sat down in it, and he looked at her, looked into her, and for just a moment he saw her sitting in that chair on a patio behind a house they lived in together, her hair touched with silver, her face bearing the lines of several decades.

When he pulled his focus back into the room—*this* room, the living room of the apartment of the woman he'd been seeing for nearly a year and had fallen in love with—his vision went blurry, his eyes turned damp, and he repeated his last three words, a simple, devastating phrase: "The whole thing."

"Just don't do anything impulsive," she said again.

"Meaning what?"

"Meaning, whatever you do has to be thought out, and it has to be for you."

He felt his head shaking. He made it nod *yes*. "I know."

"Not for me. Not even for us. It has to be what *you* need."

"I know." He felt his face contorting, felt a wet suck of air startle the top of his throat, and then his lungs let go and the tremor carried up his throat and straight out of his mouth, and as he wept, he tilted his face down over his coffee mug.

She didn't come over to him. She was startled, he knew. She was worried. And yet, a minute later, when the wave began to subside and he dragged the heel of his hand across his eyes and looked at her, it wasn't panic he saw in her face. It was nothing that bore Teresa's trademark. Leona looked worried and concerned, but for the two of them: together and individually. She would stay with him, but not under just any terms. If he remained like this, frustrated, angry, unstable, or if he brought radical change to his life for the wrong reasons and derailed himself in the process, she would let him go. He could see it in her face: she would be with him, or she wouldn't. Either way, she was going to be all right, and he loved her for it.

"I'm going to do...whatever I do," he intoned slowly, evenly, "for me."

"Don't make any major decisions when you're like this, okay?"

"Okay."

"Promise me," she said.

"I promise." His hands were trembling. He set the mug next to hers on the table, stood up, and walked to her chair, where he started to bend over but wound up on his knees, his arms around her, his face pressed against her T-shirt. She held him. "I promise," he said again. He kissed her once, and left.

*

The Beachcomber Souvenir Shop, where he worked as a manager, appeared to be undamaged by the storm. Roy circled the freestanding row of stores that housed the Beachcomber, and as far as he could tell the only damage to the entire building was to the dry cleaner's sign at the south end of the complex. A series of metal bolts edged in broken plastic stuck out from the building's gray façade, and the sign was nowhere in sight.

From there he followed a network of side roads that led to the back entrance of his neighborhood.

The ranch houses were made of cinder block; the roofs were gravel set into tar. The colors varied, but there were only five different models, repeating like the background of a children's cartoon. Once again he pictured himself as Charlton Heston in *The Omega Man*. When he spotted movement behind the living room window of a house half a block away from his own, he imagined slamming on the brakes, leaning out the window of the station wagon, and opening fire with an automatic weapon, his eyes trained behind dark sunglasses on a member of that deadly group of mutants known only, in the film, as *the family*.

He parked behind Teresa's Datsun, got out, and walked the perimeter of the house. There was evidence of fresh chaos here: Joe's bicycle, left out, had been carried halfway across the backyard and lay on its side in the grass. The metal bucket he used to wash the cars had been tossed due west and sat against the next-door neighbor's house, as if the ground had tilted in that direction. The taped sliding glass door that opened onto the backyard from the dining room bore the scar of something that had hit it hard enough to dislodge a thumb-size chunk of glass. But that seemed to be the extent of the damage. He made his way around to the front door and unlocked it. There was no indication of flooding; the carpet, at least what he could see of it, looked dry. He reached one shoe forward and tapped a rubber-soled toe against the fiber. Then he closed the door and locked it.

So far in his day's tally, there was only one lie. Teresa knew the parts of him that he'd shown her, willingly, over nine years of marriage. She knew parts he'd never wanted her to see: the depths to which he'd sunk after losing his NASA job; the way he could brood after one of his father's lacerating, off-the-cuff remarks about what Roy was doing with his life. But she didn't know all of him. Leona knew more, somehow. Not all, but more. She was right to advise him not to make any major decisions while he was in this state. She was right to press him, to get him to promise. But he'd lied to her.

He rode the arch of the Hubert Humphrey Bridge for the third time in under twenty-four hours, leaving the island behind him, descending back onto the mainland where the roads had been drained of floodwater. The westbound traffic lights were stuck on green: there was no excuse to drive slowly. He had a family to return to. He had the day ahead of him, already penciled in with necessities, with duties, with chores. He had a lie on his mind and a vein sparking beneath the skin of his left temple.

As the town thinned out on either side of the highway he found himself thinking again about Matt. He desperately needed to be a father figure to this kid, to pull him aside and tell him, somehow, that what he'd been doing in the bathroom of the motel didn't make him a freak, that it was normal, that *he* was normal, and that everything was okay. What devastated Roy was that a conversation about jerking off would fall so near the end of the time line. It would stand out in the boy's memory, stinging with significance because it would be one of the last intimate conversations he had with his stepfather before . . .

Roy turned into the parking lot of the Ponce de Leon and rounded the building to the rear of the motel.

Before he left them. Soon, though he didn't know exactly when. Soon, though he'd lied to Leona about not already having decided to do it. A deep breath before knocking on the motel-room door. A somber entrance. That's what he pictured. But she was standing outside, across the parking lot from the room, waiting for him, her purple purse hanging from one shoulder and her sandaled feet planted apart on the gravel. She was smoking a cigarette. She exhaled smoke and stared down his approach, waiting for him beneath the dome of this full-blown, cloudless sky bright enough to expose all secrets and lies and betrayals. His face adjusted and readjusted itself. He felt his throat try to swallow, and seize.

II

Frankie asked who Ponce de Leon was.

"The guy who discovered the fountain of youth," Joe said. "It makes everything get younger."

"Even your fish," Matt said, flopping down onto one of the beds. "Keep 'em in this motel and they're going to turn back into eggs."

"No they're not!"

"Sure they are," Joe said. "And you're going to be back in diapers by morning."

Karen pitched in, declaring the three of them morons. "In the first place," she said, "those goldfish were probably the only thing in our house that *didn't* need to be evacuated. What are they going to do if the place floods, drown? They're *fish*. In the second place, there was never any such thing as the fountain of youth. It was made up by hicks. And thirdly, even if there was, you'd have to *drink from it* to get younger, not just stay in some crappy motel named after the guy who discovered it."

"They aren't goldfish, they're neon tetras," Frankie corrected her, removing the foil top from the fishbowl and folding it into a triangle. "They're Brazilian and they live for five years."

"Maybe they'd like to live in the Ponce de Leon toilet," Karen sneered—and then her mother descended on her like a hawk.

She grabbed Karen's wrist, pulled her into the bathroom, and shut the door.

"You and I are going to talk," she whispered fiercely. She looked even thinner than usual, her shoulders drooping out of a sleeveless light-blue T-shirt and her arms folded across her stomach.

Karen leaned against the wall between the toilet and the tub. "About what?"

"I think you know about what. Did you seriously think I wouldn't find out about it?"

"*Dunno,* because I don't know what you're talking about."

Her mother's face was turning red. Her eyes were glassy

with either anger or the beginnings of tears, and as much as Karen wanted to remain cool, it frightened her to look into them. "Yes you do."

The overhead light went dark for a second, then came back on, brighter. This was about her father. He had been Karen's secret weapon, a dagger strapped to her thigh; but now her mother had pieced something together, or suspected that Karen had, and it wasn't fair because it was Karen's weapon and it should have been her own decision when to brandish it.

But instead of saying anything about her father, her mother spat out, "Just what do you think you're up to? I talked to Father Gillespie."

Karen felt her stomach contract. "So what?"

"Don't *so what* me. Don't even try it. He called and asked me to come to the church to see him. I had no idea why. We're a good family. We put money in the collection basket. So why should Father Gillespie want to see me? I drove up there thinking, it's got to be one of the children. One of them did something in Sunday school, disrupted class or wasn't paying attention. Well, what a surprise I was in for, huh? To sit there, in his office, and find out he really wanted to see me about me—*because of what you told him.*"

The conversation between Karen and Father Gillespie had occurred the week before. The meaty-faced priest made a habit of standing outside the classrooms when Sunday school let out and selecting a single student to harass. He would pull you aside, place one of his large, knotty hands on your shoulder, and thump a couple of times—like a mallet tapping a stake into the ground—while he asked stupid questions about grades, athletics, family. "Young Katherine," he'd said that Sunday morning, one hand thumping her shoulder, the other knuckling a cigarette, "how are things in a girl's world?"

Whatever that meant. She'd shrugged.

"Your mother tells me you're reluctant to go to confession lately."

"That's none of her business."

"Well, maybe not, but it's certainly yours and mine. I hope your reluctance isn't connected to that confirmation business last year. You can still confess, you know, even though you weren't confirmed."

"Confess what?"

"That would be between you and your—it would be between you and me, and God, in the confessional."

"Why don't I just tell you now?"

He'd tapped his cigarette onto the floor and stepped on the ash. "Your mother did mention a certain *boldness* that was troubling her. From you, and sometimes from your— Is it three brothers?"

Boldness. Her mother was the one who had enrolled both her and Matt in Sunday school under the last name of Kerrigan, telling them not to mention their "real father" or the name Ragazzino to anyone. "Yes," her mother had clarified, "I'm saying it's okay to lie about this one thing. Any other kind of lying is wrong, but God understands this one."

The words *real father* sounded ridiculous to Karen when it meant that loud, wide-faced talker who showed up out of the blue once or twice a year in some ugly checkered blazer, looking and sounding like a used-car salesman. She hated the lunches he took them to; it was like having to eat with the principal of a school you didn't go to. As far as she was concerned, the man they lived with was their father.

But who did her mother think she was, telling her to lie and then siccing this priest on her for not going to confession? Karen had smiled when she'd told the priest, "Actually, I've got one full brother. Two of them are halfs."

Father Gillespie had blown smoke up past his cheek, eye-balling her. "I'm sorry, child, what was that you said?"

"I said I've got one full brother—you know, from the same dad. My other two brothers are my stepfather's."

"What were you thinking?" her mother asked her now, reaching over the toilet and twisting the skin on Karen's forearm. "Do you have any idea what you could have done? Any idea at all?"

"I didn't do anything," Karen said, pulling her arm away.

"You most certainly did, and you did it on purpose. Divorced women aren't allowed to take Communion. They cut you off from the body of Christ. Forever." She made an effort to lower her voice. "I don't like that part of the church, but I can't change it. All I can do is . . . find a way around it. The church and God may mean nothing to you, young lady, but they mean something to me, and I won't be refused Communion."

Karen stared down at the toilet lid.

"Look at me," her mother said. "You will not bring down this family."

Karen felt her eyes widen. "You're nuts," she said. "Let me out of here."

She stepped around the toilet and began to pull the door open, but her mother said *"No!"* sharply and, leading with her elbow, brought the entire weight of her body against the door, slamming it shut. "That's *exactly* what I'm talking about," she whispered angrily. "I am *not* crazy, even though you're doing your best to drive me crazy. You'd love nothing more than to see me kicked out of the Church. You'd love to see this whole family fight itself to death."

Karen didn't want either of those things to happen. She wasn't even sure what one had to do with the other. She only wanted to get out of the bathroom, away from this woman. She started to cry.

"Oh, turn off the waterworks," her mother said, though she was tearing up too. "Don't you see how much damage you cause? How fragile everything is? You don't remember, you *can't* remember living in that roach trap of an apartment in Washington, just you and your brother and me. There was a crash one night—I thought it was an earthquake. I opened the front door, and the entire landing of the building across the street had just *dropped off*. The whole length of it. All those people on the first floor were looking at a pile of concrete as high as your shoulder, and those poor people on the second floor opened their doors to *nothing, to air*. Can you imagine what that was like? And I realized I was looking at all that from the landing of our building, the *same* landing on the *identical* building, and it was all I could do to run back inside and get to you and your brother, to make sure I wasn't killed, because what would happen to you then? Uncle Phil had been transferred to Arizona; he would have been no help at all. And you slept through the whole thing. The earth shook, and you slept through it. After that night I was terrified every time we stepped out the front door." She reached down and snatched a length of toilet paper off the roll, gave Karen half, and brought the rest up to her own eyes. She took a deep breath. "You have no idea how quickly things can change," she said. "*Behave*. Can you do that?"

Karen just wanted out of the bathroom. She had to *go to* the bathroom, but she wanted out of it more. She nodded yes.

"All right, then. Is there anything you want to say to me?"

"You really can't take Communion anymore?"

"Of course I can take Communion," her mother said, straightening up and sniffing. "I told Father Gillespie you were lying, that you make up stories all the time, and that's how it's going to stay." She blew her nose and opened the door.

*

The cluck of Frankie's sleep-breathing woke her the next morning. She was on one of the roll-away beds; Matt was on the other. Frankie and Joe were in the nearest double bed and her parents were in the one next to the bathroom. She was on her side, facing the front window, and from the light she saw coming in around the curtain, it looked as if the storm had passed.

She closed her eyes. A moment later she heard movement at the other end of the room. Fabric rustling. A brief flow of water in the sink. She remained still as he walked past her, and it wasn't until she heard the sweep of the door against the carpet, saw sunlight glowing orange through her lids and then saw it extinguished, that she opened her eyes. He was gone.

She got up and went to the window. Inching the curtain away from the wall, she saw the empty spot where the station wagon had been. She wasn't surprised. Everyone had seemed angry when they went to bed, but her father had seemed the angriest of all.

She'd slept in her clothes, so she only had to put on her sandals. Next to the television was the note he'd written, saying he'd be back soon. Next to that was the room key. She slipped it into her purple purse, eased the door open, and left the room.

Judy Rhodes, the tall, slender girl at school who gave her cigarettes, had taught her a game called Heads You're Right, Tails You're Dead. "If the last seat is already taken," Judy might say, approaching the bus after school, "we're both going to die of cancer." Or, while standing in the lunch line, "If they run out of cobbler before we get any, the Nazis will kill our families." It was dismemberment sometimes, or a car crash, but usually cancer or Nazis. It was a dumb game, but the kind that stuck in Karen's head whether she wanted to play it or not, and she often found herself playing it alone. One afternoon, as she was cutting through the Winn Dixie parking lot on her bicycle, she counted four blue cars parked side by side. *If I see another blue car in the next five seconds,* she thought, *I'll be kidnapped.* The next blue car she saw was the station wagon. It was sitting off by itself, aimed away from her. She stopped her bicycle two rows away. *It's our car, or a look-alike,* she thought. *If it's ours, I'll be kidnapped and brainwashed, and turned into a criminal.* There were two people in the front seat: a man who looked like her father, and a woman she didn't recognize. *If it's him,* she thought, *I'll be forced to rob banks.* It was him—she could tell by his profile. He leaned across the seat and kissed the woman on the mouth. They kissed again. Finally, the woman got out, walked quickly over to her own car, and climbed inside. Karen leaned into the handlebars and pedaled straight across the parking lot, in the opposite direction, without looking back.

From the button-down pocket of her shirt she took the cigarette Judy had given her, flattened now because she'd slept on it, and as she was rolling it back into shape between her thumb and forefinger, she remembered that her father had taken her matches. She stuck the cigarette behind her ear, followed the front of the motel to the glass door of the lobby, and pushed it open.

Behind the desk, with his wide back to her, was the bald-headed man her father had told them all to stay away from.

"Morning," she said, strolling across the indoor-outdoor carpet.

The man swung around with an exaggerated look of shock on his face, which immediately melted into a fake-looking smile. His skin had the color and sheen of Silly Putty. "Yes, we have rooms."

"I already have a room."

"You do?" His glasses had slid down the bridge of his nose, and he tilted his head back to look through them. "You're a rather young lady to have your own room."

"We're in twenty-eight, like you didn't know." She pulled the key out of her purse and waved the tag at him.

"That's right. That's right, you are. That's the room we reserve for...frisky people." He took hold of one side of his glasses and seesawed them into place, and when he gazed at her again, his eyes were magnified. "What can I do you for?"

"Nothing," she said. "Just killing time till I can get out of this dump." She ran her eyes across the tourist pamphlets in the metal rack next to the cigarette machine.

"You've got better things you could be doing, eh?"

"Than staying here? About a million."

The man cleared his throat. He leaned his stomach against the counter. "Then why aren't you doing them?"

She glared at him.

"Just asking," he said, holding up his palms. "You folks checking out today?"

"I hope so."

"Where are they? Your folks, I mean."

"My mother's in the room, asleep," Karen said. "My father's with a friend of his." She walked past the cigarette machine, running her eyes over a calendar and a map of the state of Florida, to the wall behind the desk. There was a paint-by-numbers picture of a man she guessed was Ponce de Leon, bending down over a fountain with his hand dipped into the water. "You paint that yourself?"

He was staring at her with his lips parted. She'd walked to the back of the lobby and could see behind the counter now, where he was standing next to a low filing cabinet with a laundry basket blocking his feet. "A girl I know did it," he said.

"Your wife?"

He shook his head, his mouth still hanging open as if he were drying his teeth. "Just a girl. Another girl I know did that one."

He lifted a finger toward the wall over the filing cabinet, where a latch-hook rug of a pelican on a pylon bulged out from a wooden frame.

"That one's ugly," Karen said, taking a book of matches from a basket at the end of the counter.

The man's eyes were moving across her. She saw him spot the cigarette behind her ear. "You think so? Do me something better, I'll hang it right there." He pointed toward the wall next to the pelican.

"I don't paint," she said. "And I don't 'hook,' in case you were about to make that dumb joke."

He squinted at her from behind his glasses. "Let me ask you something," he said. "Why are you in here talking to me?"

"Because my father told me not to. Why are you talking to *me*?"

His face locked up in its moronic gaze. Sparking suddenly, he grinned and said, "Any port in a storm, honey."

She saw his wide brown shoe lift over the laundry basket and land on the grassy carpet between them; then his other shoe appeared and moved farther, planting itself equidistant between her and the basket. He was literally growing before her eyes.

"I've got lemonade," he said. "And Little Debbies."

She fled the lobby, hurting her wrist when her purse snagged on the door. She ran halfway down the cement walk, and when she finally stopped and looked back, there was no sign of him. Her heart was pounding. As she made her way toward the room, she took the cigarette from behind her ear and placed it between her lips.

Anyone might see her with this cigarette. One of her brothers might step outside, or her mother, and look her way, and the day might take a whole new shape. Mostly, she imagined her father in the station wagon rounding the corner she'd just traversed on foot. Spotting her. Parking and getting out of the car to confront her, or stopping right next to her and rolling down his window. *Just what do you think you're doing?*

If a car doesn't appear in the next ten seconds, she thought, *I'll die in a plane crash.*

She walked, and counted.

If a car doesn't come around the corner in the next ten seconds, the Nazis will kill my family.

She kept walking, and counted to ten again, and without looking back she dug the stolen matches out of her purse and lit the cigarette. She stood across the parking lot from the door to their room, counting for the third time. At last she heard an engine, heard tires moving over gravel and leaves and twigs, and she turned around, planted her feet apart on the asphalt, and drew on the foul-tasting cigarette.

The station wagon rounded the corner.

She knew how it would go: he wouldn't like it, her standing here smoking; he would be angry, and would tell her mother. But she didn't care. She stared the car down and exhaled a cloud of smoke, happy to have him back.

That Daring Young Man

1986

There were times when I saw Frankie as a kind of prodigy. There were other times when he just seemed weird. After coming out at fourteen (before I even realized I was in the closet), he declared himself a gay alien at fifteen, and by the time he turned sixteen he was human again (and still gay), claiming his previous incarnation hadn't been him but a "proxy clone" marking his place while he explored the galaxy. He wore his clothes backward every third Wednesday throughout his sophomore year because he claimed it helped reset his gravity. He took Grant Jenkins, the drum major, to his junior prom and slow-danced to "I Want to Know What Love Is." His senior science fair project was a thoroughly illustrated plan to colonize—exclusively with homosexuals and macaws—an as-yet-undiscovered planet called Gaystar. And still, somehow, he managed to make it out of high school without once getting beaten up.

I'd graduated the year before, and because of lousy SAT scores I'd landed at the community college. Frankie, on the other hand, surprised everyone by mopping the cafeteria floor with his college boards and got accepted to Florida State University with a partial scholarship in graphic design. He opted to start in the summer, and two weeks after his graduation he was gone.

When he called home from Tallahassee one night, I carped and complained about how miserable I was, and how badly I wanted to get off Merritt Island.

"Wow," he said when I was finished. "Mr. Cranky-Pants."

"Sorry. I just feel like I'm going to be stuck here for the rest of my life."

"So transfer to FSU."

I'd thought about it before, but by the same screwed-up logic that made my coming out seem all the more impossible once Frankie had done it, his moving to the state capital virtually sank my feet into the foundation of Merritt Island. I said, "My SATs stink."

"You can retake them."

"They probably wouldn't transfer all my credits."

"That's a reason to stick around? Come on, Joe, you ought to give it a shot. Trust me, you'll love Tallahassee. And I think it'd be good for you. You could, you know, be *yourself* up here."

Dodging the implications of his remark, I said, "I don't know. I'll try."

" 'Do, or do not,' " he said, slipping into his Yoda voice. " 'There is no try.' "

As strange as he could be, I missed him. I had visions of us signing up for the same classes, eating meals together, being known across campus as the Kerrigan Brothers—assuming the powers-that-be accepted me.

They did, in a cold letter no more than three sentences long. The following August, I moved to the panhandle.

❋

McGarry Hall was the dorm where Frankie had lived his first two semesters, and the one he'd told me to request. I'd been lucky enough to get a room on his floor, but I found out from the R.A. that he'd moved out just before I arrived.

When I got back to the dorm that first evening, my phone was ringing. A synthesizer wailed through the receiver. "Hello?"

"You made it!" Frankie said over the music. "Great!"

So far, nothing had been great. I'd spent the entire afternoon in the Civic Center just off campus trying to sew together a schedule, standing in one registration line after another, only to find out most of the classes I wanted were filled. On top of that, McGarry Hall was a huge, filthy city of a dorm. It was made of aluminum and mud-colored brick, was ten stories tall, and was home to over eight hundred students. In its center was a narrow, hermetically sealed airshaft they called a courtyard, the top covered with a fiberglass dome the color of an eggshell—the only source of sunlight for the inner rooms. No one had access to the courtyard other than from the windows, out of which had been dumped (over years, I guessed) garbage, books, mattresses, and broken furniture. My window, on the second floor, was half-submerged in refuse.

"Where *are* you?" I asked.

He explained that a great opportunity had come up, a friend's roommate had split town at the last second, and Frankie had filled the slot. He was living in an apartment now across Tennessee Street. I asked him where that was. "You're kidding. I'm ten feet away from you! McGarry's on Tennessee, and I'm right down the road on the other side. You can almost see me from your window."

"There's garbage outside my window. This place is a dump. Why didn't you tell me you were moving out?"

"I didn't know till yesterday. Don't be such a sorehead."

I apologized. I asked him when we were going to see each other.

"Oh my god," he said, "tonight!"

But I never saw him that night. He had to find out where a particular party was going to be held and said he would call me back with the location, and then he called hours later only to say the party was a bust because the host's ex had shown up with the ex of the host's current, and it was too much for the host to deal with.

"Cool," I said, faking comprehension, hoping he wouldn't pick up on the disappointment in my voice.

❊

Purely by eavesdropping—in the student union, in the cafeteria, in McGarry's smoky, war-torn lounge area—I learned that in an ideal schedule, your classes were lined up one right after another and dominoed over two days. The classes I'd ended up with were spread out all over campus five days a week, separated by huge chunks of time. I could have walked back to the dorm during these idle hours, but I had quickly begun to hate it there. In the first week of the semester, the guys on my floor (all of whom seemed to know one another already) had poured rubber cement down the shower drains, turned the hall into an all-night bowling alley using a baseball and empty wine cooler bottles, and torn up the carpet in front of the elevator in order to have a Tide slide. After the R.A. lectured them, they painted his door with rubbing alcohol and set it on fire. This last stunt had all eight hundred of us standing outside at three A.M. while firemen wandered the building. The R.A. was furious, but no one would admit to the arson. The following day, someone carved COCKSUCKER into the door's blackened varnish.

I began hanging out in the Strozier Library. It was a good place to study because people had to behave, and for someone who suddenly felt stripped of all privacy, Strozier was an excellent place to masturbate. All over the building, tucked into the elbows of the stairwells, were men's rooms: narrow, institutional green boxes divided by granite slabs, antiseptic and silent. Having left home to come to this strange new place where I felt overwhelmed, the library immediately became a vital part of

my survival: a quiet cubicle, a door with a latch, and a few soli-
tary moments to jerk off.

Tap your foot for head someone had scribbled with a ballpoint
pen over the door latch. The words were written in every stall
of the third-floor men's room in the annex, and they sounded
like a line nixed from the Hokey Pokey, but I knew what they
meant. Only I wasn't looking for anonymous sex. I wasn't looking for sex at all. I wanted to do my business alone and get back
to my carrel. But at the beginning of the second week of classes,
someone came through the door just after I'd gotten started.
There were four stalls. I was in the last one. Soft footsteps
crossed the tile and hesitated. Then a body settled into the stall
next to mine.

He could hear my heart pounding, I was sure. I eased my
head away from the granite wall that separated us, and then
brought it down just enough to see his left shoe. It was a red
canvas sneaker with three white stripes running down the side.

He tapped once against the floor.

I tapped once back.

There was a long pause. He tapped again. I tapped back.

We did this several more times, like musicians who'd fallen
out of sync. The system was far too vague, I thought; we needed
more than one signal. Which one of us was offering to *give* the
head? Finally, I heard him sigh, and heard the squeak of his
stall door and his footsteps as he left the bathroom. I felt both
frustrated and relieved, since I would have been terrified if anything had actually happened.

But when I got back to my carrel, I saw him. He was
hunched over a bound periodical, his red sneakers tucked beneath his chair, teetering on their rubber-soled toes. He had
horn-rimmed glasses, and hair so black it was nearly blue; enormous biceps stretching the sleeves of his burgundy FSU T-shirt;
a superhero's jaw, right down to the divot.

When he tossed his backpack over a shoulder and left the library, I followed him. I'd never tailed anyone before and I wasn't very good at it, for when he turned unexpectedly—say, to cut across a lawn instead of following the sidewalk—and put me in his peripheral vision, I stopped short and began looking around like someone who'd just dropped his keys, even glancing up into the dogwood trees to see if they'd landed there. He didn't seem to notice. In tandem, we made our way through a patchwork of buildings, on paths shaded by enormous pines. I concluded he was heading toward the football stadium, which would explain the arms. But before we got there, he veered off to the right. The buildings thinned out and the sidewalk turned to grass. The grass wore down to dirt, and then opened onto a clearing, and there before us stood an enormous white circus tent. A woman was coiling rope around a wooden spool near the entrance. She said hello to him. He high-fived her, and disappeared inside.

Frankie and I spoke several times over the phone during that first week. He apologized for not having seen me and said he was "swamped with stuff," and I lied and told him it didn't matter.

We compared notes about the disparate architecture of the campus, and talked about how awful the meal plan was (he hadn't signed up for it again, and had forgotten to warn me about it). I asked him about the circus tent.

"Isn't that great?" he said. "I think we're the only state school in the country where you can major in clown."

"So it's an actual program?"

"Sure it is. Why? You want to switch majors?"

Several more days went by before we at last made solid plans to see each other—at another party given by one of his friends.

The place was mobbed. It was just off campus, in the up-stairs apartment of an old house that shook with voices and a thumping bass. At the top of the landing, I pushed through the crowd and stepped right up behind a young man with dark curly hair who I thought was Frankie. I tapped his shoulder. "You rang?" he said, looking at me with tired eyes.

"Sorry. I thought you were..." I glanced at the surrounding T-shirts and multicolored heads of hair. It was like being in a field of tie-dyed sunflowers. "Do you know Frankie Kerrigan?"

"I don't know last names," he replied. "There's Big Frank and Little Frank."

"Here's Big Frank," said the girl he'd been talking to, and she reached for the arm of the person behind her.

Big Frank wasn't Frankie. He was at least six two, was nearly bald, and had an indignant-looking face tempered with one of those five o'clock shadows that seemed tattooed on. "What's your last name, Big Frank?" the girl asked.

"My last name is *Who-the-fuck-wants-to-know,*" he replied. Then he focused on me and his mouth widened into a smile interrupted by a gap in his front teeth. "Hello." He extended a wide hand. "Who be you?"

"Joe." I shook his hand.

He could see only a wedge of me, but he made a quick assess-ment of my clothes, my haircut, or both. "Rush week is over," he said. "But I can still be your big brother."

"I think he wants Little Frank."

"Oh, who doesn't?" Big Frank's teeth disappeared. He glanced around the room. "Over there, in the corner."

Arms lifted to let me through. My shoulder brushed an elbow and was splattered with beer. At last I reached the corner, where a cluster of people were sitting at knee level on overturned milk crates. I spotted Frankie among them. He'd gained a little weight, I thought; his wiry body had filled out just enough so that he no longer looked like a little kid but like a handsome young man. He'd cut his thick, dark curls down to a soft-looking brush and dyed a bright blue patch the size of a cracker into the hair above the left side of his forehead. He was wearing jeans that were snug against his legs and a plain white T-shirt with a wide neck hole that exposed his collarbone. He was talking a mile a minute to the guy sitting next to him. The music was too loud for me to hear what he was saying. Then abruptly he turned. His eyes brightened, his cheeks lifted, and he looked like a child again. "You sneak! They were supposed to announce you! I had your theme song all cued up on the stereo!"

I couldn't imagine being "announced," and if I had a theme song, it was news to me. But he looked elated. "I crept in the back way," I said as he rose to his feet and hugged me. "Check out your hair."

"Yeah. They've been calling me Simon. Remember that game where you had to knock out those color patterns? People keep mashing their hands down on my head."

"I thought they were calling you Little Frank."

"Yeah, that too." He introduced me to a half dozen people, and pointed out and named countless more. I got the impression there wasn't anyone at the party he didn't know. The guy on the milk crate next to him stormed off toward the bathroom ("That was Brian—trashed") and another one took his place ("This is Chip—the trasher"). Chip was blond and much thinner than Frankie. He laid one spindly calf across a knee, then reached up and pulled Frankie down beside him by a belt loop. They kissed for an entire verse of whatever was playing on the stereo. When their mouths separated, Chip looked up and said, "So you're Little Frank's brother."

"I am."

" 'I am,' " Chip repeated in a voice deeper than the one I had used. He mugged at Frankie. "So serious."

"Drinks," Frankie said. He got back up and turned around dramatically. To Chip: "Behave, and keep your hands off him." To me: "Don't worry, Chip's a nice one. And it's a mixed party, by the way. AC *and* DC. Just so you know it isn't all scary."

He darted off. I glanced down at Chip. "I'm a nice one," Chip said, smiling.

A few minutes later, the crowd pushed back to allow for a handful of people who had started dancing, and through this gap I saw Frankie emerge from the kitchen. He was holding three plastic cups of beer. He hesitated in the doorway as another guy stepped up in front of him and held something under his nose. When the guy stepped away, the Talking Heads song "And She Was" began to punch out of the speakers, and Frankie perked up. *"Yes,"* he mouthed to no one in particular. *"I love this song!"* Some of the beer spilled from the cups and he grinned and closed his eyes. His face turned blood red. For a few moments, he just stood there, flushed, between the kitchen and the living room. Then he made his way back to the corner. "Intense," he said, handing me a cup.

I stayed longer than I wanted to. Frankie talked to me for a while, but he was a busy man. He hung on Chip for a while, and kissed him several times; then Brian showed up again and hung on Frankie; then Chip pulled Brian onto his narrow lap and made out with him, while Frankie occasionally glanced over and applauded. Three different people came up and whispered in Frankie's ear. Each time, he glanced at Chip, dug something out of the pocket of his jeans, and palmed it over to them, like an uncle bestowing quarters. At one point, Big Frank sidled up to us and asked me to dance. Frankie burst out laughing.

"What?" Big Frank wanted to know. "Is that so funny?"

They both looked at me. I held up my hands and said, "Sorry. I don't really dance."

"He doesn't dance," Frankie confirmed. "Nothing to be

done about that. It doesn't mean you're not pretty, though," he called after Big Frank, who was already wandering off.

"I'm going," I said.

"Don't," he said. And then, "All right. But I'll call you this week. We're going to see each other."

"Good," I said. And then I couldn't help myself. I felt a wave of desire to be part of his troupe. I dredged a nickname from my memory, one my sister had used for both of us, indiscriminately, and I reached up and smashed my palm down onto his patch of blue hair. "Dingus."

At the foot of the stairs, I met the host. He was short and thick-waisted, standing with one hand on the newel and the other pinching a cigarette; he couldn't have been more than twenty, but he talked like a middle-aged mobster. "Thanks for coming, Little Frank's brother," he said, for that's how I had introduced myself. "I, ah, wouldn't go out there just yet, if I were you." He was staring intently at the screen door that opened onto the front porch.

"Why?"

"Thugs," he said. "Across the street, there, next to the cemetery. They've got nothing better to do; they've been hanging out, staring at the house, shouting the F word."

"Fuck?"

He took his eyes off the screen door and blinked at me, as if I'd asked him what planet we were on.

✳

It isn't all scary.

I knew what my little brother was getting at. Not only had I never clarified which side of the fence I was on, sexually; I hadn't indicated that I even knew where the fence was. An all-scary party would be one filled entirely with homosexuals.

I'd always secretly felt that Frankie owed me one for playing the gay card just when I was beginning to figure things out for myself. Even as I observed the world's slowly growing tolerance, I understood that, with this one announcement, he'd used up all the allotted gay goodwill in the family. No one had *two* in one household, in one generation. Gertrude Stein's mother had Leo. Even Liberace's mother had George. Just what I would have done if Frankie had turned out to be straight (or had kept his mouth shut) was difficult to imagine; if nothing else, I had earned the right not to have to answer that one. Such was my occasional righteous moment.

He called a few days later and said he was glad I'd shown up at the party. I thanked him for inviting me.

"They're great people, right?"

"Really great," I said, trying to sound convincing.

"Oh, and for the record, I don't know what Chip told you, but don't listen to him. He exaggerates."

"Chip didn't tell me anything."

"No?" He seemed caught short by this. The line went quiet.

"What would he have told me?"

"Nothing, I guess."

"Something, or you wouldn't have said that."

"You know, just stuff." Frankie cleared his throat and started talking faster. "Just that Chip can be a real sourpuss sometimes, you know, saying stuff about people—like, he says most of those people are 'vapid,' stuff like that. He got so bent out of shape that night, later on. Brian wanted me to go home with him, and it's not like *that* hasn't happened before, and Chip said fine, but he was really wasted and probably wanted it to be a threesome, I don't know. Anyway, he got pissy about it. But I've never really been big on the guessing game, you know?"

I felt like we were playing a version of it now.

"Hey, do you swim?"

"I taught *you* to swim," I said. "I taught you how to body-surf."

"I mean *swim*. Like, in a pool. For exercise."

"Sure."

He told me he did laps several mornings a week and asked if I wanted to join him.

We met the next day at seven A.M. in front of an old, Gothic-style gymnasium off Landis Green. I was hardly awake and had bought a cup of coffee along the way that was still too hot to drink. Frankie was so wound up, he couldn't stand still. He led me down a darkened stone stairwell to a locker room in the basement, where we changed into our suits. As kids, we'd shared a bedroom and had gotten undressed in front of each other countless times. But suddenly I felt self-conscious about my soft stomach and sunken chest. Frankie was clearly in better shape. His shoulders and chest had the definition of someone who exercised. His stomach was so tight, it looked like bongo skin stretched over his hips.

We walked down another flight, from the locker room to an enormous pool sectioned with lane dividers and flanked by high, caged windows just beginning to glow with morning light. I commented that the entire building seemed to be empty. "It won't be," he said, slipping into the pool. He pushed off the wall with the grace of an Olympic swimmer.

I was anything but athletic. I loathed sports, which were drenched in a sense of competition I was unsuited for. But I wasn't about to be shown up by my little brother when it came to something as basic as swimming. I inched down into the water and drifted away from the wall. My arms slapped at the surface; my legs scissored to little effect. Frankie was already at the far wall, waiting for me. As I grabbed hold of the ledge, he said something about keeping my arms close to my body. "Uh-huh,"

I gasped, as if I knew that and was just trying something different, this one time. I struggled back to our starting point, and
managed another lap, while Frankie glided from one wall to
the other, over and over again, like a porpoise in captivity. I felt
vaguely nauseated as I climbed out of the pool.

When he was finished, I followed him back to the locker
room, where we stripped off our suits and stepped into an open
shower. "I'm out of shape," I said, my hands brushing against
my stomach.

Frankie was sanding a bar of soap against his head. He let
out a small laugh. "No, you're not. You look fine. You're just . . .
uptight."

"I don't think I'm uptight," I said—or tried to say; halfway
through the rebuttal, the heat of the shower did me in. I folded
over next to him, and if there had been anything in my stomach,
it would have come out right then and there.

"Wow," I heard him say as I felt his hand on my back. "Are
you okay?"

Standing upright a few moments later, I said, "I'm great."
He was looking at me, one eye squinted against a tributary of
soap. "Swimmer's cramp," I said.

When we came out of the shower, there were several men in
the locker room: morning regulars, it seemed, silently changing
into bathing suits or gym shorts. One of them took off all his
clothes and stood holding his swim trunks and fiddling with
the drawstring. He had the longest penis I had ever seen. Its
presence was almost threatening. I don't know how long I'd
been staring at it when I glanced over at Frankie, who was
watching me as he tied his shoes.

"It can get pretty cruisy in there," he observed as we were
leaving the building.

I told him I had five minutes to get to my eight o'clock class.

We were hardly turning out to be the brother/brother team I'd envisioned. Our paths rarely crossed unless we arranged it in advance. We never spent an entire day together. We never hung out in my dorm room or in his apartment (I had the address but, a month into the semester, I had yet to be invited). Basically, he worked me into his schedule. He had his classes, his friends, his dates, and the people he had to "see"—a category that smacked of something lurid. It wasn't hard to figure out that it had to do with Chip, and with what Frankie was dispensing at a regular series of parties held around the perimeter of campus. I showed up at a number of them, and he was like a turnstile half the party passed through on its way to fun.

I didn't press him about what he was really up to. Instead, I went on supposition: it was speed coming out of his pocket, or quaaludes, or little plastic envelopes of cocaine. But the drugs were just part of my concern. I'd seen him leave—arm in arm, on different nights—with at least ten different guys, sometimes two at once. How did he *do* it? How often was he splayed out unconscious on a living room floor, surrounded by drugs and sex paraphernalia and strangers who used both? And beyond that, I wondered, when did he study?

Meanwhile, I lugged my books all over campus. I took the same carrel in the library most afternoons and gave myself a headache looking down at the page and up every time someone walked by. I read all of *Aspects of the Novel* in the third-floor men's room of the annex. I lingered around the circus tent for weeks. One day, as I sat on the ground at the foot of a tree, reading and waiting for the guy from the library to show up at the tent, I spotted him through the open flap.

He was hanging upside down from a trapeze. There was an

enormous net stretched beneath him and a harness around his chest, which was tied to a safety line that ran up to a scaffolded system of pulleys. He was wearing what looked like white footy pajamas. His glasses were gone. His arms were folded across his chest and his thick black hair was hanging in the shape of a pope's hat. On the ground, a gray-bearded instructor was yelling at him. "You will be laughed out of the ring, Margolis! You will be dead on the floor, and the last thing your lazy-ass soul is going to see before it floats off to lazy-land is a whole tent full of people laughing at your dead body! Now, how about you show me you've actually practiced this glide, or *am I wasting my time?*"

Margolis. Even though it was upside down and from a distance, I could see the scowl of frustration on his handsome face. He tightened his stomach muscles, folded upward, then dropped and commenced swinging. I waited for him to take hold of the opposite trapeze, but it was the swing and the reach he was practicing; after a few carefully executed grabs at the air just in front of the second bar, the instructor yelled, "*Thank* you!"

Other than learning his last name, I hadn't really accomplished anything, but I felt elevated as I repeated it to myself. When I got back to the dorm that night, I exited the elevator onto the second floor and sailed across an inch of water, landing flat on my back. The drinking fountain had been ripped from its foundation. One of my neighbors, dressed in baggies and flippers, burst into a laugh, then stuck his head out the window that overlooked the entrance to the building.

"Hey, bitch! Lose some weight!"

❋

There was no number on his apartment door. I checked the numbers on either side, and knocked lightly. I knocked a second time. A voice exploded from somewhere inside, a single

blast of sound I didn't recognize as a word. Then I heard
Frankie's voice: "Jason, hold on! I'm coming!" The chain rattled and the bolt unlocked. When the door opened, Frankie
was standing in front of me in his underwear and a T-shirt,
squinting against the sunlight.

"It's not Jason," I said.

He looked confounded by the sight of me. Then his face
snapped to life and his head dipped as if he were laughing hard,
though he wasn't. "Wow! Look at you! What are you doing
here?"

"I thought I'd drop by, finally see your place."

"Wow," he said again. "That's great." He glanced back, his
head disappearing behind the door. "You just showed up." His
head reappeared. "Well, come in."

The apartment was rectangular, the living room opening
onto the kitchen. There was a yellow vinyl couch, a chrome and
glass-topped coffee table, a pair of wooden dining room chairs,
and a makeshift stereo cabinet comprising a long plank of ve-
neered shelf board set on cinder blocks and supporting two
sophisticated-looking turntables; on the carpet beneath the
board, hundreds of record albums were lined up against the
wall. It was just after three P.M. "Did I wake you?" I asked.

"No." He picked up a pair of shorts from beside the couch
and pulled them on. "Just, you know, getting stuff done. Missed
you this morning."

He meant the pool; I hadn't been back since that one time.
"It's a bit early for me," I said. "When do you sleep?"

"In shifts. A couple of hours here, a couple there. I like it that
way." He was in constant motion: kicking things under the
couch, emptying an ashtray, gathering dirty dishes that were
scattered around the carpet. "Sit down. I'm just going to, you
know, crank up the bulldozer."

I told him not to bother. I sat down on the couch, which

exhaled at the seams, and looked at the opposite wall. A blowup of an album cover for Roxy Music and one for something called *The Queen Is Dead* were thumbtacked side by side, and beyond these, adjacent to the refrigerator, was the tanned Calvin Klein underwear model I recognized from my squirreled-away copies of *GQ*.

"No spaceship designs?"

"I had them up in the dorm, but, you know, I share this place. You want a Sprite?"

He poured us each a Slurpee cup of soda and ice, and sat down across from me in one of the chairs.

We complained about our classes for a few minutes. Then we fell silent. I wanted to come out and ask him, *Why aren't we seeing more of each other?* But pride kept me from it. "So," I finally managed, "do I get the tour?"

"Mmm." He nodded into his Sprite. "Of course. Definitely. The thing is..." He glanced toward the bedroom door, and at that moment, it opened.

Chip stepped out in a peach silk robe. His blond hair was standing up on one side, and he looked as if he'd been punched in both eyes. He glared at the two of us. "I thought Jason was here."

"Not yet," Frankie said.

"Christ. Didn't he say three o'clock? Why the hell am I hiding in the bedroom for your brother?"

He walked toward the kitchen cabinets as if his bare feet were sinking into the floor. I smiled at Frankie, who looked nervous, who was making me nervous. "We have to hide from Jason?" I asked, trying to sound amused.

Frankie shook his head no, smiling.

"Bingo," Chip snapped with his back to us. "*I* have to hide from Jason. The narc." He opened and closed one cabinet after the other. "I can't sneeze without worrying about the door being kicked in by some fag-hating friend-of-a-cop who's got his own little one-man sting operation going. I'm a veritable prisoner in my own home."

Frankie rolled his eyes at me. "He's a veritable drama queen," he whispered.

Chip wheeled around. He may or may not have caught Frankie's comment. Holding an empty cereal bowl like a primitive tool meant for digging, he asked me, "Are you a fag-hater?"

"Um, no," I said.

"Are you a cop?"

"Hardly."

"Go back to sleep, Chip."

"Fuck you, *Little* Frank." Chip waved the bowl through the air, ran his eyes across the ceiling, and then drilled them into mine. "Are you a fag?"

I looked at Frankie. He stood up and took the soda from my hand. "Thanks for coming over, Joe."

"You're throwing me out?"

"No," Frankie said, sidestepping Chip and carrying both our tumblers to the kitchen counter.

"Your little brother would never be so mean," Chip told me. "He's the sweetest, most popular thing on the planet. *Everybody* loves him. Granted, he's a good lay, but I should get points, you know, for boosting his popularity. If it weren't for me—"

"Yes," Frankie said, taking my arm, "I'm throwing you out."

"I guess I should have called first," I said.

"See ya!" Chip called as Frankie escorted me to the door.

When we were outside, he said, "It's okay. Look, I'm sorry about Chip. It's just probably better if you go. This guy's coming over..."

"Jason."

"Yeah. What are you doing next Saturday?"

He told me about another party, promising this one would be a real blowout. I said I'd be there. He hugged me, said "Sorry" again, and kissed me on the cheek. Then he retreated into the apartment.

I'd come over with the crazy notion that we might talk about living together, that maybe there was room for him and me and his roommate (I hadn't realized the roommate was Chip) in the apartment, and if so, I could bail out of McGarry like he had. Now I let go of the notion. I would never be able to move in with him, and the more I thought about it as I walked back to the dorm, the more I realized that Chip wasn't the reason.

※

It turned out that on a campus with one student union, one post office, one bookstore, one video arcade, and one main cafeteria, it wasn't that difficult to stalk a person who wore the same pair of shoes almost every day. I watched him eat breakfast and check his mail. I watched him play Asteroids. I watched him read a textbook and nap and perform the occasional set of push-ups on the grass next to the Business Building. And I watched him practice his craft. The day he was allowed to grab the second bar (still not yet at the point where he could release his legs from the first), I nearly applauded.

A girl tapped my shoulder. "What are you doing here?"

I was sitting on the bleachers just inside the entrance of the tent. People seemed to be wandering in and out all the time. Entire art classes sat around sketching. I hardly thought I stood out. I'd seen this girl harnessed up with four different safety lines, carrying a pole across a tightrope: she was official circus. "Research," I said.

She tilted her head to one side. Her hair was pulled up into a biscuit that sat on top of her head and her hands were in her back pockets. She looked entirely wound, and I had the feeling she was going to spring forward and pounce. But something flickered in her eyes. With a fluid motion, she released her hands and entwined her arms over her stomach. Her head drifted back to north. "What for?"

"Exposé on the circus," I said, digging my notebook out of my pocket. "For the school paper."

She smiled, introduced herself, and told me she was from Tampa. Then she talked for twenty minutes straight while I took notes and tried to look interested.

I had other things to do, of course, and I did them sufficiently. While learning that Margolis chatted about the weather with the woman who worked the card-reader at the cafeteria, and that he liked to squeeze his hand grips while running at the track, and that he belonged to the Sigma Nu fraternity, I somehow managed to do fine in my classes—probably because I knew his schedule so well that whenever I spent time on my studies, I did so fixated on the reward of seeing him.

Most nights, after I resigned myself to returning to McGarry Hall, I spent an hour or so in the lounge off the lobby, where I could read and thus prolong my return to the second floor. I was halfway through the door of the lounge one night when I saw Margolis. He was sitting in a battered armchair, rubbing a nail file against the calluses of his palms. He glanced up through his horn-rimmed glasses, then looked back at his hands. Clearly, he wasn't there to see me. Part of my brain was relieved by this; the other part sent out signals that carried me to the love-seat crate next to where he sat with his legs splayed. One of my knees was trembling. I immediately pulled a book from my backpack and opened it and tried to slump into a casual pose. Out of the corner of my eye, I saw his head shift slightly. I heard the nail file stop sanding his skin. He said, "You're that guy."

I blinked. "What guy?"

"That freak who's been following me."

I felt my stomach turn to liquid and forced my eyes down to my book. "Whoever you're talking about, it's not me."

"Yeah, it is. I have your friggin' face memorized. I was going to call campus police, but a friend of mine said it wasn't worth it."

I couldn't speak. I couldn't look up.

"What's that all about?" he demanded.

Your sneaker, I wanted to say. *You tapped your sneaker on the men's-room floor.* Even as I realized the sentence might get me killed, its potential inaccuracy nearly made me laugh out loud. All my efforts had been the result of an anonymous shoe tapping on a men's-room floor. For all I knew, that had been the one flickering moment in his life when he'd considered having sex with another guy, and the moment had passed. For all I knew, he was having a muscle spasm in his leg that day, or was looking for someone gay to beat up.

He said only three more words to me, and he said them carefully, like a schoolteacher at his wit's end: *"Knock it off."*

Then the friend he'd been waiting for emerged from the elevator, and he shoved up from the chair and left the lounge. On his way out, he turned around and walked back a few steps, staring me down and pointing two fingers at the end of his outstretched arm. I know it was meant as a demarcation, but it looked as if he were bestowing a curse.

※

Saturday evening's party—the one Frankie had promised would be a blowout—was just that, and a bad one. But Sunday afternoon was worse.

The party was in an old U-shaped motel that had been con-

verted into apartments. I shouldn't have gone; I was still smart-
ing from Margolis's verbal kick in the teeth, still racked with
embarrassment and humiliation. The party was loud. I heard it
long before I reached it: screams and laughter and that Kate
Bush song that just wouldn't go away. Across the leaf-covered
swimming pool, on the opposite side of the complex, a handful
of guys leaned in a doorway, holding beers and watching us. I
pushed through the crowd until I found Frankie.

"Brother!" he said, throwing his arm around my neck.

For the first time in my life, the term irked me. I had no idea
why, since my recent altercation had had nothing to do with my
being someone's brother—unless that was part of it, in which
case I was even more of a mess than I thought.

"The host is *insane,*" Frankie said. "He's already threatened
to throw everyone out because somebody broke his Hummel.
He owned a Hummel, can you believe that? But he's got this
whole door-prize thing he wants to do later, so I think we're
safe."

Someone stepped between us, right in front of me, and spoke
into Frankie's ear. Frankie dug into his pocket. When the guy
stepped away, he said, "You want a beer?"

"What's that?" I pointed to his pocket.

"Nothing." He grinned. "I'm just glad to see you."

"Cough it up."

"What is this, a shakedown?"

"I want some," I said.

"No you don't."

"Don't tell me what I want. I'm two years older than you." I
was suddenly fuming. I took hold of his ear.

"Ow!"

"Give it," I said.

He jerked his head away and stabbed his fingers into his
pocket. "Here, grouch. Do you even know what it's called?"

He'd extracted a single beige capsule and was holding it in his palm between us. I shrugged as if it didn't make any difference. "MDA," he said. "Which is . . . ?"

"I don't care."

"Care," he said. "It's just about everything out there right now, combined into one."

"Do you take it?"

"Occasionally."

I scooped it out of his palm.

"Half," he said. "You'll be flying if you take the whole thing."

"I want to fly." With that, the capsule was on my tongue. I borrowed a beer from the nearest person, and swigged.

"Jesus," Frankie said. He looked at me with the gravest, most adult expression I'd ever seen on his face. "Stick close, okay?"

I didn't want to. Chip walked up and smirked at the two of us. I found a beer of my own, and shoved off into the crowd.

There was a girl there from Luray, Virginia. I remember that, and a few other things, with clarity. She was elfin, wore a Springsteen T-shirt, and had a beautiful mountain accent that reminded me of Sissy Spacek in *Badlands*. She asked where I was from, and I told her; then I ran through the usual list of clarifiers to place Merritt Island on the map: "The NASA area. Cocoa Beach. Cape Canaveral."

She brightened up. "*I Dream of Jeannie!*" Her hands locked together over her head and she gyrated her hips. Then she stopped abruptly, dropped her arms, and laughed in my face. When I didn't laugh back, she narrowed her eyes and said, "Luray's where the pottery comes from."

I realized she was wired on something. I also realized, looking around the crowd, that she was the only female at the party except for a tall, auburn-haired woman who stood with her back to us across the room.

"Yep," she said, reading my mind and glancing around, "all boys. All boys who like boys. I live next door, and that's the only kind of party they ever have here. It's a lose-lose situation, as far as I'm concerned."

I looked at her and said impulsively, "Do you want to get out of here?"

"Mmm . . ." She sized me up. "No thanks."

Fighting the crowd, I made my way over to the tall, auburn-haired woman. She turned around just as I got close.

"Hey!" Big Frank said. "I wondered if you were coming. You're the only person here who hasn't met Butter Rum." The hair looked real, but he wore no makeup. He hadn't even shaved. He smiled coyly, reached into his purse, and handed me a piece of candy.

"Thanks."

"Hey, Butter!" said a red-faced boy, stepping out from behind Big Frank and drumming his hands on the hairy forearm that supported the purse strap. "Is Chip here?"

"Travis," Big Frank said in a cordial voice, tilting his head back and staring down the bridge of his nose, "have you met Joe?"

"No." Travis gave me an impatient glance. "Is Chip here?"

"Yes. Joe is Little Frank's brother. He moved here in August."

"*That's* who I'm really looking for," Travis said. "Little Frank. Where is he?"

Big Frank huffed, and pointed.

When Travis was gone, I said, "Don't you get tired of doing that?"

He took a piece of candy from his purse, unwrapped it, and

stuck it in his mouth. Around it, he said, "What, playing 'Where's Frankie?' *Somebody* has to do it. He casts a pretty wide net, when it comes to people."

"Yeah, I wonder why."

Big Frank didn't pick up on the sarcasm in my voice; he responded as if I'd asked him a question. "Because everyone likes him. And he's nice, you know? He'd give you the back off his front, if you asked for it."

"You mean shirt off his front."

"I was tweaking," he said.

"No, that's not right, either. Back off his shirt? How does that go?" I immediately became consumed with how it went. I mouthed the words silently: *shirt, front, back, shirt.* "*Front* is the bad one! *Front* shouldn't be in there! He'd give you...the *shirt*...off his *back*!"

Big Frank was studying my face. He said, "Yikes."

"What?"

"I'm not the only person who's given you a piece of candy tonight, am I?"

With that, I began to trip. And speed. And slide. I couldn't tell who was drunk, who was sober, who'd taken the same drug I had and might be riding the same heady waves. I wandered into the bedroom, found the fragments of the shattered Hummel, and thought they were teeth.

Frankie was in front of me at one point, speaking directly into my face. Then he was across the room, four swimming pools away, and it looked as if he was putting something up his nose. I lurched toward him. Big Frank caught me. We danced in each other's arms.

Someone screamed.

The music stopped, and we all froze like a field of possums caught in a flashlight beam. A guy's head was bleeding. He had his hand up to his brow and was shouting "Damn!" when a beer bottle in the hand of another guy exploded. There were several pings and pops, and I looked down and saw marbles collecting on the floor.

The girl from Luray curled her hands up against her ribs and cried at the ceiling, *"They're shooting at us!"*

Across the way, the trio of drunken guys was playing target practice with slingshots. The host ran forward, using a couch cushion as a shield, and slammed the front door shut.

Eventually, our attackers got bored—or passed out—and marbles stopped pelting the door. Thereafter, I experienced a moment that came close to lucidity, and decided to make a run for it.

I was crossing the parking lot when a deep voice came out of the darkness from above: "Good evening, Jack."

I spun around—which I shouldn't have done, because it turned the parked cars into carousel horses that kept moving after I'd stopped.

"Up here," the voice said.

On a small balcony above me, a shirtless man in white sweat shorts leaned forward and planted a pair of enormous hands far apart on a wrought iron railing. He had a head of wiry hair and a barrel chest that seemed to glow.

"I'm not Jack," I said.

"I don't care what your name is," he replied calmly. "I'm a deputy sheriff. That car is my cruiser."

The carousel horses were slowing down. I followed his pointing finger and saw a squad car parked several feet away.

"I'll make this as plain as I can," he said. "I'm going back to bed now, and if I'm awakened one more time by your friends and their stereo, I'm going to get dressed and go to the station. And if I go to the station, I'm taking people with me. Is that clear?"

His mouth didn't appear to be moving much, and his voice

sounded as if it were coming from a distant P.A. system. He was a robot, maybe—something out of *Westworld*. I nodded yes.

"You might want to pass on the good word."

"I'll do that."

He winked. "Night, Jack."

"Good night," I said, and continued walking until I got to McGarry Hall.

Early the next afternoon, I called Frankie.

"What happened to you?" he asked, as soon as he heard my voice. "You left without saying goodbye."

"Poison happened to me." My hand was shaking around the phone receiver. "I haven't even closed my eyes. How do you take that stuff?"

"I told you last night, I *have* taken it. I don't *take* it."

"Well, I want you to stop. I mean, having anything to do with it. And whatever that was I saw you snorting up your nose, I want you to quit that, too."

"What, poppers? That's not exactly cocaine. Jeez, you really haven't slept, have you?"

I was pacing as much as the three-foot phone cord would allow. "I want you to stop carrying this shit around in your pocket at these fucking parties."

"Really? Too bad."

"I'm not kidding about this, Frankie."

"Neither am I. You know, you're the one who wanted it. I said no, and you just...*took* it from me. You haven't even come down from it yet, and you're lecturing me."

"Because if anybody knows how nasty this stuff is, it's me. The last fourteen hours have been hell." Actually, there had been three pretty great ones in between the walk home and trying to sleep, but I didn't want to tell him that. "If you owe Chip money, we'll take care of it. You don't have to work for a creep like that."

"You don't know what you're talking about."

"He's there now, isn't he?"

"No. Listen, I'm not *working* for Chip."

"You're dealing for him. That's working."

"I'm *not* dealing. I'm helping him out. I don't see what the big commotion is. Chip got into a little trouble last year, and he doesn't want to get busted again, that's all."

"Again?" I barked like a mother into the phone, "You could go to *jail,* Frankie."

"No one's going to jail! Technically, he's not selling anything. People just come up to him and give him money."

"And you're, what, the pickup window at the pharmacy?"

"No, because you *pay* at the pickup window. I don't take any money; I just have some stuff on me. Never that much. So neither one of us is bustable."

"Bustable. Well, you know, I hate to sound like a *sorehead,* but you're *bustable* if you have your pockets full of this crap. You really don't see the danger in this, do you? You're floating out there in Frankie-land, where everybody wants you and everything's just . . . happy-go-lucky and perfect."

"Wow," he said in a voice suddenly juked with revelation. "You're jealous."

"That's such a laugh. Jealous of what?"

"Me. There's no reason to be, Joe. I know I have a lot of friends up here, but you could, too, if you'd just loosen up a little."

"I don't know what you're talking about."

"Come on. You just can't take the leap, can you? You have no trouble showing up at all of these parties and staring holes through . . . certain people . . . but you never let on what's really happening with you."

"Well, if it's that obvious, why should I?" I wasn't sure if that helped his argument, or mine. In fact, I was losing track of mine fast.

"I could help you," he said. "I know you don't like to think that, but it's true."

"I'm not discussing this with you. This isn't the conversation we're having."

"*What* isn't the conversation? Can you even say it? It doesn't have to be a big deal, Joe."

"*I'll* decide when…and *if*…there's something to talk about."

"If you don't go bonkers first."

"Let me tell you something. I don't need a helping hand from a…from a drug dealer. You don't have to come to my rescue, okay? I don't have to be part of Frankie's Fan Club. *I'm* the older one here."

"What in the world does that have to do with it?"

Nothing, I thought. Everything. I said, "This is idiotic. Maybe we should just hang up."

He did.

❋

We didn't speak after that for several weeks—a stretch of time that felt much longer, and that made me realize I missed him even more now than before I'd moved to Tallahassee. I felt as if I'd sworn off a particular food, only to find I'd been drawing some crucial nutrient from it.

I started noticing gay people almost everywhere I looked. They grouped together in the cafeteria. They hung out on the grass between the English and humanities buildings. I hovered near them. Of course, I had no more chance of being subsumed than a pilot fish has of being absorbed by the skin of a shark, but the fact that I was thinking about them seemed a step in the right direction.

One afternoon, I saw a flyer on a campus bulletin board for "New Wave Night" at a bar called Diggs, and I got brave enough to consider going. Diggs was the only gay dance club in Tallahassee. Monday was their slowest night, and the New Wave angle was their attempt to lure a wider client base—all of which I'd learned from Frankie ("New Wave" in a gay bar ad equals "straight," he'd told me, rolling his eyes). I had no one to go with, but if I could get myself through the door, I thought, I could safely mingle in a "mixed" crowd. I took a bus downtown to a quiet grid of streets behind the Capitol building. As I walked toward the club, its unmarked door opened and closed with foot traffic, the music wheezing out and drawing in as if from an accordion. A woman behind a counter, standing in front of a spice rack of poppers, said, "Not so fast, sweetheart." I stopped, momentarily convinced that it was her job to ask me whether I was gay or straight. "Two bucks," she said.

"Absolutely." I scrambled for my wallet. "The New Wave cover charge, right? It's a bargain, you know, if you're really bored and you've just got to get out. I love this song."

She smiled warmly and said, "Exhale, honey."

Most of the first level, including the dance floor, was empty. I walked upstairs to a large, open room with a scattering of round tables and a center bar, over which spun an illuminated, multicolored soccer ball. I bought a beer and anchored myself against a drink rail along the back wall, and from that darkened vantage point I watched the crowd. There was a circle of guys in fraternity sweatshirts and baseball caps regaling one another with arm punches. There was a straight couple making out against a pool table, and a gay couple that appeared to have fallen asleep in a corner booth. There were a few loners who sipped drinks and stared at a video screen playing a muted rerun of *Remington Steele*.

I recognized most of the songs: British, androgynous sass I'd come to like. I nursed the beer and watched one of the guys sitting at the bar bobbing his head to the music. He had white-blond hair and was dressed in jeans and a T-shirt that read HAVE A NICE DAY on the back. His face was turned away from the screen. I shifted my focus to the far end of the room and saw what had captured his attention.

In the middle of the circle of fraternity boys, a pair of legs had been hoisted. As the boys whooped and cheered, the legs came together, topped by a pair of sneakers, their toes aimed at the ceiling. Even in the swirl of colored lights, I could see that the sneakers were red, with white stripes. The boys clapped and backed away to make room, and there was Margolis, his hands gripping the edges of a table, his arms bulging from his wrists to his shoulders.

I looked back at the blond sitting at the bar. He made two distinct claps with his hands. Then he turned abruptly away from the spectacle and from the video screen, planting his elbows on either side of his glass, and at the same moment that he noticed me, I recognized him.

I had the crazy notion that he was in disguise, and was following me. He wasn't. He was just as surprised to see me as I was him, and I'd like to think that if I hadn't moved, he would have come over to where I was standing. But it suddenly became important for me to be the one who approached first. When I reached the corner of the bar, Frankie spoke, and I could tell the moment he did that he was a little drunk. "Are you lost?"

"No. What do you think of that?" I indicated the inverted Margolis.

"I think he's a closet case."

The remark stung, and was probably meant to. "He's not a closet case."

"Well, he's not out. Not in khakis and a tank top, sorry."

"Maybe he's straight. Is that even a possibility?"

"Nope." Frankie stared forward now. Behind him, Margolis

walked his hands around the table, his shoes turning like a pair of giraffe heads.

"It's really easy for you, isn't it? You practically sent a telegram ahead of your birth telling everyone you're gay, and the rest of us—" I stopped myself.

He glanced up. "Yes?"

"That guy happens to be a friend of mine," I said. "I happen to know him."

"Go back to what you were saying about 'the rest of us.'"

"A *good* friend of mine," I said, sounding ridiculous even to myself. "Why do you want to needle me? Why are you such a prince with everyone else, but all you want to do with me is poke, poke, poke?"

He looked forward again and shrugged. "I like you best."

Margolis dropped his legs and dismounted the table without much grace. One of his friends handed him a beer. Another handed him his glasses.

Watching him, and keeping Frankie in the corner of my eye, I said, "Then let me go at my own pace."

He sipped through the little red straw in his glass. "I will if you will."

"That's not the same. What you're doing is dangerous. I'm genuinely worried about you."

"What, my worries aren't genuine? You think I'm just faking interest? Tell me what the deal is with you and the acrobat."

"Nothing."

"See? What am I supposed to do with that? You're so mysterious, I can't stand it."

"Mysterious?" I huffed. "I haven't understood you since you were *five*."

"It's like you think I can't handle whatever you're doing," he said. "Well, guess what? I can handle it fine. *Excuse* me."

He'd gotten louder; I thought he was about to start yelling. But he leaned sideways across the empty stools and reached for Margolis, who was walking past us on his way to the rest room. Frankie's fingers brushed his forearm.

"Sorry. Just one second. My friend here knows you, apparently quite well, but he's too shy to introduce us."

"Frankie, shut up."

The blood was still swirling behind Margolis's face from being upside down for so long. He squinted at me through his glasses.

"I told you I didn't want to see you," he said in a low rasp. He glanced across the room, where his friends were filing outside onto the patio. "I told you to get lost."

"Wow." Frankie darted his eyes between the two of us. "You *do* know each other."

"I didn't know you were here," I told Margolis.

"Bullshit."

"You dated," Frankie said. "Jeez, you two *dated*. I can hear it in your voices." He poked a finger into my ribs playfully. "You've been leading a secret life!"

"I have *not*."

"*Look,*" Margolis sneered at Frankie, "why don't the two of you kiss and make up, because *he's* a freak, and *you* can have him."

"We're not a couple," I said. I could have been addressing either one of them.

"*I don't care!*" Margolis was practically spitting now, his anger verging on panic. "Don't talk to me. I'm here with friends, do you understand that? *They* wanted to come, and they dragged me along. I knew this whole 'straight night' thing was bullshit."

Frankie received all this with a certain alarm, and then lost interest. He gave me a glance that hovered between commiseration and conspiracy—a glance that I instantly loved him for—and, turning back to his drink, said, "Aw, go stand on your head."

It was so appropriate, so simple and well delivered, I couldn't help but laugh.

Margolis pushed him off his stool.

The rest happened very quickly. Frankie was still in the act of falling (his somewhat stewed body rolling down to the floor with a harmless finesse no sober muscle horse could have ever achieved) when I dropped my beer and shoved Margolis as hard as I could. He stumbled backward only half a step, but it was enough to lock one of his sneakers around a leg of the nearest barstool, and when he started toward me, the stool went with him. It tipped and slid up his shin; he went down with a crash. Frankie was on his back, laughing. Margolis thrashed about and cursed and brought down several more stools.

A bouncer who looked like a circus strongman appeared out of nowhere, hauled Margolis and Frankie to their feet, and walked the three of us downstairs to the front door. Margolis got mouthy, and after he'd been tossed outside, I pleaded with the bouncer to let us stay or we'd surely be pummeled as soon as we stepped onto the sidewalk. The bouncer asked me if I had any money. I told him yes, thinking he wanted a bribe, but he called us a cab, which took nearly thirty minutes to arrive and cost a relative fortune, but got us home safely. On the way there, I told Frankie about my library men's-room encounter with the trapeze artist and my subsequent obsession, and he just laughed, and continued laughing all the way to McGarry Hall.

✳

Within a year, Frankie picked up his colored pencils and compass and protractor again, and resumed designing spaceships on his exam sheets. After one very bad night spent on a sub-par gelatin dot of acid, he abruptly stopped taking drugs of any kind, eschewing even aspirin and caffeine. When the appearance of German measles rocked the campus, Frankie was one of the few students suspended from classes because he wouldn't get immunized. Ultimately, this antidrug resolve brought on his refusal to take AZT in the early days of the AIDS crisis (before anyone knew that taking AZT alone could kill you). In short, his weirdness saved his life.

I endured another half a semester in McGarry Hall until I could get myself transferred to one of the older dorms, where it should have turned out that no matter where you lived, there were troublemakers, but where, in fact, it only confirmed that McGarry was full of degenerates. I walked around campus with a mortal and eventually dwindling fear of running into Margolis, until, one evening during my senior year, I found myself sitting next to him in a gay discussion group (he pretended not to recognize me; I didn't bring it up). In terms of romance, during our college years, neither I nor Frankie would have any relationships that lasted longer than a month.

We did, however, become pals for a while.

We didn't know we'd been banned from Diggs for fighting until we tried to get back in. Frankie suggested that we dye our hair in order to disguise ourselves. He turned me into a redhead, and from the same bottle he'd used to create that patch that had made people call him Simon, he went entirely blue, right down to his eyebrows. And he looked fantastic.

A Door in St. Augustine

2 0 0 2

"This place is so...*faisandé*," the boy says, and then nods in agreement with himself. The end of his chin is whiskered—a wiry, meager attempt at a goatee—but the face above it is smooth and clean, his cheeks and nose slightly sunburned, his light-brown hair gelled into a mop. He lifts an eyebrow as he glances around the room: at the Moorish arches cut through the far wall, at the columns flecked with remnants of gold leaf, at the shallow midnight-blue dome set into the ceiling, its plaster striated with cracks that emanate from a chain supporting a teardrop chandelier. "That's French for when they hang a pheasant up by its feet and, like, let it rot until they can scoop the meat off with a spoon," he says. "Perfect, right?" He bends forward and, without using his hands, brings his lips to the beer in front of him. An instrumental from *Camelot* trickles from a pair of hidden speakers. Overlapping this, a faint, rhythmic scratching issues from the Discman headphones around his neck.

He's taken the last chair at the bar, closest to Karen, who sits at a round marble table near the window. Other than the two of them, the bartender, and a small silver-haired man in a powder-blue suit seated on a sofa next to a grand piano, the cavernous room is empty. The boy's tennis shoes knock lightly against a backpack nearly half his size propped against the brass foot rail. With a beer-foam mustache outlining his upper lip, he looks at Karen and, as if the two of them have been exchanging remarks, says, "I mean that in a good way. Most of the old grand hotels in the South have been chewed up by fat-cat millionaires looking for a tax write-off. Those guys always want to gut the place and 'redo' it, you know, all that faux marble, those faux murals they paint in the morning and then, like, rub with sandpaper in the afternoon to make them look old. When, really, something's nice when it's just *naturally* old, you know? Like this place. It's kind of crumbly, kind of falling apart, but it's natural. It's like an old face."

Karen is thirty-nine by a week and two days: old enough to be the boy's parent. She meets his gaze out of politeness and does her best to maintain a reserved, neutral smile. One of her hands holds her glass and the other rests low on her thigh, making sure her skirt is as close to her knees as she can get it before she crosses her legs.

"I like older faces," the boy clarifies, smiling back.

She doesn't know what to say, feels it might not be proper to say anything, just as it isn't proper to be here, in St. Augustine, in the bar of the Lutie Matanzas Hotel. Still, the boy, for some reason, holds his smile in anticipation of her response, and she is prepared to say *So do I,* for lack of anything else, when a voice from across the room declares, "You won't."

The boy looks over his shoulder. "Won't what?"

"Like old faces. Not when you see one in the mirror."

The voice is vowel-heavy, more like what Karen has become accustomed to in her current life in Savannah than what she remembers from her Florida childhood. It belongs to the little silver-haired man who easily looks old enough to be *her* parent. He crosses his legs just as Karen is crossing hers and, with the slightest movement of one hand, rattles the ice in his highball glass.

The boy glances at Karen in an assumed alliance. "It was a metaphor."

"Your metaphor is moot. This hotel is already sold."

Karen watches the boy frown as he turns off his Discman. "No way."

"I'm afraid so," the man says calmly. "And while I do have plans to remodel, I would hardly call myself a *fat* cat."

The boy looks to the bartender, but she, a young woman in a starched white shirt and yellow bow tie, only confirms this—and her alliance to her new employer—by nodding and smiling professionally.

An awkward silence ensues. Karen glances at the three of them, in turn, and is alarmed to find them all looking back at her. She has the urge to let go of her club soda and flee the room.

"No *drastic* remodeling, of course," the little man tells her warmly. "A few nips, a couple of tucks. Just because we're married to gravity doesn't mean we can't cheat with style."

✳

She finally got away from her hometown when she was twenty-one, but only as far as Kissimmee. She arrived with no real money, no plans other than being someplace that wasn't Merritt Island, and she festered there in the humidity for the next six years, working in delis and restaurants. For a while, she shared an apartment with a pair of hard-edged girls who were both named Becky and who called themselves Splitsville. It turned out that Splitsville had been the name of a strip joint where the Beckys had worked, and since the club was now closed, their plan was to keep the name and start up a freelance strip troupe of their own. Birthdays and bachelor parties. No slutty stuff, they emphasized. Just dancing and being friendly and getting naked—slowly—while their friend Anthony manned the tape deck and doubled as security. Two hundred dollars for two hours work. They taught her how it was done in their living room (Anthony gave pointers), and Karen did it professionally—once. The event was a retirement party for the CEO of a Kissimmee land development company. The CEO, in the middle of Karen's disrobement, passed out, but the CFO tried to join the dance and perform his own drunken striptease. In one flailing swoop he got his ankles twisted in his trousers, went down on a marble coffee table, and took Karen with him, shattering his kneecap and vomiting across her neck.

She saw the evening as an omen: get out of Kissimmee.

She moved to Orlando, feeling more than ever like a loser girl from the sticks who would never amount to anything. She took her own apartment and a hostessing job at Buffalo Jack's—a position that rescued her from waiting tables but chained her to a maître d' stand in a cowgirl costume. Another four years passed without seasons, highlights, or milestones. She had always worked, had tried to live frugally, but she'd acquired over $18,000 in credit card debt. She had mildew growing in the closet of her apartment, and a molar that was changing color and occasionally throbbed but that she had no money for a dentist to examine.

During her break one busy evening, she stood in the ladies' room washing her hands in front of the mirror, glaring at the little white cowgirl hat anchored to her hair with bobby pins. Back behind the maître d' stand, she fantasized about mouthing off to the next customer who walked through the door. *What is this,* she thought of asking, *National Eat Out Night?* The door opened. She smiled.

"Now *that,*" said Daniel James Luckett Jr., "is a pretty smile."

He was from Savannah, in Orlando to attend a convention at one of the nearby hotels. "It's just up I-4," he told her, "a stone's throw." He showed up five consecutive weeknights, always alone. He wanted her to call him D.J. and, when he found out her last name was Ragazzino, told her he never would have guessed it because she didn't look Italian. He chatted about the food, about the area, about the sensible overhaul of the Orlando International Airport. He spent nearly as much time at the maître d' stand as he did at his table. He was tall and trim and solid, with good bone structure and a high, smart-looking forehead. He didn't seem to blink, though after a while she realized that of course he blinked; it was just that his eyes were set a fraction wider than most people's, his gaze slightly—and perpetually—intense. He wore his clothes like a mannequin: free of wrinkles and carefully tucked, as if a team of people had dressed him moments before he walked through the door. She felt like an idiot in her cowgirl uniform. On Friday, after he'd paid his check and was telling her good night, she complimented his tie, then touched the red bandanna knotted around her neck and said, "I hate this thing."

"*Hate*'s a strong word." He gazed at the bandanna as if transfixed by it. Then, perking up, he said, "I'm going to take a chance here. My convention is over, but I don't go back to Savannah till Monday. Now, you just answer honestly. Whatever you say is okay. Would you like to go to Disney World with me?"

✳

The boy hops down from the bar chair and then hops up again, backward, as if mounting a horse. He folds his arms over the brass studs that outline the chair's leather back and studies the little man on the sofa.

"So, how many hotels do you own?"

"Three. Not counting this one."

"All in Florida?"

The man peers at his drink, then drains what's left of it. "I feel like I shouldn't be forthcoming," he says casually to Karen. "He looks like an activist, doesn't he? For all I know, he belongs to some Greenpeace for hotels."

"That's funny," the boy says. He pulls his wallet from his back pocket and shows the man—and Karen—his Greenpeace membership card. "Registered Green Party, too. And, of course, a dues-paying member of..." The end of this sentence is his ACLU card, raised before them like the apogee of a magic trick.

"Good Lord, the boy's practically a Soviet." The little man lifts his glass as if raising a toast to the bartender. She comes out with a bottle.

"Drives my dad crazy," the boy says, putting away his wallet. "Talk about *faisandé*. The man's entire set of political beliefs—which are totally wrapped up in ZOG paranoia—went into overdrive on 9/11. He thinks al-Qaeda has infiltrated Greenpeace. He really believes that! If you're liberal, you're vulnerable, he says."

"Explain 'ZOG.'"

"The Zionist Occupation Government. The *real* government, if you listen to my dad. As in, even the White House answers to ZOG."

"Oh, yes," the little man says, as if recognizing a name he'd once heard. "I always forget I'm a ZOG-ist. My card is around here somewhere." He taps the breast of his suit coat and winks at Karen. "And you, Ms...."

"Smith," Karen lies.

"Ms. Smith," the little man says. The hand that was pretending to search his coat touches the buttons of his shirt. "Landon Jessup. And I have no intention of asking your political affiliations; you've been so kind and silent. But, as the newly established proprietor of the Lutie Matanzas Hotel, I would like to offer you a drink."

She no longer has any idea what her political beliefs are. She is, at best, selectively informed about the world, knows only what spills into the house through the one approved television channel and the commentary provided by her husband. The boy is looking at her with some kind of interest she can't fathom. Mr. Jessup, who has been kind enough not to solicit a political statement from her, is smiling, waiting for her to respond to his offer. "Thank you," she says, "but it's just a club soda, and I'm fine."

"Todd Gladbach." The boy waves at the two of them. "Nice to meet you both. Lager?"

"Please, Hannah," Mr. Jessup says, "give the boy another lager. We'll assume if he's old enough to vote Green, he's old enough to drink. Is that Gladbach of the Maryland Gladbachs?"

"Yep," Todd says.

"The Maryland drywall Gladbachs?"

"Right again."

"Well, forgive me for asking, but what business do you have being critical of hotel renovators who utilize, among other materials, a substantial amount of *drywall*?"

"I hate the family business," Todd says. "I *hate* it. It stands for everything that's wrong with this country. Minimum wages, outsourcing, union-busting, a complete disregard for architectural aestheticism, not to mention what it's doing to the environment, all in the name of lining people's pockets."

"Pockets like your father's."

"Exactly."

"And have you stood firm on your political beliefs and renounced the family money?"

"I will," Todd says, jumping on the question. "As soon as my book comes out. I have to finish my research, first, is all. I need travel money."

"I had a hunch you weren't local."

"Nope." He kicks at the backpack behind him with both heels as if he's wearing spurs.

Mr. Jessup runs his eyes around the vast room. "You've chosen some fancy digs for a"—he searches the options and seems to settle on a phrase that is far from his first choice—"rugged type. What is this book about?"

"It's about you."

Consumed with what she shouldn't be doing, preoccupied with the running list in her head of every action she's taken in the last eight hours that she shouldn't have taken, Karen is, at best, half in the room when she hears the boy say this. She pulls out of herself long enough to wonder what sort of book might be written about Mr. Landon Jessup, and how he might react to the writing of it. But then she finds Todd looking directly into her eyes, and hears him say, "You too."

"Well," Mr. Jessup says, "this is exciting. If it's a romance you're writing, let me be the first to say, I'll need some pointers. Not that you," he tells Karen, "wouldn't be motivation enough for a romantic adventure, but I wouldn't exactly call myself the best man for the job. Mr. Gladbach, would you be willing to give me pointers?"

"It's about real people," the boy clarifies, speaking directly to Karen. "It's about post-9/11 insecurities that *seem* to have everything to do with the fear of terrorism but have nothing to do with terrorism at all. How they've purposefully broken down our systems of comfort, and how we've bought into the corporate myth of America and turned it into a psychological safety net. Have you ever read *The Air Conditioned Nightmare*? It'll be like an extension of that; I might call it *The Code Yellow Daydream*. You know, Howdy Doody in the White House. Halliburton as puppeteer. And Mr. and Mrs. Average America just shoveling it all in like a trusty bowl of Wheaties. Tell me that doesn't ring some bells."

"Oh, it'll ring some bells," Mr. Jessup says, glancing up at the teardrop chandelier. "Though I think I liked it better when it was a romance."

"It *is* a romance. It's very sexual." Todd dismounts from his chair and, with one fluid motion of his wiry body, lands himself in the vacant chair at Karen's table, suddenly less than two feet away from her. "But not in a dirty way," he tells her. "Well, okay, it's dirty, but it's tragic, too. It's like *Romeo and Juliet,* only she knows she isn't faking death and he doesn't know he's poisoning himself. It'll be a good read."

The boy's skin is beautiful. She wants to touch his cheek, and at the same time she wants to ask him if his parents know where he is. Are they together? Divorced? Perversely, she wants to know if they cheat or have secrets. There's a minute quake through her body caused by the desire to know and the desire to touch, and its epicenter resides somewhere below her stomach. The bartender is gliding past for a second time with a bottle in her hand. Karen should call Savannah. She wants to use her phone to put the boy in touch with his family. He reaches across the small table, lands his fingertips on her hand, and asks, "Do you read—for pleasure?"

✳

Because her nose was turning red in the sun, Daniel Luckett bought her a hat with a long duck's bill that honked when you squeezed it. When she lost this in the metallic chaos of Space

Mountain, he bought her a hat with dog ears that flapped against her shoulders. She felt silly wearing it, but she couldn't remember the last time a man had bought her something, so she wore it for a few rides, then purposefully forgot it in their scoop-shaped carriage at the Haunted Mansion. "You're going to cost me a fortune in hats!" he said, smiling, steering them toward another shop. "Wait," she said. "I just remembered, I have this." She took a small bottle of sunblock from her purse and rubbed some onto her nose, then gave him a dollop. His fingers left smears of white over his brow and along his hair-line. She laughed and told him he looked like a cupcake, then reached up and smoothed the lotion into his skin.

The day, parceled over different lands, subdivided into historical wormholes and fantastical digressions, seemed to last a thousand hours. She'd been to the park before, every couple of years while growing up, but she didn't mention this, and whether or not he'd been there, too, didn't matter; they continued to swap expressions of surprise and delight. Over burgers in a crowded eatery that was reminiscent of *The Jetsons,* he caught her studying his left hand. "Did I make a mess?" he asked, glancing at his fingers, though what she was looking for was the stripe of pale skin that might, on other days, have been buried beneath a wedding band. A few minutes later, dipping a french fry into a little paper bonnet of mustard, he said, "I wouldn't be here with you today if I was married, you know."

"Oh, I . . . wasn't wondering about that."

"Sure you were. And it's okay. I know there are men who do that sort of thing, but I'm not one of them. I run a clean ship, Karen."

"Well, that's good to know," she said.

"And I'm thirty-five. I'm always up-front about my age—especially since this gray coming in makes me look a little older."

"Thirty-one," she volunteered.

"Gosh, you don't look it. Twenty-five, maybe. I will tell you this much: I was engaged for a while. Fairly recently. To a girl in Savannah."

"Really? For how long?"

He frowned. "Not quite a year." The frown lingered in his mouth a fraction too long; he looked pained. "She and I ... saw the world differently."

"I'm sorry," Karen said.

"No, it had to be. That's just what it was. Anyway"—his eyes brightened—"today is starting to feel like a—well, like a date, I hope you don't mind me saying that, but I thought I'd be up-front. You know, fess up." He mugged again, lifting his brow and flashing his teeth, playing down the moment with a look of exaggerated fright.

"Well, I can fess up to something as well." The words fell from Karen's mouth impulsively; she had only wanted to sound involved in the conversation, but now that she'd offered to di-vulge something, the list of choices felt longer than her reach. She was in debt. She was a high-school dropout. She'd been, for a while, a raving, reckless young woman and had landed her-self in some sticky spots. In fact, it might have been easier to confess what she *hadn't* done (or what hadn't happened to her): clarify which of her many short-lived relationships with men over the years *hadn't* ended in broken engagements or been drowned in boozy bickering or flat-out crashed and burned in altercations involving mild violence, property damage, and, more than once, the police. "My name is really Katherine," she said. "Mary-Katherine. I started going by Karen when I was a teenager, and I still go by it, obviously. But I prefer Katherine." She didn't. And then, suddenly, she did. She wanted to be Katherine, with him. "Kind of a stupid confession," she added.

"That's not a confession at all. It's a beautiful name. Katherine."

In the sluggish line for the Peter Pan ride, she asked him what sort of convention he'd attended, and he told her it was a church thing. He asked her if she went to church. An elaborate network of railings had the line tripling and quadrupling back on itself, so that they were folded up against people on both sides. Karen found herself inches away from a bewigged old woman who had heard the question and was staring at her, waiting for her response. "Sometimes," she lied.

Then, as they were hanging from a track over Neverland, their little ship tilting toward dioramas of piracy and rescue, he leaned into her and said gently, "Catherine Deneuve cries in the night."

It was such a strange comment. Sexy, somehow—as if he were whispering the first of what might become an entire language of obscure, private remarks they would exchange only with each other. A secret code. She gazed over the safety bar of their ship at the shivering statue of a young girl in a light blue dress. "Does she?"

"I'm asking if *you* do."

They rounded the final bend. The pulley suspending them rattled in its track and a treadmill of black rubber appeared beneath them. The mass of people waiting to get onto the ride stared at them like a bemused congregation. She realized what he'd asked her. *Katherine, do you have Christ in your life?*

"No," she said. A young man dressed like a pixie took hold of the safety bar and pulled it back, warning them to be careful as they got out. Daniel—D.J.—knew almost nothing about her. His question alone revealed that, and it made her mind scramble as if it had come under fire. Did she have something even remotely resembling Christ? Was there anything that she really believed in, or could fall back on in a crisis greater than the perennial one that was her life? He took her arm to help her from the ship, his expression hovering somewhere between concern and disappointment.

As they were exiting the pavilion, she said, "I want to." The foot traffic was heavy. He was still holding her arm, gently escorting her through the crowd, and because she liked it, because she couldn't remember ever having been escorted before, she added, "I feel like I should."

"It's the greatest thing on earth," he told her, squeezing her arm. "Honestly, Katherine. It's the most amazing love you'll ever know."

❋

" 'We are all part of creation,' " Todd tells them, " 'all kings, all poets, all musicians; we have only to open up, only to discover what is already there.' "

"Testify, brother," Mr. Jessup says languidly. The side of his face is cradled in one hand, the elbow propped on the arm of the sofa.

"I'm quoting Henry Miller, in *Sexus*. All that stuff they don't want us to know anymore, and that most of us *don't* know, because they've castrated us."

"Oh, *they*," Mr. Jessup says. "They get on my nerves. Ms. Smith, can you imagine the burden of carrying around so much knowledge? And a backpack? In *this* heat?"

"No," Karen says. The boy's hand has remained in the vicinity of hers, and he occasionally taps her wrist as he makes his points. He's serious about what he says; she can see that in his eyes. He's also hitting on her. She can't deny this obvious fact and so tries, instead, to consider the possibility that he might be dangerous, but to little effect.

"The American citizen," he tells her, "is down, but not out. Can I?" He lifts her drink and takes the bar napkin from beneath it. Then he tilts back on two legs of his chair, which has the effect of drawing his crotch out from beneath the table and raising it slightly, featuring it, like an object ready to be unveiled. And, indeed, it is ready; his jeans are baggy, and his enthusiasm is nearly eclipsing his belt buckle. So positioned, he digs a pen from one of his front pockets. Then he lowers himself again, uncaps the pen, and unfolds the napkin. "I can't go everywhere and see everything. I mean, I could, but it would take my whole life; I'd never get the book written. So here's how I'm doing it." The napkin is damp with condensation from her glass. The pen is a felt-tip. As he draws, his lines turn into caterpillars.

"Georgetown," he says, making a dot that immediately becomes a blob, "was my starting point. I was a poli-sci major, but I dropped out right before Christmas. Going to classes was like going through a whole chain of restaurants where they pre-chewed your food and were just waiting to shove it in your mouth. Hello? No. So I went south, did Amtrak for a while, and a Greyhound for six hours, which was totally Jon Voight because this lady wouldn't let me turn off the reading light and kept complaining about my headphones. I did some walking, some hitchhiking, and voilà, YOU ARE HERE." He draws an arrow at his approximation of the northeast coast of Florida. "And I'm going to keep moving: down to the Keys, back up the gulf side, across the bottom of Texas and up the California coast. Then I'm heading straight across the top all the way to Maine, and back down to D.C. Assuming Dad hasn't cut me off by that point, I'm going to cross the middle of the country—in a car, if I can find one of those great old convertibles—then backtrack to the middle, head up to the Canadian border, and straight down to the Rio Grande. That way, I've done the perimeter and a cross-section, which should be a pretty good representation of who's out there."

"Hold that up," Mr. Jessup says from the sofa.

Todd lifts the now ink-sodden napkin and twists around in his chair to display it.

"I feel like I'm at a pattern party," Mr. Jessup declares. "Honestly, son, besides sounding dreadful, that voyage would use a whole lot of gas."

"It only sounds dreadful because ninety-nine out of a hundred people would be too terrified to do it."

"Actually, it's a dreadful idea because ninety-nine out of a hundred people are uncivilized—and dull—and you'd have to see them, and talk to them, town after town."

"That's the whole point," Todd says, smiling at Karen. "Find out what's passing for intimacy these days. Find out how fear and mistrust and depression have practically become . . . aphrodisiacs."

She stays in this moment, inside the parameters of his gaze, until she hears Mr. Jessup make a throat-clearing noise that diffuses into a groan. "Excuse me," she says, pushing away from the newly generated gravity of the room. She takes her purse and walks the length of the bar, the blood rushing out of her brain from having risen so abruptly, her eyes shifting right and left until finally she sees a short hallway that leads to the rest rooms. She opens her purse and digs for her cell phone. But at the last second she puts the phone away and veers off to the door marked with a large brass W.

The powder room is oval and the pale lavender color of Wellbutrin. There is a vanity on either side, and their mirrors play off each other as she passes between them, cloning her in both directions like the front line of an army that is simultaneously advancing and retreating. She pushes through the inner door to a room covered in black and white tiles, but stops at the row of stalls. Nervousness, or panic, has absorbed whatever liquid she's ingested: there is nothing to pass out of her. There is only a needling sensation—a little like thirst and a little like hunger.

Back in the bar, Mr. Jessup is still perched at one end of the sofa with his face cradled in one hand, but his eyes have closed. The bartender is nowhere to be seen. Todd has pulled his back-pack over to the little table and is sitting with his legs on either side of it, watching Karen as she crosses the room. The intensity of his gaze is still there, and she's thankful that she's found enough bravado to squeeze a little more life out of the impulse that made her leave Savannah. She looks at Mr. Jessup as she sits down and pretends to have just noticed his dozing. She mouths the words, *I think he's asleep.*

"Yeah." Todd hoists one end of his mouth into a grin. "It must be exhausting to be that cynical."

"He's nice," Karen says, in case the little man is still registering.

"Anyway, you're just the sort of person I want for my book. I need real people who . . . what's your job, anyway?"

"My job?"

"Like, for a living. What do you do?"

"I don't have a profession," she admits.

"Are you rich?" he asks, frowning.

"No."

"Good. That's exactly what I'm *not* going for."

"I'm . . ." She hates *housewife,* and while *homemaker* is more accurate, the word itself is like an Easter egg tinted gray from having been dipped into the pastel voice of nearly every woman she knows. "I don't have a job at the moment."

He's already nodding. "I understand. The economy's in the toilet. All those tax refund checks went out right before the World Trade Center, and then, boom, the country's on its ass. I mean, when the dust settled, they had all these misdirected 're-venge' plans in place, and all these speeches prepared about here's what we're going to do to defend democracy—but no plan for helping ordinary people. And who's standing up and asking the question, Why did 9/11 happen? I mean, who said anything at all about *why*?"

The president did; Karen saw him do it on television. He asked the question, and then answered it by saying terrorists hated freedom. Jerry Falwell asked it, and said the homosexuals and abortionists had brought the attack on the rest of the country. The pastor of her church asked it loudly, over and over, and then said Satan himself had steered the planes because the Twin Towers symbolized a "righteous, prosperous people." But she doubts this is what Todd is after.

"Noam Chomsky," he whispers. "Gore Vidal. Susan Sontag—and, man, she took a beating for it. Meanwhile, Mr. and Mrs. Average Joe have their flags out and their sights set on their next SUV, and they don't really care why it happened. I don't mean to include you in that. What I mean is, I don't know what you—or your husband—drive. Have you mentioned a husband?"

The boy has a technique, she'll give him that much. He's pushing his crotch against his backpack. She says, "I haven't."

"You know"—he glances up at the chandelier as if it might be bugged, then leans into her until she can smell the beer on his breath—"I'm staying here. I have a room."

"Do you?"

"We probably wouldn't risk ... bothering anybody ... if we talked up there."

She realizes now that Mr. Jessup was the last vestige of propriety in her afternoon. Simply by closing his eyes, he has gone from being a charming, silver-tongued host to a drugged watchdog. "I don't know," she says, reaching for her empty glass. "I haven't made up my mind about staying."

Todd smiles. He leans in closer. "You're lying."

❊

They didn't sleep together. They didn't even kiss each other goodbye. The day after their trip to Disney World, she drove him to the airport and saw him to the gate, where he boarded a plane back to Savannah, and when she started her car in the parking lot, she realized he'd set her radio to a religious station out of Tampa. She kept it there because it reminded her of D.J. Some of it made her laugh. One song in particular sounded like a call to cannibalism, because the only words were "Jesus is good, feast on Him." But there was another song they played repeatedly, about a woman who went to bed "on the good side of the Lord," died in her sleep, and woke up in heaven's court-yard being serenaded by angels. The song was catchy enough to sink into Karen's head, and she caught herself humming it sometimes.

D.J. flew back down to Orlando twice more (they went to Epcot Center and SeaWorld), then bought her a ticket to Sa-vannah for a weekend. They took the historic tours and visited the tile company where he worked as a sales manager. She slept in his guest bedroom. He asked her politely, almost ceremoni-ously, if she would attend church with him, and when they ar-rived that Sunday there was a full-fledged revival under way, and people there already knew her name.

"Katherine," an attractive, portly man said, smiling, his eyes glistening as if she were a family member whom he'd feared dead, "welcome." She was smiled at and hugged more in that one afternoon than in all her previous days combined. A line formed in one of the aisles that pie-wedged the massive congre-gation, and D.J. squeezed her shoulders in the fold of his arm and said, "if you really want to do this, we're here for you." Her eyes followed the line up to the stage, where the pastor had re-moved his suit coat and was pivoting about in a white shirt turned the color of a peach from perspiration, shouting into a microphone he held so close to his mouth that the sound of his lips scraping the mesh dominated the speakers. A pair of suited church members steered the people in line onto the stage. Another pair presented them to the pastor, who shouted into their faces and mashed the heel of his free hand against their foreheads, causing them to fall backward into the arms of yet another pair of church members, one of whom held a second microphone to the mouths of the saved. As they collapsed, these everyday-looking women and men began to prattle like auctioneers.

Karen went with it. She felt like a spectacle, and then like a failure, for as that sweaty hand swung like a door into her face, she knew nothing was going to pour out of her, and when it hit her forehead and she fell, nothing did. So she faked it. But when she faked it, she felt . . . something. Halfway through her babbling, some other force took over, and by the time they were holding her shoulders a foot off the floor, speaking encouragement into her ears and extending her mike time as if she were a jazz musician running with a solo, her tongue was writhing and her lips were spasming and her jaw was jumping around in what amounted to the closest sensation she'd had to an orgasm in years. In his home that night, D.J. got teary-eyed describing what it was like to witness the event. Then he kissed her, told her he loved her, and, to her great surprise and relief, began to help her out of her clothes.

In the morning he proposed.

It was only after she'd accepted, and after they'd prayed together to ask God's forgiveness for jumping the gun, that he eagerly inquired about her family. She no longer ranked herself above any of them, as she'd done when she was a teenager; in fact, her opinion of herself was far lower than her assessment of anyone else in her family—except maybe her stepfather. Still, she didn't have it in her to conjure them up for D.J. and then watch the scaffold of his handsome face begin to collapse one joint at a time as she filled his head with this roster of "sinners" from which she'd sprung. She considered inventing entirely new people, but the logistics of maintaining such a charade seemed overwhelming to her, and doomed to failure.

Her parents, she told him, were dead. Her father when she was a teenager; her mother two years ago, from cancer. She had no siblings.

"Sweet babe," he said, tearing up. "Sweet babe." He put his arms around her.

He didn't want her touching herself. He embraced the idea of oral sex if he was the recipient but not the other way around (in fact, he wouldn't touch her vagina with anything but his penis), and he pulled the plug on the whole production if she tried to talk dirty. But he loved her—fiercely, sincerely. She would maintain the household, but a job, he told her, was out of the question. There was the home-based education of their future children to consider, and for that, she should save her energy. Meanwhile, he wanted to help her make peace with the loss of her family. God saw straight into this great void in her life, D.J. said, and He intended to fill it.

※

"I don't understand guys freaking out about going bald," the boy says, studying the dark, tousled density of his hair in the mirror. "Henry Miller? Brilliant writer, *genius,* a real ladies' man—and bald as an egg. You know why women didn't care? Because *he* didn't care. It's just like a job interview: you know you've got flaws, you know you're not perfect, but that stuff doesn't matter if you know you can do the job. So you walk in with confidence and say what you have to say. Speaking of that, Miller was hardly your average Joe because he was 'diabolically truthful,' but he got *his* job done. 'I see a long night settling in and that mushroom which has poisoned the world withering at the roots.' You know what he was referring to?"

Stop talking, she thinks. She's sitting with her legs crossed on the low table meant for a suitcase at the foot of the bed. Her purse is beside her. His backpack is on the floor next to the closet.

"America," Todd says, turning around to face her. With his arms hanging limp at his sides, he lifts one foot, then the other, knocking his heels against the carpet and causing both his sneakers to fold up and fall off.

She's done this before: kicked away from who she thought she was, jumped into who she thought she wasn't. She's found herself, repeatedly, in a skin that isn't hers. In the eight years that she's been married to D.J., she's kissed him goodbye on his way to work in the morning and then gotten into her car and driven straight out of Savannah no less than a dozen times. Always heading south, into Florida. Sometimes to a restaurant, sometimes to a bar, occasionally to a hotel room and a situation like this one. D.J., in a way, is a willing participant in these ventures. If she isn't there when he gets home from work, if she pulls into the driveway long after she should have started preparing dinner, he asks where she's been, but he doesn't press for more information when she responds, "On a drive." "The sky was so beautiful today," she sometimes adds. Or "I've never seen leaves so green." Like any sensible person, he wants his life to hold together, and like Karen, he is willing to settle for imperfection in order to make that happen. With him, she has pretended to pray for pregnancy. Privately, she prays for the opposite. They've continued to attend church and have become pillars of the community. There have been seven subsequent revivals. He's a good husband, she loves him, and the fact that she has remained childless all these years has become the strongest confirmation of her own brand of faith. God, she believes, understands.

"You told me you were unemployed," Todd reminds her, crossing his arms over his waist and lifting his T-shirt above his ribs, where it bunches up level with his collarbone for a moment, then slips off his head, resetting the mop of his hair. His torso is pale and smooth, just slightly meaty. "You didn't say what it was you used to do."

"It doesn't matter."

"Sure it does. For my book." He unbuttons his jeans. They drop to his ankles. He steps out of them, kicks them aside, and, using his toes, pulls off his socks and tosses them on top of the jeans. He stands before her on display: smiling, with his arms held wide and his erection pulling the waistband of his shorts away from his stomach. Then he moves as if to step toward her.

She lifts the hand that's been resting on her knee. "That's good."

"You think?" the boy asks, glancing down. "I've never had any complaints."

"I mean, that's good, right there. Stop." He's as close to her now as when they were sitting at the table. His arms drift down to his sides. "You like to talk," she tells him.

"I guess."

"But you don't swear, do you?"

"Mmm, not around ladies. I try not to. Hey, are you going to get naked?"

"You can swear around me."

He shrugs. "Okay."

"I'm telling you to." She feels a jurisdiction over him in a way that is almost parental. "In fact, Todd, I don't want to hear you say anything else unless you're swearing."

"Wow," he says. And then, "Damn."

She motions for him to lower his shorts, and he shucks them

halfway down his thighs. His cock stands out of proportion to his skinny body like a bowsprit on a canoe. When he tries to move forward again, she shakes her head no. With one hand, she suggests that he take hold of himself; with the other, she unzips her skirt.

"Wow," he says excitedly, "you just never know, do you?"

She cuts him a glance.

"Damn," he says.

An hour later, the sun just starting to set beyond the curtains and the boy asleep in the wingback chair in the corner, she opens the door and steps out of the room. Mr. Jessup stands in the hall, sideways to a wall sconce that has failed to illuminate. He wiggles its stem and taps its glass shell with a fingernail. When he looks over, he squints as if half-recognizing her through a haze of elapsed time. "*Ms.* Smith." He sounds mildly shocked. His focus shifts, then shifts again, until he is looking past her into the room, where a bare shoulder is visible in the chair. "You depraved soul," he says calmly, and though his lips try to close around a nugget of disapproval, he grins. "You're old enough to be that boy's lover."

"It's a very nice hotel," she says, closing the door behind her. "I'll recommend it to my friends."

"Please do."

She walks past him, down the hall, through the lobby and the grand front doors. The air outside is so hot and damp, it's almost liquid. Two hours to Savannah, if the traffic isn't heavy. She'll get home just as he's finishing a dinner of leftovers. She'll kiss his cheek, squeeze his hand, and tell him the sky was beautiful today. And there'll be no arguing with that, because it's true.

There's Nothing Wrong with Gus

2000

On Sunday afternoon, I eat lunch at the Red Lobster because there's no food in the house, and I have one of those ridiculously tall, narrow beers that looks like it's going to tip over just sitting there. The beer loosens my brain a little, and for the third time in as many days I catch myself thinking about calling Teresa.

I do other things instead. I coast by my old house. I get an ice cream cone at the Dairy Queen where we used to take the kids. And for the first time in twenty-five years I drive out to Jetty Park—one of the places I surrendered after the divorce—and mosey around the pavilion in a sugary, beer-fuzzed haze.

The little girl in front of me at the snack bar is maybe eight years old. She's barefoot and wearing a lime green bathing suit, her hair knotted in a thick braid that hangs down her back. Clutching a dollar and drumming both hands against the counter, she says, "Skittles, please, Skittles, please, Skittles, please," until the man hands over the candy and takes her money. She skips away.

I buy a ginger ale and carry it up to the roof of the pavilion.

People are standing around in the sun, most of them on the east side, looking out at the ocean. I take a spot along the railing and just stand there along with them. On one side of me, a young couple is having an argument next to a baby stroller. On the other side is a pair of ancients—so old, they're probably past all arguments. The husband has on a Doc Holliday–style straw hat and a pair of sunglasses as wide as welder's goggles. His hands are resting on the sun-bleached wood of the railing, and he appears mesmerized by the sight of the Atlantic—though my guess is he's just old and no longer holds his mouth closed. His wife watches the ocean as if she's waiting for it to impress her.

Suddenly, the young woman raises her voice over the breeze and the surf. "You know, if you're going to contradict every single thing I say, then maybe we should just drop the subject."

"You're doing it again," the young man says.

"Doing what?"

"Channeling your mother when she's not even dead."

"That's it, I'm through," she says, glancing down. "The baby's going to fry if you don't get him out of the sun."

The baby's wearing orange sunglasses. His hands are holding a little steering wheel mounted to the front of the stroller, and his head is leaning to one side. He looks like a miniature drunk driver.

The young man uses his foot to drag the stroller into his shadow and says, "He's not *in* the sun."

"Another contradiction?" the woman snaps.

A marital fight is the last thing I feel like witnessing right now, so I head back down the stairs.

❄

Nothing looks the way I remember it. They've dredged sand from the bottom of the ocean and added it to the beach, and it's twice as wide as it used to be. The port's been gutted into a pair of turning basins for cruise ships. Even the jetty's been renovated with a fancy cement overlay and metal railings. My loafers take in sand as I walk toward it.

A pair of chunky retirees are parked a little ways down the cement walk, fishing and watching a golf game on a battery-operated television. Farther out on the jetty is a foursome of rednecks: two men, two women, six poles. They've staked out a little area for themselves with Budweiser cans, a bait bucket, and a radio playing one of those "long highway back to you" songs. They have tattoos all over their backs, even the women.

I walk past them and lean into the railing.

One of the rednecks grins in my direction. He tilts a beer can up to his lips and drinks. Then he says, "When's your birthday?"

"Me? October."

"Mine's today."

The woman next to him makes a remark about how everyone on the goddamn beach already knows it's his birthday. She suggests he tell the goddamn fish. "I'm sure they'd like to know."

"Hey, guess what?" he asks her.

"What?"

"Chicken's butt." He turns back to me. "You know what time I was born?"

I shake my head.

"Twelve minutes after midnight. Twelve-twelve. How's that for a lucky number?"

Over his shoulder, a cruise ship is inching toward us. It gets bigger and bigger as it steers away from the port and into the channel. There hardly seems room for it. On the deck, passengers are waving at us, the last land-bound faces they'll see before leaving the coast behind. As the ship creeps past the jetty, the redneck who announced his birthday stares at it and holds up his middle finger for a solid minute.

*

"Crab, please, crab, please, crab, please," a voice says. I look farther down the jetty, and there's the little girl in the lime green swimsuit, clutching her bag of Skittles and ducking under the railing. She's alone, from what I can tell. I walk farther out until I'm even with her, and by then she's several yards out from the walkway, her legs apart and her bare feet resting on two slanted rocks.

"Miss," I call to her. She doesn't look up. She's bending over, reaching into one of the crevices. "Little girl," I say. And then, "Hey!" for it seems certain she'll topple headfirst down the jetty.

She looks up and says, *"What?"*

"You should come back to the walkway," I say. "You're not supposed to be out there."

"Who are you, Mr. Cocoa Beach?"

"I'm Mr. Kerrigan," I say. "Come on, now, you don't want to get in trouble. It's dangerous on these rocks."

"I'm trying to catch a crab," she says, looking down around her feet.

I tell her the crab is gone. I tell her I saw it jump off the jetty and swim away, that it was probably following the cruise ship. She rolls her eyes at that one. Then, as graceful as a gazelle on a mountainside, she hops here and there, arms out, braid swinging, and returns to the walkway. She says, "You're nosy."

Fair enough, I think. I ask where her parents are.

"Dead!" she cries in a delighted voice. "Everyone's dead!" She skips back up the walk, past the rednecks and the chubby retirees, all the way to the steps and then down onto the sand.

I watch after her, thinking how Teresa would have had a heart attack right there on the spot if one of our kids had climbed out onto the jetty like that. She once read an article about how sharks eat the small fish that feed off jetty rocks, and from then on we had to walk clear down to the other side of the beach before the kids could get in the water. She read about rocket fuel sweeping outward when it exploded, and that was the end of our viewing the launches from the employees-only field, a mile away from the launchpad. "You know," I'd told her, "it would take a *lot* of burning rocket fuel to spread out over a mile." But logic like that didn't matter, once she'd made up her mind.

I follow the little girl as she ambles along the waterline, and she looks back every so often. I see her bend over and draw something in the wet sand with her finger. She skips on, and when I reach the spot where she's been, I see the word HI!

She charges straight into a resting flock of seagulls and sends them flapping. She bends over and writes in the sand again. When I reach the spot, it reads, S'UP, OLD MAN!

The next message, several yards ahead, reads, WHERE AM I?

I look around. She isn't farther down the beach. I scan the families separated by twisted ropes of seaweed. A woman is shaking out a blanket, and as it drifts onto the sand, I see the little girl squatting and watching me, seesawing her shoulders in the air. She laughs, then jumps up and runs.

Long before I catch up with her—I'm trying to maintain a casual gait—I see her go into the water. She hits a lot of breakers, and turns around to face the shore each time one smacks into her. As I get nearer, I watch her make a few meager attempts at bodysurfing. A small wave takes her by surprise after she straightens up, and just behind it, a larger one knocks her over. Where in the world, I wonder, are this girl's parents? I sit down on the sand, narrowly missing a spot of tar that would have ruined my trousers, and prop my elbows on my knees.

Remember how we used to use turpentine to scrub the tar off the kids' feet? I imagine asking Teresa. *Remember the time Joe put tar in Karen's hair because she broke his ViewMaster?* But that only makes me remember how I tried to rub the tar out of her hair with turpentine, and what a mistake it was. How I then stupidly followed Matt's suggestion and tried peanut butter. How the boys were all cracking up and Karen screaming bloody murder while I cut the mess out with a pair of scissors. One more little failure on the road to disaster.

❊

The little girl is nowhere to be seen.

I stand up and stare at the ocean. I walk toward it. Wave after wave breaks and smoothes out, and still there's no sign of her. I look behind me and see a white lifeguard tower, but it's empty. I step closer to the water.

Not too far out, I spot a pale shape bobbing with the motion of the tide. Shoulders, arms, a braid floating on the water. She's facedown. *This isn't happening,* I think. *This can't be.* I holler "Hey!" toward the floating shape, and then "Help!" to the beach in general, and a moment later I'm running into the surf. All I can think is to get her onto the sand.

As soon as I touch one of her arms, she springs up like a jack-in-the-box.

"Ha ha ha!" she laughs. "You're wet! You're all wet in your clothes!"

I'm almost up to my crotch in the water. She's thrilled, doing a victory paddle no one but me is close enough to appreciate. Then she springs back to the shore with giant steps that bring her knees rocketing out of the waves.

Back on dry land, I take off my shoes and drain out the water. When I put them back on, the sand clings to them like flour to chicken parts. I'm dripping wet from the waist down. Score one for the leaders of tomorrow.

I walk slowly back to the pavilion and the parking lot. As I reach my car, I hear a voice say, "What gets into your head?"

The young couple with the baby stroller stands several yards away. Cowering in front of them is the girl in the lime green swimsuit. She's standing with her arms folded, her head bent down, dripping dark spots onto the asphalt.

"Did we know where you were?" the woman asks. "Did we?" Her hand sweeps across the girl's cheek with a sharp crack. "I hope you had the time of your life, because you worried us *sick*."

"All right," the husband says, "let's just go home." The baby, still wearing his sunglasses, looks oblivious to this turmoil, but the little girl looks miserable.

❊

The day is still bright. I drive back to the island but don't feel like going home yet, don't want to be in the house, so I stop off at the Galaxy Lounge. The place is nearly empty, only a couple of guys drinking beer and talking at the revolving bar. I take a stool a little ways down from them and order a Glenfiddich and water. I'm thinking that, as crazy as things got with me and Teresa, we were never the kind of parents who slap their kids around. We never hit them, never even spanked them. No parent deserves an award for that, I guess, but I like thinking we did at least one thing right.

I order another Glenfiddich and sip it, watching the room slowly turn around me.

"No, no, no, I remember that," one of the guys at the bar is saying. "I remember it clearly. Grissom panicked."

"He didn't *panic*," the other guy says. "The hatch malfunctioned."

They don't know each other. Or they didn't, before they came in here; they're sitting two stools apart. They're around my age, early sixties, one of them a little lighter than me and the other one a little heavier. They look like the guys who played Doc and Festus on *Gunsmoke,* though I'm pretty sure both of those actors are dead.

Festus says, "You know, I've been hearing this for years. 'The hatch malfunctioned.' Well, pardon my French, but *bull-crap*. They were having trouble hooking up the chopper cable, and Grissom didn't want to wait. He got scared and bailed out. End of story."

"And you were there?" Doc asks him.

"Of course not. But I know what I know. I know he didn't follow procedure. I know the chopper pilot told him to wait, and he didn't wait. That's common knowledge. And who paid for that capsule? The taxpayers, that's who. You and me."

I remember hearing about the incident, though it happened years before I started working for NASA. Grissom splashed down after a suborbital flight and they got him out of the water unscathed, but his capsule ended up at the bottom of the Atlantic.

Doc brings the end of his index finger straight down onto the bar over and over. "I want to see you in that capsule when the hatch blows and the water starts coming in. You think you know brave? They were blasting our boys a hundred miles into space, and the only way to get them back down was to toss them into the ocean. Drowning was a very serious risk for those guys. Sometimes they *had* to break procedure. I'm telling you, there was nothing wrong with Gus."

These two are ex-NASA, I'd put money on it: sitting in a bar in the afternoon arguing about the Mercury project, a little too invested. They sound like the photographers at Techni-color who had nothing to do in between launches but smoke and pitch rumors in the break room across from where I worked: mean stories about whose bowels had turned to water at T-minus ten seconds; whose monkeying with the cooling system may have caused the AS-204 fire. Grissom had died in that fire, six years after the hatch incident. It was considered bad form to criticize him.

Sitting there, nursing my drink, I decide I'm with Doc. Even if Grissom *did* blow the hatch early, give the man a break. Honestly, when you get right down to it, who wants to go down with the ship?

I order another drink, and a joke comes to mind, one I remember the photographers telling. It's not a good joke, but I'm starting to feel my drinks and want to chip in. So I clear my throat and say to the two guys, "Hey, what do you get when you cross twenty billion dollars of taxpayers' money with three thousand pounds of moon dirt?"

They glance over, as if suddenly realizing I'm there.

"I don't know," Doc says.

"Three thousand pounds of moon dirt."

They don't laugh.

Festus says, "That's real funny, pal."

"I'm with you," I tell Doc. "There was nothing wrong with Gus."

Doc gives me a cautious nod, as if worried I might want to join their conversation.

Festus mumbles, "Who asked you?"

Coward, I think. *How many drinks is it going to take for you to work up your nerve to call her?*

I stand.

"You all right, there?" Doc asks.

"Gus," I say, and I give him a thumbs-up. Then I make my way toward the door, and for just a moment, when I cross the ring between the inner and outer orbits of the bar, I feel one wet shoe slide toward the other in a way that borders on slapstick.

✣

The sky is dark by the time I get home. I leave my loafers in the garage and walk straight to the dining room, where I pull the Cutty Sark from the sideboard. I take down one of our nice glasses from the china cabinet and pour out a half inch. Just a sip, standing there in the dining room, looking at all this beige carpet, all this tasteful furniture, all this space.

"Goddamn it," I say out loud.

My cell phone is in the kitchen, in its charger, topped off because I haven't touched it in weeks. I scoop it up and drop it into my pocket, along with a pen, then carry the bottle and the glass out to the backyard.

At the end of the yard, near the canal, is a pair of lawn recliners: rusted and weather-beaten from having been left outside for the past six months. I sink down into one of them and set the bottle on the grass next to me.

After I've finished my drink, I take the phone out of my pocket. For a long time, suspended halfway between sitting and lying flat, I do nothing but stare up at the sky packed with stars. I'm not bad with constellations, but tonight I can't make out a single one. Not the dippers. Not Orion. It's like they've all been stirred up when no one was looking. Finally, I squint at the phone and dial my old number.

"Hello?"

"Teresa," I say, "it's me. Roy."

Silence. The last time I did this—called her out of the blue—was at least five years ago. Leona and I had just had a fight about something, I can't even remember what, and

I dialed Teresa without knowing what I'd say. The call didn't go well. This time, though, I have something to tell her.

"How are you, Roy?" she finally asks.

"I'm okay. I just ... I wanted to let you know ..." How hard can this be?

"Wanted to let me know what?"

"Leona died."

Silence again. "Oh," she says. "Roy, I'm so sorry. I really am. What happened?"

"Leona was—" Suddenly I have no air in my lungs. I take in a deep breath, and tell her about the cancer. I keep the details to a minimum, mostly for my sake. "She fought it," I tell her. "We *both* fought it. But there's only so much ..."

"Oh, Roy," Teresa says again. "I'm really so sorry. When is the funeral?"

"The funeral? No, I'm not calling about that. The funeral was two months ago. She died in January. I've been wanting to tell you, and didn't quite know how to do it. You and I haven't really kept up, over the years."

"No, we haven't. But ... you're doing all right?"

"I'm hanging in there," I say. "You know, I drove out to Jetty Park today. First time since I'd been there with you and the kids."

"You haven't gone for all these years? Why?"

"I don't know. It felt off-limits, I guess. All those places we used to go—as a family—I just sort of ... avoided. I even avoided the mall for a while. It just would have been awkward to run into you and the kids while I was, you know, with Leona."

"I guess that's why it never happened," Teresa says.

"I was thinking about how you wouldn't let the kids swim near the jetty because of the sharks. And remember how you wouldn't let them see the launches close up? Because of explosions? I was thinking: None of them were ever bitten by a shark, or burned up. *You* did that." I'm trying to pay her a compliment, but it hasn't come out right. The Scotch is starting to get in the way. "How *are* the kids, anyway?"

"They're fine. Are you—are you in contact with them … at all?"

"I've been terrible about that," I admit. "And I don't want it to be that way. I mean, I'd like to get back in touch with them, if they want to hear from me."

"I'm sure they do. If that's what you want." She doesn't sound quite as sincere as she did a moment ago, but at least she hasn't hung up on me. "You know, they're all in different places now."

"Really?" A stupid reply; of course they are: they're grown-ups. I wait for her to speak again.

"Joe lives in Chicago."

"No kidding. Chicago. And Frankie?"

"Frankie's … in Jacksonville."

"Well, at least *one* of them hasn't abandoned Florida. How about Matt and Karen?"

There's another long pause, and I suspect she's deciding what she will and won't tell me.

"Everyone's fine, Roy," she says.

It's that use of my name that puts up the wall I know will be there for the rest of the conversation.

I hear a man's voice in the background asking who's on the phone. "One of the neighbors," she tells him. Technically true. We live on the same island.

"Teresa," I say, "I should let you go. I just wanted to, you know, check in."

"I'm really sorry to hear about Leona."

"Thank you. And I—I hope you're doing okay."

"I am."

"All right, then. I'll talk to you."

"Goodbye, Roy."

Is she remarried? The possibility never occurred to me. I feel like hitting redial. I'd say, *Teresa, just for the record, I don't think our marriage was a complete bust. You'd at least agree with that, wouldn't you?* And then I'm remembering how, for the first few years after I left, I received a card from the kids on my birthday, and on Father's Day. It occurs to me that those cards were probably Teresa's idea. She probably followed each of them around the house with a pen, haranging them to sign.

I pour a little more Cutty Sark into the glass. The stars are brilliant, even if they're all stirred up. I dial information in Jacksonville.

"Frankie Kerrigan," I say.

But there's no Frankie listed. No Francis. No F. Kerrigan. He's either moved or unlisted, or Teresa was lying. If she was, I can't say I blame her, but the thought irks me. I don't know where else to look for Frankie, so I decide to try the rest of them.

Matt, as far as I know, is still in Utica. I have the phone wedged between my ear and shoulder, the pen poised over my palm. I give the operator the name, but there's no listing for a Matthew Ragazzino in Utica or the surrounding area. I ask the man if there are any other Ragazzinos listed and he says there are around a hundred.

"What about a Dermot?" I ask. No Dermot. I take a shot in the dark. "How about Karen Ragazzino?"

I hear clicking for a few moments. "No sir."

"What about in general, then?"

"You mean all of New York?"

"The country," I say. "There can't be that many Karen Ragazzinos in America, can there?"

"We search by area code."

"Can't you just put in a name and zip across the whole database? I'll bet the FBI can do that."

"This is Information," the man says.

"All right. Bear with me a minute." I try to think of where else Karen might have landed. D.C. Hollywood. These kids could be anywhere, doing who knows what. They could turn up in *People* magazine tomorrow, for all I know.

"Sir," the man says, "do you need another number?"

I say no and thank him. I lay the phone on my stomach and balance the glass on my chest. Reclining on the lounge chair, staring up at the stars, I realize I'm in the exact posture of an astronaut. One of the old boys. John Glenn in the *Friendship 7*. Space, Glenn told ground control, wasn't black at all; it was blue. He reported something about being surrounded by dancing orbs of light, outside the window of his ship. He wasn't scared, just amazed and exhilarated, but the more he talked about the lights, I'd heard, the more the men downstairs began to worry he was losing it. I can imagine what the guys in the Galaxy Lounge would say about that one.

Then I open the phone, dial Information, and try Chicago.

There are two listings for Joseph Kerrigan. I write both numbers on my palm. As I dial, I can feel my heart thumping.

An answering machine picks up. It's a man's voice, but it's so hurried and monotone, there's no telling whether or not it's Joe. I'm not sure I would recognize his voice now, anyway. "Um, listen," I say after the beep, "don't have a heart attack or anything, but this is your father. Your dad. I have...something I want to tell you, but I'll wait until we can actually talk. I hope you're well." What else is there to say? "I love you," I say, and hang up.

Because the odds are fifty-fifty, I try the second number.

A woman answers.

"Is Joe there?" I ask.

She tells me to hold on.

A few seconds later, another voice comes on.

"Joe?" I ask.

"Yeah, this is Joe."

"It's your dad."

"No it's not," he says. "My dad's dead." He doesn't sound affronted or even sad. He sounds amused. I hear snickering in the background.

"Well, then, it's your dad calling from beyond the grave. I just wanted to touch base with you, see how you're doing. We haven't talked in a while."

"That's true."

"So how are you?"

"I'm fine. How are you?"

"Well. Leona passed away. That's part of the reason I'm calling."

"Leona," he says.

"I know you didn't really know her—"

"I didn't know her at all."

"But I wanted to tell you about that."

"Well, thanks." I hear more snickering, and shushing.

"Listen," I say, staring up at all those unfamiliar star patterns. "I just want to say I'm sorry. For everything. I'm sorry for what I did, letting go of you kids. Can you forgive me?"

"Sure," he says. "Why not? I forgive you."

"Honestly?"

"Yes. I honestly forgive you for everything you've ever done." The room at the other end of the line erupts into laughter.

"I don't have any good excuse," I say.

"You don't need one. You're perfect just the way you are."

That really sends them howling.

"Well, thank you. That—that means a lot to me."

We both fall silent for a few seconds.

"Was there anything else?" he asks.

"No, I don't think so. That covers it. But...is this really Joe?"

"Honest to god," he says, "it's Joe. And you are...?"

I think about how I might answer that. Then I fold up the phone, put it in my pocket, and reach for my glass.

Love at the Dog Fight

1 9 6 9

They wrestled in their sleep. According to the game, whoever was pinned when they woke up had to submit. That morning it was Roy.

Teresa was behind him, one arm curled around his middle, the other draped over his pillow and across the top of his head. Her right leg was folded over his, the heel of her foot locked against his shin. He felt her breath on his neck: an even tide that told him she might still be asleep. Slowly, he stretched out his body within her hold. He turned himself like a dowel, and was in the process of lifting her arm from around him when he heard her mumble, "Cheater."

He faked a yawn. "Hmmm?"

She bit down gently on his shoulder.

"I'm just stretching," he lied.

"Go ahead and stretch, but I'm the boss."

He wriggled around to face her. "Can I be the boss this time? Please?"

She tightened her grip. "Shush, young man."

He was completely aroused. He tried to make this apparent, but her hold on his legs prevented him from moving his hips forward. "I could owe you one."

She kissed his forehead. "You're cute when you don't get your way." She kissed the spot between his eyes, the end of his nose, his mouth. "Lie flat on your back."

There was a knock on the door.

"What?" they called out in unison.

Katherine's voice penetrated the thin, hollow wood. "Frankie wants out of his crib."

"Tell Matt to get him," Roy said, and then, whispering to Teresa, "I'll owe you two times as boss. Just let me have this one. I'm in that kind of mood." He tried once more to press against her.

"Wait." A yawn stretched Teresa's face, inches from his. When it subsided, she said, "Matt won't do it."

"He can't get Frankie?"

"He won't."

There was another knock on the door. "Matt says he doesn't have to do anything on his birthday."

Teresa smiled thinly for Roy. Letting go of him, sitting up, she said, "Can you just give Frankie his cup, then, honey? Make sure the lid is all the way on. I'll be there in a minute."

"So you're forfeiting?" Roy asked her.

"It's not a forfeit if we get interrupted." She tugged on his ear and tossed out the word *cheater* again as she got up from the bed.

He put on his robe, brushed his teeth, combed his hair. He smoked a cigarette. When he stepped into the living room, Joseph ran toward him and grabbed hold of his legs. The boy barely came up to the middle of his thigh. "Morning," Roy said. He looked over at Frankie, already tucked into his high chair. "Morning to you, too."

Frankie raised his sip cup as if he meant to throw it, but then just held it there, suspended over his head.

Staring up at Roy's face, Joseph announced, "I use Brylcreem because it makes my hair look natural."

"Bingo," Matt said from the dining room table, where he

and Katherine were waiting for breakfast. "And what kind of bra do you wear?"

"Cross Your Heart," Joseph replied.

Roy rubbed the top of the boy's bed head as if smoothing down feathers. "Can't you teach him to say something he actually needs to know?"

"Like what?"

"I don't know. How about, 'The world is round.'"

Matt snapped his fingers to get Joseph's attention. "Joseph. Hey, Joe. Say, 'The world is flat.'"

"The world is fat," Joseph said.

Both Matt and Katherine burst out laughing, and Joseph jumped up and down, chanting, "The world is fat! The world is fat!"

Roy bent over and scooped the boy into his arms. "Has your older brother taught you how to say 'Happy Birthday'?"

"He already knows that one," Matt said.

"Does he know 'Happy Birthday, smart aleck'?"

"Joseph's not a parrot," Teresa reminded them all from the kitchen.

"That's exactly right," Roy said, "he's *not* a parrot." He lowered Joseph onto his booster seat on one of the dining room chairs. Joseph looked across the table at Matt and said in a voice so soft it was almost a whisper, "Not a parrot."

"What am I getting for my birthday?" Matt asked.

"That's for us to know," Roy said, sitting down at the head of the table.

"A new bike? That's what I asked for."

"Well, we can't always get everything we ask for, so let's just wait and see."

"Sounds like I'm getting a new bike. Maybe a Sting-Ray."

"I didn't say that." Roy glanced at Teresa, who was carrying in a large bowl of scrambled eggs and a plate of bacon.

"Grandpop asked me if I wanted a puppy."

"He asked you? Or you told him that's what you wanted?"

"I told him I wanted a Sting-Ray."

"Well, I know you're not getting a puppy, so forget about that one."

"But I don't have to do any chores today, right?"

"That's right," Teresa said. "No chores for Matt. You don't even have to make your bed."

"And I get to tell everybody what to do?"

Katherine wailed a complaint.

"Sorry, champ," Roy said. "You can be king for the day, but it doesn't make you boss."

*

It was a fine day for a birthday. A Saturday, when they could all be home together. A day with a bright, cloudless sky. Teresa had successfully smuggled the cake into the house the previous afternoon without Matt noticing, and had hidden the box behind the toaster and the Charles Chips can on top of the refrigerator. Their refrigerator. Their house. A mortgage existed with their names on it, the $2,800 down payment scraped together with the help of Roy's parents. It made even scrubbing the toilets feel good. Having lived in apartments for most of her adult life and in a hotel for the duration of her first marriage, she caught herself wondering if property—ownership—had been the missing element all along. Her life had been a whirlwind, and this house secured it, like a paperweight holding down a stack of appliance warranties, the children's birth certificates, their marriage license.

They'd moved in the month before, after renting an apartment in Cocoa for nearly a year. There were still a few boxes to unpack, and the walls were mostly bare; in the dining room hung a handful of school portraits, and over the television a pair of metal-framed photos Roy had recently brought home from work: group portraits of the astronauts from *Apollo 9* and *10*. Autographed, as if Roy knew the astronauts personally, though the signatures had been reproduced and the photos had been handed out to every Technicolor employee. It was part of the impetus for moving to Florida, this promise of employment at NASA, along with a higher standard of living, the warm weather, the nearby beach: enticements emphasized over and over again in the Chamber of Commerce booklet Roy's father had mailed to them in D.C. "Brevard County—The Future for Your Family, Today."

Florida felt more prehistoric than futuristic to Teresa. All those gargantuan flying palmetto bugs, and lizards curled up inside the mailbox waiting to jump onto her hand. Still, she liked it here. Roy seemed to like it here, too. And while Matt, who was turning nine today, sometimes spoke of how Florida was "crummy" and D.C. was better, and of the father he still remembered and missed, Katherine never seemed to think of Dermot at all, and Joseph and Frankie were so young that wherever they were when they opened their eyes in the morning was home. She could see herself content as a resident of Brevard County, on this island, in this house, for the rest of her life. Not that she cared much about the space program. *Apollo 11* was heading toward the moon at that very moment, twenty-four hours away from landing, if things went according to plan, and Teresa seemed to be the only person who wasn't excited about the event. She was a thirty-one-year-old woman with four children and a good husband. They had their health, they owned a home. What could she possibly want with the moon?

She was clearing the breakfast dishes when Katherine—too young at six to have any common sense when it came to surprises—asked what kind of cake they were having.

"Shhh!" Teresa said, darting her eyes toward Matt. "There is no cake."

"There *has* to be a cake," Matt declared.

"They were all out of cake. Not a single birthday cake left on the island. Katherine, would you keep an eye on Joseph for me while I finish cleaning up? He's in the living room."

"No he's not. He's in his bedroom."

"Well, could you go play with him, please? And Matt, could you get Frankie out of his high chair and put him in his playpen—even though it's your birthday? That would be a big help."

"Some birthday," Matt grumbled.

"And be careful with him."

As Matt reached for him, Frankie swept his tiny hand back and forth across the high-chair tray, scattering bits of scrambled egg and chopped-up bacon onto the floor. "Smooth move," Matt said. "Joe might not be a parrot, but you're a pig."

"Frankie is not a pig." Teresa sank a frying pan into a sink-ful of soapy water. There was movement in the corner of her eye, and she looked over to see Roy standing in the doorway of their bedroom, still in his pajamas, his robe hanging open. He was waving her over.

Teresa pointed to the stack of dirty dishes.

Leave it, Roy mouthed.

She turned off the water. She dried her hands and, glancing around to make sure the coast was clear, crossed the dining room and stepped into the bedroom. He closed his arms around her waist as she shut the door behind her. "What was all that about a bicycle? Does he really think he's getting one?"

"Hope not," Roy said, dipping his head down to her chest.

"His bike works, right? I mean, he doesn't *need* a new one, does he? I don't even know how much a bicycle costs these days."

"Everything's fine," Roy murmured against her skin.

She felt his hands lifting her nightgown inside her robe. "Hey. Who's the boss here, anyway?"

"Doesn't count. It's a whole new game now."

"I keep forgetting I'm playing with a cheater." She pushed away from him, took hold of his shoulders, and guided him until his back was against the door.

"Let me. Please?"

"Please, my foot."

He leveled his gaze upon her and crimped his mouth as if exasperated.

She smiled. "My little palace boy. My little . . . beck-and-call servant." The right words, she knew, could put him into the role. She watched his unshaven face readjust itself, and then relax into subservience.

He asked, "What's your bidding?"

She thought about it. Before she could speak again, Matt's voice sliced through the door behind Roy's back. "They're here!"

"They're *not* here," Roy said quietly, hopefully.

"What time were they supposed to arrive?"

"Eleven."

Teresa looked at the clock on the nightstand. It was ten A.M. A car horn tapped out shave-and-a-haircut. "That's your dad," she said. "And I was just about to get creative."

When the two of them emerged, dressed, through the front door, her in-laws were standing in the driveway next to their car. Helen, her auburn hair freshly coiffed into a bouffant, was bent over Katherine and Joseph, hugging them. Walter was holding a rolled-up magazine and had his other hand clamped onto Matt's head, tilting it up toward the sky.

Teresa carried Frankie across the yard. Roy held back a moment to light a cigarette, and she heard him say from behind her, "You're early."

"Ten," Walter said, looking at his watch. "On the dot."

"We said eleven," Roy countered. Teresa glanced at him, and he waved the cigarette in front of his chest casually. "It doesn't matter. How are you?"

"We're on time, according to schedule," Walter said. He hiked up the waist of his checkered pants. "I was just telling this astronaut here that the men upstairs are about to enter lunar orbit. It's probably happening as we speak."

He was an older version of Roy: the same sharp, dimpled chin, the same blade of a nose, a pair of large, chocolate eyes fixed beneath brows shaped like little furry triangles. The part in his silver hair was a carefully executed line just a couple of inches above his left ear. The hair, waxed and shining, covered his forehead like a visor and bore the tread marks of his comb.

Frankie held on to the pocket of Teresa's blouse.

"We're going to grill hamburgers for lunch," she said. "Hot dogs, too."

Helen winked at her. Walter told Matt, "They have to fire that main rocket just right. Too soft and they'll get pulled into the moon's gravity and just circle around it. Too hard and they'll smash into the surface."

"Pop," Roy said. "I don't think we have to worry about that right now."

"Who's worried? I'm not. They've got this whole deal worked out to the inch, and they'll do it right. I'm convinced of that. By the time Matt's up there, he'll be able to pick which city he wants to live in. *These* two"—he indicated Joseph and Frankie—"will be stopping on the moon to get gas before they head off to Mars."

"It's Matt's birthday," Roy reminded him.

"Why do you think I'm holding him away from the car? I don't want him to see his present."

"It's in the backseat." Matt beamed. "There's a blanket over it. It's huge!"

Roy stepped forward. "Well, let's bring it inside."

"Negative," Walter said. "Let's leave it right where it is until he's ready to open it."

"Is that a good idea?" Helen asked him.

Walter glanced at Teresa. "I'll bet you have a beer for me."

"I think so," Teresa said. She shifted Frankie to her other arm. "I have iced tea and Hawaiian Punch, too."

"I'm thinking a beer." Walter aimed Matt toward the house. "Steer us indoors, pilot."

The boy charged across the lawn. Katherine ran after him. Joseph pulled at Helen's hand until she lifted him into her arms. She told Teresa, "You look so rested."

"Do I?"

"It's a wonderful age, isn't it?" Helen nodded from behind Joseph's head, toward Frankie. "Just before they turn two. Two to about three and a half is awful. And the first six months is even worse, because you feel so helpless and tired. But look at that little angel. A-look-at-it. All it wants is to be right where it is."

Teresa liked Helen, who never argued with anyone, who let all remarks and opinions exist around her like molecules in the air. Because her own parents had been dead for so long, and because she so earnestly wanted to please her in-laws, she'd even gotten used to calling Helen "Mom." But the woman had a tendency to talk in circles. And it was odd hearing her discuss child rearing as if it were an industry she'd worked in all her life. She'd only raised one child.

"How are things at Sears?" Walter asked her.

"They're good."

"You're selling, what, maintenance agreements?"

She nodded. "We just got new headsets. They're much more comfortable." Walter stared at her for a moment with his eyes narrowed against the sunlight. He'd worked a dozen years at a metal foundry in Grand Rapids, had put in five years with the army, and then another dozen at the foundry. After retiring into restlessness for a few months in Florida, he'd taken a job reading meters for the electric company. He was proud that Helen had never worked a day of their marriage, and he'd made it clear that he thought it a shame Teresa had to work at all. With what she hoped was a pleasant shrug, she said, "How's the meter reading?"

"Excellent. Florida Power & Light is a decent company, as companies go." He turned to Roy and tapped his chest with the rolled-up magazine. "How about you? Any word on the promotion?"

Roy blinked. "What promotion?"

"You told me they were expanding the department. I just assumed that meant there was more opportunity."

"I said they were expanding the *break room.*"

"Well, you've been there almost a year now. Aren't people being promoted?"

"Probably."

"They've got to get you out of that cage, Roy. At least get you doing something that'll give you some arms." He touched the magazine to his own bicep, still hard from his years at the foundry.

"I'll look into it, Pop."

"Do." Walter glanced behind him as they reached the porch. "I don't know what you're putting on your lawn, by the way, but it's not working."

Teresa held the screen door open and watched Roy's face as he passed her; he was clenching and unclenching his teeth, pulsing the hinge of his jaw. "I'm going to start up the grill," he said a little louder than necessary. "Pop, you want to come with me and show me how to do it?"

"You're the man of the house here." Walter shrugged. "But I'll keep you company, if you'd like."

They all stepped inside. The men walked straight to the back, out the sliding glass door, and onto the patio.

"Those two are like chalk and chalk," Helen said, depositing Joseph on the living room carpet and setting her purse on the coffee table.

Teresa lowered Frankie into his playpen. He grabbed at the netted sides, looked at Joseph and said, "Zoom."

Helen's eyes rested on a large unpacked box marked BRIC-A-BRAC next to the television. "How's the settling-in going?"

"We're getting there. We actually don't have enough to fill the house. It's a mansion compared to what we're used to."

"I'm just so glad that you're all here together," Helen said, as if the odds hadn't been in their favor.

Teresa opened the refrigerator. "Iced tea?"

"I would love some."

As she was taking out the pitcher she asked, "What's 'chalk and chalk'?"

"Instead of chalk and cheese. If Walter and Roy were chalk and cheese, they'd be so different, they might just get along. Not that they don't get along. I guess when people say 'chalk and cheese,' they *do* mean two people who don't get along. But you know what I mean."

Teresa didn't. She poured.

"I watched it happen back in Grand Rapids, when Roy was a teenager," Helen continued. "He was more like his father every day. But there wasn't a thing you could do about it."

"You didn't want them to be alike?"

"I wanted them to like each other. That would have been nice. And I think they do, now; they just don't realize it. They're still getting used to being around each other."

"Well, I think Roy *is* happy that we moved down here."

"Oh, I know he is," Helen confirmed.

The sliding glass door opened. Roy entered first, followed by

Walter. "I'm just saying that lighter fluid is a scam. That's my opinion. Charcoal was made to *light*. Lighter fluid's just an extra tacked on by some joker who's probably a millionaire by now."

"And all your marketing research has proven this?" Roy asked, glancing at Teresa as he walked over to the sink.

"I'm just saying," Walter said again.

"Yes, Pop," Roy volleyed back, "that's all you're doing: saying."

Teresa looked at her in-laws. Walter had wandered into the living room and Helen was looking down into her glass. In that moment Teresa reached over and spanked Roy on the butt. He shot her a look. *Behave,* she tried to say with her eyes, and because he didn't seem to get this message, she leaned into his ear and whispered, "Bad boy."

*

As if it were possible to get more channels than they did, Walter bent over in front of the television, turned it on, and popped his way around the dial several times. "Nothing," he said, frowning at the screen. "It's the biggest event since the *Mayflower,* since Columbus set foot, and they're showing all the regular programs. Would you come over here, Roy?"

Roy grimaced. He pecked Teresa on the cheek and walked into the living room, past his mother, to the television, where his father was stooped over. "What?"

"Am I doing this right?" The man motioned with the magazine for Roy to bend over with him.

Roy squatted down. "Are you turning the dial right? I guess so."

When their heads were level in front of the screen, his father's voice dropped to a whisper. "I know we butt heads. It's just what we do. But really, I want you to know I think you're doing a decent job here."

Roy watched the screen as it popped through its four stations. "What are you talking about?"

"Don't be difficult. I'm talking about you, the job you're doing."

"As a father, you mean."

"I'm not going to paint you a picture," Walter told him. "I'm saying, it's good to see. Mind you, I don't retract anything I've already said. If you don't take care of that lawn, it's going to be dust one day. But I'm glad to see that, in general, you're...rising to the occasion." He straightened up.

Roy followed. "What occasion?"

Ignoring him, Walter asked in a softer voice, "Did their other, uh...Teresa's first husband—did he send any kind of present? I mean, is he still in the picture?"

"Dermot? He sent a card and a hundred-dollar bill," Roy said with a certain amount of humility; it was far more than he and Teresa could afford to spend. "Teresa's got savings accounts set up for each of the kids. She's already deposited it."

His father pulled at his nose and pointed a finger toward the screen, as if the television had anything to do with what they were discussing. "Well, that's good. That's sensible."

"What occasion am I rising to?" Roy asked again.

Walter turned toward Teresa, who was now standing just a foot away, offering him a can of beer.

She said, "There's iced tea, if you'd rather."

"This is fine, honey."

"What occasion, Pop?"

"That was a private remark," Walter grumbled, after bringing the can down from his lips. "You never could take a compliment."

Roy looked at his father. He looked at his wife, whose arms and neck were moist despite the air-conditioning. He wanted a break from the old man. He wanted to be alone with Teresa. The damp hollow of her neck had an opal glaze.

He said, "I think we should let Matt open his presents before lunch."

✳

Walter still wouldn't let them bring the present in from the car, though he went out and fiddled with it while Roy and Teresa dug the other gifts from under their bed and carried them to the backyard. They unfolded lawn chairs. Katherine sat on the grass and tugged up handfuls of it and sprinkled them over her legs.

"We're doing this outside?" Matt asked. "Makes sense."

He was still thinking about the bicycle, Roy could tell. None of the gifts they'd set on the patio table was larger than a shirt box. But this mythical Sting-Ray wasn't hiding around the corner of the house, or locked in the storeroom, with a big red bow tied to its handlebars. It made Roy's chest sink beneath his shirt, knowing Matt was going to be disappointed. The boy was maybe even wondering if a disassembled bike was waiting for him under the blanket in Walter's car. Roy caught himself wondering the same thing. Would his father do that? Trump him with a gift so much nicer than anything he and Teresa could afford? Did bicycles come disassembled?

They'd written "From Joseph and Frankie" on a set of plastic army men packaged in a miniature U-boat, and "From Katherine" on a diver's mask and snorkel. "Thanks," the boy said politely upon opening each gift, but with the enthusiasm of someone receiving a consolation prize. The largest box, "From Mom and Dad," Teresa lifted herself and plopped down on Matt's lap as if to impress him with its weight, though it was certainly lighter than anything he could ride down the street. He tore off the wrapping paper and stared at the box. "What's a Slip'N Slide?"

"You haven't seen those commercials?" Roy asked. "The kids in those commercials are going out of their minds with fun."

"*I've* seen them," Helen said. She was holding Frankie in her lap, bouncing him up and down. "That's the best gift anyone could ever receive."

"How is it a slide?" Matt asked, tilting the box, frowning at its size.

"Just open it," Roy said. "Something tells me we might need the hose for this. And bathing suits."

Katherine let go of a handful of grass. "Can I put on my swimsuit?"

"Absolutely."

"Swimsuit!" Joseph parroted from between Walter's legs.

Matt was still staring at the present. "I don't get it."

"Well, open it, honey," Teresa said. Matt took the lid off the box. What lay inside looked like a deflated life raft, or a rain slicker. He lifted the folded mass of bright yellow vinyl and bent it in half.

"Watch this," Roy said. He got up from his lawn chair and took the present out of Matt's hands. With a few snaps of his arms, the slide expanded into a twenty-five-foot runway that drifted down across the lawn. "Now for some water." He stepped around Walter to the side of the house where the hose lay coiled on the grass. Tugging the free end around the legs of Walter's chair, he stretched it across the corner of the patio. There was a nozzle in the slide, and he screwed the hose onto it, then fast-stepped back to the spigot.

"Maybe I should go get our present out of the car now," Walter said.

"*Wait,*" Roy snapped. "Just stay where you are. Watch the slide." He turned on the spigot. After what felt like a long delay, the slide rippled from near end to far, and tiny threads of water arced from its outer edges toward its middle. As the vinyl glistened in the sunlight, Roy so wanted everyone to be impressed by the sight that he heard himself declare, absurdly, "It's the yellow brick road!"

"Follow the yellow brick road!" his mother chimed in, and because the rest of them were shifting their eyes from the pathetic, wet slick of rubber to him as if he'd lost his mind, Roy shouted, "Waa-hoo!" and ran forward, throwing himself down onto the nearest end of the slide. To his surprise and great satisfaction, he slid all the way to the other end, like a car hydroplaning in a rainstorm.

It was far from a convenient gesture. He was wearing trousers and a sports shirt, socks and shoes. He'd been holding a lit cigarette, which was now a soggy nub between his fingers. But when he pulled himself up onto his feet and looked back toward the patio, they were all laughing and applauding—even Teresa, who'd never heard of the product when he'd come home with it and had doubted its qualifications as the main present for a nine-year-old's birthday.

"So how about those swimsuits?" he asked, smacking his hands together and sending beads of water into his face.

Matt and Katherine and Joseph were already running into the house. "Matt," Teresa called after them, "would you help Joseph get into his suit?"

Roy walked back over to the patio. Walter leaned into him. "Very clever. You haven't been, uh..." He teetered his beer in front of his mouth.

"No, Pop. It's not even noon."

"Just asking. Well done, in any event. Sometimes a man has to play the clown to win over his audience."

"I wasn't *clowning*." Roy flicked the wet cigarette onto the lawn and looked at Teresa. She gave him an appreciative smile. She handed Frankie to Helen and glanced toward the house.

"Pop," Roy said, "would you and Mom watch the kids for a few minutes while they play on the slide? We've got some other birthday things to take care of."

"Sure. But I really do want to get that present out of the car." Teresa walked into the house.

"Soon," Roy said. "Real soon."

"You are a stitch," his mother told him. "I was just thinking of that Red Skelton impression you used to do. That pigeon person. You were so funny when you were little."

When he pulled open the sliding glass door, he heard the commotion the kids were generating in the scramble to change into their swimsuits. A moment later, they were running past him on their way to the backyard.

He found Teresa in the bathroom off their bedroom, combing her hair with her fingers. She grinned at him in the mirror. "That was really something," she told him.

"Thank you."

"That earned you points, I think."

He started to pull his damp shirt over his head, then stopped. "Get me out of these clothes," he said, "quick, before we get interrupted." He raised his arms and she peeled the shirt off his torso and tossed it onto the floor next to the tub. She unbuckled his belt, unfastened his trousers, and let them drop down his legs.

"You're a nurse," he told her. "I've just been brought into the emergency room. There was a storm, a shipwreck, and they found me on the beach."

"We have to get you warm," she said.

He felt her lips on his chest, on his stomach.

"No, no, no, honey! Ask your mother!" Helen shouted from the patio.

Teresa paused.

"I'm freezing," Roy said, trying to hold her in the moment.

"Really, now," Helen called out. "Mattie, Katherine, listen to me. You should ask your mother about this first."

"I'm dying," Roy said. "I'm about to go into shock."

Teresa stood up, shook her head no so subtly that it was almost a tremble, and left the room.

❖

Walter was nowhere to be seen. Joseph, dripping wet, was running circles around Helen's legs. At the nearest end of the Slip'N Slide, Matt and Katherine were holding Frankie—were *swinging* Frankie—low to the ground and counting in unison, "Three . . . two . . . one . . ."

"Stop it!" Teresa yelled, but their voices overlapped hers.

"Blast off!" They launched the baby. Teresa froze on the patio. She felt her heart squeeze in on itself like a fist. Frankie, who'd been stripped down to his diaper, had landed on his back, and as he sailed down the wet yellow strip, he somehow rose into a sitting position and began to rotate.

She watched him become a blur and realized it was because she was no longer frozen; she was running toward him. "Jesus, Jesus, please," she said.

She reached the end of the slide just after he did. Two thin fountains of water were batting against either side of his head. He was laughing.

"We do not throw Frankie down the slide!" she hollered, picking him up.

"He's not hurt," Matt said.

"You don't know that! He could have broken his neck!"

"Yeah, but"—Matt shrugged—"he didn't."

Frankie's diaper squished against her arm. "Young man," she said, walking back to the patio, "you can be restricted on your birthday. Don't think that can't happen."

"Restrict him," Katherine said, smiling.

"And *you*." Teresa glared at her daughter. "Since when do you think it's funny to put your little brother's life in danger?"

"*O*-kay!" Helen nearly sang. "It's all fine. And it won't happen again, thank goodness for that."

"Matthew the birthday boy!" Walter shouted from a distance. "Driveway, front and center!"

Roy, in a dry set of clothes, was just stepping out onto the patio. "What's going on?"

"My present!" Matt said, and ran past him into the house.

Helen picked up Joseph and motioned for Katherine to follow her. They all filed past Roy. He looked after them, then turned to Teresa. "What happened?"

"I have to change Frankie's diaper," she said, trying to calm down. She glanced at his shirt. "You missed a button." He opened his mouth to speak, but she stepped around him and into the house.

※

A large cardboard box was sitting on the driveway in front of his father's Chrysler. It wasn't wrapped. It said Sears on the side and had a picture of a lawn mower. "It's not a lawn mower," Walter was saying, holding Matt by the shoulders, "and it didn't come from Sears. I just needed a big box."

"I know what it is," Matt said.

"You think so?" Walter took his hands away. "Open it."

Roy stepped up next to his mother, who had a pensive crimp in her mouth. Matt leapt onto the box and pulled at the flaps, which weren't taped but had been folded into one another. As soon as he pulled back the first flap, the rest flew open, the box jostled, and something large and blond and furious scrambled out of it, lunging for Matt's face.

"Whoa!" Walter yelled. "Dwight, knock it off!"

Matt screamed and reared back. The cocker spaniel, half in the box, half out, tipped the entire thing over and emerged, growling and snapping at the air. Matt ran behind his grandfather.

"Bad!" Walter reached down and popped his hand against the dog's head. Dwight immediately dropped onto the cement, panting.

"That's Dwight," Roy said with a numbing sense of recognition.

"He's just a little edgy. We had him in his travel crate, under that blanket in the backseat. He didn't like going from the crate to the box."

"That's your dog."

"Yes." Walter sounded annoyed. "I know that. He's a good dog, and Matt's always been fond of him."

Roy saw Matt peek around Walter's hip timidly. There was a long pink scratch on one of the boy's cheeks. "Pop, it's your *dog*. You're giving Matt your *dog* for his birthday?"

"He's a fine dog."

"Yeah, but he's, what, twelve years old?"

"He's *eleven*. He just turned eleven. Matt's always loved Dwight, haven't you, Matt?"

"Where's the bike?" Matt asked, not so much frightened now as confused.

"Pop." Roy looked at his father. He looked at his mother, who smiled at him weakly, and at the dog, who appeared exhausted from its lunge and was sagging on its side, its chest heaving against the heat. There were several small, knobby growths on the top of its skull. "You're not serious about this."

"Matt has always loved Dwight!" his father shot back.

"He's your *dog*. You've been complaining about him for years. You told me just last week that he chewed up your footstool, that you thought he was crazy."

"Watch this," Walter said. He bent down and snapped his fingers. "Dwight. *Dwight.* Shake hands." The dog glanced at him without moving its head. One of its paws lifted a few inches off the driveway. "See that? Is that a crazy dog? Dwight, *up.*" The dog struggled to its feet, its head drooping in a near-surrender to gravity. "He's a *smart* dog, is what he is. Who's your best friend, Dwight? *Speak!*"

Dwight barked. It sounded like a tiny amount of air squeezed through a folded rubber hose.

"That's right," Walter said. "*Rarf!* means 'Matt,' and Matt's your best friend." Matt had, by now, inched out from behind his grandfather and was standing beside him. Walter placed his hands on the boy's shoulders and guided him forward. "Happy birthday, Mr. Astronaut."

The boy took a step toward the dog. He rubbed the scratch on his cheek and glanced at Roy. Roy shook his head no. "You don't have to touch him. You don't... We're not going to... Christ, Pop, what were you thinking? That you could just dump this thing on us?"

"He's not a thing," Walter said. "He's Dwight. All Matt does when he comes over to our house is play with Dwight."

"That's because there's nothing else to do."

"Roy, don't sass your father," Helen said in a voice that sounded almost pleading.

"Mom," Roy said, "I can't believe you'd even go along with this." But she was a peacekeeper at all costs. And now that Roy thought about it, she'd never wanted a dog, had never liked Dwight very much, had been making gentle complaints about Dwight's smell for almost a decade.

Matt edged closer. The dog collapsed again onto its belly. When Matt took another step, the dog exhaled and rolled over onto its back, its legs sticking up into the air. For a moment, with a sense of horror that clashed with his sense of relief, Roy thought the dog had died right there on the spot, in front of everyone. But then Matt reached down and touched the dog's belly, and the ratty tail began to wag.

"Aww," Helen cooed.

The screen door opened and Teresa stepped out of the house, holding a dry and freshly diapered Frankie. "What's Dwight doing here?"

"He's Matt's present," Walter informed her.

"No," Roy said. "He's not. He's *visiting,* and he's going home with Grandma and Grandpop."

"I want to keep him." Matt's voice sounded small and younger than it usually did. It sounded like Joseph's. He was rubbing Dwight's belly vigorously and the dog's tail was sweeping the driveway.

Roy watched Teresa's face go from confusion to refusal, and finally twist into a hesitant surrender. She caught Roy's eye and the look she gave him said, *What choice do we have?*

Roy turned to his father. "You think I'm doing a decent job here? You think I'm rising to the occasion? We're not taking this wreck of an animal off your hands."

He knew instantly that his wording had been too strong for everyone but his father. Walter's arms were swelling beneath the sleeves of his polo shirt, his legs were hardening inside his golf pants; he was ready for any confrontation. But it didn't matter, because the issue didn't reside between Roy and his father anymore. Helen was *aww*-ing, and Katherine had joined in the rubbing of the dog's belly. Most dire, Teresa's focus had shifted to the smile on Matt's face. "Well, birthday boy," she said, "looks like you've found a new friend."

"They've *always* been friends," Walter emphasized. "Dog is

man's best friend, and Dwight is Matt's best friend. You don't have to be a rocket scientist to see *that*."

Roy closed his eyes.

✳

Dwight walked the perimeter of the backyard, following the fence and sniffing the ground and lifting a trembling hind leg every few feet. Matt watched Dwight with an increasing calmness and, Teresa thought, a growing sense of ownership. They'd never had a dog; she and Roy had never wanted to bring one into an apartment, either because an additional pet deposit would have been required or because they'd feared that a dog might damage a rug or a piece of furniture that wasn't theirs. Now they were homeowners. She knew Dwight was old and cranky, but she'd inspected the scratch on Matt's face and found that the skin wasn't broken and the line was already fading. The boy clearly wanted the dog. Her in-laws had contributed to the down payment on the house. How could they refuse?

"What about this?" Roy suggested, reading her mind, standing over the grill with a spatula in his hand. "You guys keep Dwight, who's got one paw in the grave, and we go out and buy a puppy."

"Oh, it's a *nightmare* to train a puppy," Helen said from one of the lawn chairs. "This breed, in particular. They're so stubborn and aggressive."

"I didn't say we'd get a cocker, Mom."

Walter, sitting in the chair next to hers, tapping the rolled-up magazine against his palm like a billy club, cleared his throat. "You're getting a good deal, Roy. Dwight's already trained. He's already broken in."

"You make him sound like a used car," Roy muttered. He turned hot dogs and flipped burgers.

"Is there another beer somewhere?"

Teresa felt as if she were watching a business deal suddenly go south. For a moment, she forgot that she could have any voice in the matter; it all seemed to be between Roy and his father. But part of this investment was hers. Bouncing Frankie in her arms, she said, "Matt seems happy."

The dog had finished circumnavigating the yard. It was standing at the edge of the patio, and Matt was squatting down in front of it with his arms held out.

"That's not the point," Roy said.

She caught his eye. "Maybe it *should* be the point."

"Listen to your wife," Walter instructed.

Roy tilted his head in her direction. "You want this dog in our house? *This* dog? He can't even control his bladder anymore."

Dwight collapsed in front of Matt and the boy scratched his hands up and down the dog's back.

Helen shifted in her chair. "Roy always loved pets when he was little. He used to put on shows for us. We had a fox terrier he taught to jump through a tire and roll over. For about two weeks, once, we took in a cat while the neighbors were on vacation, and in no time, Roy had it meowing whenever he said the word *Shanghai*. A cat. Can you imagine that? He even trained a chicken to follow a clothespin tied to the end of a string." Her expression popped as if she'd felt a minor electrical jolt, and she looked down at her lap.

"Yeah, what about that chicken?" Roy asked.

"He loved animals," Helen said, locking her hands together.

"Tell them about the chicken, Mom."

Helen said nothing. Walter grinned. "That was a *good* chicken."

The spatula was bobbing up and down in Roy's hand. "She was one of those little tinted chicks you used to buy in front of the supermarket at Easter," he told Teresa. "There were six of them. They came in an egg crate, remember? Well, I was, what, ten years old? And I wanted to keep those chicks, but Pop said they weren't really pets and they wouldn't live long. And, sure enough, they started dying off one after the other." He flipped a burger. "But not the pink one. She was a trouper; I named her Rita. She turned brown, and lived in the backyard and ate feed out of my hand. All my friends thought I was the bee's knees because I had a chicken for a pet. And then one night Mom made a roast for dinner. You can see where this story's going."

"Oh, don't be so sensitive," Walter growled.

"That's exactly what you told me that night."

"And you still haven't taken my advice."

"I didn't *ask* for your advice, Pop. I didn't ask to *eat* my *pet*."

"For godsake, chickens are food!" Walter snarled.

Matt, thankfully, didn't seem to be listening to this exchange. He was on his knees in front of Dwight and looked completely enraptured, scratching his hands along the dog's spine. Teresa felt the need to say something, anything, to change the subject. The meat on the grill was starting to smoke. She stood. "Who's hungry?" she asked, still holding Frankie and rocking him frantically.

"Me!" Katherine shouted.

"Me!" Joseph echoed.

"Dwight wants a hamburger," Matt announced.

"Oh, no, honey," Helen said, "that'll ruin his stomach. He'll be sick for *days*."

"I'll get the bread," Teresa said. "Help me, Roy."

Roy wiped the back of one hand against his forehead. "Help you what?"

"Get the *bread*," Teresa said, motioning toward the house with her head.

Roy handed his father the spatula and asked him not to let anything burn. A moment later he was standing beside her in the kitchen, one hip against the counter, his arms folded across his chest. "Please don't tell me you want to give in to them."

"That's horrible about the chicken. You never told me that story."

"It's not something I think about a lot."

"You know, your mother made a comment—"

"*She,*" Roy said, "likes to seem oblivious, but she's totally aware of Pop's game, and she's *for* it. She's like his...political base."

"She's not very confident in us. I think she's surprised we're still together."

"She said that?"

"Well, something close to that."

"She didn't mean it. But listen, you don't want to let them get away with this, right?"

"I don't know," Teresa said, one of her hands resting on a bag of hamburger buns. "I know how you feel. I do. But it just seems like we don't have any choice but to go along. They've done so much for us."

"Oh, God." Roy dipped his entire body. "This is my father, through and through. He loves to play this game. He feeds me this crap about how I have to be the man of the house, then he pulls some stunt so I have to cave in to *him.* It's his specialty. You know that, right?"

"I don't think it matters," Teresa said, choosing her words carefully. "We should just...accept this. Things can't always be exactly the way we want. We have to compromise."

"It's not a compromise to let them dump their problem in our laps."

"Matt likes the dog."

"I'm going to lose this, right?" Roy looked up at the ceiling. "I'm going to lose this. Pop's going to win."

With one hand Teresa untwisted the tie from a package of hot dog buns. "We should think about Matt."

"Matt wants the dog because he knows I *don't,* and because we didn't give him a bicycle. A month from now that mutt'll be shitting up and down the hallway and Matt won't want anything to do with it."

"It's his birthday," Teresa said. "The dog isn't going to live long, anyway." Roy's posture, the tight knot of his arms around his middle, suddenly seemed like a bad omen. Dermot had stood that way when he was anxious. He had stood that way for hours at a time, and she'd been too young, too naïve, to realize that it was a sign of restlessness, unhappiness, that he must have been holding himself down because he so desperately wanted to be someplace else. She let go of the bread bag and all but thrust Frankie onto Roy, who had to uncross his arms to receive the child. Frankie registered the shift by reaching up and fastening a hand around a wing of Roy's shirt collar. "It would be a nice thing," she said. "We can adjust to it. And it would help us all stay . . . content."

He smacked his lips once and looked down at the dark, curly hair that covered Frankie's head.

She pulled apart the hot dog buns and set them on a plate, waiting for him to respond.

Finally, softly, he said, "I'm content with things the way they are now."

"Me too."

"If I go along with this, will it . . . buy me points?"

"We're not talking about that. We're talking about Matt and his birthday and your parents."

"Yeah, but will it buy me points?" he asked. "Significant points?"

She looked up. The tension and annoyance were suddenly gone from his face. His mouth was curled on one side and his brow was raised inquisitively. Still holding on to his shirt collar, Frankie smiled and said what sounded like the word *shirt,* though it may have been *hurt* or even *shit.* Roy kissed the top of his head. The two of them, father and son, were leaning toward boyishness from opposite directions, and it was such an endearing sight that she wished there were film in the camera, wherever the camera was; she wanted to freeze the moment in time, already afraid that it was some sort of summit they might never reclaim.

Still, she didn't want to give up the game entirely.

"Half," she said, and tried to bend her mouth to match his grin.

"Half what?"

"Points."

❋

After lunch and the devouring of the birthday cake, they turned the water back on and let the kids wear themselves out on the Slip'N Slide. Walter unrolled the magazine he'd been carrying around—a brand-new issue of *Life* called "Off to the Moon"—and tried to show Matt a series of profiles on the three astronauts, and then, when those failed to compete with the slide, a color diagram of *Apollo 11*'s projected flight plan. "A hundred and twelve hours in space before they even set foot on the moon. Can you imagine how long that is?"

"Doubleheader!" Matt yelled, dragging Joseph by the hand to the nearest end of the slide and yanking him into a dive that sent them both across the yard.

Walter leaned sideways in his lawn chair. "Hey—I'm trying to show you something!"

"Let him play," Helen said, coddling Frankie, who was sound asleep in her arms. "He can read it later."

"He won't read it. Anyway, I'm not leaving the magazine here. I'm not finished with it."

"But you're finished with the dog, right?" Roy asked. He'd settled into one of the chairs on the opposite side of the patio and had one leg folded across the other, his left loafer bobbing in the air.

"We've already settled the matter," his father said evenly. "Haven't we?"

"I just want to be clear. You're not going to be asking for your soon-to-expire, twelve-year-old dog back anytime soon, right?"

"Roy," his mother said.

"No," his father said. "We're not. And he's eleven."

"I just want to be clear," Roy said again. He could see Teresa through the kitchen window, standing at the sink, washing the plates and glasses. The window was closed to keep in the air-conditioning, but she was glancing out every few seconds—trying to lip-read, he thought.

"Armstrong's a cigar smoker," Walter said, holding the magazine open with both hands and squinting at it. "I might take up cigars again."

"Not if you want to kiss *me,*" Helen said. She winced at Roy, and then smiled.

Half-points, Roy thought. He wanted his parents to leave, wanted all the kids to fall into deep naps, so that he and Teresa could get back to the bedroom. But what were *half*-points, anyway? She was the one who had introduced the whole point system into their sex life. It was fun, it was exciting, but all of a sudden it seemed like something Walter might have concocted when Roy was a child to gauge how accurately Roy had cleaned the rain gutters. And why was he settling for half-points?

"How about that," Walter said. "Buzz Aldrin's a West Point man. Top of his class, '51."

The dog had lumbered up to the near end of the slide and was licking at one of the water jets.

Roy leaned forward in his chair. "Come here, Dwight."

Dwight didn't move.

"You have to snap," Walter said.

Roy immediately began snapping his fingers. "*Dwight.* Come here."

Moving his mouth away from the spray, licking at the air, Dwight glanced at Roy skeptically.

Roy snapped. *"Here."*

"He'll warm up to you," Helen said. "Just give him time."

Roy snapped again. Dwight walked lazily over to the lawn chair and sat down between Roy's feet, his tongue hanging limp now over his remaining lower teeth.

Helen looked at Walter. "Did you tell them about the ketchup?"

"We haven't gone over the details yet," Walter said to the magazine.

"He likes a little ketchup on his food," Helen told Roy. "Canned food. He won't eat the dry. And just a little ketchup or he'll turn into a fountain at the other end, and you won't want *that.*"

Roy scratched the dog's neck.

The sliding glass door opened and Teresa stepped out onto the patio, dusting her hands. She smiled cautiously. "So are we all decided on this?"

"We're kind of…*half* decided," Roy said. He continued to pat Dwight's head and with his other hand hooked a finger beneath the dog's leather collar.

"What half is that?" Walter asked, sounding suspicious.

Roy looked at Teresa. The set of her face had instantly changed; she looked panicked. "We'll take the dog," Roy said— to all of them, keeping his eyes on Teresa. "But he has to live in the backyard."

"Dwight lives inside," Walter said.

"He used to. From here on out, he's a backyard dog. Which means we'll need a doghouse."

For what felt like a long stretch, all adult noise dropped away; there was only the sound of the children as they hustled up and down the slide. His father, Roy knew, was weighing the matter.

Finally, Walter said, "Well." He cleared his throat. "You can get one of those at Babcock's."

"You'll have to get it for us, Pop." Roy scrubbed the top of Dwight's knobby head with his fingernails.

"We can do that," Helen said. "Can't we, Walt?"

Walter cleared his throat again. He tapped the leaves of the open magazine against his knees. "Sure. We can do that."

"All right, then." Roy smiled at Teresa. "We're all decided."

The panicked, edgy look on Teresa's face softened like a sandcastle in a rain shower.

His father commenced reading aloud from the back of the magazine a full-page letter by Charles Lindbergh about the moon launch and the flight of the *Spirit of Saint Louis*. He read in a strong voice, as if they'd requested the reading and were eagerly attentive. But Helen started cooing over Frankie's sleeping face, and Roy, after a few moments, released Dwight, got up from his chair, and walked over to the grill. He took the wire brush from its hook on the side of the grill and started scrubbing off the grit from their lunch. Teresa stepped up behind him. She closed her hands around his stomach and said softly into his ear, "Clever boy."

"You think?"

"I didn't really want that dog in our house anyway," she whispered.

Walter read on, and Dwight meandered from the patio over to the slide to resume lapping at the water spray. Within the circle of Teresa's arms, Roy turned around. He couldn't bring himself to be physically aroused in the presence of his parents, but he felt it in his mind, and, facing Teresa, he brought his hips against hers and kissed her. When their mouths parted, he said, "So I guess we've got a pet."

"I guess we do. It'll be okay."

"Dog food. Trips to the vet. All that crying when he kicks the bucket."

"Don't," she said, and touched a finger to his mouth.

"Is anyone listening to this?" Walter asked them. "There are important things going on in the world."

"Everything's important, Pop." At the far end of the slide, Joseph was pushing both his hands against Katherine's lower back. Katherine was pushing Matt's shoulders. Matt, crouched down and half-hidden by Walter in the lawn chair, was shoving his weight against something, and in the next moment all three of them pitched forward out of sight, and from the other side of Roy's father, Dwight came sailing down the yellow runway. He was balanced on his back haunches, his front paws dangling in front of his chest. His tongue was lolling out one side of his mouth. *They'll kill him,* Roy thought, *he'll have a heart attack.* But Dwight lifted his snout and aimed his face into the water's spray, oblivious to his velocity, or surrendering to it. Enjoying it, even.

Believe It or Not

2006

He reads the word *WE* in the stratocumulus clouds that form after a tornado one summer. He discovers *ARE* and *LEAVING* in the pattern of blinking lights on the Christmas tree the following year. Six months later, he emerges from his room, finds Teresa cutting coupons at the kitchen table, and tells her in an excited, almost breathless voice that the Visitors are on their way.

She looks at him over the tops of her reading glasses. "And how do we know this?"

"I found the fourth word!" Frankie says, and then explains how he's been monitoring the static between stations on his police scanner. "They did it with clicks. N is the fourteenth letter of the alphabet, and there were fourteen clicks. Then fifteen for O. Those came yesterday, and I just got the last letter—twenty-three clicks for W. *WE ARE LEAVING NOW*. They'll be here any day. We have to get ready!"

He sits down across from her with his graph paper and a pencil and sketches out plans. He wants to relocate the palm tree in the middle of the front yard to make room for a landing area. He wants to paint WELCOME on the roof.

"Couldn't we just clean the house, instead?" Teresa asks.

"They can't land *any*where. It has to be someplace where they feel invited."

"Well, does it have to be our front lawn?" She doesn't want him digging up the yard and can just picture him breaking his neck if he tries to climb up onto the roof with a can of paint. "Maybe they could use the airport. There's a perfectly good runway less than a mile from here."

"They don't need a runway. They land like this." Frankie holds one of his hands horizontally and brings it down in front of his face.

She suggests the mall parking lot, even closer than the airport.

He groans. "They're going to be looking for *me,*" he says, patting his chest. "I have vital information."

"About what?"

"Us."

Then he hears the police scanner crackling again and hurries back to his room.

The next day, he pulls his poster boards and tackle box of markers out from under his bed and begins drawing a series of family portraits to show the Visitors when they arrive. A week later, four of the portraits are finished. But they look nothing like their subjects. They don't even look like people. The one labeled "Joe" is a picture of a melting typewriter with eyeballs for keys. "Karen" is a white bird flying upside down with feathered crosses for wings. "Matt," from what Teresa can tell, is a Greyhound bus sliced into pieces and fanned out like playing cards. And "Roy" is a trail of footprints zigzagging across a beach to a pair of boots filled with water.

"What in the world?" she asks, looking at this last one taped up alongside the others on his bedroom wall.

"That's going to be *their* question. They're going to want to know who we really are, so they can correct things."

This, she wonders, *is who we really are? How is he planning to draw* me?

Just as the thought crosses her mind, he asks, "Do you want to sit for yours?"

"For my . . . ?"

"Portrait. Do you want to sit for me?"

The other family members haven't been around for that option—and clearly haven't fared well in the absence.

"Well, what exactly does that mean, they're coming to 'correct things'?"

"*You* know," he says, waving his hands to indicate the two of them or the house or the entire planet. "Put things right."

Teresa hesitates. She glances again at the water-filled boots that represent his father, and sighs.

❊

She's 99.9 percent certain that the Visitors don't actually exist. Frankie concocted them in a feverish dream, most likely, or fixated on something he'd seen in a science fiction movie when he was sick. The tiny part of her that thinks the Visitors might be real is there only because she, in her mid-twenties, believed herself to be the reincarnation of a seventeenth-century model. No one could have talked her out of that, at the time, and she still wonders if it might be true, so who is she to say for certain that an alien race won't one day land on the planet?

They begin her portrait on a bright Monday morning in June. Frankie tapes a fresh poster board to a piece of plywood and anchors it to his easel in the middle of the backyard. He unfolds a TV tray for the tackle box of markers, and sets up a lawn chair for her. When Teresa has settled herself into the chair, he drapes a tablecloth like a barber's smock around her shoulders.

She sits for an hour that first morning, another hour in the late afternoon. At the end of the day, she asks if she can see what he's done so far, and he tells her no.

"Why?"

"Not until I'm finished," he says. "It might interfere with the augury."

By the next afternoon, she's wondering why he's covered her body. *Maybe all he needs is my head,* she thinks. Then she pictures her head severed, fastened to a kitchen appliance, and surrounded by knives, the word *Teresa* written at the bottom of the poster board. She begins to wonder how much—if any—sway she has in this process. "I hope you're not making me look old," she says. "Make me look like Jane Seymour. Or that actress with the eyes. Susan Sarandon."

He selects a green marker from the tackle box. "The whole point is to be *accurate.*"

A stiffness is settling into her neck. Turning slightly, she looks past him, at the layers of chain-link fence that separate one backyard from another all the way down the block. "There's Mrs. Bennett again," she says, spotting the woman on her patio four houses away with a garden hose in her hand. "Third time today. She must be dying to know what we're up to. Don't look over here."

"I have to," Frankie says. "I'm drawing your hair."

"Not you; Mrs. Bennett. Ugh, she's waving." Teresa smiles. She lifts a hand beneath the tablecloth, offering the slightest wave back. "And she's just *drowning* that bush."

"Is she the lady who comes by to sell you makeup?"

"That's Mrs. Granger on Bahama Drive. Mrs. Bennett is the one who's been on the warpath about that tower."

"What tower?"

"Oh, they're putting up some sort of cell phone tower in the woods at the end of the block, and she's fit to be tied."

"You know, when the Visitors get here, they might not actually speak."

"English?"

"Words," he clarifies. "What if they communicate with electronic signals? That tower could come in handy."

"Well, don't tell Mrs. Bennett. She called here twice last week asking if I'd join a demonstration in front of the phone company. Can you imagine—me, swinging a sign around and shouting at strangers?"

As if he hasn't heard her, he says, "I wonder what frequency they'd use."

"Now she wants to come by with some petition she's trying to get all the homeowners to sign. As if a piece of paper can stop a bunch of bulldozers. I'm sorry, but the pen is not mightier than a bulldozer. Yes, hello, we see you." Teresa waves again, grimacing.

"Hold still," he says.

"If you ask me, this whole crusade is really about Mrs. Bennett. She's nothing but a gossip and a snoop. She loves to get inside people's houses and find out their business."

"She wears those puffy outfits?"

"That's her."

"She's the lady who asked my computer if you drank."

Teresa flinches. *"What?"*

"Whoever came down the sidewalk got to write one question on an index card and feed it into the computer. She wrote, 'Does your mother drink?'"

"Why on earth—when was this?"

Frankie shrugs. "Remember when we got that new refrigerator? You said I could have the box, and I turned it into a computer. I stuck Lite Bright pegs through the front of it, and lit them up from the inside with a flashlight."

"That was back before . . . that had to have been 1975, at the latest."

"I guess."

"And she asked you if I *drank*? What did you tell her?"

"I wrote *yes* on the index card and fed it back through the slot. I thought she meant water."

Teresa rolls her head around. "Oh, god, Frankie."

"Hold *still*."

"She probably told half the neighborhood! She's probably been spreading that one around for years."

He drops the green marker back into the tackle box, takes out a yellow highlighter, then changes his mind and selects a red grease pencil instead. "It doesn't matter, it's not true."

"*That's* what doesn't matter," she says. "People believe what they want to believe."

"Until something drops out of the sky and tells them different." He blows on the tip of the pencil, then leans into the poster board.

✣

He's the oddest of her four children, by far. But he's the only one who never completely drifted away.

Matt's in Las Vegas, as far as she knows, doing who knows what for a living. Karen's in Savannah working as a church secretary and is so secretive about her life that Teresa suspects she's joined a cult. Joe's a reporter at a small Chicago newspaper. He calls now and then—mostly to talk to Frankie—but he doesn't come home anymore, and she'll probably never meet his partner, an architect named . . . is it Brian? Brendan? All because, when Joe finally came out to her (over the phone on his thirtieth birthday), she foolishly blurted out, "Do you *all* despise me so much that you'll never give me a grandchild?"

Frankie moved to Jacksonville after college. He drove down the coast to see her every couple of months, was there at Thanksgiving and Christmas, and for a week or so in the summers. Then, abruptly, he stopped coming home. Car trouble, he told her over the phone. On the eve of one planned visit after another, something was wrong with the car. Then his phone calls dwindled, and he became harder and harder to reach. She thought, *He's pulling away from me, like the rest of them; he's just taking a little longer to do it.*

Twelve months went by.

Then the phone rang one afternoon, and she heard a small, distant voice say, "Mom?"

"Frankie?"

"Can I come home?"

"Of course you can! Anytime. Whenever you want."

"Okay." He hung up. She tried calling him back, but the number he'd dialed from, the operator told her, belonged to a pay phone.

Two days later she was collecting the mail when she heard what sounded like the sputtering of an old prop plane. She looked overhead, and when she lowered her eyes she caught sight of his light blue VW bug rolling toward her down Bel Air Drive. Its engine was racing and its tailpipe was spitting smoke. As she watched, the car clopped over the gutter, cut across the driveway at a diagonal, and rolled to a stop with its front tires in the grass.

Maybe it *was* car trouble, she thought.

But who was this old man getting out from behind the wheel? His shoulders were little more than a clothes hanger for his T-shirt. His pants were cinched around his waist. His cheeks were so hollow, there were pockets of shadow in his face. As he walked across the front porch, a hand dusting the wall, she saw that his curly hair, once jet black, had become embroidered with gray, and the narrow bridge of his nose was crazed with red veins. It was as if he'd stepped out of a time machine that had tossed him years into his future.

"Frankie!" she said, "My God!" When she hugged him, she felt the trenches and protruding spine of his back through his shirt. "What's wrong with you?!"

"Oh," he said lethargically, almost casually, "I'm AIDS-y."

He'd been tested but had never gone back to the doctor after he'd gotten his results. He had no interest in taking medication because he was waiting for *somebody* (the Visitors, it turned out) to show up and fix all of his problems. When he was too weak to argue anymore, she drove him to her GP, who took one look at him and recommended a specialist in Orlando. A nurse took six or seven vials of Frankie's blood (Teresa was amazed he had them to spare). Two weeks later, they went back for another appointment.

"Things could be better," the specialist told Frankie, who was drowsy from the car ride and was blinking slowly at a plastic brain sitting on the desk.

"Tell me," Teresa said. "He's too sleepy to pay attention."

The specialist cleared his throat. He explained in simple terms how the virus went about its business, what the viral load count meant, what a T cell was. He told her Frankie's viral load topped two million, and that his T cells were very low.

"Well, how many should he have?"

"I'll try to put things into perspective. The average, healthy person has about a thousand T cells. Your son has seven."

"Seven!"

"Seven," Frankie repeated in a sleepy voice.

"Can he have some of mine?" Teresa asked.

"I'm afraid it doesn't work that way," the specialist said, frowning.

They drove to the pharmacy and—at Frankie's request—the arts and crafts store, and came home with a small stack of art books and a bag of pill bottles. Next to the books on Modigliani, da Vinci, and Watteau, she laid out one of each pill across the coffee table and read off their names for him.

"They're ugly," Frankie said, eyeing the pills suspiciously.

"This one's not ugly. It looks like a little pearl."

"It looks like fertilizer."

"Well, look at this one. That's kind of a sky blue, isn't it?"

"There's no such thing as 'sky blue.' It's one of those made-up colors, like 'fire red.'"

"Periwinkle, then."

He liked periwinkle, but still he refused to take the pills. When the Visitors came, he said, there'd be no need for medicine.

At her wit's end, she called the specialist and asked what could be done if her son refused to take his medication.

"Admit him to the hospital," the voice on the other end of the line said.

The advice made sense, but she knew, somehow, that if she followed it, he would never come out again.

She hung up the bedroom phone and walked back into the living room. "Frankie..." she said.

"Ape marathon!" Frankie exclaimed, pointing to the television. "They're showing *Battle for the Planet of the Apes*! Will you watch it with me?"

Exhausted, she nodded and sat down next to him on the sofa.

Not long into the movie (the apes had yet to begin their battle), her eyes started tearing up. She rubbed at them. "You can take a nap, if you want," Frankie told her. "I'll catch you up on what happens."

She sank a little lower on the sofa, and finally stretched out with her head in his lap, and fell asleep. When she woke up, he'd placed one of the sofa pillows beneath her head. He told her about the battle she'd missed, and said they were almost to the crying-statue scene. "It hurts your *brain* when you think about it. The first nuclear bomb left the apes in charge, but they didn't detonate it; *we* did. And we blew up the world the second time, too." He was rocking forward and back gently, as if floating on a raft. "They're all the descendents of one talking baby monkey. They all come from the same ancestor. He's the one who...*Look!*" He pointed to the television. It showed a close-up of an ape statue, a tear running down its face. "He's crying for the *whole world,*" Frankie said. "He's crying for *everyone.*"

"Frankie," she said, sitting up, dragging the heel of one hand across her eyes. "I want you to listen to me."

He waited until the credits appeared, then clicked off the television with the remote, and looked at her.

"The Visitors aren't coming."

"Yes they are."

She took a deep breath. "Okay. They're coming. But we have no idea when, and if you don't take your medication in the meantime, you're going to die."

"They told me that might happen."

"Well, you know what? *I'm* telling you it's *not* going to happen. Because you're going to start taking your pills. Today, no arguments. And I'll make a deal with you," she said, because he was just beginning to shake his head no. "The minute the Visitors arrive, you can stop. I promise: not one more pill after they get here. But until then, we're going to do this my way."

He dropped his gaze to the blank face of the television for several moments. She tried to arrange the right words in her head, ready for anything that might come out of his mouth. But when he looked at her again, he said, "Okay."

"Really?"

"They probably already know I'm going to do it."

"They probably do," she said. "And I think they understand."

*

Several days into the portrait, just as they're finishing lunch, the doorbell rings. Teresa gets up from the dining room table and steps toward the front window, peering through the gauzy curtains. "Oh, lord, it's her."

"Who?" Frankie asks.

"Mrs. Bennett."

The doorbell rings again. Teresa moves out of view of the window and glances back at Frankie, who's holding a soup spoon in front of his chin, watching her.

"What'll I do?"

"Open the door."

"The snoop. I can't stand her."

He shrugs. "Then don't open it."

"She already knows we're here. She's seen the car."

Finally, as the bell rings a third time, Teresa smoothes a hand over her hair and opens the door.

"Hiding?" Mrs. Bennett asks with a smile. She's wearing a billowy turquoise jogging suit and white tennis shoes. Her fuchsia-colored eyeglass frames are so large that they encompass—and magnify—both cheekbones and two scoops of forehead. The better to snoop with, Teresa thinks. When Roy left in '76, Mrs. Bennett was so curious to know *why* that she questioned not only Teresa but Karen as well. She cornered Matt one afternoon when he was only twelve and asked him if he was the person who'd dropped the hypodermic she'd found in her yard. And now this business about asking an eight-year-old boy if Teresa drank. And Frankie told her yes! Teresa feels like slamming the door in her face, but worries about the rumors that might ensue. *What do you suppose is going on in the Kerrigan house that Teresa would slam the door on me?* she would ask, and then spill out a list of options: *Drugs? Illicit sex? Drinking?*

Mrs. Bennett has a clipboard in her hand and a smile plastered on her face.

"We weren't hiding," Teresa says, trying to sound pleasant. "We were just finishing lunch."

"Don't let me stop you," Mrs. Bennett replies, but then just stands there.

Teresa unlatches the screen door and reluctantly eases it open. "Would you like to come in?"

The woman steps into the house as if entering a museum. She runs her fuchsia-framed eyes over the drapes, the furniture, the carpet, looking for anything out of the ordinary that might be worth talking about later. "Do you know I can't remember the last time I was in your home? *Ages.*"

Never, Teresa thinks.

"I was just down the street at the Pattersons'," she says. "Bill's liver cancer has accelerated, and the poor man's the color of a lemon. He *claims* he feels fine, but I swear he's last-stage. And Dora may as well be on cloud nine, rattling on about next year's Kiwanis flea market while her husband is sitting there in his BarcaLounger about to expire. It really is shocking. Is that Frankie?"

"Hi, Mrs. Bennett," Frankie calls from the table.

"My, you certainly have...grown up."

She's noticing his drawn face, his gray hair, Teresa thinks. *Grown up means ill when she says it. She probably told Mr. Patterson he looked spry.* "Would you like something to drink?" Teresa immediately feels the need to clarify. "Water. Or Pepsi. I'm sure that's all we have."

"No, thank you. This really is a business call..."

Mrs. Bennett's voice trails off. Her roving eyes have settled on one of Frankie's drawings, framed and hanging over the stereo. In the drawing, his VW is suspended in midair over a field, held in place by a beam of light that emanates from somewhere above the top of the frame. "That certainly is an...interesting picture. Is it original?"

It's a print, Teresa wants to say. *I bought it at the Salvation Army.*

"I did it," Frankie says. "Do you like it?"

Mrs. Bennett's head tips gradually to one side. "I love original art," she finally says. "What inspired you?"

"One time, I drove to Alabama to see this prophet, and right after I left his house—"

Teresa cuts him off. "So this petition, what exactly is it for?"

"I'm trying to get as many signatures as I can to protest the relay tower. As home-owners, we have a say. Just because this town's not incorporated doesn't mean the nearest local government gets to decide who tears down our woods."

This is going to take a few minutes, Teresa can tell. She holds her hand out, indicating the sofa, and Mrs. Bennett sits down at one end. Teresa sits in the armchair next to her.

"Honestly, I wish you'd shown up at the demonstration. Things like that can really make a difference. We were on the local news."

"But aren't they supposed to start bulldozing any day now?" Teresa asks. "It seems a little late for a petition."

"Call me an optimist. I know we can't stop the construction at this stage. But it's still going to take them a while to get the tower up and running, and we might be able to slow that down." She slides the clipboard forward across the slick legs of her jogging suit. A pen is attached to the top with a little piece of Velcro.

"I haven't really made up my mind on the matter," Teresa says.

Mrs. Bennett's eyes narrow. She gives Teresa a *get real* expression, then looks down at the end table and its cluster of brass-framed photographs. "Look at the whole gang!" She reaches over and picks up an old school photo. "This is Matthew, isn't it?"

"Yes."

"He and William used to spend so much time together. Did I tell you William's slated to be chair of the economics department at Dartmouth?"

"Really?"

"It's a done deal, from what he tells me. Where is Matthew now?"

Teresa glances over at Frankie, who's done with his soup and is getting up from the table. He gathers their plates and bowls and carries them into the kitchen. She hears him turn on the faucet.

"Matt's at Yale," she says, lowering her voice a little. "He's a research scientist."

"*That's* impressive. What field?"

"General."

"And Joe?"

"He's in Chicago. He runs a newspaper there."

"I don't envy him that. From what I hear, management's a tough one. And this must be Katherine. She has your ex-husband's eyes. Wait, that's not right. She has a different father, doesn't she?"

"Yes."

"And Matthew too?"

"Yes."

"They *each* have a different father?"

"No," Teresa says leadenly; Mrs. Bennett already knows all this. "They're from my first marriage. They have the same father."

"And where is he?"

"Dead."

"Oh. I'm sorry." Mrs. Bennett sets the photo down. "It's

terrible, the way divorce scatters a family. And what's Katherine doing now?"

"She's in Paris," Teresa says. "Designing fashion."

"Good for her. I always used to say that girl had a look that could burn a hole through leather." She laughs, sighs, and re-adjusts herself on the sofa. One of her fingernails taps against the clipboard.

The kitchen faucet shuts off.

"Seriously, Teresa, this petition isn't just about the woods. There are health issues at stake. Let me ask you something: do you have a cell phone?"

"No."

"Me, either," Mrs. Bennett says. Then, as if singing a line from a jingle: "But a lot of people do."

"Well, then, maybe we need the tower."

"Oh, please. Those people are making *millions* of calls a day, and for no reason at all. Who knows how bad that is for you, all those signals flying around? If they put up this tower, we're go-ing to have phone calls burning tumors into our heads just so teenagers can tell each other what's new on the hit parade. I don't think you want that any more than I do."

I hate you, Teresa thinks. *You're just a busybody. You don't care about any of this; all you want is to be able to move on to the next house and talk about poor Mr. Patterson's liver cancer and poor, al-coholic Mrs. Kerrigan and her decrepit son.* "I haven't decided," she says.

"I see." Mrs. Bennett sits back on the sofa. She pulls the pen off its Velcro patch and reattaches it. "Well, how are things? I noticed you and Frankie have a little project going on in the backyard."

"That's just a picture he's drawing."

"It's her portrait," Frankie says, emerging from the kitchen and drying his hands on a dish towel. "It's for when the Visitors arrive."

"Oh, are you expecting company?"

"Big-time," Frankie says. "You know, Mrs. Bennett, there's no reason to worry about brain tumors from those cell phones."

She laughs gently. "There most certainly is."

"I mean, it's not hard to prevent them. But we need that tower. The Visitors are going to want to communicate with us, when they get here."

"Well, they can pick up a landline like anybody else."

"No they can't," Frankie says, raising his voice a notch. "They won't be connected. And it only makes sense to do whatever we can to understand them, after they've traveled all the way across the galaxy. Right, Mom?"

"Oh," Teresa says. "Maybe."

"I forgot my pills." He turns around and walks back into the kitchen.

Teresa looks at her lap and scratches lightly behind one ear.

Mrs. Bennett asks, "What was all that about?"

"The thing is," Teresa says, "I don't have anything *against* the tower. I really don't have an opinion on it one way or the other."

"Then why not just sign? Come on, Teresa, you're talking to the woman who shut down the phone company parking lot for two hours. I can certainly plant myself here until you buckle and put your name on this piece of paper."

Teresa doesn't want to sign, but the thought of Mrs. Bennett staying much longer is unbearable.

Pill bottles rattle. Mrs. Bennett glances toward the kitchen. Then she leans forward and lowers her voice. "May I ask you something?"

Teresa nods.

"Is he...okay?"

They hear the metallic crackle of aluminum foil being ripped from a roller.

"What do you mean?"

Mrs. Bennett taps one fuchsia temple of her glasses.

Feeling the muscles in her forehead tighten, Teresa says, "In my book, he is."

A moment later, Frankie comes back around the corner wearing an aluminum foil helmet. He's twisted the foil into antennalike horns at both corners of his forehead. "This'll block the cell phone signals from getting into your brain," he says. He has the roll of foil in his hand.

Teresa watches Mrs. Bennett's eyes widen.

"But I really need that tower," Frankie says. "If they use electronic signals to talk to me, I have to be able to *receive* them."

"Who are *they*?" Mrs. Bennett asks.

"The *Visitors*."

"Frankie." Teresa turns around in her chair. "I don't think Mrs. Bennett is interested in the Visitors."

"Should I be?" Mrs. Bennett asks.

"They're nobody," Teresa says.

"Mom! They could be listening!" He removes his helmet, tears off another sheet of foil, and lays it across his head, twisting the front corners into horns. Stepping forward, he places this new helmet on Teresa.

She's about to yank it off, but the look of confusion bordering on fear creeping into Mrs. Bennett's face is so satisfying that Teresa leaves the helmet where it is.

Frankie pulls another sheet of foil from the roll, fashions it into a third helmet, and approaches Mrs. Bennett. "Here you go."

"No, thank you!" Mrs. Bennett presses back against the sofa.

Frankie looks at the helmet. He looks at Mrs. Bennett. "What about tumors?"

"I'm okay for the moment," she says.

He sets her helmet on the coffee table and puts his own back on his head. Then he begins to pace in front of the television. "If I were you, Mrs. Bennett, I'd *want* them to be able to talk to me. Because if I can't get their signal, I won't know who they're asking me about. What if they ask about you? There they are in their ship, hovering over the neighborhood, making a list of who to incinerate. And there *I* am with no relay tower to pick up their questions. They get no answer from me, so they put you on their list, then you step out of your house, feel the ground start to shake, and *wham!*" He smacks his hands together. "You're toast!"

The clipboard nearly slides off Mrs. Bennett's lap. She catches it, and shoots Teresa a bewildered look. "If you don't want to sign this petition, I have other houses I need to get to."

"Certainly," Teresa says. She's flushed from embarrassment and anger—or maybe the foil helmet is just making her head warm.

"Well, don't say *I* didn't warn you," Frankie says, dropping down onto the sofa just as Mrs. Bennett stands.

Teresa gets up as well. Mrs. Bennett brushes at the sleeves of her jogging suit, adjusts her glasses, then leans into her and says, "When I decided to come here this afternoon, I didn't expect to feel threatened."

Despite her anger, despite the satisfaction she feels at how the visit has played out, Teresa has the impulse to apologize. But before she has the chance, Mrs. Bennett walks out of the house.

After she closes the front door, Teresa turns around and looks at Frankie, now stretched out on the sofa with his legs crossed.

She pulls the helmet off her head. "You scared that woman half to death."

"That's okay," Frankie says.

"She's heading for one of the neighbors right now to tell them how crazy we are. She's probably telling them we're dangerous." Even as the words leave her mouth, Teresa pictures Mrs. Bennett being zapped off the face of the earth by a laser beam, her empty tennis shoes smoking on the sidewalk. "And what was all that about incineration? You never mentioned anyone being incinerated before."

"I just threw that in to get rid of her," Frankie says, removing his own helmet and wadding it up into a ball. "They're not going to incinerate anyone; they're just going to...correct things." He rolls the ball of foil between his palms and then holds it up above his face. "Did you know that Giotto is the only person *ever* who could draw a perfect circle?"

"No." She doesn't care about Giotto. She has no idea who Giotto is. She wants to ask him to put away all of his quirks for five minutes and explain to her what he thinks needs "corrected."

"Let's work on your portrait," he says, getting up from the sofa.

*

Whether or not she's done it in a previous life, she decides she doesn't like modeling. It's nerve-racking. It involves nothing more than sitting in a chair for an hour at a time, yet it leaves her exhausted, as if she'd spent the hour doing yard work. Even the thought of finishing the portrait makes her feel tired. According to Frankie, they're in the homestretch, but she feels rattled from Mrs. Bennett's visit and tells him she needs to take a nap first.

She doesn't sleep. She lies down across her bed and stares at the ceiling, thinking: *What needs to be corrected?*

Everything, really. Her nonexistent love life. Her relationship with her other three children. Frankie's health. His blood work is stable now; during the past ten years, the virus has evolved into something he's living with rather than dying from. But still she wishes she could have done more for him. She understands why he wants something to drop out of the sky and fix all their problems. Let them start right now and work backward, by all means, until the home she tried to create can be remembered as something other than a smoldering battlefield.

But that's not what's going on in his portraits. He's mutated Karen, sliced up Matt, and melted Joe. He's drowned Roy right out of his shoes. How clean can Teresa's own record be, in his eyes?

She remembers Jennifer Woodrow—often, and privately: whenever she drives past the house where the Woodrows used to live, sometimes just out of the blue when she's gazing at Frankie—and suspects that this one unfortunate episode is more than enough reason to have her "corrected."

Roy was a wreck. He'd lost his job that summer and did nothing but mope around the house. Suddenly he was telling Teresa that he didn't want Frankie going over to the Woodrow house anymore, or having anything to do with "that sick girl."

"Why?"

"Her mother's a loose cannon," Roy said. "She threatened to sue us."

He didn't look her in the eye when he said it, and she didn't believe him. *He* was the loose cannon. But they'd fought constantly since he'd been laid off, and Teresa was tired of fighting and desperate for things to get back to normal. So she agreed.

Frankie, who was seven, cried the entire afternoon.

And as far as Teresa knows, he never saw Jennifer again. The girl lived only another five years. Teresa heard the news at the grocery store, from Mrs. Bennett (who else?), and she didn't have the heart to tell Frankie. He found out soon enough, though; Karen announced it during dinner.

"She didn't die," Frankie replied.

"She did so. I talked to Sue Gallo, who lives next door to the Woodrows. Jennifer died two weeks ago. Sue said Mrs. Woodrow hasn't left the house since the day of the funeral."

"She didn't die!" Frankie yelled. He wasn't looking at any of them, just staring down at his plate. Teresa felt mortified. She had the impulse to cut her eyes over to Roy, but Roy was long gone by then; she was sitting in his chair at the head of the table.

Frankie calls to her from a distance.

She doesn't want to see the portrait. Ever. But how will she avoid it, when it's going to be hanging in his bedroom? Anytime she walks past his door, she'll risk catching a glimpse of her "corrected" self.

He calls to her again, his voice rising out of a thick silence that makes her think she might have fallen asleep for a few moments. She pushes up from the bed and walks through the house, pulls open the sliding glass door off the dining room. The afternoon sky over the backyard is cloudless and the grass is a dark, rich green. Frankie is standing beside the easel; the lawn chair is waiting for her a few feet away. Barefoot, she steps across the grass and takes her seat. He drapes the tablecloth over her body.

"You're almost done?" she asks him.

"Just about. And just in time, too, I think."

Teresa glances up at the sky. *Have I done such an awful job?* she imagines asking him. And then, after a deep breath, "Do you ever think about Jennifer Woodrow?"

"Sure," Frankie says from behind the easel.

"That situation wasn't handled very well."

"What do you mean?"

"Your father—" She stops herself. She doesn't want to blame the whole thing on Roy; it wouldn't be fair, or accurate. "*We* stopped letting you go to Mrs. Woodrow's, then you and Jennifer stopped being friends. And then, well . . ."

"She died," Frankie provides.

"Yes. It doesn't do much good to say it now, but I've always felt bad about that. I think we were wrong not to let you go back over there."

"I liked Jennifer."

"I know. It's so hard to be a parent, Frankie. In some ways, it's even harder when there are two of you, because it's not like two people splitting the work. It's more like you have a coworker you can't completely trust, and you have to constantly check up on what he does...." She's pinning it on Roy again. She clears her throat. "It wasn't right, what happened."

"It doesn't matter," he says.

Doesn't it? She isn't sure what he means by the remark. She should have apologized for what happened with Jennifer—for everything—long ago, before he ever started the portrait. But then she feels a pang of annoyance. Just how much weight is she going to lend this piece of poster board? There's no way to alter it now, anyway, if he's so close to being—

"Done," he says happily. He steps back from the easel, capping a highlighter.

"Really?" Teresa swallows. She tries to smile. "You're finished?"

"Yep. Want to see?"

"I don't know. I don't have to."

"Come on," he says. "Take a look."

You get what you deserve, she tells herself. *There's your past, and there's your future, and right now is all about owning up to one and dreading the other.* She stands, keeping the tablecloth around her, and walks slowly toward him.

When she's halfway between the chair and the easel, the ground begins to shake.

Just barely—a tremble that courses through the dirt and vibrates the grass against the bare soles of her feet. A rumbling sound rises out of the quiet afternoon. She runs her eyes across the sky again. She glances at Frankie.

"You feel it?" he asks.

She nods.

"Come here! I want you to see it first!"

"I do feel something," she says.

He waves her over. "Hurry!"

Her heart is thumping beneath the cloth. The trembling grows as she moves up alongside him and looks at the portrait.

The woman centered in the middle of the poster board isn't on a lawn chair; she's in a high-backed silver throne. Instead of a tablecloth, a paisley robe drapes her body, its swirls made up of every color in the tackle box of markers. She has the neck of a Modigliani, the face of a Watteau. Her eyes are fixed directly on the viewer and her mouth is curved at one corner, like the *Mona Lisa*'s. A narrow, golden crown rests on top of her head. Behind her, a valley rolls out, full of meadows and miniature trees and tiny animals: dogs, zebras, rhinoceroses, alligators— right out of the pastel pages of a children's illustrated Bible. In the top right corner of the sky, so small that Teresa has to lean forward to distinguish its shape, is a saucerlike craft. Her ship, she thinks, either leaving or about to land. At the bottom of the poster board is the word *Teresa*.

Frankie's head is tilted back. He's staring straight up. She glances toward the street, visible in the gap between their house and the next, and sees a dump truck crawling past, then a crane, and finally the massive yellow hull of a bulldozer.

"It's beautiful," she says, looking back at the portrait, her eyes going damp. She reaches out and rests a hand on his shoulder.

Still staring at the sky, rising up onto his toes, Frankie wraps his narrow arm around her waist. "It's you."

Acknowledgments

The support and encouragement I've received from Michael Carroll over the last twenty years, along with his friendship, have profoundly and positively shaped my life, and I owe him a world of gratitude. My mother, Beverly Neel, kept the faith against all odds; for that and a thousand other reasons, she's a woman to be celebrated.

Susan Kamil, my editor, is a dream come true: warm, wise, committed, and a source of constant reassurance at every turn. Lisa Bankoff, my agent, believed in this book from the beginning and worked wonders in the interest of finding a good home for it. My friend Andrew Miller devoted himself to plowing through the early drafts with a red pen and improved every page.

Special thanks to my family, and to the following people who have provided various and sometimes crucial forms of support recently and over the years: Denver Butson, Daniel Casey, Chet Childress, Noah Eaker, James P. Elder, Will Fabro, Craig Ferguson, Thomas Lee Jones, Rhonda Keyser, Jack Lynch, David Masello, Joe B. McCarthy, David McConnell, Lee Morrow, Duncan Osborne, Mark Pitman, Anna Schachner, Hannah Tinti, Don Weise, and Tina Wexler.

And if it weren't for the amazing Fred Blair, none of it would have been possible.

About the Author

Patrick Ryan was born in Washington, D.C., and was raised in Florida. A graduate of the writing program at Bowling Green State University in Ohio, he has published stories in the *Yale Review,* the *Iowa Review, One Story, Denver Quarterly,* the *Nebraska Review* and other journals. He lives in New York City.